I0679081

Copyright © 2020 by TV Scribner

Published in 2020 by TV Scribner

Printed in the United States of America.

ISBN: 978-1-7346663-0-4

www. tvscribner.com, 1st ed.

Cover design by Carissa Andrews

Cover © TV Scribner

ACKNOWLEDGMENTS

To all my family and friends who believed in me, and never doubted I could write this book.

I also wish to thank several men, women, and a few family members, who allowed me to use them as sources, for technical parts of the story.

I must also thank, my guru, Carissa Andrews, who helped guide me through the tangled web of learning how to publish this book.

THE SUITCASE

TV SCRIBNER

PROLOGUE

R ussia's history of corruption begins as far back, as the 1700s when the Tsarists took control. Under their rule, with wealth and power concentrated in their hands, the masses struggled. Many countrymen reverted to robbing the few in power, by roaming the countryside and attacking government entities, in order to help the people. They became the people's champions, by robbing from the rich and giving to the downtrodden, until the end of the 1800s.

During the Russian Revolution of 1917, a large group of radicals, called Bolsheviks, led by Vladimir Lenin, ousted the Tsarists. Lenin proceeded to found the Communist Party, during which time, corruption continued, despite his efforts to abolish the criminals, and it even continued to be a problem following his death, in 1924.

Joseph Stalin, Lenin's Secretary-General, became Dictator of the Union of Soviet Socialist Republic (USSR), inheriting Lenin's corrupt underworld. Stalin ruled with an iron fist, in an attempt to rid the country of corruption. However, his stringent policies created a man-made famine, killing millions of his countrymen.

Leonid Brezhnev rose to power, following Stalin's death in 1953, and freed millions of criminals, whom Stalin had incarcerated in gulags. Unfortunately, many of the freed convicts joined forces with corrupt government officials, causing corruption to spread even further in his regime. By the 1970s, when Brezhnev died, illegal activity had increased, and the black market flourished.

Under the rule of Mikhail Gorbachev, who was Brezhnev's successor, the USSR collapsed, and the Mafia took over the struggling economy. Chaos developed in the country, as it attempted to become a democracy, which served to help the criminal element experience an increase in profits. The Mafia leaders and their groups organized with corrupt government officials, and eventually managed to export their corruption to many other countries.

Boris Tazvoshenko, saw an opportunity and capitalized on it. He was born in Dolgoprudny, in a Moscow oblast (a zone or area), about thirteen miles, northwest of the Moscow City Center. Orphaned at a young age, he was put in an orphanage and was poorly treated.

Tazvoshenko ran away from this orphanage, and as a teenager with no place to go, witnessed the workings of the Mafia. Within his first month of freedom from the orphanage, he managed to join one of the large Mafia organizations, and over time, became well-known for his fearlessness, taking on *any* task assigned to him.

The leadership skills of Tazvoshenko developed to the point where he managed to form a Mafia organization of his own, in which he held the position of *Pakhan*—the leader who controls the entire operation. Over the years, he built it into one of the largest Mafia organizations in Russia, and re-located towards the outskirts of Lyubertsy, in a Moscow oblast, approximately fifteen miles southeast of Moscow's City Center.

To call Boris Tazvoshenko ruthless, did *not* do justice to the type of heavy-handed violence he meted out to his rivals or the extent of criminality with which his organization was involved. Its specialties consisted of anything and everything. He dealt with all varieties criminal activities such as extortion, loan sharking, counterfeiting, auto theft, tax fraud, blackmail, assassinations, homicides, kidnapping, racketeering, drugs, gun trafficking, Visa forgery, passports and any other valuable papers needed to travel the world freely *or* even disappear.

However, Tazvoshenko's long suit included trafficking in guns and weaponry of all sorts, including larger military weaponry—tanks, armored transport vehicles, even shoulder-fired missiles (MPADS)—for major clients, who wished to deal in international weapons.

His Mafia organization spread its tentacles into almost every country, including the United States, and offered services to the highest bidders, including Mid-Eastern countries, terrorist groups, the North Koreans, South Americans and African despots, or any radical militant groups, who might want to buy what he had to sell.

However, in 2012, he was onto something very big—bigger than anything he'd ever handled, and his top *Brigadier* (second in rank) was going to help him acquire what he referred to, as *the chemodan*. In 2015, he sent his Brigadier to Brainerd, Minnesota, a city in the mid-west area of the state, to focus on this unique project. A small cadre of men traveled with him, plus several young recruits, to assist with the acquisition of this item.

The project would take time, to gather the clues and add

them to those he already had, as to the *chemodan's* whereabouts. Tazvoshenko relied on his comrades' area research, to find the final clues, and ascertain the exact location, of that which he sought. When the time arrived to complete the work, his plan included sending extra support to the same general area, to help extract the item. Because of his greed, Tazvoshenko was obsessed with the *chemodan*, as it would bring in the most money from his buyers, of anything he'd ever procured.

CHAPTER 1

SUNDAY, MAY 14, 2017

Pinecrest Minnesota

Gregore Kamorov was exhausted. It had been a particularly busy afternoon at Ben's Burgers, due to the fact he'd been out all night Friday and Saturday, drinking with some of his reprobate friends. Today was Sunday, and thankfully he pulled the late afternoon to midnight shift. Even though he arrived for his shift at Ben's Burgers by 4:00 p.m., his roaring headache was still pounding because of his debauchery of the last two nights.

Kamorov's college computer classes began at eight the next morning, which made him even more anxious about ending his shift. With loads of homework (because of his procrastination over the weekend), it was imperative to finish his work so he could go home and have time to study to pass his finals the next day. As a result of past bad behavior, he was on probation, and his student visa was dependent on his school performance. Therefore, he couldn't afford to fail any class, or his visa might be revoked, and he'd be sent back to Russia.

Six months ago, at the age of twenty-two, Kamorov entered the computer engineering program at Pinecrest College, to get his degree and all required certifications. He'd been a tech phenom when he was younger, winning acclaim from his "so-called" friends by spending untold hours gaming and hacking into computer systems. During his earlier school years, his objective was to wreak as much mischief and damage as possible with his amazing computer skills.

Born in Russia, Kamorov's parents were murdered in a gang warfare incident, when Kamorov was a teenager, His cousin and only relative, Medved Grinko, was authorized to be his guardian even though Grinko belonged to a local Russian Mafia group, but the authorities didn't care. It wasn't long before Grinko drew Gregore into the Mafia *and* its criminal elements, because of Gregore's extraordinary computer skills. It wasn't long before he was in demand to perform all illegal services needed by the Mafia members.

Boris Tazvoshenko, Grinko's Mafia boss, sent Medved Grinko to Minnesota to help an arm of the Mafia group in the Minneapolis area. Gregore accompanied him under the guise of attending college on a student visa.Gregore's antics at school were such that he was put on probation almost immediately, and shortly thereafter, his cousin was killed in a gang fight in Minneapolis. Rather than return to Russia, Gregore appealed his case, and the authorities allowed him to stay in Minnesota, on two conditions—he was to start school in the spring and find employment.

He was placed with two fellow Russians in Brainerd, Minnesota. Yury Panuken (also a student), and Pyotr Zolotov, who was his sponsor. When Gregore applied for college, he managed to talk his way into the IT program at Pinecrest College. The authorities allowed this, contingent upon four things: he must stay out of trouble, attend college, keep his grades up, and find employment. Gregore applied immediately for a job at Ben's Burgers and Ben hired him.

It wasn't long after Gregore began his job before he fell into bad company, because besides computer hacking, his other favorite pastimes were drinking and gambling, which landed him in trouble again.He was arrested several times for driving under the influence, and once for petty theft. His employer, Ben Wister, owner of Ben's Burgers, generously gave him a second chance.

Since then, he'd performed his duties diligently, kept his grades up, and Ben rewarded him with the position of night manager. Kamorov told himself he didn't have to change—he just needed to be more careful in his off-duty hours. Because he ignored his own advice, the headache from the weekend's drinking on his off-hours still hung on, and as far as he was concerned, midnight couldn't come quickly enough.

As soon as the last customer left, he said, to his co-worker, Bill, "You go home early. Only fifteen minutes to end of shift." Bill, used to Kamorov's Russian way of wording things, hustled to the back room where he retrieved his jacked and car keys, then waited at the side door for Gregore to shuffle to the back room and unlock it.

Gregore let Bill out, locked the door brushing his straggly dark hair out of his face, shuffled back to the kitchen area, and continued performing the remaining tasks necessary to close for the night. Gregore was a slight man with dark, deep-set eyes, set in a round face with a sallow complexion and thin lips revealing a gap in his front teeth, *if* he smiled

After Bill left, he entertained himself with thoughts of his well-planned scheme, which would facilitate his strategy to ditch the burger place, the town, and the state. He could hardly wait for its implementation. This plan, the best one he'd ever concocted, would make him a wealthy msn, and he was just days away from its execution. It excited him to think about it.

The trash can made a screeching sound across the cement floor as he dragged it to the backroom to empty it. While heading back to the front to get the other trash sacks from their containers, he turned off the outside neon lights, then continued to finish the remaining tasks upfront. But Gregore was roused from his thoughts by a light knock on the side door. He stood for a moment listening, and just as he decided he'd heard something, he heard it again, rap, rap, rap.

There it was, and this time thinking it was Bill, who had forgotten something, he jogged back to the side door he'd just locked, took the key ring off the hook, and unlocked it again. The door pushed inside, causing him to back up, and instead of Bill, he was startled to see, one of his so-called friends, an ex-con. He'd partied with this guy and several other losers over the weekend. The element of surprise made it easy for the intruder to brusquely shove his way past Kamorov and push the door closed before Kamorov had a chance to react.

Kamorov said, with his prominent Russian accent, "Hey, what are you doing here? Place is closed. You are not to be here."

The man dressed in black pants, a hoodie, and watch cap, slithered to the front of the place, then turned and leaned back against the counter, propping himself up with his elbows. He settled there for a moment sneering, his thin lips stretching across a set of crooked teeth, as he eyed Gregore with his cocky smile erupting on his face, then said in a raspy voice, "Gregore, my man, we need to have a little talk," and with a smile more like a grimace, waited for him to reply.

"I need to close...we talk later." Gregore brushed him off

and resumed his work, dragging a trash bag towards the back room, annoyed with this interruption.

"No, I think we're talkin' right now, my friend," he said, staring at Kamorov as he walked away.

Kamorov slowly put the bag of trash down, turned, and said, "What is so important it cannot wait?" He could smell the booze from where he stood, as it mingled with the odor of stale burgers. It was then he noticed the wild look in his friend's dark eyes. Slightly unnerved by his friend's demeanor, Kamorov tried to shrug him off, "Looks like you are still partying, I'm still hungover from weekend too, I need to finish work...you go sleep it off."

"Oh—kay," the man said, as he dragged out the word like syrup slowly running off the sides of a pancake, "have it your way. I'll get right to the point. I want to go halve-sies on your little scheme—simple as that," and he sat down on a stool, watching to see Kamorov's reaction, after having spilled his purpose into the room. Kamorov, trying to ignore him, turned and continued walking, but stopped abruptly and carefully slid back several steps, squinting his eyes as he turned and stared, then said, "What scheme?" Kamorov's face was beginning to radiate his irritation. He did *not* want to have this conversation!

"The scheme you talked about while you were so drunk-out-of-your-mind last night! *That's* what scheme I'm talkin' about, and it's *all* you talked about while I drove you home. Ivan and I *both* thought it sounded pretty good at the bar—even better than pretty good!" He leered at Kamorov."No, I remember nothing! I was drunk," he said defensively, shaking his head and looking at the floor, noticing it still needed mopping. But now, he needed to get rid of his friend—immediately! His headache was pounding even harder, and he still needed to head home to study.

The friend scoffed, taking a step towards Kamorov, "Well, *I* remember *everything*! Bragging about how you stole it, how you have buyers already, and last but not least, you told *us* you keep it on you at all times!"

Kamorov's face registered shock, and like a jigsaw puzzle, he put the pieces together, slowly realizing he must have divulged the information last night...he broke into a cold sweat, saying, "You are mistaken, and as calmly as he could, in an effort to call his friend's bluff, he said, " I was drunk! I don't know what you talk about...I don't know what I say!"

"How about taking it out? Lets' have a look at it," he urged.

For Kamorov, there was a moment of clarity and sensing danger, he began slowly backing away. "*No!* Go away, or I call police!" Kamorov walked around the corner of the counter into the kitchen area and headed down the hallway, dragging the trash bag behind him to the trash area in the back, where he knew a telephone hung on the wall, just to the right of the restaurant's cooler door.

With an abrupt one-eighty in his tone, the man growled, "Come back here, you *Russkie*! I'm in no mood to play games! We can share this because I'm sure there will be enough money for two!"

"Go home! I have work to finish!" Trying not to show panic in his voice, he reached for the phone on the wall.

His visitor sneered, "And *now*, guess what? If you don't cooperate, I'm not even gonna split it with you—I'll be takin; it for myself! He lunged toward Kamorov and knocked the phone's receiver out of his hand before he could dial. He gave a hard push to Kamorov, throwing him off balance and causing him to fall backward, landing on his back. Enraged, he jumped on Kamorov, and they struggled.

"Tell me where it is *right now*, and maybe I'll let you live! Is it in your pockets? Is it somewhere hidden in this burger place? The freezer, maybe? Is that why you ran back here? *Tell me!*" he yelled.

Kamorov's arms were pinned to his sides, "*No!*" he yelled and began to writhe, attempting to free himself because he was choking...it became difficult for him to breathe!

"*Tell me!*" the intruder insisted, in a menacing voice, as his anger rose. "Did you make a deal with Ivan? *That's it!* You and Ivan are working together, aren't you?" he said in a calculated tone.

You crazy? I'm *not* woking with Ivan. I *never* tell Ivan, *or* you!" Kamorov choked out the words, as his face turned red and his breathing became ragged, "Stop!" His voice gurgled, and was almost inaudible, "I...never...!" Unable to speak anymore, he could only look at the terrifying expression on the face above him and make one last attempt to break free. But he could no longer breathe and became aware that his life was in the hands of a man crazed with hatred and anger, fueled by drunkenness, and probably drugs. He knew he was dying.

In a rage, the man lifted Kamorov's head, and like a wild animal, banged it repeatedly on the floor of the cooler, while continuing to choke him. At last, Gregore resisted no longer.

CHAPTER 2

MONDAY, MAY 15, 2017

Paisley Ingles lived in the small town of Carpenteria, California. After graduating from the Carpenteria Police Academy the previous year, the local police department hired her. Six months later, they promoted her to the position of detective in the small precinct. Instead of fighting crime and solving murders, her work consisted of overseeing office chores such as handling stacks of paperwork, typing computer reports, doing some computer forensic work, and participating in uneventful stakeouts.

Paisley's duties at the Carpenteria Precinct, did not reflect her detective status, so she decided to move to Minnesota, in the spring of 2017, when the Pinecrest Police Department (PPD), in Minnesota, hired her to fill the position of Forensic Computer Specialist. Also offered was the opportunity to move into a detective position after three months on the job. She accepted, knowing her status as a detective would enable her to assist in investigating murder cases, which is what she *really* wanted to do.

Although the job was considered part-time, she intended to gain enough experience in the field to fulfill her plans down the line to perhaps, open a private detective agency!However, for the time being, computer forensics remained her ticket into the department and would do for now. She settled into her great Aunt's farmhouse in Brainerd, a small city next to Pinecrest. Her Aunt was somehow related to someone on her mother's side of the family, and this would only be temporary until she had time to find a place.

As a young girl, Paisley dreamed of being a detective—ala Nancy Drew. She also loved archaeology and after high school, registered in the archaeology program at a nearby university, where she studied for two years, until deciding she needed a more practical profession.

She withdrew from the university and, instead, decided to attend the Police Academy, in Carpenteria. Wasn't detective work a lot like archaeology? Both were involved in investigating and uncovering mysteries, new and old. Someday she would continue archaeology classes again, but she needed to earn money to support herself right now.

A distant cousin on her father's side of the family, Mandy Dillard, had moved to Pinecrest, the previous year, from Iowa, enrolling in classes at Pinecrest College, and Mandy contacted Paisley, when she arrived in Minnesota. They met over lunch to get acquainted, establishing a close friendship and discovering both had a passion for running.

Monday, May 15, 2017 Brainerd Over the weekend, Mandy informed Paisley her finals had been moved to Monday and would start mid-morning and last until late afternoon, which meant Paisley would have to run solo. Their usual route began near the college along a wooded trail, which after a mile or two turned towards town and into residential streets, finishing at Ben's Burger's, by the Pinecrest Mall. So, Sunday evening, Mandy followed Paisley's car to the parking area at Ben's, then drove her home, so she'd have a car the next day after her run.

Monday's early morning weather was the usual clouds-disappear-sun-comes-out type of morning, typical of upper Minnesota. Paisley forced herself out of bed and began her morning routine. Not *every* day was good for running in Minnesota, because the weather varied so much. People warned her that fall was too cold to run much past September, and too cold in March and April, to begin. However, since Paisley's arrival in Brainerd, she'd been lucky, because beautiful weather had arrived earlier than usual, or so she was told.

Shutting off her alarm, Paisley stretched her arms towards the ceiling, yawned, and stood for a moment, before walking to the closet to claim her running attire. She chose a raggedy pair of gray sweats, her favorite well-worn T-shirt with her old college logo on its front, her comfortable faded blue zip-up sweatshirt (with its small tear on the side pocket), then dressed quickly.

She stepped into mud-spattered running shoes and headed for the mirror on the back of the bedroom door. Standing in front of it for a moment, she stared, then gathered her bronze unruly curls and pulled them away from her face into a pony-tail, wrapping it with an elastic band, and an old ball cap added to protect her fair skin. Taking a last look in the mirror, she hurried out the door into Aunt Olga's car, who planned to drop her off at the starting point of her run.

"Thanks, Aunt Olga, I appreciate the lift."

Aunt Olga smiled at Paisley, "No trouble my child, I go see Vlad at hospital for hour or two, he has small operation today. It starts early."

Paisley smiled, as she adored her little Aunt with the Russian accent, but was scared to death to drive with her. Aunt Olga was up there in age, and Paisley wasn't sure *how* far up! "Please say hello to Uncle Vlad and tell him I hope his procedure goes well. See you later," and she waved goodbye as she stepped out of the car, glad to have arrived without incident.

Her run dragged without Mandy's company. However, forty minutes later, she rounded the last corner and sweating profusely, finally caught sight of Ben's Burgers. Located on the main street, in front of the Pinecrest Mall parking lot, Ben's had a large red neon arrow pointing to a giant sign, which read, **Ben's Burgers.** She jogged a little faster, thirst spurring her across the parking lot until she arrived at the entrance a few minutes before the place officially opened.

Pinecrest With time to cool down and stretch for a minute or two, she was ready when the doors opened promptly at seven and strolled in and over to the counter ready to order. Ben's Burgers, was a popular fast-food place in Pinecrest, especially with the college crowd. The decor was pseudo-fifties with bright red Formica counters and matching Naugahyde seat covers. Formica topped tables sat on chrome legs with red chair seats, all of which added a cheerful touch.

Eclectic framed prints consisting of old fifties' celebrity caricatures, such as Elvis, Sal Mineo and James Dean, adorned the walls along with a poster of Jackie Gleason and Alice, with a banner that read "To The Moon". Red plastic baskets lined with wax paper held burgers and fries and condiments adorned each table. Ben's Burgers wasn't the newest *or* biggest place in Pinecrest, but certainly the busiest. Customers chose to eat inside because of Ben, who created a welcoming atmosphere, treating each customer like a neighbor.

"Morning, Julia, I'll have the usual," Paisley said and took a seat at the counter. She glanced around, as the customers filed in, it looked like another busy morning.

"Coming right up," Julia called out, her ponytail bouncing as she headed to the fountain to get a Diet Coke for Paisley. Julia was familiar with Paisley's and Mandy's penchant for stopping at Ben's after their twice-a-week run and was always ready for them with a friendly smile and their favorite beverage.

"Does Mandy have classes this morning?" Julia set the Diet Coke down in front of Paisley and handed her a straw.

"Yep, the semester is almost over, so she has finals today."

"Hey, you want anything else this morning? We have..." but Julia never finished her sentence.

"*Help!*" A piercing cry was coming from the backroom, startling everyone in the place. Paisley jumped up, running towards the kitchen to see what happened.

Julia followed close behind when one of the cooks, Jerry, nearly knocked them both down, as he raced around the corner from the backroom into the kitchen still yelling for help.

As they adroitly avoided a collision, Paisley and Julia simultaneously said, "What happened?" Jerry struggled to speak, silently moving his lips and waving his hands as if he were a mime—pointing and gesturing to make himself understood. His oval face was ashen and his brown eyes registered shock, at whatever-it-was he'd encountered. Looking unsteady on his feet, Paisley rushed forward, stabilizing him and gently shaking his shoulders to help him focus.

"It's...the freezer! It's...!" He stared blankly at her for a moment, finally mumbling his words again, as she endeavored to decipher what had happened to cause such agitation. It was useless...he continued to stutter incoherently.

Paisley didn't wait for him to say more, but instead, asked Julia to take him up front where he could sit down, and she could call the store's owner. Taking Jerry's arm, Julia led him away, while Paisley turned, racing through the kitchen, around the corner, down the hall, and past the manager's office. She paused to get her bearings before turning right towards the cooler, which led to the freezer.

The morning manager, Steve, heard the commotion and fell in behind her. Once inside the cooler, she noticed the freezer's door standing slightly ajar and motioned Steve to stay behind her. Not knowing what to expect, she slowly crept further until she reached the freezer's heavy metal door. Steve stood watching, as she used her foot to tug the unwieldy door open several more inches in order to peek further into its interior.

The freezer was a large room, approximately ten feet wide, by twelve feet deep. The ceiling was low with two light bulbs—one towards the front of the freezer and one at the back—both encased in metal cages. When the door opened, they turned on, flooding the freezer with light. The electric circuitry, encased in metal pipes, traveled up one of the walls to a metal fan, with two vents. Paisley stepped forward on the cement floor and noticed a dark reddish-brown trail leading towards the freezer's back wall. She avoided stepping on this trail, as it resembled dried blood.

The freezer held cases of frozen food, and a small dolly used to wheel the cases in and out, but no light switches. The lights had been wired to go on automatically when the door opened, so she surmised that they probably automatically turned off when the door closed. The door itself was almost ten inches thick with rubber gaskets to seal the freezer when it closed.

Although surprised to see no internal handle, she did notice a temperature gauge on the wall closest to the door. It was also imprisoned in a wire cage, presumably to keep it from being hit, as cartons of frozen foods were rolled in and out on the dolly. The temperature gauge registered zero degrees.

The drastic drop in temperature assaulted her as she haltingly edged deeper into the freezer to investigate, keeping her eyes on the rusty-brown line, trailing across the floor. Her body involuntary shuddered, as she traveled further into the freezer's depths, where metal shelves reached almost to the top of the low ceiling.

The shelves were stacked with cardboard boxes of all sizes, containing foods needed to run the burger place. There were large bags of frozen French fries and onion rings, boxes of frozen hamburger patties, bags of fish fillets, chicken strips and chicken nuggets, five gallon containers of ice cream, and smaller boxes full of dessert pies and ice cream treats.

Shelves extended to her left *and* right, almost eight feet into the freezer, with a large shelving unit across the back wall, opposite the entrance. Pausing for a moment, she gazed at the shelves lining the freezer's walls, and there it was! Paisley covered her mouth with her hand and uttered a low gasp, stopping briefly to steel herself before moving forward.

A voice from further behind her said, "What is it? Do you see something?" It was Steve, sounding impatient, as he stood at the freezer entrance. He was middle-aged, a little on the short side, with a crew cut, a weak chin, and a slight paunch. He craned his neck from the freezer doorway to see what she'd spotted. Tending to be on the bossy side, he said, in an authoritative voice, "I'll be careful, but I'm coming in too...I want to have a look!"

Paisley held up her hand, signaling him to wait for a moment. Her attention was riveted on the toe of what looked to be a boot, partially protruding from a space between the two shelving units. There was a small alcove created by the shelving, that didn't quite meet the wall in the left-hand corner. Boxes of frozen foods blocked the alcove, causing her to move forward and peer around them to see if it *was* a boot. Despite her request, Steve pushed forward into the freezer, carefully following the path she took.

As she stared into the recess, he came up behind her, peered over her shoulder, then let out a yell, *"Oh, no!* The legs—it's one of our employees! Is he...dead?"

CHAPTER 3

"Stay right there! Don't come any closer...I'll find out." She moved forward into the alcove, stared a moment, then said quietly, "I think you'd better call the police."

Steve needed no further urging. He turned, running from the freezer into the cooler area, yelling, "Make way!" And shoved past several employees, who had just arrived for their shift and were crowded by the cooler's door wondering what had happened.

Carefully, Paisley stepped closer into the recess of the alcove and couldn't help but recoil, as she viewed the grotesque tableau before her. The body sat on a cardboard carton labeled hamburger patties, perched on it as if he were a discarded rag doll. His face was a sickening whitish blue, while his head lolled against the back wall. The sight was horrifying. The right arm, bent at the elbow, rested atop a carton of fish patties. Wide-open eyes bulged and stared at her, while a swollen blue tongue protruded from the side of the corpse's mouth. The left arm hung limply to the side as its hand looked like it clutched a discarded burlap bag in a feeble attempt to draw some warmth from it.

Even though it seemed apparent this poor soul was dead, she stepped even closer, carefully putting two fingers on the side of his neck to determine if there was a pulse—just in case. Of course, there was none. At first, she thought it must have been some horrible accident. However, when she checked his neck for a pulse, she also noticed bruising, confirming that it *might* be a homicide. She knew the investigators and Medical Examiner would have to make that determination. Quickly backtracking through the freezer door into the cooler where it was marginally warmer, she encountered a few workers still hovering in the cooler.

"Please," she requested, "return to your posts and take care of the customers. I assure you, once the police arrive and do their work there'll be more information. Although I *am* a detective on the police force, I don't have the authority to comment on the situation right now" The workers accepted this and dispersed to their stations, mumbling quietly among themselves about the shocking discovery.

Jerry rounded the corner and entered the kitchen, at the same time that Paisley exited the cooler, and they almost collided! He'd been looking for her.

"Gregore!—It's Gregore," Jerry said, "because, as I entered the freezer this morning to get a box of hash browns, I saw this shoe and went closer to look—I *had* to look! Is he dead?" Jerry asked. He'd obviously recovered his voice and wasn't stuttering this time, as he blurted out his question, his eyes wide with emotion.

They were interrupted when Steve said, "I called the police as you asked!"

"Great, thanks." Paisley said, then turned towards Jerry and answered his question, "Yes, Jerry, to the best of my knowledge, he's dead, but we still need to wait for the official word from the police."

With Jerry's loud comment, he let the proverbial cat out of the bag, and the few people close by, who heard him were stunned. They filed back to their stations in silence with Jerry and Paisley close behind. The workers resumed serving the customers, and neither Jerry nor Paisley said anything else.

Once in the dining area, she watched out the windows, waiting for the police to arrive, but didn't have to wait very long. She heard the sirens before she seeing the vehicles drive up the street and pull into the parking lot. The doors flew open and two officers hustled inside the building. Paisley stepped forward to greet them and, acting as the spokesperson, directed them towards the back of the burger place to the freezer where the body sat.

Officer Ryan immediately recognized her from the precinct and introduced her to Officer Smith, as they hurried along, and then asked for a quick description of what had taken place. She was relieved to have Officer Ryan present. He had helped acquaint her with the precinct when she was hired, so it was reassuring to see his familiar face.

Both officers were filled in, upon arriving at the entrance to the freezer, then she pointed to what she believed to be, a dried blood trail on the floor and they circumvented it, as they made their way further into the freezer, to the alcove. They glanced in at the body while she explained the circumstances of her discovery.

"At first, I thought it was some horrible accident, but when I felt for a pulse, I noticed marks on the neck, and I decided it might be a homicide," Paisley said.

Several more officers arrived, and Steve directed them

towards the back. Paisley hurried to greet them, guided them to the freezer, then stepped aside at the freezer entrance, as they surveyed the scene. She mentioned the dried blood trail on the floor again, then stepped a little further to the left of the door to keep from blocking the doorway.

As she did so, her foot stepped on something hard, and looking down, she noticed a small object partially lodged under the edge of the door. Realizing her chap stick must have fallen from her pocket, she hurriedly picked it up and put it in her hoodie pocket where it belonged. By this time, the two new officers had greeted Officers Ryan and Smith.

Officer Ryan introduced them to Paisley Ingles, as Officers Beck and Mead, and mentioned to them that she was new to the department. They both looked at her quizzically, and nodded their heads, as she stood by the door, then turned back to look in the alcove. Ryan briefly filled them in and directed Beck to call the Pinecrest Bureau of Criminal Apprehension (PBCA) and the Medical Examiner (ME).

Beck turned, noticing Paisley still standing against the freezer wall, and stared at her momentarily. She could see by his face that he wasn't sure whether he'd seen her at the station or not. Ryan noticed, explaining to Beck, as he was leaving, "I want Ingles to remain. I want to question her further about what happened." He looked directly at her, saying, "Ingles, I want to extend my appreciation for handling the situation so well before we arrived."

Paisley smiled.

Officer Smith turned and quickly reaffirmed, that the victim was deceased, then instructed Officer Mead to put up crime scene tape in the dining area, to keep customers out of the way. The PBCA and photographer were next to arrive and were hurriedly ushered into the freezer.

The photographer began taking preliminary pictures of the crime scene and the body *in situ*. With white attire and latex gloves, the crime scene technicians looked more like mad scientists, as they proceeded to spread a plastic sheet over the freezer floor to protect the area. Although the paramedics had arrived, they would have to wait until the preliminary investigation was over before they could remove the body.

Minutes later, the Medical Examiner sauntered in followed by another detective, also briefed on the situation. He brushed by the ME and Paisley, joining the others in the freezer, which had filled up fast! She stayed by the doorway and watched, as the ME shambled into the freezer and nodded to acknowledge those present. A moment later, all officers left, heading towards the front to interview witnesses—except for Officer Ryan.

Pinecrest had two medical examiners, and Dr. Hyde, the head ME, was the lucky one to get the call. He was a perfect prototype of what one might expect a medical examiner to look like, who bore the name, Hyde. An older man of average height, he appeared shorter, because of a slightly hunched-over back. With a thin, corpse-like face, his black bushy eyebrows appeared rather startling on his pallid face.

He dressed in an out-of-date, drab brown suit, with wide lapels, no tie, and the top button on his shirt unbuttoned. He peered at those in the freezer over small round wire-rimmed spectacles, which rode low on his hooked nose. With thin tightly pressed closed lips, it all served to create a grim visage.

Dr. Hyde shambled towards the rear of the freezer to access the alcove where the body rested, to determine its condition. A minute or two later, speaking in a scratchy voice, he said, "This man is deceased!" then stood back seemingly satisfied with his pronouncement. Paisley watched closely, majorly underwhelmed and could not help but roll her eyes, as the ME continued to gaze at the body.

Presently, the technicians, a tall man and an older woman brought something resembling a tackle box into the freezer...it was their crime kit. Dr. Hyde stepped towards the corpse again and proceeded with his examination, while the two technicians scurried about gathering samples from the freezer's interior.

When Dr. Hyde stepped back to pen a few notes, the technicians swooped in to check the body, pulling invisible evidence from its clothes with tweezers, and putting the particles in small test tubes, or plastic packets to take back to the lab for analysis. Included, were dried blood samples from the cement floor under the protective plastic sheeting.

The forensic techs dusted the surfaces for fingerprints, while the photographer was directed to take more pictures of the space, from the doorway to the corner, where the corpse resided. Resuming his examination, the ME peered closely at the corpse's eyes, ordering more photo close-ups of the face, marks on the neck, and each hand.

Dr. Hyde cleared his throat, noting aloud, "Since the body usually cools one degree an hour, it obviously cooled more rapidly in the freezer and rigor mortis set in." He stopped to clear his throat again. "Because the eyes are still open," he continued, as he viewed the body from different angles, "a thin cloudy film has formed, which usually happens two or three hours after death." Stepping back once more, he jotted down a few quick notes, tapped his pen on his notepad, and stared at the corpse. A moment later, he wrapped up his cursory examination and was ready with more pronouncements. But just as Paisley, growing weary of this man was about to exit, he began again, so she paused.

"The victim," he said, "is—was—a Caucasian male." Dr.

Hyde declared loudly, as if the room were packed with people. But by this time, the only ones still in the freezer with Paisley were Officer Ryan, and one technician...the other tech had escaped to the PBCA van. The volume of Dr. Hyde's voice was out of place, and Paisley let out a sigh, as he continued.

"He was approximately twenty-five to twenty-eight years old, perhaps of northern European decent," then added, "approximately five feet, ten inches tall, weighing somewhere around a hundred and sixty, to a hundred and seventy pounds!"

This is unbelievable, Paisley thought. This is torture! She noticed Officer Ryan shifting from foot to foot, (obviously he too, wanted the ME to finish), and the technician was only staying, in case asked to perform another task.

"Death probably occurred sometime last night, after 11:00 p.m., and before 2:00 a.m., this morning." He droned on, "The male may *not* have died of natural causes, so I will request an autopsy." Paisley and the other two waited impatiently in the freezer for him to finish, but he forged ahead.

"Most likely, the body hit the cement floor with the back of his head, and he was either scooted or dragged to a sitting position on the box in the alcove, in which case, there *is* some evidence of attempted strangulation. Death 'could' have occurred from either one of those events...*or* perhaps he was still alive and froze to death? The cause needs to be determined."

"Are you finished, Doctor?" the female technician finally asked.

Ignoring her comment, and to everyone's consternation, he had even *more* to say! "In the meantime, as soon as you people finish with him, make sure to bag his hands and call in the paramedics to wrap him up to be transported to Ramsey County Coroner's Office, for the autopsy. Good day!" He said this in a cheery tone, volume up, and shuffled towards the freezer door.

He glanced at Paisley, as he passed her and stopped for a second to stare, giving her what *she* considered to be, the evil eye!

"*That*, was creepy!" she thought and shuddered. Chilled to the bone, she realized it was time to leave the freezer. Dr. Hyde's weird performance would probably haunt her, she thought, as she carefully edged her way through the door into the cooler, where it seemed at least thirty degrees warmer.

Paisley headed through the kitchen to the outer dining room and sat at a table in time to see the paramedics drive to the back of the building. Glancing out the front windows, she was momentarily shocked to see the conglomeration of vehicles: the police cars, the ambulance, and the PBCA van. Turning her gaze to the dining area, she noticed several detectives sitting at tables in the far corners with notepads and pens, busy conducting interviews.

Julia approached her table. "I made you another Diet Coke, Paisley—I can't believe what's happened! Everyone's saying it was Gregore, who froze in the freezer! How did it happen? Poor guy...I didn't know him very well, because our schedules rarely overlapped, but it's a horrible thing to have happened—and at *my* workplace!"

Paisley, half listening to Julia's rambling, said, "I'm sorry. I don't have answers for you right now. The police are busy trying to determine what happened and how. So, everyone will have the information when they uncover the facts. The authorities will probably be here for a while—don't be surprised if they want to take a statement from you." Paisley put her arms on the table and leaned back in her chair, attempting to relax. It seemed as if she'd been here for hours, but it had only been forty-five minutes.

"But I don't know anything? I barely knew him!" Julia said.

"Well, they'll even want to know that! I'm sure they'll take statements from all the employees to find out as much as they can about him," Paisley added. Just then, Ben Wister, the owner, came around the corner, and when Ingles spotted him, she hurried over to express her sympathy for the devastating occurrence.

"Paisley, I just arrived...all the police vehicles outside...I can't believe it! All I know is one of my employees is in the freezer, and he's dead—is that true?" he asked in a distraught voice.

CHAPTER 4

"I'm afraid so, Ben. I was here when the body was discovered, and there's not much to tell yet, except according to Steve, his name is—was," she corrected herself, "Gregore—not sure of the last name."

Ben appeared shaken to hear an employee died, and in *his* fast-food establishment! "Excuse me, Paisley," he said, "I have to check this out," and he headed for the freezer to see for himself what had happened.

Paisley followed, but a tall, lanky police detective blocked their way. "I'm sorry sir, no one is allowed back here just now," the Detective said firmly.

"But I'm Ben, the owner, and I demand to see what's going on!"

"I'm sorry sir, but there's an on-going investigation. One of the Detectives will be out soon to talk with you, so it's best to return to the dining room and wait for an update."

Ben would *not* acquiesce, causing Paisley to intervene and explain, "Ben's the owner, and I'll be happy to escort him, as I'm a detective on the force." The officer regarded this request, but looked at her with doubtful eyes, noticing her unconventional attire. "You can ask Officer Ryan for corroboration," she said.

The officer was one of the late arrivals and hadn't been introduced to her yet, so he left them standing, while he went to talk to Officer Ryan. Upon returning, he said nothing, but led the way to the freezer and when rounding the corner to the cooler, he reluctantly stepped aside. "Please stay close to the freezer door. Don't get in the way of the investigation," he said and returned to the dining area.

Ben was about to see for himself when a gurney entered, and the paramedics said, "Excuse us! Please make way...!" The gurney rolled through the back door, through the cooler, and into the freezer. The attendants began gingerly retrieving the victim's body, lifting it onto the gurney, placing it in a body bag, and zipping it up, ready to go.

Cobbling back across the freezer's cement floor, the gurney passed by Paisley and Ben, then bounced over the door jamb, and exited the freezer into the cooler. There was a crinkling and crunching sound, as the gurney, with the body aboard rolled over the plastic, which the technicians had also used to cover the cooler's floor. The gurney was pushed through the back door, as quickly as possible, to avoid gawking customers and employees in the main dining room. From here, the body travels to the Ramsey County Coroner's Office for the autopsy requested by Dr. Hyde.

Both Paisley and Ben returned to the dining area and sat at a table by the side windows. Ben put his elbows on the table and his head in hands, covering his face for a moment. When he looked up, there was concern in his dark eyes. He straightened in his chair, "This is horrible! Gregore is dead! Such an awful thing to happen! I'm sure the employees are scared and upset!"

He ran a hand over his wrinkled forehead and across his closely cropped thinning hair, then sat back in his chair, looking around his establishment. It almost seemed normal. Workers carried on with their work, and the delicious smell of burgers and fries wafted into the dining area.

Paisley sympathized, "Ben, there's really nothing to do right now. The authorities are just beginning the investigation, so just keep the employees calm and take care of business as usual. The police will do a thorough investigation and get to the bottom of this," then she sat back in her chair, too. "In the meantime, as I was telling Julia, the police will interview you. They're questioning some of the employees now to obtain information about Gregore. Maybe someone knows something that will help us find out what occurred?"

"I'm sorry Paisley, but this is *so* difficult...I'm upset! But of *course,* I'll make sure things run smoothly. I've been worried about other things which have been happening here lately, too— and this is just the clincher!"

Paisley started to ask Ben what these things were. Still, the image of Gregore involuntarily flashed into her thoughts, and she momentarily relived the sight of him sitting on the container, with his pallid complexion, blue lips, bulging eyes, and even ice crystals on his eyelashes! She couldn't shake the sensation of the feel of Gregore's skin when checking for his pulse...suddenly, she felt chilled and shuddered involuntarily.

Noticing this, Ben abruptly stood in case she needed help, saying, "*Paisley!* Is everything all right?"

"Oh, I'm sorry. It all caught up to me for a second...I've been running on adrenaline since I arrived this morning, and I switched into clinical mode when I saw the body. After sitting for a minute, it kind of hit me, but I'm okay, thanks." Still feeling chilled, she zipped up her hoodie a little more, struggling to gain her composure.

Police officers were putting up more yellow crime scene tape now that the PBCA technicians and ambulance were finally gone from the freezer area. They instructed employees not to cross the tape since it was now an official crime scene. Paisley was still pondering the events of the morning, when a Detective strolled over. He recognized her, said hello, and turned and introduced himself to Ben. Sitting down at the table across from Ben, he extracted a small notebook and pen from his jacket pocket, then proceeded to tell Ben what little information there was, concerning the death of his employee.

While Ben and the Detective talked, Paisley retreated towards the tables at the front of the fast-food place. With the Paramedics and the Medical Examiner gone from the freezer, there was more room for the Detectives to take a closer look at the entire back area, so a more careful determination could be made, as to how a murderer was able to enter, commit a murder, and escape. Paisley was deep in thought about ideas concerning the incident when Julia surprised her by appearing at the table again.

"Hey Paisley! I've been trying to get a Diet Coke to you all morning! Here's a fresh one!" and she set down another Diet Coke.

"Oh, my gosh! Thanks, that's so sweet!" Paisley took a long sip, "Ahhh!" Suddenly, she was aware of someone tapping her shoulder.

"Excuse me?"

Turning to see who was there, she was surprised to see a man she didn't recognize standing behind her, and said, "Oh! Are you speaking to me?"

"Yes, I am." His tone was business-like. "I was told you were one of the first people to arrive on the scene when the employee called for help."

The man wasn't in uniform like the other officers, but before she had a chance to ask who he was, he said, "I'm Detective Boone, with the Pinecrest Police Department, and I wonder if I might ask you a few routine questions?"

"Well, I..." she stammered. This morning had been stressful, and her reply wasn't coming out clearly. "I...guess so?" Paisley tried to gather her wits about her, which wasn't easy because right now, all she really wanted to do was relax a moment and quietly enjoy her Diet Coke! To make things worse, hunger was now rearing its ugly head, and of the two drinks Julia had served, she'd only managed to take one sip! And now, here is this detective!

At first glance, she had to admit he was a nice looking man, and obviously he wanted whatever information he could get concerning the murder. Immediately, however, she was self-conscious, realizing her appearance was one of a rumple-haired, sweaty woman dressed in an old faded T-shirt and sweats, with a worn-out hoodie—and wouldn't you know it—her dirtiest, mud-stained, used-to-be white, tennies! Knowing the interview was inevitable, she restrained the temptation to roll her eyes.

Detective Boone suggested they move to different table near a larger window, which faced the parking lot further away from customers because it would offer more privacy. She followed him. "Have a seat," he gestured and pulled out a chair for her.

Glimpsing out the window, she noticed most of the police cars had departed, and the ambulance was gone, along with the veritable traffic jam of emergency vehicles, which littered the parking lot earlier. The scene had dissolved into a typical mid-morning parking lot for Ben's Burgers. Only two police cars remained to bear testimony to the morning's events.

The detective seated himself on the opposite side of the table, and she turned her attention to him. But before he could speak, Julia scurried up and deposited another drink in front of Paisley, saying, "It was on the other table—it's still cold, and I thought you'd still like to have it!" What a welcome sight for Paisley, and she took a long drink.

Julia barely stepped aside when a pushy photographer ran up to the table and began snapping pictures. "I'm from the *Brainerd Daily Newspaper*, and they said, you were the one who discovered the body...is that correct?" There was an eager look on his face as he stood, waiting for an answer.

Before she could say anything, the camera was clicking away, causing the Detective to stand and say, "Could you please come back later? Right now, I'm conducing an investigation."

A *Pinecrest Gazette* reporter was standing next to the cameraman, and heard the rebuff, "Sure! Sorry," the photographer said, and he and the reporters backed away apologizing for the interruption, then scattered to collect pictures and comments from the workers.

The Detective sat down and began again. "I'm sorry to detain you...I'm sure you have things to do, but I'm Detective Boone, and several officers said you were the first person on site after the employee yelled for help." Taking out a small notebook and flipping the pages, he slid a pen from his pocket and looked up at her with the most penetrating eyes she'd ever seen. His eyes were the color of blue denim! Then in a business-like tone-of-voice, he continued, "May I have your name and occupation?"

"Certainly," and Paisley found herself flustered by his formal demeanor. The Detective's hair was slightly graying at the temples, blending into darker, somewhat curly hair, with a casual unruly look. It was difficult to discern his age, but because of his rugged look, she guessed he was in his mid-to-late thirties, or maybe even early forties? Considering his deeply tanned face and hands, he obviously spent a great deal of time outdoors in much sunnier climates. His stern countenance was slightly intimidating, and, she decided, his eyes *might* crinkle at the corners, *if* he ever smiled.

He even dressed in a conservative manner—dark jeans, a dark well-worn leather jacket, sunglasses hanging in the V-opening of a light blue T-shirt, *and*, without looking, she'd bet he was wearing cowboy boots, too—he just seemed the type. Suddenly, she was aware he was asking questions and taking a guess, quickly offered what she hoped was the right answer,

"Oh...uh...my name? It's Paisley, Paisley Ingles," she stammered, as she continued to gaze into his blue-denim eyes, which were busy sizing her up. She said, "I'm *also*, a detective for the Pinecrest Police Department...currently working as their Computer Forensics Specialist." How embarrassing! She was aware of how much her attire did *not* speak to her position! She wanted to crawl under the table.

His eyebrows rose slightly, and with a touch of surprise in his voice, he said, "Oh! I'm sorry, no one mentioned your connection to the department. So, Ms. Ingles," he paused a beat, "would it be possible to obtain a statement later this morning at the precinct? It would free me to help the rest of the officers here with employee interviews so we could wrap up sooner, rather than later...I'm sure you understand."

"Of course," she said, much relieved. "That would be fine. What time would you like to meet? Besides," she added, "I need food and a shower before coming to work." Why did she have to say that last bit about a shower? Anyway, she thought, she wouldn't mind looking at those mysterious blue eyes again —*that's* for sure!

"Well," and glancing cursorily at his watch, "how about meeting around one this afternoon? Does that work for you?"

She pondered for a moment or two, "Sure,...where will I meet you?"

"I'm not exactly sure which office I'll be using this week, because I've come here on assignment and I don't have a permanent office yet, so I'll wait for you at the receptionist's desk, or perhaps outside on the steps. I'll have a temporary place to meet by then." With that, he stood and nodded, shook her hand, started to turn, then paused and looked back. "Ms. Ingles, please be careful on the way home...you never know who may be watching."

CHAPTER 5

Paisley nodded her head, turned, and though puzzled by his comment, shook it off and began threading her way through the tables to the door. Several police officers watched her exit Ben's Burgers, and once outside, she took a deep breath to clear her head. Today's hubbub at Ben's had lured people from the surrounding mall establishments, curious about the cause of the extraordinary police presence, and many had wandered over to see what happened.

Apparently, an event of this magnitude in Pinecrest, was *not* an everyday occurrence. Several people were standing near the entrance, talking about the earlier commotion to a man from the local TV station, while his cameraman recorded them. Hoping they hadn't noticed her, Paisley pulled her hood over her head, crammed her hands in her hoodie pockets, and skirted around those still gathering as the news spread. Head down, she failed to notice a photographer, snapping pictures of her, hurrying towards her Jeep.

Fortunately, she had parked her Jeep Ranger off to the side

in the parking lot, enabling her to make a quick getaway. As she neared the shiny white Jeep, she inhaled the aroma drifting out of Ben's, of burgers cooking, reminding her that she hadn't eaten breakfast. Fumbling in her pocket for keys, she beeped open the door and slithered into her seat with a sigh of relief.

The used Jeep Ranger, which Paisley bought shortly after arriving in Brainerd, was referred to by those who knew her, as the White Tornado—not just because of its color—but because most of the time, she drove too fast. It was a bad habit from California, where drivers viewed a speed limit, as just a suggestion. However, slumped in the driver's seat, she felt relief coupled with exhaustion. Today, she felt no compulsion to speed. The horror of the morning's event was just beginning to register.

The weather had warmed and as the temperature increased, so did the number of people heading for the stores, which would soon be humming. It was the season, to buy bug spray, mosquito repellant, grass seed, fertilizers, and annuals to brighten yards after the long Minnesota winters. Fortunately, she hadn't experienced mosquitoes—yet! Paisley turned the key in the ignition, and the Jeep roared to a start...well, maybe roar wasn't quite the word, but the engine *was* running.

She eased out of the parking lot and turned left onto the highway, heading southeast towards Brainerd and her Aunt's farmhouse. Once she crossed from Pinecrest into Brainerd, eight more miles and she could turn south, onto County Road 38. Fifteen minutes later she made the turn, stepped on the gas and flew down the road into the countryside's freedom, putting the murder behind her for the moment.

Brainerd Open land, with thickets of oak and birch trees, drew her attention. Most of their leaves had already emerged, with the rest creating a celery-green haze across some of the still visible, tree trunks and branches. Cows meandered towards giant round hay bales, which looked like over-sized tan polka dots decorating the fields, which were still recovering from winter. She passed a farm with a small herd of sleek Arabian horses cantering across a field attempting to rid itself of the last vestiges of snow, which hid in shaded areas of the land.

In the distance, she noticed a murder of crows. She loved the group designation for the scavenger birds, who pranced around on the road ahead, stalking some newly found road kill. She made a mental note to avoid running over whatever-it-was, as she disliked the thought of further adding to what was already an unsightly mess! By the time she neared, they all took flight—but not until the last minute—how daring, she thought!

Several more farms loomed in the distance, and she passed them without so much as a glance because she'd finally spotted the large red barn and farmhouse belonging to Uncle Vlad and Aunt Olga, in its rustic setting on a heavily wooded piece of land. She looked forward to a shower, a change of clothes and something to eat because it was already midmorning, and so far, she only had a few sips of her soft drink. The Jeep bounced down the long dirt driveway of the quaint farmhouse, and Paisley parked, turned off the engine, then hurried into an entrance on the south side of the house. This entrance led into a small mudroom, where she deposited her dirty tennies, before entering the farmhouse kitchen.

She was eager to tell Aunt Olga about her unbelievable morning at Ben's Burgers, as she walked into the spacious kitchen—her favorite room—and set her keys and purse on the end of a rustic oak dining table. The kitchen felt homey, like something out of the magazine, *Farmhouse Journal*. There were old copies of this magazine piled by the large brick fireplace, and Paisley enjoyed perusing some of the issues.

The enormous claw-footed oak table sat at one end of the

kitchen with chairs on three sides and a bench on the other. A delicate ecru crocheted lace tablecloth, adorned the table, with a round wooden bowl planted in the center containing a variety of fruit. Open shelves on the back wall were filled with things you'd expect to find in a pantry, like canned goods, large glass canisters of flour, sugar, various types of noodles, beans, and corn for popping.

Shelves covered a wall next to the counter where all the various pots and pans resided, while the cupboards over the counters, with their glass doors, held dinnerware and glassware. On one end of the room, a cozy breakfast nook contained a small tea table and chairs with a view through a large bay window onto a beautiful flower garden, which Aunt Olga obviously tended with love.

Paisley's Aunt heard her enter, and turned to greet her, as Paisley ran towards her with a big hug saying, "Oh, Aunt Olga! I'm so glad to be back from my run, and you'll *never* believe what happened today! But first, I need to freshen up."

"Okay, I make some food." That was Aunt Olga's go-to for anything—good news, bad news, gossip, or visitors—the first thing she'd say was, "I make some food," then she'd make coffee, and whip up something special.

Without giving her Aunt a chance to say anything else, Paisley grabbed a glass of orange juice from the fridge and picked up her purse and satchel as she exited the kitchen and headed towards the bathroom. Ready for a relaxing shower, she turned on the water, shed her clothes, and stepped into the warm water, where she luxuriated for fifteen minutes. After drying off, she went to her bedroom to get dressed.

She chose a pair of dark blue jeans and a pale pink cotton shirt for her return to the precinct to meet with Detective Boone, both of which accentuated her lithe body and long legs.

After drying her hair, she pulled back the curly bronze tresses, fastening them with a clip. However, wisps of hair always seemed to escape and fall to the sides of her face, drawing attention to her amber eyes and long lashes.

She yanked the sweaty hoodie off the bed and threw it towards the hamper, causing several objects to fall out of the pocket and onto the floor. Leaning down, she picked them up and tossed them in her purse. A swipe of lip gloss across her rosy lips, and with a quick evaluation in the mirror, she scooped up her satchel and purse then headed to the kitchen, rushing into its delicious aromas. She settled into a chair positioned close to the stove, which resembled the old fashioned cast iron models with claw-footed legs raising it half a foot or more off the floor.

Aunt Olga hustled towards the oven to check on the blueberry muffins and said, "Here...have coffee, my dear...blueberry muffins, ready in minute or two. You like this snack?" Aunt Olga spoke with a thick Russian accent, which Paisley loved, because of the staccato way she put her words together...it was endearing.

"Smells *so* good," Paisley said, closing her eyes and enjoying the aroma filling the kitchen, then she headed to the refrigerator across the old fashioned braided rug centered on the oak plank kitchen floor. She poured herself a second glass of orange juice, and grabbed the jar of homemade butter for the muffins, and then sat on the other side of the table closest to the raised hearth, beckoning to her, with its fireplace full of logs warming the kitchen. Aunt Olga mentioned how years ago, during cold winters, a kettle of boiling water hung over the roaring flames everyday to act as a humidifier for the farmhouse during the frigid, Minnesota winters.

Wearing a vintage red gingham apron, her Aunt carried a tray to the table, "Ready to eat?"

Paisley stared at a picture of her Aunt and Uncle, which hung over the fireplace, and turned towards her Aunt, eyeing the muffins and said, "These look delicious! Of course, I'm starved!"

She turned back to stare at the picture over the fireplace again, while she ate and thought, that her Aunt looked much the same now, as she did back then. She wore a floral print dress in the picture, with long sleeves, just like she wore now. It seemed all the dresses Paisley saw her in were the same as the one in the photograph, except made from different prints. No matter how warm it was in the house, she always wore dresses with long sleeves and sometimes a sweater. How odd, she thought?

Looking back towards her Aunt, she smiled, as she grabbed two more muffins from the plate and sipped her coffee. She told her Aunt all the exciting events of the morning, and needless to say, Aunt Olga was shocked to hear of the murder at Ben's Burgers. Concern spread over her face, "I worry for you!" she said.

The last thing Paisley wanted was to give her Aunt more reasons to be upset, and immediately said, "I don't want to worry you—everything's fine."

Her Aunt, changing the subject, confessed, "I'm glad you come to stay here, dear. I miss having Vlad at house with me, and it's nice to cook for you. I am not lonely."

Paisley, reaching for another muffin and referring to her Aunt's last comment, said, "I'm grateful for everything you do for me. I *never* cooked while attending the Police Academy in California. I filled my freezer with cheap frozen meals, and most nights, I resorted to fast-food places for sustenance." She chuckled, and so did Aunt Olga. Even though Paisley wasn't always sure her Aunt understood her humor, it seemed whenever Paisley laughed, her Aunt always joined in.

Since arriving in Brainerd, several months ago, Paisley's fondness for her Aunt had grown. Staying at the farm gave her a chance to adjust to the area before having to find an apartment. Her Aunt's round face, rosy cheeks, and gray eyes, which squinted when she smiled, made her happy and the move to Minnesota, more manageable. Although her Aunt was short and overweight, in a plump sort of way, it didn't slow her down, as she scurried around the kitchen and the farm. She wondered how old her Aunt was but didn't want to be rude and ask.

"Eat, eat!" Olga repeated.

"Honestly, I'm stuffed!" Paisley moaned, as she eyed another muffin, and reminiscing about visiting her Aunt years ago. She said, "When our family came to visit one summer, so many years ago, I was only six years old, but I still remember how much fun we had. You made blueberry muffins then, too," and she added, "who would've thought I'd ever move out here?"

Paisley knew very little about her Aunt...only a few sparse facts from family members. She remembered her Father telling her years ago, that Aunt Olga Shenkovsky, was originally from Russia, and immigrated to America, as a newly-wed with her husband, Vladimir, in their early twenties. Her Dad told her that he remembered hearing that the Shenkovskys came to Minnesota, worked hard, and eventually purchased the Brainerd farm, adding more acreage as the years progressed.

Apparently, the Shenkovskys had twin sons, who, according to family rumors, were killed in a helicopter accident while in a branch of the armed forces. Paisley was very interested in learning more about her Aunt's past, but every time she brought up the subject of family, *or* Olga's Russian history, Olga changed the subject. It made Paisley curious, and she wondered, did her Aunt have something to hide? Clicking on the oak flooring, suddenly came from the mudroom. It was the nails of paws, tapping on the floor.

"Oh! Abby...I get food," and Aunt Olga hurried out of the kitchen into the mudroom, mumbling to herself. She'd explained to Paisley, how Uncle Vlad found Abby years ago, abandoned alongside the road, when she was a pup. They adopted Abby, and she lived with them ever since and was like a child to them. Abby was well trained and came into the mudroom, but only as far as the kitchen doorway, then waited, as Olga waddled out to feed her.

Paisley watched and smiled while finishing her coffee. Aunt Olga explained, "Abby is Australian breed... a Blue Heeler... breed makes good cattle and horse herder. They are smart...easy to train. Good guard dog."

Abby was all that, Paisley thought. She loved being in the pasture with the cows and horses, barked whenever strangers came to the door and was protective of the Shenkovsky's farm —*and* Paisley, who loved her, too!

CHAPTER 6

"Abby, miss my Vlad, too," Aunt Olga said, coming back into the kitchen. Paisley noticed her Aunt's expression had turned to one of sadness. Olga's husband, Vladimir, had been in the hospital for four weeks, while the doctors ran tests to determine what was wrong. Since he was very ill, Olga visited him in the hospital, as much as possible. Several weeks ago, the Doctors finally revealed he had terminal cancer and wasn't coming home. This was when Olga began going to the hospital almost every day and sometimes staying overnight.

Paisley, seeing the anguish on her Aunt's face said, "Hey!" then stood up and went to her, giving her a big hug. "Don't be sad. Uncle Vlad wouldn't want you to worry...look, I'm going to work now, but when I get home tonight we'll pop corn and play some card games, okay?"

The dark cloud disappeared from Olga's countenance, as quickly as it had come, and when her Aunt lifted her head, she said, "We play tomorrow...I see Vlad tonight and stay."

"Then, please say hello to him, for me...and give him my love. I'm sorry...I have to go now," she said, walking to the table and grabbing her purse and satchel. She gave her Aunt a big smile, threw the satchel strap over her shoulder, took her purse and keys, and headed for the mudroom.

"Bye, Abby!" Exiting the farmhouse, she bent to pat the dog, who licked her fingers. Wondering what lay ahead at the office, she climbed into her Jeep. Okay, Detective Boone, I'm on my way, she thought, and found herself looking forward to the meeting. But first, one more piece of business to take care of... she needed to call Ben Wister.

Starting her car, she drove down the dirt driveway and onto the paved road towards town. The atmosphere of the Midwest rural setting was exactly what Paisley needed. Paisley's Mother had suggested she leave California after her divorce, and the two difficult years that followed. "It will give you a place to start over," her Mother said, so she finally decided to make the move. Now, after being in Minnesota for such a brief time, she realized the much needed change of scenery was working!

But her thoughts were abruptly interrupted, when the voice on the radio said, "...And later, clouds will gather, and there will be possible thunderstorms, lasting into late evening..." The radio droned on causing her thoughts to drift back to California, and her decision to leave.

Her feeling of contentment, as she breathed in the cool country air and surveyed the beauty of the fields, blew thoughts of California away. The rest of the day was going to be fine despite the unsettling events of the morning. The sun moved from behind a cloud, causing her to reach for her purse to retrieve her sunglasses. Eyes on the road, she fumbled in her purse until out of frustration, she pulled onto the shoulder and stopped. Dumping its contents onto the passenger seat, everything fell out except the sunglasses, which apparently, were stuck in the bottom. She pulled them out and put them on then began returning the items on the car seat, to her purse.

It was then she observed two small objects. One, was her new chapstick, which she unceremoniously dropped in her purse. Picking up the other object, she turned it in her fingers realizing it was the item she rescued from under the freezer door, at Ben's. She stared at it. It was a flash drive, but not one of hers. The only ones she used were PNY drives, but this one was not a familiar brand—in fact, it was *no* brand. Realizing the flash drive must have belonged to Ben, she made a mental note to return it. Didn't a*ll* flash drives have a brand, she thought?

According to her watch, she had plenty of time to get to the precinct, so she decided make a quick call to Ben before getting back on the road. Paisley found his number in her contacts and punched it into her phone, then put it on speaker and resumed driving.

When he answered, she said, "Ben, this is Paisley. I'm on my way to work now and thought I'd call to see how you're doing."

"Oh, thanks for asking, Paisley...I'm hanging in there. The police wrapped up their investigation about an hour or so after you left this morning. What a relief to have them gone!"

"Okay...just wanted to make sure things were going better. By the way, I'll probably be by a little later."

"That'd be great. There's a couple of things I'd like to talk about," he said.

"Sure...we'll do that," she said, and wondered what he wanted to talk about?

Pinecrest Ben Wister hung up, after speaking with Paisley. Since he'd purchased the eatery, in 2002, freezer safety had never been an issue. Although, he did recall a time several years ago, when a teen worker was fooling around and hid in the freezer, but, he was discovered several minutes later when one of the workers entered to get frozen chicken nuggets for the cooks.

As a rule, many workers were in and out of the refrigeration area and it never posed a problem, but now there was a reason to replace the existing door with one having an inside handle, as a safety measure. He also considered calling a company to install video cameras outside...maybe it was time to do that, too? But first, he needed to handle the freezer safety issue. Before making the call to the refrigeration company, he checked the front dining area to make sure his assistant manager had things under control.

Boy, I hope the murder doesn't have a detrimental effect on my bottom line, he thought. Second guessing himself, he wondered if he'd made a mistake hiring Gregore—and I even gave him a second chance! He was strange from the get-go...I should've listened to my wife. I'll listen next time, he vowed to himself. Ruminating on this, he remembered it was almost time to go to police headquarters to see Detective Boone.

"Now, where is Gregore's personnel file?" he muttered to himself. Detective Boone wanted him to bring it along, so he began a search of his office for the file. Drawers were opened and closed, but he found nothing. This mess needs straightening, he realized, and began rifling through papers. That's when he noticed the employee files scattered on the desktop mixed in with some packing slips, which also needed filing.

However, as the employee files caught his attention, he also noticed a locked drawer in his desk, which appeared to have been pried open and carefully closed again. A tug on the handle, and sure enough, it was not locked anymore. He could even make out tiny scratches on the metal lock. This drawer held spare keys for the various entrance doors, registers, etc., but all the keys seemed to be present and accounted for. How odd, he thought?

Why would anyone be looking through these drawers, when nothing was missing? Turning his attention to the rest of the office, he methodically searched through other drawers in a small corner desk, then the large filing cabinet, located in the corner of the office. He was satisfied nothing else had been taken. Whoever did this, obviously was looking for something, but what? The office had been searched by someone, who left it just as messy, as he found it.

Ben returned to the personnel files on his desktop and could tell they were out of place, and for *this* reason, he knew someone really *had* been in his office! Ben scanned the files, found Gregore's and put it next to his jacket until time to leave for the precinct. He resumed another search...this time, for the refrigeration company's business card. He finally located it and called.

"Hello? May I please speak to someone regarding a replacement door for my commercial freezer?" Several minutes later, a salesman came to the phone. "Yes, this is Ben Wister, owner of Ben's Burgers, in Pinecrest. How soon can someone come out to replace the door of my walk-in refrigeration unit? A new door is needed...a new one with an inside handle." He waited on line for a few minutes, then said, "Model number? Let me see," and he looked through a few invoices. "The unit is a CC5-54."

Paisley arrived at the precinct at the appointed time, and noticed Detective Boone standing outside, on the entrance steps of the station. The station itself, was a two-story building, taking up almost the entire block of Euclid Street, with replicas of antique three-globe Victorian light posts lining the parkway. The precinct was located opposite a two-story courthouse and jail and was situated next to a law building on the left, and a large parking lot flanked by an office complex on the right.

Seedy little bail bond store-fronts were further down the street and around the corner, for those unlucky enough to need them. The cement feel of the precinct's structure was softened with parkway trees and small shrubs planted strategically in front of the building. A bronze statue of a police officer stood near the steps, ringed by a flower bed filled with colorful spring tulips. After parking in the police lot, Paisley climbed out of her Jeep and walked the rest of the way.

Nearing the steps, the colorful flowers were beginning to bloom, attracting her attention for a moment, then she looked up at Detective Boone, waiting on the top step. When she neared, he seemed taller than she remembered from their brief encounter at Ben's Burgers. Her attention had been on so many other things at the time, but looking at him now, she guessed him to be six-feet plus, and with his tan face he looked like he'd just returned from a vacation in a warmer climate.

By the time she stood in front of him, she thought OMG, there they were! His blue-denim eyes sparkling in the sunlight! The toes of his boots peeked out from the bottom of his jeans, as he stood, leaning against a pillar, arms crossed over his chest, and one foot crossed over the other. Paisley couldn't help but silently congratulate herself for being right about the cowboy boots! His smile widened when he greeted her, which of course, displayed his beautiful white teeth...and she tried hard to ignore his good looks.

"C'mon, let's go in." He motioned her to follow, ushering her inside the double doors of the precinct and into the building. She took her sunglasses off her nose and pushed them up on her head, as they both approached the front desk.

"May I help you?" the receptionist said to Paisley, while buzzing Boone through. Paisley didn't recognize this girl and wondered where Jane, the regular receptionist was, who would have recognized her and waved *her* through also!

Before she could answer, Detective Boone spoke to the receptionist saying, "She's with me...she works here too...we're having a meeting."

While the receptionist was batting her eyes at Boone, she buzzed Paisley through, who now had to pick up her pace to catch up to Detective Boone, with his long stride. Slightly miffed by the exchange at the receptionist's desk, she felt like an underling, which of course she was, but that was beside the point! Where was the respect? She decided to set her irritation aside—for the time being.

Boone made an abrupt turn to the right, down a putty-colored hallway lined with pictures of old police cars from the 1950s, and photos of the precinct itself, before it was expanded and remodeled. There were portraits of past officials handing out achievement medals, and before turning left, they passed portraits of previous Police Captains, with brass nameplates on the mahogany frames, encasing their portraits. The hallway continued past rooms and offices and at the end of the hall, there stood an open door.

This was the room Boone had garnered and they entered. An espresso-colored rectangular table and four matching, wooden office chairs, sat in the middle of the room with papers and pens on one end, and a laptop sitting on the opposite end. A tall olive-drab filing cabinet with three or four reference books of some sort stacked on top, was positioned next to the only window in the room.

"Please have a seat, Ms. Ingles," he said. "It *is* Ms., isn't it?"

CHAPTER 7

"Thanks. Yes, it's Ms." He's *much* too formal she mused, as she gracefully sat in an uncomfortable-looking, straight-backed chair, which would have been more appropriate in an interrogation room. She'd have to work on his formality, if they had to cross paths often!

"I'm sorry to take up your time today, but since you were on the scene first, I'm looking forward to hearing what took place." His tone became serious. "This is a curious case. Right now, it's an open investigation because the actual cause of death has yet to be determined. There's going to be an autopsy, and in the meantime, we need to get all the facts we can to determine how it happened, who did it, and why."

Paisley stared at him. He sat stiffly in his chair. She felt like saying, "Ya, I know!" But instead replied, "I'll give you all the information I have." It was Boone's turn to look at her without any distractions, and he found himself noticing how cat-like her amber-colored eyes seemed—and how they contrasted with the pale pink of her shirt, *and* how different she looked from their meeting earlier, at Ben's.

She waited for him to continue, her long jeans-clad legs crossed and her arms jauntily resting on her knees, hands open to the floor, as they dangled on either side of her legs. She was ready and willing to offer up any facts that might be helpful.

"This meeting is perfect, since I had to work this afternoon anyway, Detective Boone," she began.

Staring at her for a second more, he caught himself, and quickly looked down at his notes, "Now, if I could, I'd like to ask you a few routine questions, as to what occurred when you first arrived at Ben's Burgers this morning."

"Of course," she answered demurely. She presumed he would want the events to be recounted exactly as she remembered them, during which time, she assumed he'd make notes on the worn yellow legal pad sitting on his desk, and later request an office employee to type up his notes.

"I'd been on an early morning run and arrived at Ben's a few minutes before it opened at seven. When the doors were unlocked, I went inside to get a Diet Coke, then Jerry, one of the employees, came running out from the back of the kitchen in a panic and yelled something about the freezer." Watching, as Detective Boone scratched down a few notes, she asked, "Am I talking too fast?"

"No, no...you're doing fine," and he looked up at her adding, "please continue."

"Well, I ran back to see what had happened, entered the cooler and noticed the freezer door was ajar, so I cautiously pushed it open. As I entered, I saw a boot sticking out from the recess between two shelving units at the back of the freezer, and stepping towards it there he was—a dead man. I felt his neck.

There was no pulse, so I had the front end manager, who had followed me into the freezer, hurry up front to call 911."

"Did you see anything amiss? Did it look like there had been a struggle? Anything else you can tell me?"

"Hmmm, I remember when I put my fingers on his neck to feel for a pulse, that I had to move his collar, because it was buttoned, and when I did, I saw reddish-purple marks on his throat. It appeared to me he might have been strangled. As for any other details, I think I'd like to sit down in a quiet place and carefully go over the morning's events in my head, there was so much commotion around..." her voice trailed off and she thought for a moment, "...but, if you like," she perked up, "I'll write a detailed report, and this way it will give me a chance to think everything through and I can have it ready for you in the morning!"

Detective Boone sat there with scribbles on his notepad and contemplated what she offered. "A great idea, I'm sure you didn't expect your morning to turn out this way, but before I forget, were you talking to the owner of Ben's Burgers? Did he have access to information about the murder before I arrived?"

"Not really," she said, "everyone was in a state of shock, and with so much confusion I decided to say as little as possible to anyone, so as not to give out misinformation."

"Good police procedure," he acknowledged, and nodded his head.

She repositioned herself in the uncomfortable chair. Was his comment a pat on the head, she wondered? She continued, "Ben wanted to see who the dead employee was for himself. I obtained permission from Officer Ryan to take him back to the freezer for a quick look, and Ben verified that the employee was indeed, Gregore Kamorov."

Hesitantly, Paisley decided to ask for any information

Boone had been able to ascertain from the employees, just to fill in the blanks for her. Still, he wasn't very forthcoming and the few answers he gave were vague. She contemplated his demeanor for a moment, deciding not to pursue it any further.

"Any more questions, Detective?" she asked. "

"Nope! I'll be looking forward to your written report."

"Then I'll start on it now, and detail everything I can recall." She stood up to leave, but on second thought, changed her mind and said, "Before I go, *I* have a couple of questions for *you!*"

"Go ahead, I'll answer them if I can." The Detective also stood up.

"Well, I was wondering when we'd find out the actual cause of death, it seems awful to think Kamorov just sat there...do you know what I mean? And then there're the red marks I saw on his neck...so, I'd like you to inform me concerning the autopsy's findings."

"The autopsy should tell the tale," he said. "It will be conducted in the next day or two, depending on how busy things are at the morgue. The body is at the Ramsey County Coroner's Office, so hopefully we'll have the results soon."

"Do you suppose...well...would you tell me when you find out the results?" she asked again.

"I'm sorry, only department people assigned to the case are allowed access to that information," he explained, "until it's released to the press." He observed a slight disappointment register in her cat-like eyes, for just a moment.

Not liking this answer, she felt it was time to take a stand! In a defiant tone, she replied, "Well, I *do* have authority to view records, and if you check with Lieutenant Banks—he'll vouch for me—since my position falls under *his* jurisdiction. Also, I can show you my credentials!"

Startled to see how defensive she became, he tried to assure her, "Oh, no...that won't be necessary..." he said, backpedaling, as he attempted to pacify her.

Ignoring his comment, she continued, "Actually, I *am* a detective, hired part-time at the moment, as a Computer Forensics Specialist. I'm also associated with Peter Higgins, the District Attorney, as I do some work for him on occasion. A desk and computer are my tools of the trade...for the moment, anyway. When I'm here at the precinct, I share an office with one of the secretaries, Millie, on the other end of the building. I *also* go out in the field frequently, with different officers, to analyze computers of various suspects and many times they're collected and brought here to the computer lab for me to hack into, to discern their contents!"

After her lengthy diatribe, Boone could do nothing but stare at her. He was unable to hide the surprise on his face at her reaction.

Back-pedaling again, he explained he hadn't fully realized what her position was, at the department. "I'm fairly new here, too," he said, "and, I apologize, Ms. Ingles—Detective Ingles..." he corrected himself, and at that moment, his phone rang.

Boone answered and carried on a conversation, which consisted of perfunctory yeses and noes, ending as abruptly as it began. Paisley decided they'd finished their conversation for the time being, because she knew he had work to do.

However, before she left, she said, "Okay, but one more thing, why did you give me the warning earlier when I was leaving Ben's Burgers...the part when you said, I should be careful, as I left? Did *you* know something, which *I* should know?"

The detective deftly side stepped the question by saying, "It's just police procedure. I wanted to remind you that perpetrators can still be lurking at crime scenes, watching. It was only a precaution."

Accepting this explanation, she finally turned to leave. Detective Boone jumped up and came around the desk to shake her hand and assure her he'd check with the lieutenant about keeping her in the autopsy loop. He handed her his card, then *she* reached into her purse and handed him, *hers*! With that, Paisley left the room and strode down the hallway.

Boone went to the door and peered out. He watched her determined stride as she hurried down the corridor. When he looked down, her card was still in his hand, a precinct-issued card, just like his, with the police shield logo, her name, and the number of her office phone.

Back at his desk, he sat down and realized he'd been caught off guard by this woman. Smiling to himself and turning his attention to matters at hand, he managed to shuffle a few papers before Ben Wister arrived. Boone hadn't interviewed him earlier, because Wister needed to get his establishment back to normal and running smoothly, following the morning's disruptions. He hoped Wister remembered Kamorov's personnel file.

Paisley was dying to look back, as she strode down the hall, to see if Detective Boone was watching, but pride prevented her from giving him the satisfaction. She hurriedly passed the front desk and turned right, into a different wing of the precinct, which led to a small office at the end of the corridor.

Millie Adams, a department employee who handled the precinct's voluminous paperwork, shared the office with Paisley but wasn't at her desk when Paisley entered. She put her purse in her lower desk drawer, sat down in a dark gray Naugahyde rolling office chair, scooted up to her standard- issue gunmetal gray office desk, powered on her laptop and waited for it to boot.

As she gazed out the small office window into the precinct's back parking lot, her thoughts drifted to Detective Boone and the meeting, which had just transpired. She wondered, who *is*

Detective Boone...really? She had questions. Why didn't the department's lead detectives, Barnes or Ryan, who'd been on the force for years, interview her? And why had Boone been made the lead detective on this case, since he was as new to the force, as she was? It made no sense.

Paisley turned her focus to her computer and began her report. After forty-five minutes of methodically chronicling everything which transpired earlier at Ben's, she finally finished and realized the report was longer than she'd intended. She included every detail, every movement, every conversation she could recall, to make the report accurate. This was her first opportunity to write a murder report, and she wanted it to be perfect! She couldn't help it—she was a hopeless perfectionist and overachiever.

CHAPTER 8

As Paisley was about to print out her report, the door opened with a flourish and Millie stood for a moment, before dragging herself into the office from her lunch break and plopping down in her desk chair (hers was black). In an exasperated voice she declared the day a disaster. The black-rimmed professor-style glasses, which usually slipped down on her nose, gave her round face the look of a stern librarian—or perhaps, a mad scientist? Paisley couldn't decide. Millie's sandy blond hair appeared a little mussed, and she was *definitely* out-of-sorts!

"What's the matter?" Paisley asked, surprised to see her so frazzled.

"For the entire time I've worked here, *never* have I typed this many interviews!" she snapped back. Then as soon as she'd uttered this, she said, "Oh...I'm sorry Paisley, I didn't mean to sound so cranky...and I *certainly* didn't mean to take it out on *you!*"

Paisley, amused, accepted her apology, "I can imagine how

you must feel! I just finished typing my statement, and it took me almost an hour. This has been *quite* a day!"

"Why did *you* have to write a statement?"

"Oh? I guess you haven't heard, believe it or not, Millie, *I* was there when the body was discovered and was the first one to check him to see if he was dead!"

This caught Millie's attention. She stared at Paisley, replacing her quizzical look, with one of interest, instead. "Wow! How *exciting*! Hey—wanna go out for a bite after work? I've gotta hear all about *this*!" she said eagerly, as she blew upwards, to fluff her bangs, which were in her eyes—again.

"Sure, that would be great! Unless, of course, you're planning to suggest we eat at Ben's Burgers!" Paisley chuckled, and Millie laughed out loud.

"Good one, Pais!" and her mood lightened.

Just then, Paisley's phone rang, "Paisley Ingles, may I help you?"

"It's Ben here, returning your call. I'm back from my meeting with Detective Boone—it didn't take very long."

"Oh, perfect," Paisley said, "I want to stop by for a few minutes and meet with you before things get busy at your place...if that's okay? Besides, I could use an ice cold Diet Coke," she laughed, "I never finished the ones served to me earlier!"

"Yep, that works fine, see you soon," he said

She powered off her phone. "Hey, Millie, I'm running over to Ben's Burgers for a while, and when I return we'll decide where to eat. In the meantime, I'm printing my report and I'll deliver it to Detective Boone's office, myself." Paisley pushed print.

"Gotcha, Pais," Millie answered, over the noise of the printer.

Paisley's new nickname amused her. Only Millie called her "Pais". She grabbed her things, turned off the computer, put the report in a folder, and rushed out of the office. Boone wasn't in his office when she stopped by, so she set it on his desk and left the precinct.

The drive to Ben's Burgers was uneventful. Fifteen minutes later she parked in front and was immediately accosted by the aroma of burgers being broiled over an open flame. This served to remind her she hadn't had anything to eat, except Aunt Olga's muffins. Entering the establishment, she observed a slight air of uneasiness and concern among the employees, still prevailed.

Ben, a concerned look on his face, brightened when he saw her enter. She took off her sunglasses and put them on her head —as usual. She had a habit of wearing them all day long--either on her nose or her head! When people asked why she left them on her head, she laughed, "Because then, I always know where to find them!"

Ben greeted her and called for someone to bring a large Diet Coke. It appeared instantly and he handed it to her, with a smile adding, "If you'd like anything else, it's on the house."

"Hey, thanks!" She took a long drink to quench her thirst before saying, "Ahh...that's *much* better, and if it's not too much trouble, I think I'd like a small Ben's Burger—I can't resist—it smelled so delicious when I entered from the parking lot."

"Done—hey Max—a small Ben's Burger for Paisley," he yelled to the cook.

As they walked towards the back, she began, "Ben, you returned from police headquarters a little while ago, and you've spoken with Detective Boone, but *I'd* like a chance to ask a few questions before you have to go back to work."

"Sure, what can I do for you? Come on, step behind the

counter here and we'll go to my office where we can talk privately."

"Thanks, Ben."

They threaded their way through the kitchen, where cooks were busy making chicken sandwiches and dumping fry baskets onto trays to be salted. Max handed her the burger she requested, in a red plastic basket with some added fries, as she walked by, and she thanking him, continued to follow Ben.

With the basket of food and her drink, her hands were full. They stopped at a small office off the hallway, which led to the cooler and freezer. Paisley glanced at the cooler and gave an involuntary shudder before turning to enter Ben's office. Although the office was small, Ben managed to find a folding chair for her.

"Have a seat and fire away," he said in a weary voice. Turning to face her, he leaned against the edge of his desk, crossing his arms over his chest.

She took a bite of her burger and had to finish chewing before speaking, "Sorry, this is so delicious! Getting to the point, I'm sure you answered these questions for Detective Boone, but I want to ask anyway. What do you know about the victim? I have a few more questions, too."

"Here's what I know. Gregore came here on a work Visa from Russia, and although he'd been in a little trouble with the law, I'm the kind of guy who likes to help others—even give second chances to people who are down on their luck!"

"Yes, I know what a kind person you are," Paisley smiled. "However, maybe you were *too* kind, in this instance."

"Maybe," Ben hung his head for an instant, then continued, "but, when he first started working here he did a great job, until he got in trouble for violating his probation...he was involved in some minor shoplifting. I almost fired him. I had second thoughts when he came to talk to me...he was *extremely* remorseful. He made restitution and was *very* sincere about wanting a second chance rather than be fired, so I agreed to keep him on staff. He is—was—a very capable worker after that, and I had no problems with him at all."

Paisley, had devoured the last of her burger, nodded her head, and continued to eat her fries, while listening. "How long did he work here?"

Ben thought for a second, then said, "A little over six months, I guess? He enrolled at the college as part of his student visa requirements and was a good student. But, to keep his parole officer happy and retain his visa status, he had to keep his grades up and stay gainfully employed."

"Do you have *any* idea what happened, or who would do this?"

He sighed, "No idea...no idea at all. At first, I thought maybe it was a robbery-gone-bad, with Gregore caught in the middle. So, I checked all the registers to see if they'd been tampered with, but I found nothing unusual."

"Did you find anything at all, missing?" Paisley asked.

"Not really, until I went to find Gregore's personnel file to take to Detective Boone. When I first walked in, I noticed things seemed slightly out of place." As he said this, he moved his arm in a sweeping gesture around the room. "As you can see, there's a *lot* of stuff in here, and I'm the only one who would know, if something was out of place. The employees would never be able to tell because, sad to say, I keep a pretty messy office all the time anyway! However, *I* could tell."

During his explanation, she managed to finish her fries and pop, before asking again, "Did you find *anything* missing?"

"No," he answered, "it was just that things seemed a little

out of place, so I checked for the important papers, and nothing was missing, as far as I could tell."

Gazing around the small office, Paisley couldn't deny that its appearance was *very* disorganized. It was as if someone opened a window in the middle of a hurricane, and it had its way with the paperwork! Paisley knew people who functioned perfectly in situations where their office and desktop always looked like a tornado had passed through it. Their stacks of essential files and papers were in piles, with no apparent rhyme or reason, as to their placement. She always marveled at their ability to seemingly find anything they needed in the chaos—Paisley was *not* one of these people!

"So, as far as you can tell, nothing is missing?" she repeated.

"Not exactly, what I *did* see, was employee files apparently disturbed. I always keep them on top of the printer, and when I entered, some were mixed in with the papers, on my desktop. However, nothing was missing, so I don't see how this has anything to do with the death of Gregore?"

"Every piece of information helps," she said, "could it be vandalism? Could Gregore have caught the vandal or vandals in the act, and then they 'accidentally' killed him? What was Gregore's last name, again? I forgot what you told me earlier today." Paisley searched for a waste basket where she could throw her cup and food wrappers away but didn't see one.

"His last name was Kamorov."

"Yes, now I remember." Paisley thought for a moment and asked, "Do you recall which files were mixed in the papers on your desk?" She craned her neck to glance around again, for a waste basket, and still finding nothing, gave up.

"Yes, now that you mention it," he said contemplatively, "one of the files *did* happen to be Gregore's!" His face brightened at the recollection.

"And the other files?"

"I don't remember, because they were all scattered amidst my other papers, so I gathered them together to take care of later, but I *do* remember Gregore's file, because I was looking for it to take to the meeting, with Detective Boone. It was on the top of the pile, and I thought, what a coincidence? So I had one of my assistant managers put the rest of the files away because I was called to the front to handle an unhappy customer."

Paisley stood to leave, but hesitated a moment, remembering the tiny black flash drive, and reached into her purse to retrieve it, then held it out to Ben.

"I found this on the floor earlier this morning and picked it up so I wouldn't step on it...at first I thought it was my chapstick, but obviously it wasn't, so I figured it must belong to you."

Ben took it from her. "What is it?" he asked, rolling it over in his hand.

"It's a flash drive."

"What's a flash drive?" He stared back at her with a confused expression on his face and handed it back.

"It's used to store information from a computer," she informed him, puzzled at his response.

Looking at her perplexedly, he replied, "For a computer? Nah, *I* wouldn't have anything like that! I leave all the computer stuff to my wife, who handles everything to do with the business side...I don't know my way around computers at all and have no desire to learn," he held up a hand, "no offense or anything," and his brow furrowed with concern, his thin lips pursed and his brown eyes, which usually sparkled, exhibited stress, instead.

"I understand," she said kindly, "computers aren't for every-one. Well, if this isn't yours," she persisted, "would you ask your wife and your employees if they're missing a flash drive? Please let me know when you find its owner—I'd be frantic if I lost one of mine! Call me as soon as possible if you can, because if I can't find out who the owner is, I'll have another mystery on my hands—and we wouldn't want *that!*" She laughed.

"Will do! Thanks for your concern, Paisley," he smiled.

"I'll check in again, if I find out anything else, Ben."

"Please do," he said, "our talk was helpful. It would be great if you figured out what happened. Also, please give your Aunt my best."

Paisley said she would and urged Ben once more, to poll his wife and the employees about the flash drive, then starting to leave, she turned to him and pressed her card into his hand, "Call me as soon as you find the flash drive's owner."

Paisley left his office and wound her way through the kitchen, around the counter, and before she went out the door, threw her cup and burger wrappers in the nearest trash receptacle, pausing to wave at Julia and Jerry, as she continued to her Jeep. Now, it was back to the office to take care of a few more things before going home to change clothes and meet Millie for dinner.

CHAPTER 9

Brainerd Paisley and Millie had agreed to meet for dinner at Applebee's, which was in Brainerd, not far from the precinct, in Pinecrest. Millie arrived first, parked and waited at the door. When Paisley arrived, she greeted her as enthusiastically as a puppy, whose owner just came home.

"I can't believe how fast you tore into the parking lot Pais— you're gonna get a ticket one of these times!" Millie said, and laughed.

"Coming from California where everyone speeds, didn't prepare me for the slower pace of a small town—I guess I'm still not used to it?" She said, in defense.

They entered Applebee's and the hostess greeted them. Paisley noticed her friend had changed from her office attire into a casual pair of jeans with a muted blue sweater and a light brown jacket. Paisley, still wearing dark jeans from work, had changed her blouse to a long-sleeved shirt and jeans jacket, instead.

Paisley always had fun with Millie Adams, who was a year or two older and also divorced, which gave them something in common. Occasionally, they grabbed a bite to eat or caught a movie. Slightly taller than Paisley, Millie always seemed to be dieting even though she didn't need to.

"I have to watch what I eat, or I won't fit in my clothes," Millie reasoned. Her sandy-blonde hair was worn in a medium bob, with bangs a little too long, giving her face a look similar, on occasion, to an English Sheep dog. She needed to continually fluff her bangs off her face so she could see.

The waitress seated them in a window booth and handed them menus, which they both studied amidst a flurry of conversation about the day. Their two personalities meshed well because they both had a sense of humor, which made office sharing fun, even though their work styles were *very* different. Millie tended to be more chaotic in her approach, while Paisley's style was ordered and neat—not a problem—so far!

Both enjoyed shopping, but lately, since the weather turned milder, they bundled up and rode bikes. Paisley preferred to run, but Millie didn't, so they rode bikes instead, to enjoy the beauty of Minnesota. The Paul Bunyan Bike Trail was easy to access, stretching from Brainerd, to Bemidji, which was situated in the northwest corner of Minnesota, not far from the Canadian border. They never went far...only an hour or so up the trail and back again.

On their last ride, Millie said, "I know a couple of great guys, Pais, and I'm gonna set you up with one of them so we can double date!"

And Millie *did* set her up! However, after one blind date, which didn't go very well, Paisley told her, "Thanks for the help, Millie, but I'm just not interested in getting involved with *anyone,* right now."

"All right," she'd said reluctantly, "I'll stop playing cupid—butI'm not totally giving up—just in case I find a special guy for you!"

As long as Millie understood, Paisley grinned and said, "Okay, but he'll have to be *very* special."

The waitress returned to take their orders. Paisley decided on boneless chicken wings and a side salad, while Millie ordered the Chicken Dinner Special, which included fries, a side salad, and mixed vegetables. Paisley smiled to herself as she listened to Millie's order—so much for her diet! The menus were collected, and as soon as the waitress left, they continued their conversation.

"Ahh, it's nice to finally sit and relax," and as soon as Paisley said that, the waitress came, bringing the Diet Cokes they'd ordered.

Once again, the waitress left, giving Millie to put her arms on the table, lean forward eagerly, and say, "Okay, spill it! I want to know *everything*! What did you see? How did the dead body look...and who did it? I've been waiting all day to hear the details!"

Paisley grinned and said, "All in good time," loving her chance to keep Millie in suspense.

"C'mon, Pais!" she whined, "I've been patient—don't keep me in suspense any longer—*tell* me!"

"Shhhh!" Paisley cautioned, "Not so loud, people are looking at us," she said, in a low voice, "and I don't want them to hear what I have to say."

She scanned the room and peered surreptitiously, over both shoulders. Having satisfied herself that the diners had turned their attention back to their meals, in a whisper, she recounted everything—including what it was like and how it felt when she first saw the body!

"I literally switched into clinical mode! It was amazing!" Embellishing the details a tad, to make it sound more gruesome than it really was she laughed, as Millie listened with rapt attention *and* respect.

"Wow! You handled that situation *so* professionally!" She loved every minute of Paisley's story.

Paisley glanced down demurely, "Well, I certainly didn't expect a day like this one when I woke up this morning!"

"Oh, it sounds positively exciting—you're a real Nancy Drew!" And as she spoke excitedly, Millie waved her hands around and almost knocked over her drink.

Paisley looked around again, to make sure people weren't looking at them."Not quite," she grinned, "but thanks for the acknowledgement and take it easy—not so loud!" She shushed her again. "I think you're getting a little carried away, but the whole thing sure did get my adrenaline going!"

Their food finally came, and they continued talking about the murder between bites. "I learned a few things too," Millie said, "from the Ben's Burgers employees' statements, which I typed up, this afternoon."

"What did you find out?" Paisley paused and looked curiously at Millie.

"For one thing, someone searched Ben's office—probably the killer—and several workers reported the freezer was ransacked!"

"What? The freezer was fine when *I* was in there?"

"It's true!" Millie said, "but, boxes of frozen foods were opened, their contents dumped out, then returned to their containers in great disarray. The flaps were re-closed, and the containers put back on the shelves, making everything look untouched!"

"I can't believe it!"

"No lie! This came from two of the employees' statements,

who were tasked with cleaning the freezer after the investigators gave them the okay."

"That's such a peculiar thing to do?" Paisley remarked. "What would some killer be looking for in a fast-food place—especially in the freezer—*and*, in boxes of frozen foods?"

"I know," Millie quipped, "maybe he—*or* she—was looking for some cold, hard cash!" And they both began laughing.

They dropped the murder talk and indulged themselves by sharing a giant chocolate covered brownie, topped with a dollop of whipped cream. They decided to call it a night and go their separate ways, so Paisley paid the bill, and they headed out into the cool spring night.

"Your turn to pay, next time," Paisley called out to Millie, as she waved goodbye.

Slipping into the front seat of her car, she started the engine and drove away, making a left onto Washington Blvd, which took her to the northeast edge of Brainerd. When the sign for County Road 38 appeared, she turned right, noticing that the headlights behind her, made the same turn.

That's odd, she mused. Seems like the same car has been behind me since I left Applebee's. This thought immediately brought back Boone's words from earlier, when she left the burger place. "Be careful," he said, "you never know who might be watching!"

Feeling paranoid for a moment, she shook it off. Ridiculous! She chalked it up to allowing his words to spook her. Determined not to let herself get carried away by thoughts of mystery and intrigue, she summarily dismissed the idea and turned on the radio to calm her nerves. It didn't work, because the news was on, discussing the details of the morning's murder, so she flipped it off and instead, grabbed her favorite CD—a String Quintet by Mozart—and inserted it into the CD slot in her car.

As she listened to the violins' mellifluous strains, it drew her into the music, and all other thoughts were pushed aside for the moment. Within minutes, she neared the farm house and glanced once more in her review mirror. Thankfully, there were no headlights to be seen. Whew! Whoever it was, must have turned off the road. How silly! Why would anyone follow me anyway? She pulled into the farmhouse driveway and turned off the engine, experiencing an overwhelming feeling of relief, as exhaustion swept over her. The day's events had taken their toll.

"I'm *not* a wimp, " she said out loud, to dismiss her fears. I've seen a dead body before—at a morgue while taking courses at the police academy! But somehow *this* is different, she thought. It's the first corpse I've ever seen *in situ*!

The cool crisp evening had taken on a humid feel, and she heard this would bring the promise of mosquitos in the days and weeks to come if temperatures remained mild. The weather might be temperate again tomorrow, or pour down rain—after all, it *was* Minnesota.

Rousing herself from her thoughts, she stepped out of the car and locked it. The deafening silence of the night, caused her to pause and stand quietly, as she listened and gazed at the plethora of stars. They sparkled as if someone had tossed hand-fuls of glitter into the heavens. She'd witnessed nothing like *this*, in California, because the city lights dimmed all, but the very brightest stars. She also detected the pungent smell of farm animals in the night air as it drifted across the fields.

Paisley remained there for several moments, looking up at the big and little dipper, then hurried up the pathway to the house. Unlocking the door, she stepped into the mudroom that led to the kitchen. The ticking of the antique grandfather clock, which resided in the living room punctuated the silence. It seemed sonorous in the stillness of the house. She could hear it

tick from the kitchen doorway. This evening, she had height-
ened senses.

Once again, Paisley felt her heart race, as she experienced
fear conjured up by her furtive imagination. Where was Aunt
Olga? She was probably in bed already, unless she'd stayed at
the hospital overnight with Uncle Vlad. She quelled her
emotions, and tiptoed through the living room, down the hallway, and into her room.

After closing the door behind her, she leaned against it with
her back and breathed a sigh of relief. With the door closed,
Paisley finally felt safe. She dressed for bed, then climbed under
the covers, and as soon as she turned the bedside light off, she
fell into a deep sleep. She never heard the dark car, when it
turned silently into the farmhouse driveway with headlights off.

Its occupant, quickly noted the color, make, and model of
her parked car, then jotted down the license plate number. It
backed quietly out of the driveway, and stopped at the mailbox
by the road's edge, and the address was written down, before
continuing onto the country road. It drove for half a mile in the
darkness, before turning on its headlights.

CHAPTER 10

Tuesday, May 16, 2017
Pinecrest

Early Tuesday morning, Deedrick Boone arrived at the precinct and went straight to his office, intending to make a to-do list. First on his agenda was organizing the fact cards, which he'd randomly placed on his white evidence board the day before. Next, he wanted to re-examine Ben's Burger's employee statements, which were all typed up.

The Ramsey County Coroner's Office where the Pinecrest ME, Dr. Hyde, had transferred the corpse, would be sending the autopsy report in a day or two, so he'd have to wait for those results. Sitting in his chair, he turned from the white board to face his desk, where Kamorov's employee file lay open, and he moved it aside, to reread the employee statements. He found nothing new from the few that he looked at, because most of the employees didn't know Kamorov very well, so he set the statements aside for the moment.

Boone, dragged the Kamorov personnel file in front of him.

From his brief overview yesterday, he felt it was surprisingly incomplete. All it offered was a home address in southeast Brainerd and several previous places of employment. Also Included was a mention of his brush with the law, listing Jack Minor, as his parole officer—this would be a definite lead to follow. Kamorov's work history consisted of a job at a Citgo gas station as a cashier, and he a job as a bartender at a bar named, Dino's. Neither job lasted for more than three or four-months, and both places were located elsewhere—*not* in Brainerd, *or* Pinecrest.

He returned to the employee statements. Several statements from Ben's Berger's, made mention of Kamorov's roommates, however, no names were known. So today, he would visit his place of residence, in hopes of finding more information about the seemingly elusive and mysterious, Kamorov. It was as if he hadn't existed. Puzzling over this for several minutes, he made a note to talk to several of these employees again. Maybe one of them might remember something —*anything*!

Boone was sent to Pinecrest, Minnesota, in April 2017, because of a special assignment by the FBI, to initiate contact with a person known to him only, as Mr. Ohm. It's an unusual name, he remembered thinking, as its definition meant—a unit of the measure of resistance. Boone's mission was to secretly meet with Ohm sometime during the first part of May, but after arriving in Minnesota, almost a month had passed, and Boone had not yet succeeded in making contact. He felt as if it was going to be a waiting game.

He figured Ohm's hesitation to make contact, concerned the sensitive nature of this informant's information, or perhaps he just had cold feet? At one point early on, after the initial contact with the FBI, Ohm indicated he was possibly being surveilled and now mis-trusted the authenticity of his contact, which of course, was Boone.

Boone 's code name of Mr. Watt, also a unit of electrical power, and he smiled at the irony. However, without any communication so far, all he could do was sit, wait, and stay in touch with Washington. In the meantime, when the Kamorov murder occurred, Captain Bowers decided to have him head up the case, to give him something to work on for the moment.

Born in Virginia, Boone was raised as an Army brat. His father, a Major General in the Army, frequently moved his family within the United States (mostly to the east coast), and then moved them again when stationed abroad. By the time Boone turned ten, the General and his family were stationed in Japan. For three years, his dad, the General, worked with the CIA, until they sent the family to Germany. It wasn't until, Boone's senior year that the family returned to the United States.

Following high school, Boone, admiring his father's military career, attended the United States Military Academy in West Point, New York. He became a cadet, otherwise known as an officer-in-training, and graduated second in his class with top academic scores. He had impressive grades in three foreign languages, because of his unusual linguistic abilities.

Graduating as a Second Lieutenant, he served a tour of duty in Germany, and a four-year stint in Afghanistan, as an operative, and was wounded by a roadside bomb, and flown back to the states to recover. During his recovery at Walter Reed Hospital, for several months, the CIA visited him after learning of his ability to speak multiple foreign languages. They wanted him to learn Pashto, but he'd already picked it up, along with being conversant in German and Russian.

After a full recovery, he joined a Special Ops group and

went to the Mideast, but after six years, he tired of the dangers, was burnt out, and returned to the states, preferring a job stateside. Boone decided to crossover, to the FBI, and trained at Quantico, then accepted a position with an anti-terrorism unit. It was in this capacity that several years later, he was assigned to Pinecrest, in mid-Minnesota, during the first week of April 2017.

Three days after arriving in Pinecrest Boone decided he would talk to the Captain right away about his assignment to the department. He arranged a Monday morning meeting, at 10:00 a.m., with Captain Bower, at the Pinecrest Police Department. Arriving on Monday, promptly at ten, he spoke to the receptionist at the front desk, who gave him directions to the Captain's office. He headed down the corridor to the elevator, rode to the second floor, and found the office.

Once in the outer office, the receptionist smiled and said, "Go right in, the Captain is expecting you."

The Captain stood with a welcoming smile, as Boone stepped through the door into the inner office, then put out his hand to shake Boone's. "Welcome, Mr. Boone, I'm Captain Bower...glad to meet you."

Not expecting this warm reception, he smiled back, "Likewise."

"Have a seat, Mr. Boone," Bower said as he sat down, and continued, "I hope you had a nice trip here to Minnesota—it's very different from Washington, D.C.!"

Boone sat in a cordovan leather, wing-back chair, facing the Captain, who sat behind an enormous oak desk, and replied, "I did, thank you, but I haven't had time to look around the city, yet."

"Well, why don't we get down to business." He picked up some papers from his desk and glanced over them. "I received paperwork from the Bureau, requesting that you be assigned to our precinct. However, that's all I know about this, and I was hoping you would enlighten me." He looked up at Boone, "By the way, would you like some coffee...or water?"

"Yes, coffee would be great—black, please."

Captain Bower made a quick request over his intercom, and momentarily the receptionist entered with a tray holding two cups of coffee, and set them down, then left the office, closing the door behind her. The Captain picked up his cup, took a sip, and waited for Boone to explain why he was here.

The coffee was hot. Boone blew lightly on his, before taking several sips and setting the cup aside. "I've been sent here to work undercover on a top-secret project." The Captain's eyebrows raised slightly, and Boone continued, "I'm to meet with a contact who 'may' have information about something, affecting our national security—but we're not exactly sure what it is. For my cover, I'm to be a detective on this police force, and I'm to be here until the informant contacts me so that we can arrange a meeting."

The Captain nodded his head, "I see." Deep in thought for a minute, he stared at Boone. "What would you like us to do, to help?"

"All I need is a cover story for the rest of the officers so I can blend into the group. In other words, I need to keep a low profile, and only *you* will be privy to my identity and any information I may give you. In the meantime, I'm just a detective— on loan."

Taking another sip of coffee, the Captain chuckled and said, "That's doable. I think we can arrange it. We'll say that you transferred here from another precinct on the East Coast—a favor from *your* Captain, after becoming a high-profile person in a sensational murder case, which you worked—and they thought it best for you to be out of the limelight for a while... that sound all right? And, if anyone inquires about the nature of the case in which you were involved, just say you can't discuss it!"

"Great! Perfect! I'll give you more information when I can, but otherwise consider me your new transfer detective and treat me accordingly." He gave the Captain a big grin, stood up, thanked him for his understanding, *and* the coffee, then shook his hand again.

"Welcome to the force, Detective Boone," and Bower, who also grinned, walked around the desk and accompanied Boone to the door. "If you need *anything*, let me know, and meanwhile, I'll have Officer Smith get you situated with a temporary office until we find a more permanent one. We'll furnish you with a badge, credentials, etc., and I'm sure you have a weapon of your *own*, but he'll see to it that you have access to a car and office materials."

"I can't thank you, enough!" Boone said, and left the office, nodding to the secretary on his way out.

That was then, and this is now, he thought as he sat at his desk, on *this* Monday morning, working on the Kamorov case. It's been a month and a half since I talked to Captain Bowers back in April, and here I am, he thought, it's the middle of May, and I'm still in this temporary office. But at least I have a case to work, to keep from being bored!

He sat, with his back to the door, focused again, on the white board hanging on the wall behind his desk. Deep in thought, he didn't hear Millie enter the office until she tossed the morning paper on his side desk...it made a loud, flat-sounding, "Whap!"

As it landed, Boone jumped and spun around in his chair, "What on earth!"

"Oh! I'm so sorry," Millie said, putting her hand to her throat, "I didn't mean for it to land so hard!"

In a calmer voice, he said, "Although it *did* startle me because it sounded like a gunshot—I managed to survive, so all is well," he assured her as he gave her a broad smile. "Thanks for remembering my newspaper request from yesterday."

"Sure, no prob," and she turned to scurry out of his office, while he picked up his cooling cup of typical over-heated-dregs, from the coffee pot in the break room, and pulled the newspaper towards his desk pad. When he unfolded it and began reading the headlines, he was annoyed. The paper made the murder sound more macabre and sensational than it really was —he *knew* it was to sell more papers.

Of all the ways to die, death by freezing is probably the least messy and not nearly as repugnant as stabbing, shooting, drowning, or torching. But that was just *his* opinion. Unfortunately, others preferred the more sensational methods, regardless of the mess.

Brainerd. At the farmhouse in Brainerd, Paisley was just waking up, endeavoring to open her eyes, as she crept out of her dream and into the reality of her room, finally struggling awake. Everything always seems better in the morning light, Paisley thought, and for some reason, a Thornton Wilder quote she'd loved from her high school literature class, came to mind:

For what human ill, does not dawn, seem to be an alleviation.

She rested for a few minutes, musing over the quote, then sprang out of bed. Even though she didn't have to be at work until one, she had reasons to get there earlier. The delicious aroma of coffee and bacon drifted down the hallway and donning her robe, she padded into the kitchen where Aunt Olga, busied herself making breakfast.

"Honestly, Aunt Olga, you don't need to cook for me *every*

morning! I'm able to get my breakfast, too. Besides, you must have come home very late last night!"

"It's okay," she said, "I go visit Vlad again this morning. I get call earlier. He is not good. He is worse, so I go there today. I see you later, or I stay all night, I prepare for both," Olga stated matter-of-factly, in her short staccato sentences, as she waddled over to the table.

Saddened to hear this news, and trying to reassure her, Paisley said, "I'm so sorry. Hopefully he'll be okay."

Olga's reply was, *"Beris' druzhno, ne budet gruzno."*

"What does that mean?"

"Old Russian saying, means, many hands, make light work." Paisley grinned, as Olga stooped, gave her a big bear hug, then yanked off her apron and flung it onto the counter, and headed for her room.

"I'll try and come to the hospital after work this evening to pay Vlad a visit."

As Paisley hurriedly finished her coffee, her Aunt re-entered the kitchen. "Thanks, my little *kotyonok*, Uncle Vlad, happy for any visits." And with that, she was out the door.

Paisley loved her Aunt's Russian accent and her Old Russian sayings. She smiled to herself, whenever her Aunt called her *kotyonok*, which was Russian for kitten. She headed for her room and dressed in a pair of black slacks, a powder blue cotton shirt with three-quarter sleeves, and added a navy blue cotton jacket.

She pulled her curly, bronze-colored hair into a messy bun and secured it with a clip, but again, her unruly wispy tendrils escaped falling around her face, making her appear much younger than her twenty-eight years. She quickly fed Abby on her way out and climbed into her Jeep. It was a thirty-minute drive to the precinct—a far cry from the hours she spent in California traffic.

This Monday morning, tractors were sketching lazy grids, into the dark earth to prepare the ground. She peered up through the windshield to see if the gathering clouds might float by or stay awhile. Thankfully, they seemed to be on their lazy way, as if they had better places to be, much like the large "V" of geese, honking their way towards the horizon, as they began returning for the summer.

She flew down the road towards town, while rummaging in her purse for her chap stick. Her fingers felt each item in her purse, hoping for the right shape. Without success, and tiring of this game, she pulled off the road and dumped out her purse for the second time in two days. There was the chap stick, among the other items. She picked it up, removed the cap, and glided it over her lips. Back into the purse it went along with the rest—a notebook, a sample size bottle of hand lotion, a comb, a small box of raisins, wrinkled sales receipts, gum wrappers, her wallet, loose change, a couple of pens, and a packet of Kleenex.

A small black object remained on the seat—it was that pesky flash drive. She hoped Ben would have an answer for her soon, as certainly, *someone* would have realized it was missing, by now! Paisley unceremoniously tossed into her purse, and she pulled off the shoulder onto the road, heading towards town. After all, she didn't want to be late! No telling what new information may have surfaced!

CHAPTER 11

Pinecrest
Paisley arrived at the Police Station a few minutes after nine, and rushed into the lobby, stopping at the receptionist's desk. Jane, fortunately, was back this morning, "Is the Captain in?" she asked.

"I believe so, Detective Ingles," she replied.

However, Jane's answer was almost lost, as Paisley flew by, and still managing to turn and call back to Jane, "Good, would you please let him know I'd like to speak with him for a minute?" And without waiting for a reply, she continued down the hallway, turning around once more to call back, "Oh, and Jane, you can buzz me in my office, whenever you're able to make an appointment."

"Okay," Jane said under her breath. Jane Goodman, a long-time receptionist for the department, shook her head at Paisley's quick fly-by. She peered over her glasses at the figure charging down the hallway, before picking up her phone to contact the Captain's office.

As Paisley rushed down the corridor, she fumbled in her purse for her chap stick again, but came up with the flash drive, and made a "Dahhh," noise, before throwing it back in her purse. She dug in again and finally found the chap stick, just as she whipped around the corner and into her office.

"Hi, Millie! How are things today?" Paisley said, trying to catch her breath before continuing, "According to the news reports on the radio, I guess everyone at the station is working on the murder! Anything new?"

"Whoa! Slow down a minute. What's your hurry?" Millie held up two hands, palms out.

Paisley dropped her purse on her desk, pulled out her chair and plopped down. "I'm sorry Millie, I guess I'm just excited about the murder, and I'm ready and rare'n to go. I want to help investigate it!"

"Wow! I haven't heard *that* expression since the last re-run of some old Western I happened to see on TV—and only because it was late at night, *and* I was too tired to turn it off," Millie added.

"Really? Well, I think my Dad used to say it to us when we were little—sorry, it just popped out," she smiled, then booted up her computer.

Millie looked at her, and folding her arms across her chest, leaned back in her chair. "Well, anyway, nothing big yet. The autopsy report won't be here for a day or two from what I hear, but once we get it, there'll be something to work with."

Paisley rolled her somewhat squeaky chair up to her desk, and spied a message on a sticky note, which indicated Ben had called. She reached into her purse, retrieved the flash drive, and set it front and center on the desk pad. Grabbing the phone, she dialed the number for Ben's Burger's. When someone finally answered, she asked to speak to Ben, and he immediately came on the line.

"Ben, this is Paisley, what's up?"

"I thought you'd like to know, I've asked my employees about the little drive, and no one claimed it. However, right after you left, this fellow came in, whom I'd never seen before, claiming to be a friend of Gregore. He wanted to know if I had Gregore's belongings and if so, would I check to see if a 'thumb drive' was among his things—a thumb drive?"

"Yes, a flash drive is sometimes called a thumb drive—it's the same thing," she said.

"Oh, okay, I didn't know. He said Gregore borrowed it, and he wanted it back. I told him that Gregore's things could *not* be disturbed because of the investigation. He seemed irritated and acted nervous. I told him you had found a flash drive had been found by you, which was the only drive I was aware of, soI told him maybe he should go to the precinct to see if it was what he was looking for and gave him your name *and* your number, in case he preferred calling."

"Well, that's peculiar! Did he give you *his* name?"

"No," Ben said, "I didn't think to ask him and he didn't say...."

Paisley interrupted Ben, "Can you describe him?"

"I only remember he was Caucasian, average height and weight and was wearing a camo ball cap, and a camo hoodie. Maybe brown eyes, I dunno, but for sure, he had a scraggily, unshaven face."

"Good to know," she said.

"Also," Ben continued," it was hard to tell, but I guessed him to be in his mid-thirties...didn't seem like someone who would be a friend of Gregore's. Sorry I didn't pay more attention!"

"It's okay, you did great, and I appreciate the information.

Hopefully, he'll get in touch with me, and if it *is* his flash drive, I'll be return it to him. Maybe he can tell us more about Kamorov? Thanks for contacting me. Anyway, have things settled down in your place today?"

"Quite the contrary! After we talked yesterday, word got around from all the publicity and more people than ever, flooded in—probably out of curiosity—it was great for business! *And,* our regular customers offered their condolences, they're all very supportive," Ben said.

At least there was a happy tone in his voice, and she was glad to hear things were going well and informed Ben she'd stop by in a couple of days. As she put down the receiver, the intercom buzzed, and a light began to blink.

She depressed the 'speak' button and said, "Yes, Jane?"

"The Captain said he would be happy to meet with you in fifteen minutes."

When Paisley put the phone down, Millie, who couldn't stand it any longer, finally said, "Aren't you going to look at the *Pinecrest Gazzette?*" She looked at Paisley with expectation in her eyes.

"Oh!" Paisley looked on top of the file cabinet next to her desk, then reached over to pick up the newspaper. "Oh, no!" she muttered. Right there on the front page was a picture of her in her old hoodie, with a ball cap on, talking to a police officer.

The headlines read: "BODY DISCOVERED IN FREEZER AT BEN'S BURGERS", followed by the sub-headline: "GREGORE KAMOROV FOUND EARLY MONDAY MORNING AT BEN'S BURGER BY EMPLOYEE AND OFF-DUTY DETECTIVE, PAISLEY INGLES". The caption *under* her picture said: *"Local police detective, Paisley Ingles, declares employee dead at the scene after the Assistant Manager takes her to the freezer to see the body he'd discovered".*

The article recounted the events following her discovery vividly, describing the body and the rest of the procedures that took place after it was removed that morning. Included, was the description of the forensic investigation process, and several media interviews with a few of the employees, who were present at the time.

"I don't need this!" she moaned, tossing the paper to the side.

"But it's exciting, Pais! Just think—you're famous now!" Millie said excitedly, "I've been waiting all morning for you to come in and see it!"

"Wouldn't you know, I was dressed all scruffy for my big debut? Nooo...!" She drew out the 'no', moaning, "*Why*, couldn't I have had my hair styled and a cute outfit on—it had to be with my raggedy running clothes—my hair a mess, and an old ball cap on my head!"

Both began laughing at the absurdity of Paisley caring more about her *coiffure* and *couture* than the fact that she just pronounced someone deceased. "Oh well," Paisley said, and kept an eye on the clock, waiting until it was time to visit the Captain. At the fifteen-minute mark, she was up and out the door.

Captain Bower's office was on the second floor at the far end of the building and around a corner at the end of a short hallway. Reaching his office in record time, she entered the outer office and gave his receptionist her name, adding, "I have an appointment." She took a seat in a guest chair.

The phone on the desk buzzed, his receptionist answered, and informed the Captain, "Ms. Ingles is here." She listened, then told Paisley, "Captain Bowers will see you now," and smiled.

The Captain's door stood slightly ajar, so knocking gently, Paisley said, "Captain Bower?"

"Come in, come in," he said in a jovial tone. Haltingly, she pushed the door open and stepped into an office, with a large, highly polished oak desk placed in front of an oak-paneled wall, displaying various awards and commendations. An American flag hung from a flag pole anchored in a circular brass stand in the corner of the room, while a medium-sized artificial potted fern (at least she thought it was artificial), sat in the opposite corner.

Behind the desk, sitting in a cordovan leather office chair, Captain Bower, with a kindly look on his face and twinkling brown eyes, smiled as she entered. Neatly combed white hair highlighted a receding hairline, and his face was like tanned leather. Despite his crow's-feet and generous laugh lines, a touch of youth was still visible in his welcoming smile.

"Take a seat," he said, as he gestured towards one of the chairs. "What can I do for you?"

"Well, sir," she said, after sitting down and attempting to control her nerves, "I know I'm fairly new here..." she hesitated.

"What's your department and position?"

"Presently, I'm a Computer Forensics Specialist."

"Ah, yes," he leaned back in his chair, "very good. How long have you been with us? I *do* recall your transfer—you came from California, is that right?"

"Yes, sir, I did—about three months ago." Did he remember that? Or did someone tell him this morning, she wondered?

"Well, what can I do for you?" He leaned forward with both arms on his desk, fingers entwined, and a hint of amusement in his kind eyes.

With all the confidence she could muster, she cleared her throat and said, "I was wondering if I might specifically, be assigned to help with the Ben's Burgers homicide case. I'm friends with Ben, the owner, and I was the first on the scene to

88

locate the body. I want to assist in bringing the person who committed this crime, to justice! I definitely want to participate in this investigation."

There! She said it! The Captain sat back in his chair again with his elbows on the chair's arms, then put his hands together, tenting his fingers. He looked at her for a minute or two, as he rocked slightly back and forth in his chair, pondering her unusual request. Finally, he leaned forward, looked Paisley directly in her eyes, and said, "Ms. Ingles, your expertise is in computer forensics and...well, I don't know how you'd be able to help on this case?"

"Sir," she began, and leaned forward, "I can help in several ways—I can do research on the victim, or any suspects or perpetrators we find, by using my computer skills. I can coordinate information with other sources, check computers or other media belonging to the victim for pertinent information, track down acquaintances and family—it would mean a lot to me!" The Captain listened to her with interest as he swiveled slightly in his chair. She barely took a breath and continued, "Besides, although I was hired on as a liaison to the department as a CFS, I am *also* a detective. I graduated from the Carpenteria Police Academy in California."

Satisfied she'd made her case, she smiled cordially at Captain Bower and relaxed her posture.

"Yes," he said thoughtfully, amused by her *chutzpa*h, "I suppose you could help track down leads with the victim's computer, which we'll soon have in our hands." There was something about her assertive attitude that he liked. "So, I'll tell you what, I'll assign you to Detective Boone, and the two of you can decide how to proceed with the investigation, and he can determine where you will be the most effective."

"Thank you, sir." She smiled, stood, leaned over the desk,

and vigorously shook his hand. He rose and walked around the desk to usher her out.

"By the way," he grinned, "that was quite an article in the newspaper about you at the crime scene!"

Paisley reddened, "I had no idea my picture was being taken...there was so much going on..." she stammered.

The Captain chuckled, "My secretary will let Detective Boone know of your new assignment and inform him to meet with you, as soon as possible."

"Thank you, sir, thank you *so* much!"

She hoped she hadn't sounded *too* gushy? Was that even a word? She tried to contain her excitement—she wanted to hi-five, jump up and down, and shout! Instead, she smiled to herself all the way down the hallway and back to her office.

Once inside, Paisley was ebullient! "Guess what, Millie?" she said excitedly!

Informing Millie of her new assignment, Paisley did a few raise-the-roof gestures to indicate her enthusiasm for being included in the investigation. Millie congratulated her, all the while shaking her head from side to side and laughing at Paisley's antics, then she returned to her typing.

Paisley interrupted Millie again, by declaring, "Hey—*this* calls for a celebration!"

Hurrying to the break room, Paisley grabbed a couple of sodas from the vending machine and hurried back.

"Catch," she said as she tossed one to Millie.

"Okay, okay—Congrats! Pais," and she gave her a big smile, and they both toasted to her new assignment.

CHAPTER 12

Boone's focus on the papers in front of him was interrupted by a call from Captain Bower's secretary. The call was to inform him a partner was assigned to him in the Kamorov murder, to help with the investigation.

"Okay," he said, mildly surprised, then asked, "and who is my new partner?" He couldn't imagine who it might be?

"Captain Bower has assigned Detective Paisley Ingles," Bower's secretary said, "to assist in the investigation." Before he could ask any questions the call ended.

It was unexpected, and he wondered how and why this had come about? Remembering how adamant she'd been about participating in the investigation, it wouldn't surprise him if she'd asked for this position. Annoyed, as he thought about partnering with her, he guessed the Captain had his reasons, so he'd make the best of it. He'd find things for her to do, and who knows, it might be fine? She could follow up on details with her computer prowess!

He was in the process of making a list of people he needed

to contact when he received the call from Bowers office. But instead, he changed course and decided his first call should be to Ms. Ingles. As luck would have it, according to the secretary, who shared the office with Ingles, "Paisley just stepped out to go to the computer lab, would you like to leave a message?"

"This is Detective Boone, could you please have her come to my office, when she returns?"

"Yes, Detective Boone—will do!" Millie said.

While he waited, he studied his evidence board. There was the body found in the freezer, approximate time of death noted. However, no suspects as yet, no murder weapon (other than the freezer and an unknown intruder), autopsy report—still pending, a list of several witnesses who discovered the body (i.e., Jerry, Ms. Ingles, and others), and no physical evidence—fingerprints or otherwise, back from the lab.

There was no wallet found on the body, but Ben Wister, was able to provide an address and phone number for the deceased. The home address belonged to a man named, Pyotr Zolotov, who sponsored Kamorov and housed him, according to parole and Visa requirements, enabling him to stay in the United States, on his student visa.

Boone called Detective Meade, in charge of accessing DMV records, and asked him to run Kamorov's name. It would help, Boone thought, to obtain information from Kamorov's driving record—tickets, DUIs, etc. Next, he was about to call the victim's parole officer to check on his rap sheet, when Ingles knocked softly on the open door.

He looked up, and re-cradled the receiver on the old-school phone, which the precinct provided. He stood up, "Please come in," he said, welcoming Paisley into his office, "...and have a seat."

He moved around the small desk and pulled out the austere

wooden armchair for her. As she moved towards the chair, he proffered his hand, and she reached out and shook it.

"The Captain called to inform me of your assignment to the Kamorov case," he began amiably.

She looked at him suspiciously, hoping she wasn't going to hear a 'but'. "I didn't realize he was going to get in touch with you so soon!" She really was amazed at the speed, with which the Captain had handled her request.

"I called you right away," he said, as he settled in his chair, "because I wanted you to know I'm happy to have your assistance on this case, and I'm sure your computer expertise will be beneficial. I've heard a few officers mention how savvy you are with the technical stuff. Me? It isn't my forte, but I *do* admire anyone who knows their way around a computer." He could have sworn she reddened a little! It was refreshing to see someone exhibit a genuine emotion, he thought.

"Thanks," she said, feeling relieved, "I'm looking forward to helping, in any way I can," she answered politely, re-folding her hands in her lap. Did he mean all these nice words, or is he patronizing me? She'd ponder this later.

He scooted his newly acquired wheeled office chair, up to his gunmetal gray desk and opened a drawer. He extracted a small red spiral notebook and pencil and handed it to her across the desk, like a teacher with supplies for pupils on the first day of school. Sitting back in this chair, he folded his hands on his desk, waiting to see what she would do.

She looked at him, noting the office furniture upgrade of the rolling chair and also noticed the twinkle in his blue eyes. "OK, now I feel legit," she quipped, not knowing what else to say and proceeded to open the notebook, then dab the pencil point on her tongue, before pretending to begin writing—like so many secretaries did with *their* pads and pencils, in the old movies.

They both chuckled and any leftover tension that may have been present disappeared, as the beginning of a new partnership formed.

"While we're working together, perhaps it would be easier if you called me Boone—just to make it a little less formal," Boone requested.

"And you may call me Paisley if you wish. I'm comfortable with using my first name, but I prefer Ingles when we're at the precinct, or on official business."

"Works for me!" he said. He took the next few minutes to explain his evidence board—which at present didn't show much evidence. She's particular about things, he noted, and suddenly, an idea occurred to him. He asked, "Would you happen to have any free time either the rest of this morning or this afternoon?"

Suspicious of the question, she answered, "Yes, there are routine tasks on my desk, but nothing urgent, just a few things which can be finished later, so I'm available now."

"Good! I know it's short notice, but I was wondering if you'd like to accompany me to the residence of the victim in order to question his roommates?"

"How did you get his address?"

"From the personnel file given to me yesterday, by Ben"

"Ahh, that makes sense. I want to get up to speed on the all the new facts," Paisley said calmly, trying not to let her excitement show. "I'll run back to my office and grab my things, and I'll be right back."

Rolling back in his chair, he stood to see her out. She did an about face and walked out the door, while he called after her, "Meet me in front of the station!"

Grabbing his Glock from the drawer, he stuck it in his shoulder holster (which he rarely wore, but decided to follow protocol on this occasion), put on his leather jacket and headed towards the precinct's garage to get his car. When he pulled up to the front of the station she was already standing there wait-ing, so he leaned over the passenger seat and opened the door for her. "Hop in!"

She stooped down, and got into the midnight black unmarked Crown Vic, then looked over at Boone, slid the sunglasses perched on top of her head, onto her nose, and said, "Okay—let's go!"

CHAPTER 13

Brainerd
Boone, slightly amused by her order to "take off", headed towards Highway 210, passing Ben's Burgers in the process, while Paisley made a mental note to stop there later to pay Ben another visit, concerning the flash drive.

"Where is this place?" Paisley asked.

"The house is somewhere over in east Brainerd," Boone said, "and from what Ben told me, Gregore lived with a couple of roommates, one being his sponsor/guardian, because of his being here on a work Visa, from Russia."

"Interesting," Paisley commented, and both said nothing else, content to ride in a comfortable silence. Paisley gazed at the city sights as the car made its way across town. Twenty minutes later, they reached the section of town where the house was located.

Boone made a left-hand turn off the main boulevard onto 5th Street, into the residential section, while Paisley glanced around and stated, "This is not a very well-maintained area."

"You're right...areas like this exist in almost every city—pockets of low-income properties. It looks like these houses were probably built in the 30s, 40s and 50s—maybe some even earlier —and certainly most of them are rentals, or are owned by the low-income sector."

"Several houses look like some remodeling has happened," she said, "but most could still use a coat of paint—it's depressing! I guess it's hard for people when the economy has been bad the last few years. The cluttered porches displayed old plastic garden chairs, and children's toys. Other objects are strewn around, made them look unsightly."

Lawns needed maintenance as the scraggly grass began to grow back, due to the warmer than usual spring, and created bare spots. Weeds sprouted in selected areas of the cracked driveways and sidewalks, while trash cans sat stacked haphazardly next to some of the houses. Some homes had junk cars parked in driveways and on lawns.

As they continued slowly down the street, it seemed as if the houses became even shabbier. Soon they came to Spruce Street, and Boone turned right, "Start looking for the house number, 11053," he said. "Looks like it's a dead-end street."

"Over there," she said, as they crept down the street. She pointed to the left, "I think it's the drab olive-green house, with dark-brown trim. The house next to it has a For Sale sign."

"I see it." He made a U-turn and parked at the curb, facing out, of the cul-de-sac towards the cross street.

Paisley climbed out of the car and cringed at the ugly fascia and porch railings, painted a dark mud brown. Most of the paint was peeling and hung with curled edges, exposing a brownish orange paint underneath. The house colors didn't match the dirty gray beat-up front door, or the rickety shutters, one of which hung at a jaunty angle from a single nail in its upper-left edge.

A small porch with a rusted wrought iron rail, flanked the steps and extended along the front of the two-story house. Several battered folding chairs sat to the right of the porch, and an old crusty barbecue stood at the other end, along with a clutter of assorted broken brooms and rakes, which leaned against the furthest porch post.

Boone and Paisley could smell some sort of odor emanating from a nearby trash can. It was unpleasant, as they made their way down the cracked cement walkway. She glanced at an old birdbath, leaning precariously next to the battered trash can, looking like some miniature Tower of Pisa. Curtains were drawn on the front windows, and the screen on the front door curled away from the wood on its bottom corners.

"Not a very cheery place," observed Paisley. "I wouldn't want to come here alone at night—that's for sure!"

Boone glanced at her quizzically but had no comment about what she said. They walked quietly towards the steps then heard a tinkling sound caused by one of the rusty house numbers, loosely nailed on the porch post to the left. It bounced slightly, as the breeze rose and fell, startling Paisley, with its ethereal sound. The house looked abandoned as if it belonged in a ghost town...the only things missing were tumble weeds, blowing across the lawn and down the street. This is so creepy, she thought!

Boone broke the silence. "I'll ask the initial questions, but feel free to jump in, if there's something you feel needs to be asked."

"Gotcha," she said.

A faint creaking sound emanated from the worn-out steps, as they slowly mounted the porch stairs. Paisley couldn't help but be reminded of an old, "Inner Sanctum", classic radio show. Once on the landing, a threadbare "Welcome" mat, met them— at least it's possible, that's what the faded letters spelled. Boone pushed the doorbell. There was no audible confirmation that it worked, so pausing a beat, he knocked firmly on the door.

"All we need is creepy incidental music!" she whispered.

The so-called curtains covering the windows on either side of the door nixed any chance of peeking to see if anyone lived here. However, they began hearing careful footfalls from inside the house, so there was hope!

Boone and Paisley, gave each other a knowing look, as a low, gruff voice spoke. "Who's there?" said the deep voice.

"Excuse me," Boone announced, "we're with the Pinecrest Police Department and we'd like to speak with you."

"What about?" came the surly reply.

Boone sighed, "About Gregore Kamorov!"

"What about him?" The voice, said.

Paisley half-whispered, half-mouthed to Boone, "Sounds like a Russian accent!"

Boone, tiring of this game already, said, "Please open up, so we can discuss this with you. I'm Detective Boone, with my assistant, Detective Ingles, and we need to ask you a couple of questions."

There was a stillness followed by a clacking of chains against the door jamb, the sliding of metal on metal, and the clattering of locks turning. The door finally opened a crack, as the man peered at them for a second or two, before slowly opening the door a little more, and acknowledging their presence.

"Come in," he said reluctantly, and opened the door further, allowing them to pass and ushering them into a dimly lit room. It was painted a deep tan color, which accentuated the room's gloomy ambiance. "Sit." The man motioned them to an under-sized yet overstuffed settee covered with a course gray fabric. It sat at a right angle to a threadbare sofa.

"Thank you," Boone said, and they both took a seat, Paisley choosing the sofa.

Several dingy brown chairs, one of which their host occu-pied, were positioned across from the settee, where Boone sat. Paisley's eyes drifted around the sparsely decorated room, which included a small end table on the far wall, holding an old lamp topped with a yellowed parchment lamp shade.

Two mismatched easy chairs with soiled arm rests, resem-bled freebies plucked from a curb, and were flanked by an end table near the settee. Paisley felt uncomfortable in this room and thought of the shower she'd need to take, when they left.

She saw part of the kitchen through the doorway, where several wooden chairs sat in front of a gray Formica table. The dining table/catchall, held stacks of old newspapers, a few crushed beer cans, and a wadded up jacket. She turned her attention back to the man in the living room chair.

"Now, why you here about Kamorov?" the man said.

Boone responded, "We've already introduced ourselves, so first, I'd like to verify your name."

The man stared at Boone before speaking, "My name is Zolotov."

Pulling out his little spiral notebook and pencil, Boone paused, looked up, and asked, "What is your *full* name?"

"Why is this important?" the man blurted out, but not wishing to appear uncooperative, added, "Last name is Zolotov, Pyotr, is first name, I am Pyotr Zolotov," he said defiantly.

"Well, Mr. Zolotov, if I may call you that," Boone continued, "I don't know if you've been listening to the news or seen the newspapers, but Gregore Kamorov was found dead, early

Monday morning. This house is listed as his residence, so we are here to ask you a few routine questions."

Zolotov's face displayed genuine astonishment, since it was the last thing he expected to hear. He assumed these people came because of Gregore's past *or* present escapades, but news of his death? He did *not* see this coming!

"Please, what happens?"

"Someone may have murdered Gregore Kamorov, the night before last. Although it's sill under investigation, we're working to ascertain the *exact* cause of death." Boone watched the man's response to this, as did Paisley.

Obviously shocked, Zolotov was almost rendered speechless. Many things ran through his head, not the least of which, the possibility that this could screw up everything! The *last* thing he needed was attention focused in his direction, given the critical project he was working on for his Boss! Yes, this is *no time* to have police here snooping and asking questions!

Both Detectives noted his reaction. "I'm sorry to bring you this tragic news, but right now, we're working on the assumption that it was murder. Therefore, we need more information, which will help us in the investigation. Also, we'd like to locate his next of kin." Boone said.

"How does it happen?" Zolotov said, to avoid answering Boone's question.

Ignoring Zolotov's question, Boone continued with his own, "Is Gregore Kamorov, his full name?"

"Yes," Zolotov said, still not grasping the impact of Kamorov's death on his project. He sat in still in his chair, and his lower jaw sagged open.

"This is terrible," he said, with his thick Russian accent.

As Boone continued his line of questioning, Paisley stared at Zolotov. What a frightening visage he had, she thought. His eyebrows were bushy and his deeply lined face, bad teeth, glowering eyes, and tousled head of tangled, unruly hair—not to mention his immense size—served to make him quite the intimidating character!

"Again, do you have any information concerning his next of kin?" Boone asked.

He shook his head. "*Nyet*, I know no relatives here or Russia. Is why I take his sponsorship. How is he murdered? Who does this?"

At this point, Paisley made a request. "Excuse me, may I have a glass of water, please?"

Boone and Zolotov, both looked at her with surprise. Why is she doing this, Boone wondered? "Yes, I get you water," and Zolotov lumbered into the kitchen.

Meanwhile, Boone gave Paisley a strange look, which she ignored, and Zolotov returned to the room, handing her a glass of water.

"Thank you," she said.

Zolotov asked again, "Who does this to Gregore? How?"

"I'll tell you this, he was found in the freezer of the fast-food restaurant where he worked, and as of this moment, we have no official cause of death." Deciding he didn't need to give more information, he changed the subject. "Would you to give us the names and phone numbers of his friends? Also, did Kamorov have a car? Is it one of the cars in front of your house?"

Zolotov rose and shambled to the window, pulling back the curtain/bedsheet, enough to give him a view of the street, then replied, "*Nyet*, car is not here. It must be at burger place." He rubbed his hand across the top of his head, as sweat began to bead on his brow. He felt uncomfortable, this is not good, he thought.

Paisley noticed the beads of perspiration and could see

Zolotov's demeanor change, then based on his reactions, she began making her notes.

She chimed into the conversation, "We need a description of his car, including make and model, and also the name of the other roommates, and where we can be contact them."

Surprised, Zolotov looked her way, as if he'd forgotten about her, then described the car. "It's older model Ford. Rust on bottom, gray paint. I do not know license."

Like Boone, Paisley jotted this down in her little spiral notebook, too. She was struck by how much Zolotov reminded her of Aunt Olga, with the staccato sentences, from his Russian accent. "Is there anything else you can remember about the car?" she asked.

"It is beat up. Didn't work well...Gregore always riding with others."

"Who are his friends?" she continued.

"Only name I know is Nikita. Roommate is Antonov, Yury Antonov. More friends, I don't know them. We all live here. We are busy and mind our own business. We are friends...we do not visit...we share house."

The more nervous Zolotov was, the worse his English became, Boone noticed. "And where is Yury?"

"He comes home late," Zolotov explained. "Yury is student at Pinecrest College. Stays late, sometimes 5:30, sometimes later, at library."

"And Nikita?" Boone added.

"I only see him once, twice...he sees Gregore at work. Ask those people."

"And what do *you* do for a living, Mr. Zolotov?" Ingles asked, injecting herself into the questioning again.

CHAPTER 14

Zolotov was beside himself now—this was beginning to feel like the Spanish Inquisition! Things were *not* going well.

"I am logger at Crosby/Ironton area," he said, trying to give them as little information about himself as he could, without seeming to be secretive.

Looking up from her notes, Paisley changed the subject, "Is there a chance we might see Gregore's room? We'd like to look around—*if* it's okay, that is. There might be something to help us find more information. Do you know of anyone who wanted to do him harm? Or anyone who threatened him?"

"*Nyet*, I tell you, we live in same house, we do not talk much —I see Gregore sometimes in kitchen for food, before work. We each mind our business."

There was that broken English again, and regardless of everything that Zolotov said, Boone detected an undercurrent of something he couldn't quite put his finger on. He didn't think

Zolotov lied, but instead, was hiding something. The question was, what did he have to hide?

After dragging his feet for a moment, Zolotov agreed to take them upstairs and stood up. He began plodding up the stairs, with Boone and Paisley trailing behind him, giving each other meaningful glances as they trudged up the steps.

Paisley casually asked Zolotov, "Where did you live in Russia before moving to the US?"

Thinking quickly, he said, "A city near Moscow," and hoped this answer would satisfy her.

It didn't, as she immediately asked, "Which city?"

He answered with mild irritation in his voice. "The city is Nizhny."

Nothing more was said, although Paisley paused on the step, to write the info in her notebook. When Boone looked over as she did this, she glanced at him with a mischievous look in her eyes, dabbed her pencil on her tongue, and continued to write her note. Boone held back a snicker.

Once on the landing, the bedroom door opposite the steps was partially open. A long hallway to the left, revealed two more doors further down, with a door at the very end of the dimly lit corridor, open far enough to expose a small bathroom. Zolotov glanced over his shoulder at the two Detectives, while he led them down the hallway to the end, where there was a closed door on the left.

Slowly opening the door, he peeked in, before ushering them in. Zolotov took a quick look around, mumbling, "Gregore's room."

Boone stepped in first and surveyed the meager furnishings before ambling over to the closet and pushing its sliding door to one side. Several shirts hung on the clothes rack, and finding nothing else of interest, he turned and moved to a rather dilapidated dresser and opened a couple of its drawers. All they contained was a bunch of unpaired dirty socks, faded T-shirts, and jeans.

Meanwhile, Paisley looked with interest at the wooden desk, by the only window in the small room. Noticing a computer adapter on the floor, still plugged in, she turned to Zolotov. "A couple of people mentioned Kamorov and called him quite the computer whiz. I see a router on the desk, a computer adapter on the floor and some gaming equipment, controllers, etc., but where's his computer?"

Zolotov was busy, keeping an eye on Boone, who roamed around the room, but eyed Paisley when he heard her question. His eyes shot to the desk, startled to see the computer *was* gone. He answered, "I don't know!" Zolotov couldn't hide his surprise at the disappearance of Gregore's computer equipment.

"Does he keep it with him?" Paisley asked. But before he could answer, she continued, "There are only two drawers in the desk...would you mind if I had a look?"

"Go ahead," he answered again, all the time thinking he wanted to say, "*Nyet!*" As far as he knew, the computer had never been removed from the room!

She opened the top drawer, "Hmmm...nothing here." She found no software or other media of any sort, which seemed strange. "Usually," she said, "somebody *that* techie, possesses all sorts of media with which to store information, or games of some sort—not just controllers and a computer cord! Is his computer in a different room?"

"I will search in house." But from the minute she mentioned the word storage, Zolotov began sweating in earnest. His mind went to the thumb drive he'd been looking for when the detectives arrived. Did Gregore find and take it? Was my hiding spot compromised? He could hardly concentrate on the rest of the questions and wished these two would leave as soon as possible.

"Yes, please see if you can find his computer," Paisley said, interrupting his thoughts, "and let us know if you do. Meanwhile, we'll check to see if it's at Ben's Burgers."

Paisley pulled open the second desk drawer, retrieved a magnifying glass from her purse, and stooped close to the drawer, searching its insides. After scrutinizing it, she took out her notepad and wrote something down. Putting the magnifying glass back in her purse, she closed the drawer, while Boone *and* Zolotov stared at her.

Boone spoke up, "I have one last question, Mr. Zolotov. You seemed surprised when I said Kamorov died the night before last. Didn't you notice he hadn't come home? Does he spend nights away frequently?"

"No, I did not notice...why should I? I come home tired every night. I go to bed. They—Gregore and Yury—come home all hours."

"Where were *you* Sunday night?" Boone questioned.

"I drink with friends...late into night. I come home. Bad headache! I go to bed. *Nyet*, did not notice—*or* care. Sleep late into next day—my day off. I see Yury at noon. He studies. He goes to school."

Seemingly satisfied for the moment, the two detectives followed Zolotov out of the exiguous bedroom and downstairs. Boone gave Zolotov his card and said, "Should you think of other useful information, please call this number and leave a message."

"I will," and Zolotov walked them to the door and opened it.

"Thanks, for your cooperation," Boone said, then the two Detectives walked to their car.

Closing the door behind him, Zolotov leaned against it, still in shock over the afternoon's happenings, and tried not to think of the complications this event might cause. He called his gofer, Ivan Belenski, and gave him a message to send to his boss, Boris Tazvoshenko, in Moscow. Due to these unforeseen events, an emergency phone call had to be arranged.

As soon as the two detectives were in the car, Boone said incredulously, "A magnifying glass? Really?"

Paisley looked at him unperturbed, and as he started the car, said, "Sure, I always carry one. It was a special gift from my Dad when I was younger—"comes in handy!"

At a loss for words, Boone drove off, waiting a few minutes, then asked, "So, what's your impression of Mr. Pyotr Zolotov?"

Later Tuesday afternoon, a nervous Ivan Belenski was sent to the Brainerd Public Library, by Zolotov. He hated going there, because he didn't like its atmosphere. He *never* read books. Nonetheless, at 4:00 p.m., he shambled inside the glass doors, hands in his pockets and a dour look on his face. He wore a slouchy gray sweatshirt tucked into his pants, which accentuated his tall, lanky frame and small paunch, which hung over his belt.

Cloudy dark eyes scanned back and forth over the library patrons, as Ivan aimed his body towards the front desk. With a five o'clock shadow and black slicked-back hair, he appeared more Italian than Russian. The droopy mouth, characteristic of a much older man, caused the librarian to eye him warily, as he approached the front desk.

"May I help you?" she said, as she peered up at him and waited.

He looked down at her name plate on the desk. It said Sue Mason. He looked up and uttered in a whiny voice, "Uh, I need to use a computer."

"Do you have your library card?" She said as she smiled at him.

"No, I have an ID card."

Still smiling, she said, "Would you like to sign up for our library card?"

"No, just wanna use a computer today." These procedural questions were annoying him, and sensing his impatience, Sue ceased to question him any further, hurriedly setting him up with a computer pass.

"There are no available computers right now," she said, "but as soon as number five is free, you may use that one...the time is almost up for the guest using it." Despite his attitude, Sue remained pleasant.

Uttering a low growl at this further delay, Ivan was piqued to find that he'd have to wait. He stood for a moment mulling over his options before heading to an area next to the shelves displaying magazines and slouched into one of the chairs.

Todays's newspaper lay on the low, circular wooden table in front of him, so he leaned over absentmindedly and picked it up. His dark eyes drifted to the various people moving around in the library, then glancing down at the afternoon paper, his eyes opened wide, when he saw the headline on the front page: "BODY DISCOVERED IN FREEZER AT BEN'S BURG-ERS". Then he read the sub-headline: *"Gregore Kamorov Found Early Monday Morning at Ben's Burgers, by Employee and Off-Duty Detective, Paisley Ingles"*.

In disbelief, he continued to read the rest of the article, which didn't have much information other than the events following the discovery of the body—officers arriving, people being questioned, and an investigation taking place—none of the *real* details. He couldn't believe his eyes. The last line of the article stated, "...*No known suspects or motives, at this time.*"

That bit of news puzzled him. What happened? The news frightened him. He knew the group he worked for was capable of almost anything, and he wondered if Zolotov had anything to do with the murder!

He waited impatiently for a few minutes until finally, "Mr. Belenski," the librarian called his name, "computer number five is open now..." and he hustled over to take his place.

Sue said to the girl at the counter checking in books, "That man is strange—he doesn't seem the library type...did you notice how nervous and jumpy he was?"

The other librarian said, "There you go with your imaginary scenarios, again," she said, and they both had a good laugh.

Belenski logged onto the computer and began typing an email to the contact. The message his employer, Zolotov, wanted to send, was coded. In Russian, it read, "Off track—no luck at casino. Red and Black didn't work. Need different numbers to play." It made no sense to him. Zolotov never divulged the meaning of the messages.

On one occasion, Ivan dared to question Zolotov, who responded, "It is better for your health that you do not know! I will tolerate no questions—*never* ask again!"

Ivan got the picture and knew a threat when he heard one, nevertheless, it made him curious as to what the messages meant. Zolotov treated this message as an emergency, making Ivan think something crucial happened. Could it be Kamorov's death? He hurried to finish the message, pressed the send key, and rushed out of the library.

He knew the contact in Russia, would forward the message to the Big Boss, whoever that was, and Zolotov would summarily receive a response. Information was communicated this way, and so far, it had been working, with everything going according to plan. What had happened to Gregore Kamorov?

He couldn't help but wonder and decided it wasn't *his* problem. While Ivan headed home to his apartment, he thought about the last time he'd seen Kamorov—it was last Saturday night—just before he died!

His friends, Lenny Starko and Kamorov, had been drinking at the Last Call, a seedy little bar in the worst part of town. Ivan arrived after midnight, later than the other two, and joined them in a back booth. Ivan and Kamorov talked over shots of Vodka, while Lenny left the booth, to flit around two sleazy women at the bar. He acted like a vulture, circling around road kill, buying them drinks and pestering them, in hopes of furthering a relationship, with one or the other, by the end of the evening.

As Ivan recalled the evening, he and Kamorov had laughed derisively, as they watched Lenny being brushed off by both women. Before Ivan left that night, Kamorov, in a particularly good mood after much drinking, had spouted crazy talk, when Lenny returned to the booth, about a jump drive he had, and how he was about to be rich. Although barely able to stand, Kamorov was still buying round after round, of cheap Vodka shots for Lenny and a few other patrons.

Ivan's reminiscing stopped, upon arriving at his apartment building. He parked his car on the street and went inside while shoving questions about Kamorov's murder out of his head. He only remembered leaving early that night, while *they* still partied. He and Lenny had both pressured Kamorov for access to this thumb drive, but Kamorov just laughed and said *nyet*. But he was still alive when Ivan left, so what could have happened?

CHAPTER 15

Pinecrest
Boone and Paisley parted company, as soon as they returned from the Zolotov interview. Once in her office, Paisley chatted with Millie for a moment or two, then reached into her purse to remove the flash drive, setting it on her desk.

"That pesky flash drive!" she said.

"Oh, that reminds me," Millie began, "a guy came in while you were gone, asking questions about a thumb drive?"

Paisley looked up. "Really? What did he ask?"

"He said he spoke with Ben at the Burger place about losing his thumb drive there—that's what he called it, a thumb drive—and wanted to know if it had been found. Ben told him he knew nothing about a thumb drive—only a flash drive—and gave him your card, telling him that you'd be able to help him. So, he came here inquiring about it."

"Hmmm, and what did you tell him?" Paisley said, turning on her computer.

"I told him he should talk to you, because as far as *I* knew, there was no mention of a thumb drive, so he asked if I would look for one. I told him no, that *you* took a 'flash drive' home for safe keeping, and since I'm just the secretary, I don't handle things relegated to officers or detectives."

Paisley smiled at Millie, "Perfect! Continue..."

Millie shuffled some papers, "I told him to come back when you were here and talk with you." Millie paused and took a sip of her cold coffee. "He seemed a little perturbed by this. For a moment, I thought he might try to look in your desk! I shoved a notepad and pen his way and suggested he leave his name and a number where you could reach him, and I said you would contact him."

"That's all?"

"Well, he reached across the desk and picked up the notepad and pen, mumbled something about a wild goose chase, then set them down. "Never mind," he said, under his breath, then hurried out. It was odd."

"Hmmm...can you describe his appearance?" Paisley stopped fooling with her computer and listened attentively, to Millie.

"To tell the truth, Pais, I was busy working and only glanced at him a couple of times. I didn't pay much attention to his looks."

Disappointed, Paisley considered this for a moment, then spoke again, "Do you think you could close your eyes and try to re-create the encounter? Maybe you'll recall something?"

"I don't know?"

"Let's give it a try because sometimes it works. I learned this method when I went through the Police Academy in California."

"Well, okay." Millie leaned back in her chair, closed her eyes, and remained quiet for a few minutes.

Paisley began, "Can you see his height, hair color, or what he's wearing?"

Millie said nothing, then slowly began to describe him, "I would say...medium height and build." She paused.

"Anything else, Millie? Think carefully."

Another pause, then she said, "Yes, I think he wore an old ragged ball cap, so I didn't see the color his hair, but it was kind of shaggy, hanging out of his cap in the back."

"Good, keep going," Paisley said softly and leaned forward, hands flat on her desk.

"Um, I think maybe a dark plaid shirt," then her eyes popped open, and she leaned forward towards Paisley and brightened, "I *did* notice something! He had some sort of a tattoo on the inside of his left arm, where it bends at the elbow. I remember now...it caught my eye!"

"Can you describe the tattoo?" Paisley was excited!

Millie closed her eyes again, paused then said, "It looked like a snake...the snake appeared coiled up." She was quiet again, then opened her eyes and looked at Paisley, "I saw it when he pushed the notepad back towards me because his sleeves were rolled up almost to his elbow, and with his arm stretched out, I could see it sort of peeking out from under his sleeve!"

"Great, Millie! One more thing, his age?"

She closed her eyes, "I guess...maybe...early to mid-thirties? I'm not good at guessing age, but I remember his eyes were squinty, and he seemed nervous...oh, and I remember! The snake was green!"

"Anything else?"

"That's about all I can remember. I only glanced at him a

couple of times. He came in right after you left with Boone, so it happened several hours ago. I'm sorry, I should have paid more attention. I'm surprised I remembered anything, but closing my eyes like you said, *did* help!"

"Great job, Millie—I'm amazed you remembered so much about him—you would make a good detective, too!"

"You think so, Paisley? Wow! Thanks for the compliment."

Millie's mood lightened and she smiled, then went back to shuffling the reports on her desk, which she needed to type.

"*Very* helpful," Paisley said, "I wonder who he is, and how I can get his flash drive to him? If I lost mine, I'd be going crazy trying to find it!"

Millie stopped typing and looked up again, "Hey Pais, I forgot to tell you, you have a voice mail."

"Okay." Paisley's voice trailed off.

Lost in thought, she stared at the flash drive, which now sat on her desk. Finally, she decided to take a look at the flash drive to see what it contained. Maybe it would disclose its owner? She began to back up her computer to an external hard drive, in case the flash drive contained some sort of virus or malware.

Once she finished the backup, she made an executive decision and inserted the mysterious flash drive into the USB port on her personal computer. What if this drive *didn't* belong to an innocent bystander, but instead, held information pertinent to the crime? Could it belong to the killer, she wondered?

Paisley looked up at Millie because it dawned on her, Millie was speaking. Paisley had become engrossed in her own thoughts and only heard Millie's voice, but not her words.

"What did you say, Millie?"

"It's Okay," Millie smiled, "I asked if you listened to the message on your phone. The call came in about ten minutes after you left the office to go with Detective Boone, and I let it go to voicemail since I knew you were coming back."

"Oh sure, thanks Millie. I *will* listen to it." Her voice trailed off once more, as her attention went back to her computer, the flash drive, and what she hoped it would reveal.

Millie shrugged her shoulders and went back to her paperwork, still glancing at Paisley from time to time, watching as she delved into her computer, doing whatever it was that had her so captivated.

A few minutes later, her work finished, Millie stacked the reports on her desk, turned off her computer then said, "I'm leaving a little early today, see you tomorrow, Pais." Seeing Paisley so absorbed in her work, Millie didn't bother to listen for a reply, as she bustled out of the office.

Paisley, engrossed in her quest, *didn't* notice. Her cell phone rang. She glanced at the clock—almost 3:45 p.m.! "Hello, Detective Ingles, speaking."

"Hey Ingles, this is Boone. I want you to know the autopsy is confirmed for tomorrow morning. If you'd like to go, I thought we could discuss the details tonight over dinner. How about meeting me at Casa Café on Booker Avenue...you know, the little Mexican cafe down the street from the radio station?"

Even though she sat alone at her desk, she flushed slightly and stammered out, "Sure, sure—I know the place, sounds good."

"Great! Does 6:30 p.m., work for you?"

Paisley glanced up at the clock again, then said, "Sure."

"Whoever arrives first, grabs a table. See you there," Boone said, and hung up.

Paisley put the phone back in its charging dock and stared at it. A myriad of thoughts swirled in her head. On the one hand, Boone intrigued her, but on the other hand, his cavalier attitude annoyed her. What's with his matter-of-fact way of inviting her and assuming she would automatically say yes? It's as if he thought she couldn't *possibly* have other plans! Of course, she *didn't* have other plans, but *he* didn't know that! Despite all this, she said yes, because she wanted to talk more about the case, *and* the trip to see the autopsy.

When Detective Boone finished his call to Ingles, he decided it was time to get in touch with Director White, on his secure line at the Bureau, in Washington, D.C. Several months ago, Director White selected Boone, to head the special assignment in Minnesota. An FBI agent working at the agency in Minneapolis had been contacted by a man, Mr Ohm, saying he had information about a matter of national security and was willing to sell the information.

The incident was immediately reported to the Bureau's Counter-Terrorism Special Investigation Unit (CSIU), in DC, headed by Director Woodruff White. Director White called Boone, who worked for the unit, to his office and apprised him of the situation. He assigned Boone to take charge of the investigation and make contact with Mr. Ohm.

Boone only had one short phone conversation with the man, Mr. Ohm. The call was just long enough to determine its origin to be from the Brainerd, Minnesota area, but not long enough to be fully traced. The man disguised his voice but promised another call in May to set up the conditions for a meeting. Boone was sent by Director White, to Pinecrest, a larger city next to Brainerd, in Mid-Minnesota.

Boone's assignment was to head a team to follow up on their informant's information. Boone eagerly accepted, and the following day provided a list of men he wanted on his team—all hand-picked—and gave the list to Director White. The men began preparing to travel to Minnesota—if and when— Boone needed them.

Now it was the middle of May and time to give an update to Director White. The phone rang, and when it picked up, he said, "Director White? It's Deedrick Boone, calling from Pinecrest."

"Yes," the Director said, as he swiveled his chair towards his desk. "How's it going there, in Minnesota? What can I do for you, Boone?"

"Well, sir..." Boone began, "at the moment I'm working a murder case here at the precinct, and I'm beginning to believe it *might* be connected to the contact who's supposed to get in touch with me!"

"That was quick!" Director White replied as he straightened in his chair, "Any word from the mystery contact?"

"No, not a word from him—yet! However, the murder case was handed to me on Monday morning, when a body was discovered in a nearby fast-food place. It's been something to do while I wait for contact with Mr. Ohm, but regardless, I think it's imperative to get up to speed on our operation. I want the task force to come to Minnesota now, to set up their location. We need to be ready for whatever we might discover...especially considering how important this 'could' be!

They spoke for a few minutes more then, Director White said, "I'll send all the information to you concerning the task force and its arrival plans." He cautioned Boone, "Please use every precaution, as this may turn into a perilous mission— keep me informed."

"Yes, sir!" Boone replied, "it's a shame I haven't been able to make connect with our informant, so far. We *really* need to find out what he's offering, and I assure you, I *will* take every precaution."

After ending the call, Boone grabbed the folders off his desk, threw them into a briefcase, and walked down the hallway. As he passed through the break room, several of the officers eyed him, giving each other furtive glances, which Boone noticed, but ignored. He knew they sensed something was 'off' about his presence at the precinct.

His credentials were impeccable, but a detective, is a detective, and some have a sixth sense. He could see this, especially with Officer Smith. Boone could tell his backstory wasn't completely fooling Smith. Boone glanced at the group, as he walked by the room and gave a slight nod, continuing into the corridor.

Rounding the corner Boone entered the locker room to change into more casual attire—faded blue jeans, a dark tee shirt, a blue denim jacket, and his boots. Grabbing his Glock, he stuck it in the back of his waistband, chuckling to himself, as he remembered his buddies at the CIA, chiding him about carrying it that way—a round in the chamber and safety off.

This bad habit had developed in years past when he worked undercover in Syria and Afghanistan. He couldn't help it... he liked the feel of the gun in the back of his waistband. Yes, he *knew* it was unorthodox, but he was off duty now. Raised in a military family, he was around guns all his life and learned to use them at a very early age. His first gun was a little .22 rifle with a carved butt, which belonged to his Grandpa Boone.

Grandpa Boone gave it to Deedrick on his tenth birthday, and with this gift came tall tales on star-filled nights around a campfire, on camping trips taken when Boone was young. Smiling at these recollections, Boone left the precinct, heading home to wrap up plans for the arrival of his task force, before time to leave for Casa Café.

Once Millie left for the day, Paisley became even more

engrossed in the flash drive, and after she backed up its contents, she ran a malware/virus check, just to be on the safe side. Now that she was about to open it, she felt anxious about what the drive had to offer. She hoped it would hold clues about Gregore, and perhaps even the killer!

Sadly, it probably contained the ordinary contents of some college or high school student's class notes, who'd been studying at Ben's Burgers. With a guilty feeling, Paisley assuaged her conscience, by telling herself she would find information that would help return the drive to its rightful owner.

She opened the drive. It contained ten files, which she began to open one at a time, only to find nothing of interest. The first nine files contained benign documents concerning complicated computer game strategies, school schedules, work schedules for Ben's Burgers, etc. The drive might belong to Kamorov, or some other worker at Ben's.

However, when she clicked on the tenth file, it was password protected. "Aha!" Paisley whispered excitedly. "Maybe this will reveal something interesting!" She sat tall in her chair, leaning towards her computer and with trepidation tried to decide, which approach to use in breaking the password.

The password was short, according to the number of dots in the password box—perhaps a minimum of eight characters or less. Hence, Paisley decided to use something simple, like the Brute Force method, which tries all possible combinations. The corner safe in her office contained the tools of her trade, and she procured the special disc for such a purpose, inserted it in the DVD drive, and pressed start.

After waiting forty-five minutes with no results, she decided to try another method, and moved to the Dictionary Attack, which has a dictionary of words, numbers, *and* characters to crack a password. Using some of her forensics' software was right up her alley because, as a CFS, legal hacking *is* what she did—she hacked into computers confiscated by the police needing information from them to solve crimes.

After a little over an hour, the computer stopped and a password appeared on her screen. She stared at the password now revealed—the letters spelled a strange word—*chemodan*. She thought, "What kind of word *is* this?"

CHAPTER 16

lthough puzzled by the word *chemodan*, Paisley proceeded to enter the password to open the document before her. The document displayed a more difficult-looking encryption, which might be harder to crack. She used the same software to try and decipher it, and while the software worked its magic, Paisley googled the word *chemodan* on her work computer.

The word displayed in Cyrillic characters, which surprised Paisley! Scrolling the list for something in English, she found a music group named chemodan, a restaurant in Russia of the same name, and finally, did the Russian-to-English translation. The Russian word meant suitcase. How strange, she thought?

She became impatient with the time it was taking to decrypt the document. But suddenly, the computer whirred to a stop, and as if a key had been put in a keyhole and opened a door, the screen sprang to life revealing a few coordinates and a crude map. The map contained Cyrillic characters, as did, the body of the document—just like the password. There were no clues contained in the document produced, as to what the narrative included. The encryption was a more sophisticated, and she need to be handle it later when she had more time.

Paisley felt as if she found a treasure map, and was captivated by this turn of events! Copying everything on the file to her computer, she then encrypted it, to save to a private password-protected file on her laptop, and also saved a copy to her private password-protected external hard drive.

She printed several copies, one of which, she put in a manila folder, to place in the office safe, but decided to bring the other hard copy to show Boone. The thought of Boone, caused her to glance at the office clock, "Ahh!" she said out loud. She hadn't planned to spend so much time on her computer because she agreed to meet Boone, at half past six.

According to the clock, she should have left twenty minutes ago, and here she sat with a desk still needing to be straightened before she could leave. She texted Boone, letting him know she'd be a few minutes late and grabbed the second printed copy of the file. Will I share these papers with Boone? I'll need to make a judgment call once I get to the cafe.

Instead, she stuffed the folder into her aged purse/briefcase/computer bag, which was like an old friend. It had accompanied her everywhere for years. Thank goodness it's leather, she thought, or it probably would have disintegrated long ago. Over the years, the leather had aged and cracked on the corners, yet was supple and soft from use. The leather was the equivalent of the patina on copper. Throwing its strap over her shoulder, she grabbed her jacket and ran out the door.

Boone waited for Ingles in the entry of the crowded cafe. The waitress directed him to a table and he asked for two menus, then ordered a beer. The waitress delivered it and he took a sip, looked around the room, and decided to go over his case notes while waiting.

His cell phone lit up in his pocket with the text from Paisley, but its sound was off, so he didn't notice, nor did he receive her call to apologize for being so late, which went to voicemail. While he waited, he delved into his notes, unaware of the passing time.

As Paisley drove, she puzzled over the information on the flash drive, and the effort it took to crack the file's password. Her imagination went wild. Maybe the murderer dropped it? Or perhaps it belonged to the mystery man, who had appeared in her office earlier in the day. However, it was probably Gregore's, and the encrypted part was a love letter to his girlfriend or something. Anyway, she still wanted to know what it said.

But what about the mystery man who'd tried to claim it? Could *he* be the killer, or just a friend? Pondering this, she realized both Ben and Millie, said the mystery man called it a 'thumb drive'. Coincidence? I'll have to compare the descriptions of both men tomorrow to see if they are one-in-the-same.

Other things bothered her too. I wish I hadn't picked up the flash drive that morning, because now I've compromised the fingerprints. I meant well when I picked it up, but now I can't help it...I want to see what else it contains on the chance that it reveals a clue. If it does, I'll have to turn it over to the police.

Eager to get to Casa Café, she drove a little faster, because missing this dinner meeting was *not* an option. Along with a discussion of the day's events, Boone would be interested in what she'd discovered—she was sure of it! Perhaps he would advise her to turn over the flash drive, *or* would he scold her? Ten minutes later, she pulled into a parking place.

Before exiting her car, she twisted her pony tail into a bun and stuck in several bobby pins to hold it. Scurrying towards the entrance, she failed to notice the older car, following her into the parking lot and parking further back in the lot, hidden in the long shadows of the tall trees at the far end of the parking area.

Paisley rushed into the little Mexican cafe, ignoring the stares she received from her whirlwind entrance, and glanced around until she spotted Boone. Unfortunately, as she headed towards his booth, she almost knocked down the waitress, who was attempting to seat her. The flurry of excitement and noise created, startled Boone, and he looked around to see what caused such a stir to find it was Ingles, arriving at his table.

She apologized to the poor waitress, who finally succeeded in handing her a menu, only to notice that two menus were already on the table. So much for low-key and covert, Boone thought, amused by this spectacle. People stared as Paisley sat down, and took off her jacket, then settled into the comfortable leather booth.

She rested her arms on the light oak heavily varnished table-top, and with its glassy appearance in the dim light, water spots were noticeable where the table had been wiped with a too-wet, rag. Finally, the people returned to their meals, and the chattering increased in volume once more.

When the waitress returned, Paisley ordered a Diet Coke, before turning towards Boone, to say, with a sheepish look on her face, "So sorry I'm late. I apologize."

"No problem," he smiled, glanced at the menu and said, "Let's order."

Casa Café was Paisley's favorite, and although she didn't come often, she loved the atmosphere created by the cow skulls and serapes hanging on walls, and the sizable faux cactus plants in terra cotta pots placed strategically around the dining area. Miniature sombreros were sitting on baskets of napkins, next to the bottles of fiery hot-sauce, as Mariachi music filtered through the speakers and blended with the room's chatter. It seemed a quirky place to be found in the middle of Minnesota, she thought.

The waitress brought salsa with chips, which were warm and crisp, and Paisley ordered her favorite dish—Chili Rellenos — while Boone ordered Fajitas. The waitress headed to the kitchen to place their orders, and Paisley relaxed, as they progressed from how-was-your-day to other topics.

"So, do you think this is a random murder?" She began. "Is there any speculation as to whether it will be investigated as premeditated? Or, do you think it was accidental, as in collateral damage from a robbery-gone-bad?"

She waited for his response with a questioning expression on her face, as she selected a tortilla chip from the basket the waitress had deposited on the table. When she bit into it, it fractured into pieces, which rained down on the table. She ignored the mishap while brushing the crumbled pieces into her hand, and making a small pile on the right side of the table.

An amused look appeared on Boone's face again, as he watched her do this. "Well," he paused, and looked into her beautiful amber eyes, then answered, "I think you and I both know that there's something unusual about this case," and having said this, he turned his attention to his food, which the waitress just delivered. Then, after several bites, he added, "What do *you* think?"

Her meal arrived also, but she was still reeling from his blue eyes that stared right into her being. It caused her to pause a moment, until she recovered and said, "I don't consider it a robbery since the registers weren't touched. Perhaps Kamorov had enemies, and they decided to attack him?"

Boone didn't respond, but took several more bites of his food, instead. She fell silent as the waitress arrived to see if everything tasted alright. They both answered yes, then concentrated on their meals.

Boone appeared more interested in *her* knowledge and thoughts about the case. This surprised *and* annoyed her. She gave opinions to *his* questions, but couldn't figure out why he avoided answering *hers*? When *she* asked a question, *he* found ways to change the subject to avoid answering, then turned the questions back to *her*.

"This food is delicious," she said, when they were both finished. But she *really* wanted to say, "I thought that we were working together!" Instead, she asked, "What about the autopsy? You said you wanted to talk to me about it?"

"Yes, I thought you might like to go down to the Ramsey County Medical Examiner's Office with me." He put his napkin on the table and pushed his plate away. "They sent the body down yesterday, and I received a call from the coroner, that the autopsy will take place at 10:30, in the morning. So, if you'd like to come...?"

"Yes, I would!" she said excitedly, and they agreed to meet the following morning at 7:00 a.m., which would give them plenty of time to get down to Ramsey County, by 10:30.

At least the invitation to the autopsy made her feel included, yet her intuition told her something else was going on with him. She decided to do a little checking on his background when she had a moment. She thought he seemed different from the other detectives she worked with at the PPD, but then again, maybe it was because he came from back East, where they handle things differently.

Even though she wanted to tell Boone about the information found on the flash drive, her instincts told her not to discuss it with him just yet, because after all, even *she* wasn't sure of its relevance. The flash drive would need more probing. Besides, his matter-of-fact-ness made her feel as if he had one-upped her. During the meal, she divulged more thoughts on the case than he did!

Nevertheless, she was unable to mask her excitement when he said she could attend the autopsy. She knew the hint of a smile on his face, appeared to be more of amusement, than mirth, because it was evident to her, that he totally read her facial expression, and *knew* she was pleased. Darn, she thought!

Paisley's competitive nature was activated. Now she wanted her fair share of reciprocal information, but before she could say anything more, the waitress arrived with the check. Boone stood, glanced at the bill, pulled money from his pocket and handed it to the waitress.

"Ready to go?" he asked, as he turned to Paisley, and she stood.

"Thank you," she said, and attempted to leave a tip.

"No, no," he said and stopped her hand, "I'm taking care of this." He smiled at her, then turned and led the way out of the restaurant. Once outside, they said their goodbyes and went their separate ways.

On the way back to her Aunt's farm, Paisley replayed the dinner in her head, and it occupied her mind until she turned onto CR 38. Again, she felt someone was following her, as another pair of headlights made the same turn. After several miles, she dismissed it as being her imagination. Paisley noticed the car, lagging further and further behind, and ten minutes later, turning into the farm's driveway, she parked and switched off the engine and headlights, then waited to see if the other car would drive by.

Several minutes later a car came down the road and continued South, so her fears evaporated, and she breathed a sigh of relief, then climbed out of the car and entered the farmhouse. After the busy day, she felt exhausted. When she came into the mudroom and headed into the kitchen to put her things on the table, she saw a note propped against a small vase on the far side of the table.

Paisley read the note from Aunt Olga, with great concern:

My dear Paisley,

Uncle Vlad being taken to hospital in cities, for more tests. Good friend to drive me down to be with him, and I stay with her...or at hospital. Might be gone for a while, but no worries for you. Number to call me is on refrigerator.

Love, Aunt Olga.

Paisley felt saddened by the news, but maybe her Aunt's presence would comfort Uncle Vlad, making his stay at the hospital easier. He would certainly get the help he needed from a bigger hospital, with its specialists. She left the note on the table and went to her room for the night.

CHAPTER 17

Russia
   Zolotov had tasked Ivan Belenski, to take his message to the Public Library, to be sent to Tazvoshenko, in a small town near Moscow, in Russia. Russia is eight hours ahead of Minnesota, so it would be 2:30 a.m., Wednesday, in Russia, when the email arrived. It wouldn't be seen until Tazvoshenko arrived at his office around seven in the morning.

The location of Boris Tazvoshenko's small drab office existed within the confines of an old warehouse located in a dilapidated area, on the outskirts of Moscow. His assistant, Nestor Yakimov, usually the first to arrive, let himself in and entered his cubicle, then booted up the computer on his desk. Typing in his password, he saw one message in the inbox, which according to the time stamp, arrived very early that morning.

He clicked on it, and noted the encryption and addressee, and knew Tazvoshenko was the only one who could open it, with his personal password. Yakimov jumped, as Tazvoshenko burst through the door into the ante-room, where Yakimov sat at his desk.

Yakimov said, "Important message came in last night, for only you to open."

Boris growled in response and continued to power across the small ante-room to his office, where he entered and slammed the door behind him.

Yakimov scurried over to a metal counter and sink with a small cupboard above it, to begin making his boss a morning cup of espresso. Before he finished, he heard a muffled roar from the office and knew his boss was more upset than usual. With the espresso ready, he poured a cup, set it on a tray, and with wobbly legs walked to the office door and timidly rapped on it—not sure what to expect.

"Enter!" Boris grouched.

"Your espresso, sir," he said, cautiously opening the door and scooting over to the desk, and with trembling hands, he set the small tray on the mahogany desktop.

"Stay close, Yakimov," he groused, as he reached for his espresso, "I'll have a message to send back."

"Yes, I'll be here." Yakimov said, and hurried out of the office, closing the door behind him.

Although Yakimov had worked for Tazvoshenko for two years, the anger his boss displayed almost daily frightened him. Tazvoshenko, a volatile and dangerous man, headed a Russian Mafia organization, which had grown very large and prosperous over the years. Yakimov *always* remained cognizant, of this fact.

While Tazvoshenko leaned back in his chair and sipped his espresso, he opened his computer to read the now decrypted message received earlier. Enraged, he jumped up, pacing between the door to his office and his desk, only stopping once to down the entire contents of his cup of espresso, before continuing to pace.

On his next pass by the desk, he used his powerful arm in a fit of anger to sweep the basket of papers off the desk, including the empty cup and saucer, which shattered, as it hit the floor. The papers scattered into the air and drifted to the floor, and he bellowed for Yakimov, who rushed into the office.

"Clean up this mess!" he demanded, then stomped out of the office and into the main area of the warehouse.

"Yes, sir," Yakimov said weakly, but Tazvoshenko had already traveled too far down the metal-shelved aisles, to hear Yakimov's feeble reply. Closing the office door, he began picking up the shattered china and papers strewn on the floor.

The figure of Tazvoshenko, striding down the warehouse aisle, in disheveled clothes and old scuffed boots stuffed with his pant legs, certainly did not represent the image of a wealthy Mafia leader. He used his mass of shoulder-length hair to partially cover his weathered face, while black eyes glowered from underneath bushy brows. But it was the perpetual sneer decorating his lips, which intimidated his men.

"Are the men at the other warehouse today?" Tazvoshenko asked, with his deep gravelly voice.

Pavel Gorka, his warehouse manager, startled at the ferocious tone in his voice said, "Yes, they are working here today."

"Good! If you need me, I will be at other warehouse," and with that, he headed for the side door and into the parking lot, intent on his mission. His other warehouse, located northwest of Moscow's capitol, in an industrial area, was both private *and* secure—a place to make an urgent phone call to Zolotov, *and he did't care,* what time it was, in Minnesota!

Wednesday, May 17, 2017 Pinecrest Wednesday

morning around seven, Paisley met Boone in his office at the precinct to discuss the reports from Ben's Burgers. But before tackling them, Boone said, "I thought we'd review the video feed from the businesses in the mall across the parking lot, from Ben's."

"Oh, I didn't know you had them." Paisley sat opposite him, as he angled the monitor so she could also, see the feed.

"Well," he said, with a sigh, when they'd viewed the videos, "It seems the businesses' cameras are too far away from Ben's, to discern if anyone entered *or* left his establishment that night. It's too dark from that distance."

"What a shame Ben didn't have video security," Paisley commented, "however, I believe he's considering it now. We talked about it when I paid him a visit the other day. He said nothing had ever happened to concern him enough to consider installing security equipment."

"Yes, a shame," Boone echoed, "but, we *do* have several leads coming from some of the reports and printouts, which I checked over yesterday."

"Which reports?" she asked.

"I jotted down names from Kamorov's employee file, and called a few people, whom I know in high places, to check them out, for me. One of the reports contained information on Zolotov, the guy we interviewed. They traced him to a Russian town near Moscow—and it wasn't the name of the town that he gave to us! And no wonder—since he has *quite* a colorful background."

Walking over to the file cabinet, he picked up the papers sitting on top of the opened drawer and stood looking through them for a moment.

"I'm not surprised," and she scooted her chair over to his side of the desk to review the reports, "he seemed very uncomfortable, and *my* instincts told me, that something didn't make sense."

Boone looked at her curiously then walked back to the desk and sat in his chair next to her, ignoring the fact that she'd moved her chair, so close to his. He turned to face her and said, "The fingerprints we or I should say, *you*," he corrected himself, "purloined at Zolotov's, house, have been put through the FBI's facilities thanks to your clever work, I might add!" She thought she noticed the beginnings of a smile, but he was still in business mode.

Pleased by his comment she replied, "I couldn't help myself! My intuition told me to do it, so I simply acted on it. When he brought me the glass of water, I handled it carefully, and dropped it in my purse when no one was looking, so we could test for fingerprints in the lab."

"Well, we have the prints and by using them, my contact found Zolotov in the system, and we were able to track several nefarious operations connected to some businesses of his, in Russia, and several other foreign countries."

"Really? I guess I'm not surprised," she was eager to hear. "So, what's he done?"

"He's been accused of spying, for the Russians, in Britain, and also running munitions from Russia to some Middle Eastern country, but no one could prove it."

Now he had Paisley's attention, "Wow! How does someone get away with *that?*"

"Wait," he said, "that's not all. He also involved himself in a series of robberies in France, in the early 90s, and he became a person-of-interest in the bombing of a restaurant in Italy, which killed some mafia higher-ups. "

"He has quite the rap sheet!" she said.

Boone could see she was pleased to know the fingerprints

were so helpful. "They nabbed several men for these crimes, including Zolotov, but never convicted them, because of their access to fancy lawyers. They couldn't prove any of these men were connected to these crimes. He's a slippery snake, who's managed to circumvent authorities at every turn."

"A dangerous man, like him! Why is he here in Brainerd, and what's he doing?"

Before he answered her question, he stood up and asked if she'd like some coffee, she nodded, and he left the room for a moment, then returned with two cups.

He sat the cups on his desk, "I hope you like it black?" She nodded again as he handed her a cup and continued speaking, "It seems wherever he went, trouble followed. I came across some old photos from a Russian news website, during the time of his brief incarceration, before one of the trials."

"Let me see," she said, and stood from her chair to look over his shoulder at the pictures arranged on his desk. They both examined the three photos included within the report, but they appeared blurry, grainy, and could not be identified, as Zolotov.

"One more thing," Boone said, "Pyotr Zolotov, is *not* his real name!"

"Wow! Okay," she said, then stood up and began to pace as she tried to wrap her mind around this new piece of information. Stopping and turning to Boone, she said, "Then, what *is* his name?"

"His real name, as far as we know—because he may have other aliases—is Petrov Zharco."

Paisley was quiet for a moment, then moved her chair opposite Boone's again and sat down. "Does this make Zolotov our suspect? So, he lied about his name, he's on the FBI's radar, as a very high-profile person for this area—does that mean he's a murderer?" She looked directly at Boone, "Why is he here?

Maybe he's exactly who he says he is and has put his life of crime behind him!"

"I share your frustration!" Boone moved the files to the side.

She continued her thoughts, "But why would *he* want to kill Kamorov? Is it because he didn't like the #5 Combo Burger at Ben's, and blamed Kamorov? None of this makes sense!" Almost through with her rant, she ended with, "I need to know more information if I'm working on this case too! Is there any other information that you have, and I don't?"

CHAPTER 18

"Are you finished?" he asked. She nodded, of course, and he continued, "You know the old saying, it's on a need to know basis, and right now..." he trailed off.

"I know, I know," she replied, with a calmer more resigned tone..and right now, I don't need to know!"

"Look," he said consolingly, as he leaned forward in his chair, "there's no time at the moment. I'll fill you in later, I promise! There're still a few more reports to look over and afterward, an autopsy to attend this morning. You still want to go, don't you?"

"Of course!" Paisley nodded her head again, and for the moment, it pacified her. She sighed, stared at Boone, and said nothing. They quickly perused several of the other reports with much the same results: grainy pictures, and no new information.

"Well," she sighed again, "we almost know less now, than when we started. There're so many unanswered questions."

"Come on," he urged, "we have to leave for the autopsy. On the way to Ramsey County, I'll explain what to expect. Have you ever attended one?" Boone felt he knew the answer to the question.

Ramsey County ME Office Upon arrival at the Medical Examiner's Office, they parked in the small lot designated for officers and relatives, then entered the modestl building tucked next to the Regions Hospital.

They found themselves standing in front of a secure door with a thick glass window and were buzzed in and welcomed, by a technician. She directed them to a lounge area where they could wait until the autopsy was ready to begin, since the start times were usually approximate, based on the preparations.

The two of them only waited a few minutes before another autopsy technician with a welcoming smile entered and introduced herself as Ginny. She handed them a mask and gloves to wear, including optional shoe coverings. Boone and Paisley put on all of the items, then followed Ginny to the door of the post-mortem room (which she referred to as the post room), and were buzzed inside.

Both detectives reacted to the odors in the room, but it was Paisley, who commented. "Wow! Wasn't expecting it to smell like *this*! *Potent!*"

Boone agreed, "Yes, even though I've been here before, the first whiff always hits me the hardest!"

The large room contained four stainless steel tables, with stainless steel sinks at the foot of each table, to catch fluids from the procedure. Two other autopsies were taking place when they entered the room. Dressed in the gown and mask they were given, Ginny positioned them at the head of the table to view the procedure. The body bag was already on the table.

"Dr. Raj, will be out in just a minute," Ginny said.

"Where does the Doctor stand?" Paisley asked. She assumed *he* would be standing at the head of the table.

"The Doctor stands on the right side of the table, and I'll be standing on the left," Ginny responded.

Although Ginny had on a gown, shoe covers, and a face mask, she proceeded to put on more protection. Paisley watched in fascination, as she pulled a cap over her hair, followed by a full face plastic shield over the cap, and then another set of sleeves. Paisley, was surprised once more, as Ginny pulled on a pair of heavier gloves, over the latex pair she already had on and proceeded to add a third pair of latex gloves over those!

"What kind of a glove is the second pair you put on?" Paisley asked.

Ginny giggled, "Well, it probably seems like overkill, but they're Kevlar, and with all three layers, it protects my hands from knife cuts."

Paisley nodded, "Makes sense," and leaned towards Boone, whispering, "...no wonder it feels chilly in here because it must be hot inside all that protective clothing." Looking up at him, she wondered if he'd smiled. Even if he did, because of his face mask she wouldn't be able to see it!

His response, was to lean close to her and whisper, "Are you sure you want to participate? There's still time to change your mind."

"I haven't changed my mind. I *really* want to be here," she whispered back.

"Got it," he replied quietly, all the while smiling under his mask. She is a very determined woman, he thought.

She considered asking Boone if it was okay to ask questions during the procedure. However, Dr. Raj reached the table, and, with introductions all around, they turned their attention to the body bag on the table. Since it was a homicide, Ginny hadn't done the prep work, because the Doctor had to be present the entire time, when it was a murder case.

The body bag had to be unzipped in his presence. Dr. Raj proceeded to do this, then read the tag attached to the bag. "Date: May 17, 2017, Case No: 876R44105, Name: Gregore Kamorov, From: Crow Wing County Coroner's Office." The bag was removed.

Pictures were taken of the body *in situ*, from all angles. Boone handed Documents from the Crow Wing County's forensic team, to Dr. Raj, who proceeded to read them.

"It's noted here, the body had a cursory prelim examination, befre being transferred to us, and the stats are: Kamorov, male 28 years old, approximately 177 pounds (80.29 kg), 5′ 8″ tall, Caucasian."

Paisley whispered to Boone, "This is fascinating!" prompting Boone to give her 'the look'.

Dr. Raj continued, "According to this information, death occurred sometime between midnight and 7:00 a.m., probably closer to midnight, given the condition of the eyes, and rigor. Hmmm, found in establishment's freezer..." his finger scrolled over the information, "...and immediately transferred to Ramsey County ME offices, as found, in its frozen state."

Turning to the detectives, he asked, "Can you brief me with any other facts or pertinent information you discovered or concluded about cause of death?"

Boone did the talking, while Paisley observed Ginny removing the paper bags, from the body's hands, then bagging nail scrapings and clippings along with other pieces of evidence from the clothing, to be tested for DNA. Dr. Raj turned back to the body, and the clothing was removed and set on top of a new body bag on an adjacent table.

A barely audible intake of breath, emanated from Paisley, causing Boone to glance at her, "You okay?" he asked in a hushed voice.

"I'm fine," she nodded, still repulsed by the odors emanating from the body, which seemed stronger, after removing the body from the bag and unclothing it.

Dr. Raj began examining the head, noting the laceration on the back of the skull, the condition of the eyes, mouth, throat and neck bruises. These were all noted by Dr. Raj, on a notepad.

Ingles whispered to Boone, "I thought they dictated all their notes into a recorder?"

Boone said nothing. Next, Dr. Raj examined the torso and legs to check for bruises, cuts, scars, or any other injuries. The Doctor turned, from time to time, to make notes on the pad positioned on a small rolling table, to his right, which also held various instruments.

"Note: Markings: scar on left leg directly under the lateral knee cap," he said and moving back up to the arms remarked, "Small tattoo, in the crook of the left arm. Green snake with black markings, coiled in S-shape; approximately 2 inches (5.08 cm) long..."

As soon as the Doctor described the tattoo, Paisley perked up, and just as the Doctor was about to move on, she blurted out, "May I see the tattoo?" Boone, surprised when she asked to see the tattoo wondered, what is she up to now?

"Yes, of course, Detective Ingles," and Dr. Raj stepped aside, so she could move a little closer. She stared at it for a moment, then asked, "Is there a way I can get a picture of it?"

"Sure, if either of you has a precinct camera, you're welcome to take a picture."

Boone taken aback by her request, gazed at her with curiosity, wondering what her purpose was. She turned and gave him a questioning look. Reaching in his pocket, he pulled out a small camera and handed it to her. She took it, stepped around him, then walked to the cadaver's left side, and took several pictures.

"Thank you, Dr. Raj," she said, and resumed her place next to Boone, and returned the camera to him.

The autopsy proceeded in earnest. A hard-plastic block was positioned between the shoulder blades, causing the chest to protrude, making the chest easier to access when making incisions. A 'Y' incision made in the torso, caused the body to open further, in order to extricate the organs.

Ginny, the forensic technician, proceeded to weigh the organs, and shave off thin slices to be stored in jars, to examine under a microscope. The Doctor specifically dissected the neck and neck muscles, to determine if the horns of the hyoid bone were broken, which *could* indicate strangulation.

When the autopsy was complete, Dr. Raj turned to the two detectives, "Without the lab test results, which are ordered, including Toxicology tests, here is my preliminary conclusion based on my examination. This man was attacked from the front, made a valiant effort to fight off his attacker, then fell, hitting the back of his head on the floor. However, it appears to have been banged multiple times on a hard surface, causing a concussion."

"Dr. Raj, is there any chance that he was still alive when he was left in the freezer? Could the final cause have been freezing to death?" Paisley hated to interrupt, but she was curious. Paisley pictured the suffering Kamorov would have experienced, if he had still been conscious while he froze to death! Boone and Dr. Raj, looked at her, making her suddenly feel self-conscious.

Dr. Raj answered, "Strangulation, appears to be the primary COD (cause of death). There were bruises on the front of the neck, heavier bruises on the back of the neck, and indications of a fractured hyoid bone. Therefore, this is a homicide. I suppose it's possible he was alive for a few seconds while he was being dragged to the back of the freezer, but certainly *not* conscious."

"Thanks, Doctor." Boone said, and Paisley added her thanks, too.

"When the tests are run on the evidence collected," Dr. Raj continued, "we'll know COD *and* the actions contributing to it, conclusively. Then, I'll send my full and final report."

He pulled off his latex gloves and deposited them into a container, saying," My final report will also contain the results of the Toxicology and DNA tests."

"Will that take very long?" Paisley asked.

Smiling, Dr. Raj assured her, "They'll probably be at your precinct, in a week or less. Several tests may take a little longer."

Turning to leave, the two Detectives stopped to discard their protective clothing in a container marked for that purpose. When Paisley glanced back, the bags containing the organs were being inserted into the body's cavity. Boone, noticed her staring, as Ginny continued to work.

"C'mon, let's get out of here. They'll be sewing the belly up with the bags of organs inside and putting the body, along with the clothing, into the new body bag on the other table, which was next to us. Then back to the cooler it goes, to wait for next of kin."

The autopsy lasted a little over an hour. It was a long drive back to Pinecrest. Neither of them were in the mood for a meal, even though it was almost lunchtime. Instead, they stopped at little place called, The Coffee Break, just past the city of Big Lake. The coffee shop was on a frontage road, off the main highway. Inside, they took a window seat, which looked out at a small pond, and both ordered coffee. They gazed out the window, privately reflecting on the morning's events.

The waitress brought their coffee. Boone stared at Ingles, as he stirred his coffee and remarked, "You seemed to take that autopsy in stride. It was with some trepidation, that I invited you to attend for fear that it might be too difficult for you. Some faint or become ill, and of course, there's no shame in that, as it happens to many seasoned officers. But for a first-timer, you sailed through it without a glitch, and I want to acknowledge you for that."

Her face grew warm from the praise, and she was afraid he noticed, "I went to the autopsy with no expectations. I didn't know how I'd react either, but I've always had an ability to switch my mind into clinical mode, and that's what I did!"

"Very impressive," he replied.

"I majored in math and science in my first two years of college, so I'm familiar with physiology, anatomy, psychology, and all the other '-ology's' I did my share of dissecting rats and other critters, etc., and perhaps those experiences helped!" She grinned.

Boone contemplated this for a moment, then changed the conversation to Yury Antonov, the other boarder at Zolotov's house.

"Did you read the information that came back on Yury?"

She nodded, "Yes, he appears to be on the up-and-up. I did some research on him and checked his social media profile, but I couldn't find anything there, or in Russia. I think we should meet with him to see what information he has to offer. He might have friends we don't know about, and they might have some grudge against Kamorov...I don't think we can't dismiss him as a possible suspect, yet."

Nodding his head, Boone took out his wallet and paid the tab, requesting a couple of to-go cups for their unfinished coffee. "Let's get going."

When they returned to the precinct, Boone assured her he would set up a meeting with Yury and inform her of the time and place. However, before they parted, he said, "Gonna work on some procedural things now, but before I forget, what was the tattoo picture all about?"

"Oh, thanks for the reminder, may I have the camera?" He handed it to her.

"And you wanted the pictures because...?" he asked again.

CHAPTER 19

Pinecrest
"I'll to tell you later," she answered mysteriously, with a grin. "There's no time right now because I also have a few things to handle."

And with that, Paisley turned and hustled down the long hallway to her office, leaving Boone, standing and staring after her. Entering her office after her long day, Paisley greeted Millie before plopping down in her chair. Wasting no time, she got right to work, opening her laptop and glancing over the information gleaned from the flash drive the previous afternoon.

Although dying to work on it, she wasn't clear how she would proceed. She knew it would be time-consuming, and there were just a few hours before time to go home. She pondered this, then decided to set it aside for the moment, until she handled other pressing police business.

"Well, Pais, how did the autopsy go?"

Paisley looked at Millie. "Oh, the autopsy? Well, it went great. I guess that's how I would characterize it.

After the initial shock of the odor, and the uncovered body, I managed very well! All in all, I found it very interesting—I can check 'autopsy' off my bucket list, now!" she joked.

"Not sure I could do that, so more power to you! *But*, I bet driving with that hunk, Detective Boone, worked out great!" And Millie gave an exaggerated conspiratorial wink.

"Why, Millie!" Paisley feigned consternation, at her remark, fanned her face with her hand, and batted her eyelashes. They both laughed.

"Anyway, I need to leave a little early today," Millie said, "so you go ahead and get back to work."

Not wanting to press her for more info, Millie filed her papers, and straightened her desk, then gathered her things.

Unexpectedly, Boone appeared at the office door, causing Millie to startle, then say, with a smile, "May I help you?"

With that, Paisley looked over, also surprised to see him at the door, and exclaimed, "Detective Boone, what brings you here?" What a ridiculous thing to say, she thought, and added, "Have you and Millie, been formally introduced, yet?"

Millie jumped right in and said, "No, I don't believe we have! I delivered a newspaper to your office the other morning, Detective, but I didn't introduce myself."

Paisley could *swear* Millie batted her eyelashes at him, so Paisley said, "Well, Boone, meet Millie, and Millie, meet Detective Boone."

Much to Paisley's dismay, Millie held out her hand to Boone, with her fingers pointed down, in a gesture that might look like, he was to kiss her hand, and said, "Enchanted, I'm sure!" and gave a slight curtsy.

"Very nice to meet you." Boone said, awkwardly holding her fingers, then smiled kindly.

147

"It's *such* a pleasure to meet *you*," Millie grinned, adding, "I've heard *so* much about you!"

Paisley cringed and attempted to change the subject by saying, "So...what do you need, Detective?"

"May I speak to you in the hall for a moment?" he asked.

"Oh, you can stay here," Millie said, and grabbed her jacket and purse. "I'm just leaving...see you tomorrow Pais, and nice to meet you, Detective Boone," then she rushed out the door.

"Sure...tomorrow..." Paisley said, although Millie was out of earshot when she uttered this. Relieved with Millie gone, she sat back in her chair. "Now, what may I do for you?" and she spun her chair towards Boone and waited for him to speak.

"What I wanted to say," Boone started, "...is why don't we grab a bite after work again, and discuss a plan of action for moving forward with the investigation, then we'll both go home and get some rest. Tomorrow we'll hit it running, starting with interviewing, Yury Panuken."

"I suppose it *is* time to call it a day," she checked her watch, then said, "Okay! You think of a place, and I'll gather my things, then meet you there."

Boone left her office, while Paisley began gathering her things, but just as she was about to shut down her computer, she remembered the camera. Taking it out of her bag, she removed the memory card and inserted it into her computer. Excitedly, she opened the files, which had pictures of the tattoo.

"Aha!" she said out loud, and immediately loaded them onto her flash drive, then printed out two copies...one for her files, and one for her briefcase.

Doing this brought back memories of Professor Howe, telling her college Computer Engineering class, "With all information, the key is redundancy, redundancy, redundancy." Guessing he would approve of her use of his advice, she smiled to herself. Paisley regretted not thinking to upload the pictures in time to show Millie, before she left for the day, and wondered if this tattoo would be a match to the stranger's, who came to the office inquiring about a 'jump drive'?

Boone and Paisley met on the precinct steps and walked to a little hole-in-the-wall diner, several blocks away from the precinct, for a bite to eat. They were oblivious to the car idling in the alley, with its headlights off, watching, as the two chatted on their way, to Dora's Diner. Named after its owner, Dora Turner, Dora's menu consisted of homestyle meals and had been in the same location for the last forty years.

The two detectives sat in a booth towards the back while they looked over their menus. They both ordered the meatloaf, mashed potatoes, and cooked corn, speaking very little during the meal. Since both of them hadn't eaten since the autopsy, hunger overtook them, and they even ordered Dora's famous homemade apple pie for dessert, along with coffee.

When Boone finished eating his pie he settled back in his chair, took a sip of coffee, then finally spoke. "I set up a meeting with Yury Panuken, for 7:30 a.m., tomorrow. We'll meet in the college's student union, before his first class."

Paisley nodded her head. "Why meet at the college?" Her hands wrapped around her warm cup, as she gazed at Boone.

"He has classes all day and won't be home from studying at school until late. He wanted to meet first thing in the morning, and since I didn't want to question him in front of Zolotov, I complied."

Blotting her mouth with her napkin, Paisley continued, "Here's my thought. From the statements taken at Ben's, Kamorov was a techie guy—a major gamer—but when we went through his room the next day, it was devoid of all tech stuff. So

I thought perhaps he'd put his computer in his car, but the officers already searched it, and found nothing."

"And...?" Sipping his coffee, Boone watched her over his cup rim, before he set it down.

"And," she paused, "if Ben's Burgers has lockers, maybe that's where he left his computer? But, I didn't see any mention of checking lockers in the detectives' reports. Not sure if Ben's even has lockers...I called, and they *do* have a few. If the computer *is* there, we can confiscate it, and perhaps it'll contain clues, as to whom and why, someone murdered him?"

She sat back satisfied with herself and slurped her coffee, because it was still very hot from the refill, and waited to see what Boone would say.

"Hmmm...yes, a good idea, we can go to Ben's after we meet with Panuken." Boone took a sip of water and motioned for Dora to bring more coffee. "Makes sense," and underwhelmed by his response to her idea, she decided instead to change the subject by asking him a few questions about his previous assignments.

Boone gave sketchy answers at best, although he did talk a little about his childhood. His artfulness at avoiding personal questions only served to make her more curious. She didn't press him this time, but decided to confront him at another time, and call him on his lack of candor.

Before they left, she mentioned, "I had a curious visitor to my office yesterday, who wanted to speak with me. According to Millie, he was jumpy and strange looking. Millie asked for his name, but he wouldn't say. Do you think someone who knows something about the case might be trying to come forward,?"

Boone agreed it was strange, but said nothing else...he was no longer paying attention. Rising, he threw a tip on the table after signing the check for the meal.

When they stepped outside, the night air felt chilly and damp, so they picked up their pace, hurrying back to the station, where Boone walked her to her car and reminded her about their early meeting the next day at the college, with Panuken. They said their goodbyes and went to their cars. Paisley started her Jeep, turned on the car heater, then drove to Brainerd, turning right at the edge of town, onto CR 38, as usual. The Jeep picked up speed, and she decided the Kamorov case was an enigma.

Brainerd By the time she arrived at the farm house, she looked forward to climbing in bed, reading the book she'd just started, and perhaps having a warm cup of Chamomile tea. She parked and hurried inside, turning on the light in the mudroom, then continuing, to the kitchen.

She flipped the light switch by the mudroom door, but nothing happened—how odd she thought, why is the electricity off? Reaching in her purse, she took out her small LED flashlight and turned it on, and when she pointed it into the kitchen, her jaw dropped.

"No! No!" she screamed, and stood, momentarily paralyzed, then reached for the Glock in her purse. Her hand gripped the gun, as she shined the light around the kitchen and stared, mouth agape, at the once orderly kitchen, now turned upside down!

Dishes were thrown from the open shelves and lay broken on the floor. The opened refrigerator's contents spilled out onto the floor, mixing with canned goods, raked off the cupboard shelves, in the ransacked kitchen! Turned over into the mess, was the grand table and chairs!

Horrified, she cautiously stepped through broken dishes on the kitchen floor to get to the living room doorway. She reached around the wall to turn on the living room light, but nothing happened. Stepping back into the kitchen, she carefully stepped over the mess to retrieve a bigger flashlight, from the junk drawer in the counter. Fortunately, this drawer hadn't been disturbed!

Holding her gun, she turned on the flashlight, hoping whoever did this was long gone! When she stepped through the doorway into the living room, it too had been ravaged. Glancing around the room with the light, she felt sickened at the devastation. Sofa cushions and armchairs had been slashed open, and their stuffing littered the carpet.

Everything was destroyed! Books were pulled from the oak bookcases and scattered in piles among the stuffing on the floor. Pictures ripped from the walls were strewn in the mess, their fronts slashed, with backings torn away. Paisley chambered a round in her gun, then forcing her legs to work, silently crept forward, proceeding slowly, with her gun held in both hands, arms outstretched, while moving the gun from side, to side.

She tiptoed stealthily from room to room, searching, but seeing nothing but destruction—every room a disaster! She felt numb, but convinced the perpetrators were gone, she moved back to the kitchen, picked up a chair from the floor and sat down. Staring in disbelief, she wanted to cry but wasn't able to.

Suddenly, she jumped and pointed her gun! Something moved in the darkness of the living room beyond the doorway, and it caught her eye. Straightening in the chair, she felt adrenalin pumping through her body and stood, still pointing her gun and turned her flashlight in the direction of the movement.

With a tremor in her voice, she said, "Who's there?" No answer until, to her relief, Aunt Olga's black cat, Phantom, came creeping out of the living room's dark shadows. Paisley set her gun on the table and picked up the poor trembling cat. "There,

there," she said, cooing and stroking Phantom's fur, as she held the scared cat close in her arms, trying to calm her.

Abruptly, she placed the cat on her chair, wondering about her Aunt's little pooch, Abby. Dread washed over her again, as she went through each room, calling Abby's name, hoping to find her hiding under a bed, or crouched in a corner somewhere, but there was no response. Picking up her gun again, she grabbed the flashlight and hurried to the back door. The door opened into night-blackness, as if a dark curtain was drawn, preventing her from seeing beyond it.

Gripping her gun tighter, she stood still, listening for a sound, and heard nothing but eerie silence. The porch light was switched on, but nothing happened—the yard remained pitch dark. Shinning the flash light around the yard, she called Abby's name. Still no response. Where is she hiding? Panicked, Paisley moved deeper into the yard.

She almost gave up, but as she rounded the corner of the house, she shined her flashlight further into the yard, still calling Abby's name, and spotted something on the lawn, towards the hedges, near the woods. She jogged towards it, flashlight beam bouncing and heart-pounding, and approached the form with mounting fear.

She broke into a run and found Abby laying in a pool of blood, with a bullet hole in her head. She was dead! Paisley stood up in shock and horror, backed away, and turned to run for the house. Crying and sobbing, she was unable to process the senseless killing of her Aunt's beloved dog!

She sobbed out loud, with anger and grief. "Why did Abby have to be killed, too? Why?" Aunt Olga loves her—how will I tell her? In her distraught state, she decided to call Boone for support. Still sobbing and hardly able to breathe, she attempted to calm herself as she ran to retrieve her cell phone, which rested on the kitchen table.

Once in the kitchen, she hurried through the mess, crunching glass on the floor, until she reached the table. She picked up her phone, fumbling with it in her haste to call Boone. Her hands shook as she forced herself to calm down, so she could make the call. It seemed like forever before he answered, and she burst into tears upon hearing his voice. She could *not* speak.

He was calling her name, "Ingles—Ingles! Is that you? What's the matter?"

CHAPTER 20

N ot able to get answers from her, he said, "Hang on, I'm coming over now! Are you at the farmhouse?" Boone couldn't imagine what had happened.

She managed to squeak out, "Yes."

"I'm on my way—I'll call the precinct for the address, and use my GPS—in the meantime, try and calm down, I'll be there as fast as I can!"

Stumbling out the front door and onto the front steps, Paisley sat down, put her head in her hands, and bawled like a baby. The minutes dragged before headlights from Boone's car were visible on the road. His car pulled up to the house, and screeched to a stop, his door flew open, he bounded out of the car, and ran to the steps, where Paisley sat. He crouched beside her, his arm went around her shoulder, and he pulled her towards him. She leaned her head on his shoulder and tried to stifle her sobs.

With soothing words, he attempted to comfort her, and she began to relax, gaining her composure. With his free hand, he stroked her hair and continued to speak calmly, saying, "Ingles, what the heck has happened? Try and tell me what happened."

"I'm so sorry, I don't often cry, but I can't help it." She gave a few hiccup sobs, and sat back to look at him, "But this is one of those times!"

"Shhhh! C'mon, Ingles," he said, as he helped her up, "let's so inside and get some water for you, and we'll sit down, then you can tell me what the happened!"

They walked to the mudroom door and entered. Barely inside, he peered into the kitchen, dimly lit by her LED flashlight on the counter, and said, "*What happened in here!*"

Finally able to speak, she said, "When I opened the door and came in the mudroom tonight, the light didn't work! I pulled out my LED flashlight from my purse, and entered the kitchen, to find it totally ransacked, as were the rest of the rooms, and Abby was no where in sight," she began to tear up, "...my Aunt's dog..." pausing, she tried to stifle more sobs.

"What about the dog?"

An anguished look appeared on her face, and she looked up at him, "She's dead, Boone—they killed her—shot Abby in the head! I'm devastated, and my Aunt will be devastated, too! Oh, Boone, she trusted me to take care of things here while she was gone, and look what's happened—I've made a mess of things!"

Losing her composure again, and with more tears flooding down her cheeks, Boone took her arm and led her towards the kitchen, stepping over the mess, to find water for her. But he had trouble finding an unbroken glass.

"Tell me where you found the dog," he said, and she led him through the trashed living room, towards the back of the house.

"They sure did a number on the living room!" he said, under his breath.

"She's around the corner of the house, towards the shrubs, near the trees," Paisley said when they reached the back door.

"Stay here...I want to check out the situation for myself."

Paisley ran after him, "Please Boone, I'm okay now—*really!* I am! *Please*, I want to go with you—I don't *want* to stay here by myself!"

"Okay, but stay close and follow me," and he took her hand, holding it behind him, as he walked.

Rounding the corner of the house, he shinned the flashlight around the yard and saw the form. Moving Paisley back a little, he took off his jacket and put it around her shoulders. "Stay put, while I look around."

He approached the dog, laying in the bloody grass, and understood why Ingles was so upset. What kind of monster does this to a family pet? He jogged back to her, "Stay right here— there's a tarp covering that woodpile by the back door, so I'm gonna grab it to cover her," he said.

It was a short run to the woodpile, where he pulled off the tarp, ran back to the dog, and gently wrapped the pup in the tarp. Turning to Ingles, he said, "By the looks of it, I'm sure she died instantly. I don't think she suffered. I'll help with the burial when the investigation is complete."

They walked to the backdoor steps, and sat down, her eyes swollen from crying, she asked "What should we do?"

"You stay here while I go back into the yard." Walking into the blackness, he used his flashlight to look for signs of foot prints to determine the direction from which the shots were fired. He found a spot where the ground appeared soft, and sparsely covered with grass, then walked in concentric circles until he spotted a small area towards the south side of the house, with flattened grass.

Crouching to examine the area up close, he noticed heel

marks in the grass and soft tamped down earth. He figured the shooter stood on that spot because it was close enough to the woods to provide protection and an escape if needed. Possibly, he mused, the dog heard the intruder inside the house and barked...the intruder came outside, then the dog chased him towards the trees.

Boone hurried to the area where he suspected the intruder must have turned to fire the gun. Searching the spot, he found a couple of empty shell casings. With a pencil from his jacket pocket, he used the eraser end to pick them up, then put them in one of the small baggies, which he always carried with him.

"Okay, Ingles," he called out as he hurried back towards the house. "I found something."

"You did?"

"I'll tell you later. C'mon, let's leave." They went to Boone's car, he picked up his phone and called the station to report the burglary and shooting. Boone said, "Now, while we wait for the officers to arrive, I want you to grab the things you need and pack them in a bag because I'm taking you to my place. I will *not* have you stay here under these circumstances, and anyway, the officers will be investigating the crime scene until late."

"Boone, I'm okay now—honest," her tears *had* dried, "I'm sure, whoever did this, won't be back again."

"Nope, the jury's in, I'm not letting you stay in this trashed house, without electricity, by yourself!" His stern look told her there'd be no arguing with him. "It's lucky you weren't home when it happened!"

Paisley stared at him, before agreeing. While she went inside to pack a bag, Boone pulled out of the driveway to make room for the Detectives when they arrived. She met him at the car and tossed her things in the back seat. By that time, sirens were screaming down the road, with lights flashing! The noise was deafening, as the squad cars pulled into the driveway, fanned out, and parked on the lawn. Boone, conferred with them for several minutes before they had to question her.

"I don't really want to talk about it," she said.

Officer Ryan, surprised to see Paisley again, said, "I'm sorry, but I *have* to take your statement."

She acquiesced—it was easier for her, knowing Officer Ryan would be the questioner. The police set up temporary lights, as Boone accompanied Ingles and Ryan into the house where she gave her statement. Then they went briefly from room-to-room. But, as they worked their way through the disaster in each room, Paisley found nothing missing. Jewelry, important papers, valuable artwork, and antiques, were present and accounted for (even the ruined art), and she didn't think her Aunt had anything else of value. There seemed to be no rhyme or reason for the vandalism.

Nonetheless, the detectives dusted for fingerprints, and took photographs. Boone turned over the empty shell casings to the Detectives and the officers took charge of Abby's body, to deliver to a vet for an autopsy. Perhaps two bullets were still embedded, which would match the number of casings. After the dog's autopsy, they could retrieve Abby for burial.

Boone ushered Paisley into his car, then turned the house keys over to the officers, so they could lock up when finished. Paisley felt numb and exhausted. They drove away, reaching Boone's place a little after midnight. He ushered her inside carrying her bag, and set it on the couch in the front room of the small cabin, sparsely furnished, but comfortable .

"I love your print," Paisley remarked, as her eyes took in the room. A dark leather sofa and wooden coffee table sat under the print, *Starry Night*. She focused on the large, rather well-framed, Van Gogh print, presiding over the room—it was a favorite of hers. A small electric piano was positioned on the opposite wall with another smaller Van Gogh print, *Sunflowers,* hanging above it.

A cobalt blue tufted armchair sat in the corner next to a window, while a tall counter at the other end of the room, divided the kitchen from the front room. Although the kitchen was small, it appeared neat and utilitarian. Paisley felt the serenity of the place. It was neat as a pin—no papers or mail to be seen anywhere—*and* no dirty dishes! It almost didn't look lived in by anyone! How unusual, she mused under her breath as she sat down on the couch.

"What did you say?" He called to her from the kitchen.

"Oh...nothing."

"I'm going to make some coffee. I know its late, but would you rather have tea? I'd be happy to fix a cup for you."

"Yes, tea would be great...you wouldn't happen to have Chamomile, would you?" She was sure he wouldn't.

"Coming right up! While the water boils, I'll change the bedding in the bedroom and you can sleep there. I'll take the sofa because I've turned the other bedroom into an office."

Too emotionally exhausted from the evening's draining experience to care, she put up no resistance. He hurried into the other room and came back in a jiffy, with a blanket and pillow for the couch. In a few minutes, he had a cup of coffee in one hand and her tea in the other, then sat both cups on the coffee table.

She picked up her cup, and taking a sip, said, "Thank you so much, this is just what I needed." He's full of inconsistencies, she thought. Chamomile tea—really? She sipped her tea and he sipped his coffee, both comfortable in the silence.

Finally, he stood and grabbed Paisley's bag, "C'mon, you need to get some rest," he said, as he herded her into her sleeping quarters. "Sleep as late as you want. I'll call and explain to Captain Bower, that we won't be in until later."

With an expression of relief on her face, she voiced her appreciation, "How can I thank you for everything you've done?"

"Hey, don't worry about it," he smiled, "have a good night's sleep, we'll talk about things tomorrow. Goodnight," and he closed the door behind him.

She readied herself for bed, climbed in, and pulled the handmade comforter up to her chin. She stared at it. A patchwork quilt, so beautifully made, that she wondered if it had been made by a girlfriend, an ex-wife, or his mother? Turning off the bedside lamp, she put her head on the pillow and fell asleep.

Meanwhile, Boone fixed his bed on the sofa, making himself comfortable, before pondering the evening's events. Why would someone burglarize a farmhouse, take nothing, and kill the dog? He'd have to question Ingles, tomorrow. He set thoughts of the burglary aside, turning his attention to Mr. Ohm, and why there had been no contact.

He ruminated over this for a while, before deciding to call in the troops. His primary contact at the Bureau, Dave Kaufman, was already making preparations to ready the team, waiting for Boone to give him the go-ahead. At this juncture, Boone decided it was time to covertly move his teams into the area and set up a command center, ready for action.

Boone had a nagging feeling that the death of Kamorov somehow related to the anonymous contact, Mr. Ohm. He came to Brainerd to ferret out this man and arrange a meeting, when in fact, for all he knew, could the contact *be* Kamorov? Boone was also suspicious of Zolotov, given the fact that he lied about his nefarious background and bona fides.

Boone's team needed to set up surveillance on Zolotov, his

communications, and anyone coming or going, from his residence, in order to find out what he was doing, in Brainerd.

Boone made the call, "Dave, this is Boone. Sorry I'm contacting you so late at night."

Kaufman answered, "No problem, I was going over plans for the team anyway...what's up?"

"I think it's time to round up the men I've picked for this operation, and move everyone to Brainerd, ASAP."

Dave replied, "No problem, buddy, I can put everything in action tomorrow, and we'll be ready to roll tomorrow night. We'll take three of the big choppers, which are ready to go with the necessary equipment. They're sitting on a Helipad at the military base several hours away, from Washington, D.C."

"Great, Dave! Let me know when you're here. We're still not sure what we're dealing with, but we need to be ready for the worst. In the meantime, I'm investigating a murder, which I think, 'might' lead us to the informant. Gotta go," and he hung up.

A few minutes later, Boone received Dave's email, which read, "At 4:00 a.m., EST, the Special Ops teams will assemble, board the copters and head to their rural destination. The techs will go to a safe house near Pinecrest, where they'll set up the tactical operation center."

With the operation set to go, Boone stretched out on the couch and tried to relax. Even though he turned out his light, he continued to contemplate the mission for a while longer, until sleep overtook him.

While fast asleep, neither he nor Paisley, were aware of a black sedan moving slowly down his road. With lights dimmed, the sedan paused in front of the small cabin, stopping for a moment or two, then continuing noiselessly down the road into the night's shadows, with the stealth of a black panther.

CHAPTER 21

Thursday, May 18, 2017
Brainerd

Paisley woke with a start and looked at her watch. It was a little after eight. She sat up and looked around the room, momentarily confused, she then remembered the events of the previous evening and flopped back on her pillow with a groan. The recollections flooded in, inundating her mind with all the things needing to be handled. This included calling her poor Aunt with the news about Abby and the break-in. She wondered how she'd put the house in order, and hoped her Aunt had insurance.

After laying there for a moment, she found herself focusing on another Van Gogh print hanging over the dresser, a beautiful well-framed print called *The Bedroom*. Paisley had studied art history in school and knew all the Van Gogh paintings. It seemed strange for Boone to have them hanging in his cabin, but *if* they were really his, she admired his taste. Was he a man with a subtle side...maybe?

She struggled out of bed, stretched, and rubbed her eyes before putting on jeans and a T-shirt from her bag. After winding her hair in a bun, she tiptoed down the hallway with shoes in hand, stepping into the kitchen where yet another Van Gogh print hung! *The Vase with Twelve Sunflowers*, perfectly framed, had been hung on the wall behind the breakfast bar.

What is with all these Van Gogh prints, she wondered? Glancing into the front room, she saw another she hadn't noticed the night before, in the recess of a tall, dark oak book-case—*Vase with Irises*. Van Gogh was well represented with *this* plethora of prints! She was determined to ask him about this later.

Boone, who slept on the couch, stirred, then sat up abruptly. Startled, she said, "Coffee? I tried to be quiet."

He nodded. She turned to start the coffee maker while he disappeared into the other room, returning minutes later, also dressed in jeans and a T-shirt, displaying his favorite football team's logo and it *wasn't* the Vikings!

The aroma of coffee assaulted him as he entered the kitchen, "Morning, Ingles. Are you ready to take care of your Aunt's house today?"

She put a cup of coffee on the table for each of them, while he grabbed some croissants and cream cheese from the fridge, toasted the croissants, and said, "A plate for you and a plate for me," as he set them on the table.

"Thank you, and by the way, thank you for allowing me stay here last night."

She blew on the steaming cup of coffee before taking a sip. After their croissants and coffee, he cleaned off the table, and Paisley said, "If it's all right, I need to contact my Aunt."

"Of course," he said.

When her Aunt answered, Paisley explained with great

difficulty, the happenings of the previous night. Her Aunt cried when she was told about Abby, and Paisley cried, too! "Aunt Olga, the place needs some repairs, so you probably need to stay in the cities with your friend for a few more days."

"Yes, dear, I need to be with my Vlad..no worries."

"How is Uncle Vlad doing?"

"Not good, dear, I stay longer than couple of days. He is dying." There was a catch in her voice.

"Oh no! I'm so sorry! Give him my love!" Saddened, she hung up.

"I'll call Officer Ryan now," Boone said, "and see if they finished the investigation so we can clean up the place."

Officer Ryan told Boone they could come anytime and Boone said, "Let's go, Ingles!"

Boone had to coax her into the farmhouse, but once they began cleaning up the mess, she felt better. "If you notice anything missing, please tell me," Boone reminded her.

Boone took on the kitchen with a broom and dustpan, sweeping the broken dishes into a pile and cleaning up the food. Paisley headed to the living room to salvage what she could. She dragged the damaged furniture to one corner, then grabbed plastic bags and wrestled the stuffing into them.

They both righted the furniture in the bedrooms and removed the damaged mattresses. Drawers were replaced in their respective dressers, while the items strewn around the rooms, were collected and replaced in the drawers and closets. All the while, she kept an eye out for missing items.

When they'd done everything they could for the moment, she said, "Boone, I just realized one thing *is* missing."

"What is it?"

"It's a picture of Aunt Olga and Uncle Vlad, from the late thirties or early forties...maybe later?

"Are you sure?"

"Yes, I'm positive. When I put the broom back, I noticed the picture was missing from over the fireplace in the kitchen, where it always hung. Weird, right?"

Later in the afternoon, when they'd done everything they could at the farmhouse, they retrieved Abby's body from the Vet's facility and took her back to the farm for burial. The Vet assured them he would mail his findings to the precinct.

They buried Abby in the woods at the farmhouse, according to Aunt Olga's wishes. Boone admired Ingles' stoic demeanor during the burial. Based on her upset from the night before, he was amazed at how she was able to get her emotions under control!

Pinecrest After a brief stop at the precinct, they grabbed a salad from a local take-out place and headed to Pinecrest College, for a meeting with Yury Panuken. Because of the trouble at the farmhouse, Boone rescheduled the meeting with Panuken, for later in the afternoon, and they met him at a table in the student union, to question him.

"What do you know about Zolotov?" Boone asked.

"I do not know much. I only rent from him. It's a room and kitchen—all I need. I'm there to study, not be social!"

"Did you ever interact with Kamorov?"

"No!" he said adamantly, as he picked up his book bag. "I did not like him. I avoid all of them as much as possible. I spend my time in class or at library."

Paisley asked, "Where were you Saturday night and early Sunday morning?"

Taking his time to answer, he said, "I studied at the house."

"Did you see, or talk to anyone, who can verify this?"

Frowning, Yury glared at her and adamantly said, "No!"

Yury stood up...he was ready to leave, but she continued, "Where were you born?"

"In Moscow, Russia, I have classes now. I have a test," and he walked away.

"We may be in touch again," she called after him as he headed away. He seemed to be a dedicated college student, with his nose in his books.

"You think he had something to do with the murder?" Boone asked.

"I'm not sure, but it won't hurt to investigate him a little more...he's not very fond of Kamorov, that's for sure!" Disappointed at Yury's inability to shed any light on the murder, she still wasn't convinced he'd told them everything he knew.

Back at the precinct, they went their separate ways. Boone entered his office and sat down at his desk. He opened a file when his phone rang, and he swiveled around in his chair before he picking up and answering, "Boone, here."

"Boone, this is Officer Barnes, I'm notifying you that the warrants you requested arrived. Now, you can open Kamorov's locker, at Ben's Burgers."

Paisley barely entered her office before Boone came in holding up an envelope saying, "Okay—are you up for another trip?"

"Where are we going?"

"This envelope has the warrants...we can open Kamorov's locker now!"

"Perfect! I sure hope his computer is there!"

Twenty minutes later, they walked into Ben's Burgers. Ben greeted them, and they followed him through the kitchen, and into the hallway, towards the room containing a couple of employee lockers and cupboards.

"May I?" Boone asked, glancing at Ben and gesturing with

his hand towards the lockers. "These are the warrants," and he handed them to Ben.

Ben nodded his head and folded his arms, "Gregore's locker is number 8B—on the bottom—over there," he pointed. "Not all employees use them, but they're available if needed, as long as they bring their own lock."

Boone, armed with heavy-duty bolt-cutters retrieved from the trunk of his car, had no problem snapping the lock. Once the locker opened, it revealed a Ben's Burgers navy blue windbreaker hanging to one side, some shabby spiral notebooks, and a laptop computer. Each item was put in its own plastic bag, then sealed.

"Now that we've removed the evidence," Boone said, "I'll close and lock it with a new lock, until the men from forensics can give it a going-over...hopefully that will be, as soon as possible."

"Do you have any leads yet?" Ben inquired.

"Nothing substantial so far, Ben, but we're working hard on the case," Paisley said, "and we'll let you know, as soon as we find something."

They drove silently back to the precinct, while Boone kept his eyes on the rear view mirror and side mirrors, looking for cars that might be following them. Paisley closed her eyes and leaned her head against the back of her seat. He glanced at her several times. What a resilient person, he thought, in light of everything that has happened, over the last few days.

No one is stopping *this* lady—he'd seen the determination in her eyes. Pondering this latest event, he wondered about the relevance of the break-in and dead dog. Is it connected to the murder we're investigating? I hope it isn't the case, but I can't rule it out. Did someone discover my identity, putting us *both* in danger?

By the time, Boone arrived at the station, she had awakened from her short nap, and he parked the car, then they entered the precinct. She carried the bag with the computer and the bag with the jacket, and said, "I'll drop the jacket off at the evidence room on my way to my office."

"Wait!" Boone donned a latex glove, grabbed the jacket from the bag, and checked the pockets, pulling out a small folded piece of paper. He unfolded it, revealing a hastily written phone number, he then held the note with his gloved hand and handed Paisley the pouch with the jacket.

"See you later," she said, "...and let's keep each other in the loop." They parted ways, and he smiled, giving her a thumbs up, then headed to his office to write a report, from the Yury Panuken interview notes.

Paisley headed to the lab with the bagged computer for fingerprinting and handed off the bagged jacket to forensics. She reminded the techs to call her as soon as they finished with the computer. She was eager to get it back to see what information it held.

An hour or so later, Boone met Paisley in the garage. He had persuaded her to stay for one more night, or at least until it was safe to return to the farm. She tried to put up a struggle, but he would have none of it. Her mind was changed, when he promised to make his famous Italian meatball and spaghetti dinner, with Parmesan garlic-herbed French bread, from a recipe passed down for several generations from his Italian great-grandmother.

"Okay! I guess you've made me an offer I can't refuse." Paisley chuckled.

"We'll get an early start tomorrow morning," he said.

"All right, I can't resist—especially the spaghetti dinner

part." She looked towards him, and they smiled at each other. Hmmm, she thought, who knew he could cook, too?

Brainerd That same afternoon, across town in Brainerd, Lenny Starko's phone rang. After fumbling with it for a moment, he realized he didn't recognize the number but answered anyway. "Hello?" He was surprised to hear Zolotov's voice on the other end.

"Hey Boss? Did you change your number," Lenny asked casually, as he reclined again on his couch.

"I *told* you, *never* call me Boss!" Zolotov shot back.

Uh, oh! This sounds bad, Lenny thought. "So, what can I do for you, Boss—I mean, Mr. Z?"

Zolotov discovered his thumb drive was gone, when conducting a frantic search of his house, after the Detectives' visit concerning Kamorov's death. It didn't take a rocket scientist to connect the dots! Zolotov surmised that Kamorov, was the one who snatched it, as *that* sort of thing was right up his alley!

"Lenny," he growled menacingly, "my thumb drive is stolen — I *know* Gregore did it. I demand you find my thumb drive and get it back to me! *Do you* understand?"

"I do, Mr. Z," Lenny said, trying to say it with sympathy, although *he* couldn't care less.

"Listen carefully," Zolotov warned, "it *must* be returned. Do whatever it takes! Locate and return it to me, *or else!*" he threatened and hung up.

Surprised, Lenny also wondered who had it? He'd already searched the burger place, tried the precinct, and searched the cop's farmhouse, but turned up nothing! Lenny was as frustrated as Zolotov. He thought for a while, and the only other person he could think of, who 'might' have the thumb drive, was Ivan Belenski! "Yes, of *course*! He's a cheat—I bet it's *him!*"

He remembered Kamorov talking to Belenski, the other

night at the bar! Maybe I should pay Belenski a visit? Maybe Kamorov gave it to *him*? I know Ivan works for Zolotov in some capacity, so I can't ask Zolotov for Ivan's residence information. I'll find it myself—yes— it's a great idea! I bet that Russkie gave it to Belenski! If he *did,* I'll make him cut *me* in on the money, or better yet—I'll *take* it from him!

Lenny set out to track down Belenski's address, using his own resources. Later that evening, Lenny nosed around a few of the seedy bars frequented by Ivan on his nights off, and it wasn't long before a bartender at one of Ivan's hangouts, The Loco-Motive Saloon, gave him the number of someone, who might know where Ivan lived.

He called the man immediately, and before long, had Belenski's address. With Ivan's address in hand, Lenny decided it was time to pay him a visit. I'll coerce him to turn over the drive, and then *I* will have it, plus all the information, which Kamorov divulged, the night I drove him home. He was so totally drunk, that he told me all about it!

Lenny smiled at the thought. Once I have it, *I'll* be the one to sell it for some outrageous price. If the info it contains is as valuable as Kamorov described, then I'll sell it to the highest bidder, like Kamorov planned to do, then take the money and run! He chuckled to himself.

An hour later, walking in the chilly night air, Lenny approached a rundown apartment building on the southeast side of town. He found himself in front of Ivan's building after threading his way past a half dozen beat-up webbed aluminum chairs carelessly arranged on the parkway.

CHAPTER 22

As luck would have it, one of the less-than-reputable people emerged from the entrance to the building, and Lenny asked, "I'm looking for a friend. By chance, does a man named Ivan, live here?"

The man replied dully, "Dunno," and held the security door open for Lenny to enter, before shambling down the cracked walkway and disappearing into the inky night.

Lenny was in! The entry area had poor lighting, making it difficult for him to examine the faded names on the mailboxes. Some of the names were missing altogether, or written on top of the last occupant's label. While puzzling over these, a rickety elevator landed with a thump, at the far end of the tiny lobby, and another denizen of the apartment building emerged.

This time, an older lady with a paper bag in her arms filled with who-knew-what, emerged with several plastic bags, also stuffed full, dangling from her arms. As she headed from the elevator towards the door, her appearance even took Lenny aback for a second. Frizzy, unkempt gray hair framed the crinkled leathery face. She appeared dazed with unfocused eyes, and her attire consisted of baggy faded jeans and a filthy faded pink, extra-large sweatshirt, which hung to her knees.

In his most manipulative voice, Lenny said, "Pardon me Ma'am, but does a man named Ivan, live here? He's my cousin, and I'm trying to locate him."

"Seven!" she yelled at the top of her lungs and without looking at him, limped out the door and down the steps. Her response irritated him, and if there had been more time, he would have enjoyed putting this worthless old crone out of her misery.

However, he scratched that idea, deciding instead, to take the stairs, stealthily climbing to the second floor, without encountering other residents. Apartment number seven was at the end of the hall, and he knocked on the door. Although he heard the faint sound of a radio drifting through the thin walls, there was no response.

He knocked a little harder...waited a moment and called, "Ivan? Anybody home?"

After a moment, he was about to knock again when the door opened a crack, through which, an eyeball peered at him. He presumed it to be Ivan's.

The eyeball spoke in low tones and said, "Who are you?"

"Hey Ivan! It's Lenny—you know—Kamorov's friend?" He continued in his most amiable voice, "Sorry to hear about his death, but he and I were pretty tight. We knew each other from *way* back. Can I come in so we can talk?"

Ivan eyed him a minute more, and slowly, but suspiciously, opened the door to stick his head out enough to look up and down the hallway, then moved to allow Lenny's entrance. Lenny sauntered in, glancing around the place, as he stepped toward a metal folding chair being offered to him.

He sat down and took a good look at Ivan, who looked pretty much as he remembered him, from the other night—disheveled, slicked-back black hair, squinty eyes under heavy eyebrows, and a weak mouth drooping at the corners.

Ivan stared at Lenny for a moment, "Want a beer?"

"No, thanks."

Ivan slouched over to a small fridge and got one for himself, popped the top, and took a long swig, with Lenny watching and checking out the empty beer cans strewn on top of the cracked tile of the kitchen counter.

Ivan pulled a chair up to a table centered in the middle of the small room and asked, "So, why are you here, Lenny?"

Lenny attempted to put Ivan at ease, and after a little back-and-forth concerning Kamorov, he broached the the thumb drive subject, saying, "So, were you the one that Kamorov gave the thumb drive to, before he died?"

"What thumb drive, what are you talking about, Lenny? Why *are* you here, anyway?"

"Come on, don't play games with *me*, Ivan," Lenny said in his fake, honied voice, "I told you already. *You* know I'm a friend of Gregore's—he told me all about the thumb drive, which he gave to *you*."

"What are you talking about," he said, and confused, by Lenny's assertion, he declared, "it's a lie—he *lied*!"

"Oh, so you *do* know what I'm talking about! So, he *did* give it to you!" Lenny said in an accusatory voice.

"No, he *didn't*!" Ivan said, with a bit of an attitude, at feeling accused.

"And, you *killed* him and retrieved it!"

Ivan jumped out of his chair, "Who sent you? How *dare* you accuse me?" Ivan approached him.

Lenny sat calmly...one arm draped casually over the back of

the chair, wheels turning in his brain, as he was in the process of hatching a plan to cover his *own* crime.

"We have it on good authority from some of your unreliable drinking buddies," Lenny began, "that you bragged about how you would lift the thumb drive from Kamorov—*even* if you had to kill him to do it. *And,* you were seen with him earlier in the evening on the night of his murder. It was *your* buddies, who assumed you were just blowing off steam, but *we* don't think so!"

"Who in the devil is *we*, and why should I even talk to you—get out *now*!"

Lenny stood up, knocking the chair over as he did so, and walked menacingly towards Ivan, "Does the name Zolotov ring a bell? *You,* happen to be on his payroll!"

This comment startled Ivan. "What has Zolotov got to do with this? How do *you* know him?"

"You're not the *only* one on his payroll. Ha! I came to get the thumb drive from you, so why don't we just get this over with now. You get the drive and give it to me, and I'll run along," Lenny said in a syrupy tone.

"I *don't* have it, so why don't *you* just go ahead and run along!"

"If you say you don't have it, then tell me where it is."

"I don't know that either, and if I *did* have it, why should I tell you?" Ivan replied, with a surly attitude, as he began walking towards his nearby desk.

Lenny commanded him to stop and pulled out a handgun, which had been tucked into the back of his pants and concealed by his sweatshirt, "Don't take another step," he menaced. "C'mon over to this chair and sit down."

With an astonished look on his face, Ivan answered nervously, "Okay, man, calm down, put the gun away, we can work this thing out!"

He raised his hands in the air and sat down. In a flash, Lenny jumped forward and cracked Ivan on the head with the butt of the gun, knocking him out and catching him as he fell to the side. He propped Ivan up in the chair, and with a roll of duct tape, hidden in his sweatshirt pocket for just such an occasion, he taped Ivan's hands and feet. Over at the sink, he filled an empty beer can with water and threw it in Ivan's face.

Ivan coughed and sputtered as he came to—only to find himself bound to the chair, "What's going on?" he sputtered, shaking his head to clear it.

"I don't think you understand how serious this is," Lenny said coolly. "Zolotov wants that thumb drive, and he wants it *now*. I'm here to retrieve it."

Another short discussion ensued about the thumb drive, then Lenny said, "Hey! if you *give* me the thumb drive, I'll even share the proceeds with you!"

"I'm telling you the truth, I don't *have* it," Ivan whined.

"I guess I have no choice," Lenny said, as he grabbed a rag from the sink's counter, stuffed it in Ivan's mouth, and slapped a piece a of duct tape over it. After being tied up and gagged, with a little persuasion from a very sharp knife, Ivan nodded he'd be *more* than happy to tell everything he knew about the drive.

So, Lenny removed it after Lenny promised he wouldn't yell. Scared to death, Ivan was ready to divulge everything—he was crying, "Okay, okay, I *did* plan to steal the thumb drive from Gregore and turn it over to the Russian mafia for the really *big* money."

"I *knew* it!" Lenny cackled.

Piece by piece, the story came out. Ivan said, "Kamorov didn't want to give it up—he wanted the reward for himself." Blood trickled down the side of Ivan's face from a cut, opened by the blow inflicted, from Lenny's gun.

Ivan continued, "When I confronted him earlier in the week after he bragged about it to me after work one day, I said we could share, but he said *never* because he already contacted a person from the government, who would pay him for the thumb drive! It surprised me!"

Lenny looked at him suspiciously and said, "You'd better *not* be lying to me!" He scowled at Ivan.

"Kamorov told me to go away!" Ivan said, his voice quivering with fear. "He went to the phone and started dialing 911! What could I do? I said okay, okay, put the phone down! I'll leave, and I did! I didn't want any trouble. When he put down the phone, I apologized and left."

Lenny was quiet for a moment, but his rage was building. "I don't believe you!" he shouted. "*No one* walks out on an opportunity like *that*!"

Lenny immediately rushed over to Ivan and taped the rag back in his mouth. "I'll search your place myself since you won't tell me!"

Lenny was irate, his uncontrollable temper taking over, as he proceeded to tear the apartment apart. Not finding the thumb drive anywhere, he pivoted towards Ivan, who was sniveling and crying with tears streaming down his cheeks, onto the duct tape.

Ivan saw the look in Lenny's eyes, and it was then he knew! He was going to die! Lenny paced back and forth in front of him, running his hands through his hair, never taking his eyes from Ivan's, like some jungle cat getting ready to pounce on his prey and finish him off.

Ivan's eyes pleaded with Lenny's, as the tears continued to drip down his cheeks, which flushed with panic. Besides the tears, he began trembling, as he continued to look at the dead black eyes of Lenny, who by now, was finally convinced Ivan *didn't* possess the thumb drive.

He stepped up to Ivan, drew his knife with its sharpened twelve-inch blade, then with one quick move, thrust the knife between Ivan's ribs and into his heart. It was quicker and much quieter, than a gunshot. Unfortunately for Ivan, he began to bleed out as he slumped in the kitchen chair, still tied and gagged.

Lenny wiped his fingerprints off of the few things he'd touched, and left the apartment—as-is. He peeked into the hallway to make sure it was empty, then closed and locked the apartment door behind him, with no worries. Familiar with this section of town, it would be days before anyone discovered Ivan's body.

The locals in the vicinity kept to themselves, as most were into nefarious businesses of their own. It would probably be the strange odor of something decaying, he mused, that would cause neighbors to complain, eventually goading the superintendent into investigating the source.

Looking both ways to make sure the street was empty, he exited the rundown apartment building. Once outside, he pulled the jacket's hood over his head and walked away into the night, disappearing into the shadows, which enveloped him like a heavy cloak. Ducking into a nearby alley, he wove his way through the back streets to his vehicle, unnoticed by the transients he passed along the way.

Feeling smug by now, Lenny was confident the thumb drive was in the possession of the female detective he had followed the other night to her boyfriend's apartment. All he had to do was lie to Zolotov about Ivan, and figure a way to get the drive into his own hands. Feeling *sure* it would be in his possession soon, his next chore was to communicate with Zolotov and let him know he was still on the trail of the thumb drive.

With my newly formulated plan, he thought, *I'll* be the one to find the drive and reach out to those interested in the information it possesses. The money will be *mine*! Yes, that's what I'll do, and no one will be the wiser. If I keep telling Zolotov that I can't find the drive, I can disappear, as soon as the reward is in my hands. Lenny wasted no time in calling Zolotov, when he returned to his apartment, from Ivan's.

"What happens...when you meet Ivan? Did he have thumb drive?" Zolotov asked.

"No."

"*What*?" Zolotov screamed

"Wait, just listen! I questioned him, but he wouldn't cooperate, so I had to play rough to find out what he knew. But finally," Lenny said smugly. "he gave me the name of the person who *does* have the drive."

"Who is this person?" Zolotov asked.

"It's that female—Detective Ingles!"

"What about Ivan?"

"Well, boss—I mean Mr. Z—since Ivan knew too much, I made sure he wouldn't be available to talk. He was gonna go to the *authorities*, man! I *had* to!" Lenny wheedled.

"You *fool*! What have you done *now*?" Zolotov shouted, "Cops nose around *again*!" Once more, the phone disconnected.

"*Whatever*!" Lenny said. He shrugged and put his phone in his back pocket. He was hungry. He hadn't had dinner, so he left his apartment and headed towards his favorite scuzzy pizza place! But, in *his* opinion, they *did* have really great pizza—cheesy and greasy—it was his favorite food.

CHAPTER 23

Russia
      Tazvoshenko reached the warehouse where the communication center of his organization was located. It was imperative for him to contact Zolotov, after the urgent coded message he'd just received overnight. He proceeded to the communications room and made the early morning secure call to Zolotov, in Minnesota.

Brainerd Zolotov's phone rang just after midnight, and woke him out of his sleep. He involuntarily cringed, because it could be only *one* person. "Yes," he answered coolly. It was early morning for Tazvoshenko in Russia, but middle of the night, for Zolotov. However, Tazvoshenko was *not* concerned with the time.

"What is happening," Tazvoshenko demanded, "where are my coordinates?"

"Comrade, I've been expecting your call." Zolotov said and sat bolt upright in bed. Trying to sound self-assured and wide awake, he continued, "Let me explain why I send urgent message to you. I have bad news. Thumb drive, with coordinates, fell into wrong hands, and I, Zolotov, have alerted my men to use all resources to locate it! We will have it soon, then I immediately...." He never finished his sentence.

Tazvoshenko interrupted, "What do you *mean*, fell into wrong hands!" He was livid and called Zolotov a variety of names. After his cursing and sputtering, he managed to regain his composure long enough to inquire how and why something of this magnitude occurred!

"Let me explain," Zolotov squeaked out.

"Yes, please explain to me now! I must know how something derails years of effort and places my organization in peril! How does this happen? You Idiot! People *already* pay big money to me, and will hunt to kill *all* of us—and *not* in merciful way—if I not deliver!" Slowly, in his most menacing voice, he added, "These people are ruthless! Do you understand?"

Zolotov, sweating profusely, had no chance to utter a word during the tirade, and stuttered a moment, until he found his voice again, "I, I...understand your concern..." he began, but his voice sounded strained and weak, and he was unable to continue.

Tazvoshenko began another tirade and finally declared Zolotov anathema to him. "You understand *my* concern? Bah! You trivialize and refer to this as '*concern*'? I *must* know what happens—please continue!" He made every effort to gain control of himself again so he could listen.

Zolotov threw his bed covers back and began pacing back and forth, "Kamorov, stole thumb drive before I transmit information. He was murdered. The drive disappears into hands of others, *but*...we close in on perpetrator!"

Livid, upon hearing how ineptly his top man, with his bunch of buffoons, had handled something of such importance,

Tazvoshenko responded, "Stop at *nothing* to retrieve it," he growled, then conveyed his plans for the next several days. "Make *sure* you organize group of men I transferred to Brainerd area during last six months for retrieval of chemodan!"

"Yes, yes, we will be ready," Zolotov nervously assured him.

"Now," he cleared his throat, "who is person taking our thumb drive?"

"We think is Kamorov's friend, Ivan Belenski," Zolotov said, using the original information Lenny fed him.

"Aha! Where *is* this Ivan? He *must* give you thumb drive!"

How to tell him? Zolotov thought, then said, "He did not have thumb drive, but do not worry, we took care of him. He will talk to no one, and now my man knows who *really* has thumb drive—female detective with Pinecrest Police Department, has it. We *will* retrieve it!"

Tazvoshenko couldn't believe his ears, and calmly said. "What is name of this detective?"

"Her name is Paisley Ingles." There was no sound from the Russia side of the conversation. Zolotov waited quietly.

"Who is this Ivan's murderer? Find out and kill him too—no loose ends!" Tazvoshenko finally demanded. "Now, send men to encampment—ready them for retrieval. You will need information on thumb drive! We will send another, let me know when it arrives. *Do not lose this time,* if you value your life!"

"Yes, yes, of course, I will!"

"You must be prepared for execution of mission."

"Yes, we are preparing." Zolotov decided it best to leave out the information about Kamorov, attempting to contact Feds about the thumb drive, for a big cash-out, since Kamorov was murdered before he followed through with his plan! If Tazvoshenko knew, he would be even angrier, and he was angry enough, already!

When the call ended, Tazvoshenko decided to take things into his own hands, and made several calls to his men stationed in Minnesota, to kidnap this female detective, and do whatever they needed to do, to wring out the whereabouts of the jump drive, from her.

Meanwhile Zolotov dressed and left the house, and though it was not quite one in the morning, it would take time to reach his contact's cabin. The contact had been helping them scope out the Iron Range area, as to where the camps should be based, in order to find Tazvoshenko's *chemodan*.

This contact had helped a group of KGB men hide some secret materials in a safe place. The contact was now an old man, called Crazy Abe, who lived in the wilderness, only coming to the nearest town when he needed supplies. He ranted and raved whenever he did this, but the storekeepers ignored his rantings, as long as he had money to pay for his goods.

Zolotov managed to find him and enlist his help to show him the area where the secret hiding place was. He was old and couldn't remember the exact location. Still, the information was helpful to Tazvoshenko, who was in the process of obtaining, through force, unfortunately, the exact location in that area of where the *chemodan* was buried. Now, it was time to get rid of Crazy Abe...he was useful, no more.

"There is much for you to do tomorrow!" Tazvoshenko's words rang in Zolotov's head, as he arrived back in Brainerd, from his early morning mission. Mid-morning he pulled up to his house, with his mission accomplished. Crazy Abe was dead and would tell no tales. Now, he must turn his attention to the preparations, as ordered by Tazvoshenko. It was time to assemble the men, sent from Russia to areas of Minnesota, in the vicinity of Brainerd and Crosby/Ironton.

Zolotov entered his house and placed a call to his second in command, Nicholas Illich. It rang five times, before he picked up and said, "*Dobroye utro.*"

"Good morning," Zolotov responded. "I just spoke with our leader in Russia, and he said is time to prepare. I will explain to you, but not over phone...we must meet."

"When and where?" Illich asked.

Zolotov thought for a moment, "Make it usual place...we will eat. Be there at five—alone!" The call was ended.

Storm clouds gathered all morning, and later in the afternoon after Zolotov napped, the weather finally produced a steady rain. Zolotov gathered his important papers, shoved them into a large manila folder, and wrapped it in a plastic bag to keep it dry, and then left for his meeting. As he drove, he watched in his rear view mirror to make sure no one followed. He couldn't be sure anymore, now that he knew a detective in the Police Department had the thumb drive!

Arriving in a nearby town, he parked in the small lot of a little family-owned restaurant, named Little Russia, which served great homemade Russian food. Zolotov held clandestine meetings here on other occasions, because of its discreet atmosphere. He jogged through the rain to the entrance, entered and glanced around to see if Illich had arrived. Only a few local farmers were having their evening meal, so he took a seat in the back corner to wait. He slid into a booth, and shortly thereafter, Illich entered and joined him.

After exchanging greetings, they both ordered. Illich ordered borscht and Zolotov ordered stroganoff, the house special, along with a bowl of pickled cucumbers and for appetizers—a plate of stuffed eggs. "Vodka?" He asked, and Illich nodded. Moments later, a diminutive Russian woman brought their food and drink, then paid them no attention, as she went about wiping tables and taking care of other diners.

The two men proceeded to eat in silence. When the meal was over, Zolotov said, "I spoke with Tazvoshenko, he wants us to set up designated site for operation, soon as possible." He paused to sip his vodka, then continued, "Our men must be contacted and divided into teams. You will put one team in charge of assembling trucks: one for SUV's, vans and armored vehicles, another team for trucks needed to haul supplies, and another for equipment and men. These will go to site."

Leaning back in his chair, Illich asked, "Do we know where the site is?"

Illich did not have a strong Russian accent like Zolotov, who answered, "We have general area selected for encampment." Zolotov belched, then leaned forward and folded his arms on the table, adding "Tazvoshenko will send *exact* coordinates...have Nestor Popov, plot covert directions to draw least attention to staging area. He must make maps and give copies to drivers."

"Okay, what else?"

"What about scientists, Nogorsky and Edonov? I trust they arrive?" Zolotov asked.

"Yes, they arrived a week ago, and all their equipment is organized in their van. They are ready." Illich watched Zolotov open his manila folder and shove papers towards him.

Zolotov glanced over his shoulder to see if anyone was paying attention. No one was. In a lowered voice, he said, "Here, look at these."

Illich picked up the sheaf of papers containing lists of items to be assembled from the various warehouses, where supplies had been stocked and stored over the last months. After looking over a few pages, Illich said, "This is very detailed, it will be easy to do." He took ten minutes more to glance over the rest of the papers, then looked up at Zolotov. "Okay, I'll put this in motion."

"We must be ready to leave late tomorrow, to set up camp, ready to execute mission, as Tazvoshenko gives order. You do this, Illich?"

Illich put the papers back in the envelope and answered, "Of course."

Zolotov took money from his wallet and put it on the table to cover the meal, "Most men will stay at site. You, Lev, several others and I, will be last to arrive. Make no mistakes with these orders," he menaced, "because one word from Tazvoshenko, and Viktor, or Oleg, Tazvoshenko's men, who come here as observers, will not have problem offing us. Do not doubt! Tazvoshenko's long arm stretches from Russia to Minnesota!"

"Understood." Illich felt duly warned and involuntarily shuddered, as he inserted the envelope back in the plastic bag, and rose from the table to leave. Zolotov stayed back for a moment, giving Illich time to drive away, before he exited the restaurant.

The following morning, Zolotov, in a rotten mood, dressed and went downstairs for his morning espresso. His men arrived at the appointed time, and he urged them towards a waiting van and growled, "Get in! We go to meet with others. I want to arrive before rest of men."

Seeing Zolotov's dark countenance, his men scurried to grab their weapons and toss their gear in the vehicles, ready to leave for their rendezvous with the rest of the men and equipment. Several hours later, they pulled up to a large warehouse hidden in the woods, northeast of town, where they spent the day going over plans, assembling equipment, and gathering supplies needed for the journey ahead. When all the men were ready, and the transports were lined up, it was quite an assemblage.

Zolotov gathered everyone into a clearing to explain their mission, "You are going to prearranged location to set up working camp, and wait for confirmation of coordinates. We set up, so all is ready when last information is delivered."

There was murmuring among the men, and one of them called out, "When do we leave?"

Ignoring this man, Zolotov said, "Tazvoshenko, will exact retribution should we fail. Commander Nicholas will arrive later, and I will follow when I receive final orders. You leave now!"

With that admonition, the men took their places in the vehicles, and a parade of transports, vans, SUVs, and trailer beds filled with large equipment, rolled by, all were headed for the back roads to their new location to set up. They would wait until further notice. Zolotov, Lev, and their driver got in their SUV and headed back to town.

CHAPTER 24

F riday, May 19, 2017
Pinecrest

Friday morning, traffic was heavier than usual, as Paisley followed Boone's car. They stopped to grab donuts and coffee at a gas station, and exiting their vehicles, Paisley looked up at the blanket of dark menacing clouds, covering the sky. It was already misting rain, heralding a Minnesota storm. By the time they hurried back to their cars, the mist had turned into heavy rain, creating puddles everywhere in the parking lot.

The rain slowed the traffic. When they arrived at the precinct and parked she said, "Looks like we're in for it, the rest of today and tomorrow, at least, according to my weather app. Did you hear the thunder and lightning last night?"

"A time or two,"Boone replied, "but I was so tired, I slept through the worst."

"Glad I wore my boots, and heavy coat!" With her head down, she pulled up her hood, and they both ran the rest of the way to the precinct entrance.

Once inside, they went their separate ways, after agreeing to meet just before lunch, to talk over new developments on their case and coordinate new facts. Paisley's primary objective for the morning, was to show the picture of Kamorov's tattoo to Millie, but when she entered her office, Millie hadn't arrived yet. Disappointed, she removed the photo of the tattoo from her briefcase and readied herself to pounce.

Just then, the door opened, and Millie bustled in. "Ha! I've been waiting for you," Paisley said. "As soon as you get organized, I have something I want you to see," she said excitedly.

"Sure?" Millie looked at her with curiosity, as she put her purse down and hung her wet jacket on the coat tree. "Whew! That's some storm! Now, whatcha got?" She walked around her own desk and stood next to Paisley, perched on the corner of her desk and folded her arms.

"Look at this!" Paisley laid the photocopy of the tattoo flat on the desk, smoothing it with her hands, then said, "Have you ever seen this tattoo?"

Millie, taken aback for a moment, asked, "Is that a corpse's arm?"

"Yes."

Millie leaned over the desk and stared, "Hmmm...."

Paisley couldn't stand the suspense and said, "So—does this tattoo resemble the one on the arm of the guy, who came into the office looking for what he called, a thumb drive?"

"Yes,...yes, like the one I saw. Sorry, it through me off for a minute, to see a dead man's arm!"

"I *knew* it! Thanks, Millie," and she rushed out of the office, photocopy in hand, heading for Boone's office.

Disappointed to discover Boone wasn't there, she left a sticky note on his desk, requesting him to call her as soon as he returned. Where could he be? Deflated, she headed back to her office, stopping by the lab to find out if forensics had finished with Kamorov's computer. Again, she was put off. They told her that the fingerprints tested so far, belonged to Kamorov, but there were still more tests to be run.

"Okay, but please let me know as soon as you're through...I'll be in my office."

"You weren't gone very long," Millie chided, when Paisley walked in, "however a call came in a couple of minutes ago, and went to voicemail. You might want to listen to it before getting started on something else. By the way, how are things going Pais, since...the break-in?" Millie hadn't wanted to bring up the subject too soon and upset her.

"Pretty good, all things considered."

"It's so awful! Did you stay at your house last night?" Millie asked, while sorting papers to file.

Putting her elbows on her desk, Paisley clasped her hands and answered, "No, I stayed at Boone's again. I was talked into it because he thought it was still too dangerous to go back to the farmhouse."

Millie produced a mischievous grin, "*Well*, how exciting! I think he likes you, Pais!"

"C'mon, Millie! It's not like that!" She laughed at the expression on Millie's face. "Quit trying to play cupid! We're two people working on a murder case, and that's *all*."

"I'm just sayin' Pais," and with a guileless facial expression, Millie started typing one of her reports.

"Thanks, Millie," she grinned and added, "but there's no there, there," adding, "I'm gonna listen to the message now," and with a business-like glance at Millie, she hit playback to hear her message.

It was Boone. "Grab your rain gear and meet me in the precinct garage immediately!"

Curious, Paisley called back and said, "Be right there, what's up?"

"There's been another murder," he said, and gave her a couple of details.

"Are you okay?" Millie said with concern when she saw the shocked look on Paisley's face.

"I'm fine, but I have to go with Detective Boone right now—there's been another murder, and you'll never guess who!"

"Not another one!" Millie put her hands on her cheeks, and her jaw dropped in surprise. "So, who is it, Pais?"

"One of Kamorov's friends!"

Boone was in the precinct parking lot waiting for her as she rushed out and hopped in the car. When they were on their way, she asked, "Where was the body discovered?"

"In his apartment...seems a tenant, several doors down, takes her dog for a walk every day, and as they passed one of the apartments, the dog stopped and began to bark and wouldn't quit. I guess the dog refused to leave. It just kept sniffing and barking at the door. The dog's owner knocked, but there was no answer, then knocked again, until finally deciding to contact the landlord, and the rest is history."

"Wow! That's awful!"

"The landlord reported the murder to the police and gave the tenant's name as Ivan Belenski." Boone added, "I recalled his name being mentioned as a friend of Kamorov's, in one of the employee statements."

Paisley spent the afternoon with Boone, viewing the site of the grisly murder. The victim had been duct-taped to a chair and stabbed in the chest. Blood was everywhere. There was also a gash on his head, perhaps made with a blunt object of some kind.

Forensics technicians were giving the room a thorough

going over, searching for fingerprints and other evidence. At the same time, the ME, Dr. Hyde again, examined the body, preparing it for removal.

While the police photographer finished documenting the crime scene, Paisley and Boone knocked on apartment doors in the building, hoping to find someone, who may have seen, or heard something helpful.

They came up empty-handed, except for a strange lady, who remembered talking to a man the previous evening, on her way out of the building. Unfortunately, in between her mental wanderings, she remembered nothing about what he looked like, or what he said.

When they returned to the scene of the murder, forensics was gone, but the ME was still there. The officers watched while the two detectives investigated the place. Boone found the victim's wallet in the bedroom, stuck between the bed and the wall. His driver's license indicated his name was Ivan Belenski. Boone found nothing else—no trash in the trash can, no cell phone, and no computer.

Stepping closer to the body, Paisley had an idea, "Hey, Boone! What if the duct tape over his mouth, has fingerprints on the sticky side?"

"Good idea," and Boone requested the ME, to check for fingerprints on the duct tape when it was removed in the autopsy, and get back to him ASAP!

The two Detectives left the crime scene and headed back to the precinct. The weather seemed to be getting worse. The rain had been relentless and looked like it would continue the rest of the day. Arriving in the precinct's garage, the two agreed to go to their own offices, and meet later to dine out one more time.

Boone wanted Paisley to stay at his place again, but she argued, that there were things she needed to take care of at the farm. Boone acquiesced after she agreed to allow one of the officers to keep an eye on her place at night—just in case. She headed to her office and greeted Millie, remembering she still hadn't told Boone about the tattoo.

"How did it go this afternoon?" Millie asked, looking up at her.

"Well, Millie," she said, as she gathered the papers on her desk and put them in her safe, "the site was grotesque, definitely a horrendous murder of yet, another person possibly connected to Kamorov."

"No kidding! I guess the plot thickens!" Millie said dramatically.

Paisley stopped what she was doing, smiled, and gave Millie a look, "Ya think?"

They both chuckled, then finishing her tasks, Paisley grabbed her coat and the umbrella, which she kept at the office, and said, "By the way, Millie, the weather is *terrible!*" With that, she headed out of the office to meet up with Boone.

"And where are we going tonight for dinner?" Paisley asked with a smile as she entered Boone's office. "Just so you know, I'm *famished!*"

He looked at the clock. "I'm sorry, I was engrossed in the information I've been reading about Ivan Belenski, and didn't realize it was so late! Why don't we have dinner at Dock of the Bay Grill? They have wonderful grilled salmon steaks, and a delicious house salad."

"Perfect...I think I know where it is, but I've never eaten there."

She drove with Boone to the Grill, both, failing once more to notice a pair of headlights, which pulled out and followed them at a safe distance, to the restaurant. The vehicle's occupants parked and watched the pair race to the entrance, as they splashed in puddles, arriving wet at the door, despite using Paisley's umbrella.

They were both laughing, as Boone opened the door and followed her inside. The car in the lot and its occupants watched this, realizing they would have to be patient, and parked in a dark corner of the lot, within sight of the Detective's car. The waitress greeted Paisley and Boone and ushered them to a window table, decorated with the obligatory fish net and glass balls, on the wall.

The two spent several minutes looking at the menu and gave their orders to the waitress, who brought Boone a beer and Paisley her revered Diet Coke. Taking a sip, she glanced around the restaurant at the pictures of fish along the walls, and boat rigging frought with shells of all kinds, hanging from the ceiling beams.

"Not the greatest view of the little bay tonight. It's raining so hard I can't see anything out there," Boone said, as he moved closer to the window, trying to look out. He saw nothing, but the fog of his breath on the window, so he sat back and relaxed, taking a long sip of beer.

After a long drink of her pop, Paisley said, "I have something interesting to show you." She dug in her briefcase and pulled out the photocopy of the tattoo. "Look at this," and she placed it on the table in front of him.

"Okay...a picture of a snake?" Boone took another sip or two from his beer, puzzling over the picture in front of him.

"Yes, it's a picture of Kamorov's *arm* from the autopsy, showing his tattoo! Remember, when I took the pictures?"

"That's right, you never *did* tell me what *that* was all about."

"I took it because, when I stared at it, it jogged a memory, and I couldn't remember why until I recalled Millie describing a similar tattoo." She sat back in her chair, with satisfaction.

"Okay, but what's the significance?"

The waitress arrived with their salmon, rice pilaf, broccoli, and the house salad, "Oh, this smells delicious!" Paisley said, while the waitress ground some pepper on the salad.

As the waitress cruised on to another table, pepper-mill in hand, Paisley dug into her dinner and with her mouth full, said, "The significance is, I told you about the guy who came into my office earlier in the week, and how he was looking for a thumb drive. He tried to persuade Millie to find it for him, in my desk!"

"I *do* remember you saying this," Boone said as he finished his roll and reached for another.

"Well," she said dramatically, "*he* had a tattoo on the inside of *his* arm, too! It was one of the things Millie remembered about him, and when I showed her this picture—bingo! They were the same! So, perhaps this guy is connected to Kamorov— maybe, he's even the murderer?" she asked dramatically.

CHAPTER 25

Pinecrest
Paisley stared at Boone expectantly, waiting for him to react, but instead, he seemed passive for a moment before he responded, "To go from tattoo, to murderer, is a big leap—but—an interesting connection..." He hadn't finished his thought, before Paisley interrupted him.

"But wait...there's more! I researched 'coiled snake tattoos' on the internet, and after working on it for a bit, I discovered an organization exists, which uses the coiled serpent... *and*, guess where the group is head-quartered?" Before he could hazard a guess, she blurted out, "Russia! *And*, it's connected to a Mafia organization with groups all over the world—including the United States!"

Now, Boone was interested, "Well, this *might* be a lead?"

Before she took another bite of her dinner, she added, "I think we should check the victim we found today for tattoos, and maybe even Yury, and Zolotov—they're all Russian and might *all* be connected!"

She stopped talking and began eating again, enjoying her food. Boone, also enjoying his food, but with a full mouth, noised, "Um-hmmm," assuring her they would check and then nodded.

When he finished chewing and could talk again, he told her, "We'll check it out, and now here's what *I* uncovered earlier today. Turns out, I got a hit on the phone numbers found in Kamorov's jacket. One of them belonged to our elusive, and recently deceased friend of Kamorov, Ivan! I called the number, but no one answered, and *now* we know why!"

"And the other number?" Paisley asked.

"It was harder to find...I had to pull a few strings, and found only the name—Lenny Starko. No address or other information...it's as if he's in witness protection?"

It was her turn to say, "Hmmm. Well, on another note, I barely retrieved Kamorov's computer from the lab, when you called about Ivan's murder."

When the meal and murder case talk ended, they relaxed with a cup of coffee. Boone asked, one more time, "Are you *sure* you won't stay overnight at my place, instead of driving way out to the farm in this rain? It would be safer!"

"Look, Boone," she said gently, "whoever ransacked the house, knows by now, there's nothing to take, so I doubt they'll return, and besides, I can take care of myself! I'll keep my gun with me at all times, and I'll lock all the doors and close all the blinds. I have to go back *some* time...plus, I need a shower and clean clothes, but thanks for the offer," she said, as she gave him an appreciative smile."

"I still wish you would reconsider..."

Still smiling, she continued, "Really, thanks for all the help you've been—I *mean* it, but I'll be fine, especially with the officer provided by the PPD, as a guard. I have to get back and make sure everything is okay. I need to make sure Phantom has food and water, not to mention, pick up the mail."

"Okay, if you're going to be stubborn, just keep your cell phone charged and near you at all times, and if anything happens, please call and I'll come right away—deal?"

"Deal." She grinned. His concern made her feel good, but she couldn't continue avoiding her return to the farm.

"It's time to leave," he said and paid the bill. They grabbed their jackets and headed for the door. Outside, the rain was still pouring, and a big clap of thunder startled them both, as it echoed through the night accompanied by lightning splayed across the sky, bathing the parking lot in a bright flash of light.

Paisley pulled her hood over her head, but before she opened the umbrella, Boone grabbed her hand and practically dragged her along laughing, as they raced to the car through the driving rain. They were drenched when they dove into the car.

They drove silently to the police station, where he dropped her off at her Jeep. He watched her get in and drive away, but followed her for a few blocks, to make sure no one followed *her* —or *him* either—before peeling away and heading home.

After waiting in the parking lot of the restaurant for quite a while, Tazvoshenko's men decided to return to the police precinct, figuring the detective would eventually return the girl to her car. It would offer them an opportunity to intercept and kidnap her and force her to divulge the thumb drive's, whereabouts. Tazvoshenko assured them they could use any means available.

The rain was relentless, and as they listened to the weather report on the radio, they talked among themselves, deciding the abduction would actually be easier in the storm. Shortly, the Detective dropped the girl off, and they watched, as the Detective's car followed the Jeep for a few blocks, before turning to go home. Finally, they edged out of a side street and stealthily began their pursuit.

Although Paisley noticed Boone following her before turning off to head home, she *didn't* notice the dark sedan idling on a side street with its headlights off, nor was she aware, when it slowly pulled out to make a right turn, as it followed her tail lights, at a safe distance in the storm.

Paisley headed from Pinecrest, towards Brainerd and the farmhouse, and as the rain intensified, she began picking up speed at the edge of town, because she was eager to get home, and out of the storm. Preoccupied by the strange murder of Ivan, she was oblivious to the set of lights, which had appeared in her rear view mirror as she neared northeast Brainerd.

She finally spotted lights in her rear-view mirror, appearing as a liquid blur in the storm's downpour. This made her uneasy, and even though rain pounded on the windshield, she sped up a little—and so did the lights! She began to feel paranoid again. Am I being followed, she asked herself?

Despite the rain, she increased her speed, as did the lights behind her! The uneasiness she felt soon turned to fear, and continuing to increase her speed, she saw that the lights kept pace. Approaching the turnoff to the farm, she decided it was safer to stay on Highway 210, towards the towns of Crosby/Ironton, rather than turn onto the dark, deserted road to the farmhouse. The lights followed, keeping pace, regardless of her speed. She felt scared, grabbed her phone, and called Boone.

"Hello?" His voice sounded matter-of-fact, since the call had awakened him, and he felt groggy.

"Boone, this is Ingles..."

"What do you need?" He yawned. "Is everything okay...?" *Now,* he was awake.

With a tremulous anxiety-ridden voice, she interrupted

before he said more, "Someone's definitely following me—the faster *I* go, the faster *they* go! It's raining so hard, and no one else seems to be on the road! I have a bad feeling about this!"

Boone sat upright on the couch where he had dozed off in his shorts and undershirt while reading the newspaper. Swinging his feet from the couch to the floor, he grabbed his pants and said, "Where are you? I'm coming right now!" He held the phone between his chin and his shoulder to free both hands to pull up his pants.

"I'm driving up Highway 210 towards the towns of Crosby/Ironton...I didn't want to turn off a main road...the farmhouse road is too rural and deserted!" A crash of thunder almost drowned out her last few words.

"I'm on my way," he said. "Hang in there! Do you have your gun with you?"

She could barely make out his words, over the pounding rain and the peals of thunder, "No. It's at the farm!"

Her car suddenly hydroplaned on the water-filled road, and she screamed as she fought to gain control of it, "Hurry Boone," she yelled, "they seem to be gaining on me!" She had no idea if he could hear words.

The call began breaking up, and Boone uttered expletives, under his breath, "Okay, *please* be careful and stay on Highway 210! I'm coming as fast as I can—don't take any chances! Ingles?...*Ingles!*" he called into the phone in an attempt to stay in contact, but there was no response.

Boone hung up and redialed her number, but it just rang and rang. There was nothing to do, but race to Crosby/Ironton, despite the driving rain. He threw on his shirt, boots and heavy jacket, and grabbed his gun. He picked up a pre-packed backpack for emergencies. Racing out the door to his truck, he started the engine, shoved it in reverse, and in his haste to back down the driveway, he almost hit a small tree next to the walkway. He tried calling her again...nothing!

Paisley's phone lay on the seat beside her, but she was unable to hear it over the pounding rain. By this time, the road began to curve left, then right, and caused the phone to slip off the seat and onto the floor, rendering her unable to reach it. Frantically, she tried to keep control of the car, but despite her efforts, the mystery car was gaining.

The dark sedan pulled close behind her, and as she increased her speed, so did the sedan. To her horror, she saw the driver positioning the car so that he could pull up beside her. If he did, in the worst-case scenario, the sedan could force her to lose control of her car and plummet off the road into a ditch.

Due to the torrential rain, Paisley's windshield wipers flicked back and forth, like a metronome setting the pace for *Flight of the Bumble Bee*, but even at this speed, the wipers were rendered useless in the heavy rain, and became an obstacle, as she tried to see the road.

Leaning forward, she struggled to peer through the windshield and stay in control of her Jeep as she raced around curves like a sled on a slalom track. She gripped the steering wheel so tightly that it caused her fingers to ache. She was able to speed up, just enough, to edge ahead of the sedan, and when it made its move, she cut it off, on the approaching curve.

She glanced in the rearview mirror, just in time to see the sedan swerve into a roadside ditch, and with a sigh of relief, she sped forward as fast as she dared. At her first opportunity, she squinted into the rearview mirror to ascertain if the sedan had been able to resume the chase. Still, rain made it impossible to see through the rivulets cascading down the rear window. Nevertheless, she saw no evidence of headlights in her rearview mirror *or* the side mirrors.

With thunder, lightning, and pounding rain, Paisley felt as if she were driving blindfolded and hoped she was guessing the right moves, in order to avoid the sedan's fate! She shook with fear, as adrenalin coursed through her body, but continued to drive through the storm, until the road began to wind around into the small town of Crosby, with its few blurry neon signs glittering in the rain.

Realizing she had to slow through town, she saw an opportunity to shake the sedan, by turning left onto a side street and disappearing. Having made this decision, she skidded around the corner of the next street she could make out, only to discover, it was poorly tarred. The Jeep bounced around, causing her to slow down.

Fearful of losing her cell signal, she slowed the car enough to reach down and grab her phone from the Jeep's floor to call Boone again and tell him where she turned. The peals of thunder were intense, making it difficult to hear, once he answered. As soon as she gave her location, the cell signal was gone. I hope he received my message, she thought! What a violent storm...I've *never* seen anything like *this*, in California!

Traveling further down the road, she noticed it changed abruptly, from tar to mud, with water-filled ruts. She prayed she'd be able to keep her Jeep on the road, as she hit flooded potholes, spraying water to each side.

The road grew narrower, while the monsoon-like storm continued to pound, and soon the road only accommodated one car. The terrain on either side, was populated with dense brush and small saplings, which made loud slapping noises, as they pummeled the sides of her car, making it difficult to travel—*even* in her Jeep!

Paisley had no idea where she was. The bouncing and jouncing, as she jerked around bends in the road, and splashed through mud and water, had caused her to slow—but still, there were no lights behind her—as far as she knew—and the rain seemed to lessen, which encouraged her.

"I want this to be *over*," she moaned, "I need to find a safe place to stop! Please, Boone, find me!" The windshield wipers did double duty, struggling to wipe away, not only the rain, but now the mud, which splashed onto the windshield, leaving gritty brown streaks with every swipe. And even though she hadn't seen headlights for a while, she had no plans to stop, even though the mud added a new dimension of difficulty.

Boone drove like a maniac through the rain, as he sent a cell phone transmission to Riley, at headquarters, "There's a problem," and he informed him of the turn of events. "I'll be in contact as soon as I get back with Ingles, but right now I have to pay attention to my driving!" With his eyes glued to the road, Boone made good time, forcing his truck through the ferocious storm.

Without traffic to deal with, he pushed his speed, while still contending with the darkness and rain, as it came in torrents. Before long, he reached the area where Ingles had last contacted him.

With no further information, he had to guess the path she took. He stayed on the road as it began to head toward town, and was scarcely able to catch her second communication, concerning her course change into the rural area.

Meanwhile, Paisley drove on, twisting and winding around and down small hills, and low places, like a rollercoaster, which one must be ride to the end! The landscape rushing past seemed to be changing because the brush became thicker, and the trees larger. Her car began climbing, as the hills steepened, while the never-ending downpour intensified.

She desperately wanted to turn off the road, but there was

nowhere to turn. With visibility still a problem, she began to slow the Jeep, as the road morphed into a series of sharp turns. The driver's side of the road became steeper, with a dirt wall emerging, while on the passenger side, the road appeared to drop off.

Suddenly the road veered to the right, and Paisley spun the wheel sharply to the left to avoid the roads edge, but the Jeep slipped off the muddy road anyway, plunging into a steep ravine.

Brush scratched against the sides of the car, sounding like fingernails on a chalkboard, as she zigzagged around branches and large jutting rocks. The ground leveled out, and the Jeep slowed, jolting into a shallow ditch and up onto another road.

She was relieved, until rounding the next bend. Looming ahead, she could just make out a huge tree, which had fallen across the road. With no way of avoiding it, she yanked the wheel to the right and stood on the brakes, but it was too late.

The Jeep pitched down another embankment, through dense brush, slowing the Jeep's speed as it plummeted into another deep ravine. It finally came to a stop, crashing head-on, against a tall stump standing up, in a fetid pool of ooze, consisting of mud and algae. She had no time to scream as everything went black.

CHAPTER 26

Cuyana Iron Range

Boone drove as fast as he could, repeatedly calling Ingles, with no response, until finally receiving her brief message concerning the turnoff she'd taken. Her phone cut out before he could say anything, and though he kept trying, he was unable to contact her again. Following the road through the downpour, he searched to determine Ingles' path, all the while, looking for suspicious cars. He arrived in Crosby/Ironton and slowed to look for the turnoff described by Ingles.

After a short distance, he noticed a fork in the road where he decided to turn left. Veering onto this road, he hoped he made the right choice and continued driving. Not quite a mile later, he was on a mud-covered dirt road, trying to determine if it had seen recent use, but it was impossible to ascertain under present weather conditions. However, soon he noticed signs his intuition proved correct.

Broken branches hung from low hanging trees, lining the dirt road. He stopped, jumped out of his truck and grabbed a few branches in the road, to examined them, getting drenched in the process. He looked closely at the broken ends, and saw there were signs of being recently broken.

Also, foliage appeared to be mashed into the mud, and Boone knew it only meant one thing—a car had driven through recently. But was it Ingles'? Boone felt frustrated, having no idea where he was or how to find her. Climbing back in his truck, his heavy jacket dripping from exposure to the rain, he continued driving the difficult road, all the while looking for signs of head-lights *or* tail lights.

He pressed on, remaining vigilant, as he looked for proof he was on the right track. Thunder resumed along with occasional lightning strikes. Several times he stomped on his brakes around hairpin turns, while his back end fishtailed, but he still pushed his speed. He bounced down to a secondary road.

Large rocks loomed ahead, and he maneuvered around them, running roughshod over brush and small branches, until he found himself barely able to stop in time, from sliding down a steep muddy embankment. Turning sharply, around a bend, he immediately hit the brakes, preventing his truck from colliding with a huge tree, uprooted by the storm and deposited across the road.

With his engine running, he disembarked to assess the situation, hurrying around to the front of his truck, and that's when he noticed crushed bushes at the road's edge. Taking a closer look, the crushed foliage pointed to something large, having gone over the edge, and plummeting down the steep embankment.

He stood at the road's edge, trying to see below, but visibility was nil in the darkness and rain. Boone was compelled to explore the possibility that Ingles may have come this way and gone over the embankment. Hurriedly jumping in his truck, he threw it in reverse and backtracked around the curve, continuing backward, until he found an opening in the thick underbrush, where he could drive his truck deep into the foliage, hoping it wouldn't be detected.

With a sense of urgency, he grabbed his backpack from the back seat, and scurried down the embankment, to search for Ingles and her Jeep. He tumbled through thick brush, stepped over tree stumps, and strong-armed his way through the bushes and low hanging tree branches until he almost made it to the bottom of the ravine.

There, through a small clearing in the brush, he spotted the back fender of her Jeep. It's a miracle, he thought—tantamount to finding a needle in the proverbial haystack! Breathing heavily from his arduous descent, he clambered down the steep embankment, and approached the Jeep.

Boone attempted to open its back door to see if Ingles was still inside, but the car had lodged at an angle between a large bolder and a tree stump, and almost camouflaged with brush and mud...it was impossible to see anything through the windows.

When the car door wouldn't budge, Boone ran to the other side, calling out her name, hoping she wasn't injured. The passenger door was also jammed, so he kicked in the back window, creating an opening. When he looked inside, he saw her slumped over the steering wheel, covered with remnants of broken glass from the front windshield.

He climbed through the opening and over the back seat to the front, where she slumped. He leaned over, and detected she was still breathing. "Ingles! Ingles!"...he shook her gently until she rolled her head towards him. There was a bad bruise and some blood on her forehead, probably from hitting it on the steering wheel, at impact.

"What...happened?" she mumbled and tried to sit up, but couldn't.

"Don't try to move yet," he said. "It looks like you've hit your head on the steering wheel. However, fortunately, the Jeep's airbag didn't deploy, or it might have added to your injuries."

She let out a few moans, seeming dazed, disgruntled and disoriented, as she struggled up, trying to make sense of things. Boone checked to make sure there were no broken bones, then carefully helped her out through the back window, and put his arm around her waist to help steady her.

But, she removed his arm, "I can do this myself!" She took a few steps to get her equilibrium, then thought better of it and sat down on a nearby tree stump, and put her head in her hands.

"I think you're okay, except for your bruised head. No broken bones...you were very lucky! How do you feel?"

"Yes, lucky...I feel okay. No broken bones, just a wrecked car." She made a sad face. "Thanks for coming!"

"Tell me what happened," he said, taking a bottle of water from his backpack and letting her take a drink.

She recounted the story. Boone listened with concern when suddenly, he grabbed her hand and yanked her to her feet before she could catch her breath. Off they went. He led the way, dragging her behind him. She attempted to pick up her pace as they scrambled further down the embankment and into the underbrush, when he suddenly stopped.

"Hey! What are you doing?" she asked, "I wasn't expecting this quick start and stop!"

"Sorry I didn't give you any warning, but are you able to do some moving?" They both stood there, drenched, cold, and covered with mud.

"Moving? If I *have* to—what's going on?"

Boone put his finger to his lips to shush her again, and said in a whisper, "Listen!" He stood very still and so did she.

"I hear something on the road above us, and I think I saw a light. Do you think you can run?"

"Yes, I think so?" she whispered hesitantly, and they took off down the hillside as quickly and quietly as they could, without stopping for the greater part of an hour.

Paisley, had a splitting headache and her shoulder felt achy. Once, she fell, as they were running through a thicket, and bruised her knee on a large rock, jutting from behind a tree. Boone began to slow down when he saw a spot with heavy vegetation and led Paisley into its thick center.

"Here," he said, "we'll rest for a while until we can devise a plan for returning to civilization."

She was totally in favor of *this* idea because she was exhausted and sore. Boone gathered pine branches from the nearby trees and laid them down on the drenched earth inside the vegetation, as a bit of protection from the soggy ground. They both lay down on the pine branches. While they caught their breath, he inquired how she was feeling.

"I'll live," she said, "besides my headache, my shoulder feels like I might have sprained it, and I bruised my knee back there when I fell, but I'll be fine...still a little dizzy, that's all."

The rain slowed to a steady drizzle, as the heavy vegetation kept most of it from falling directly on them.

"Sorry, Ingles—no fire tonight—might give away our position."

"Now that we've stopped running for the moment," she whispered, "can you tell me what just happened?"

"Well, I thought I heard car engines from up on the road, so even though you lost them for the moment, they haven't given up trying to locate you. I left *my* car hidden off-road in the brush, but I'm sure they know *you* didn't drive over that big tree in the road. I'm sure they searched and found my car *too*, and they'll come down the hill searching for both of us—that's why we had to put some distance between them and us."

"What are we going to do now? This is scary!"

"Here, take my backpack and use it as a pillow...I'll lean against this tree. Now we're going to rest. I'll keep watch, then we'll figure a way out of here, so we can get help. We'll talk more later, right now you need rest, so you'll be ready when it's time to move."

There was no response, so he turned his head towards her...she was already asleep. Boone awakened Ingles a scant forty minutes later, and as they emerged from their temporary shelter, he scurried further down the embankment, with her in tow.

"What are you doing?" Paisley asked, "Why are we running again—I thought we left them behind?"

"It's important to keep moving—you can ask questions later, right now, just do as I say!"

Annoyed, she followed him as they ran and half slid down another incline into deeper underbrush, with Boone picking his way through the trees and vegetation to get deeper into the dense forest. At last, they came to a small brush covered ravine, and climbed down about ten feet, over some large rocks, until Boone spotted a cave-like opening almost invisible, because of the brush surrounding it.

"Eureka!" he said.

"How corny," Paisley said, "who says eureka anymore?"

He ignored her comment, as they both entered the small hidden cave. Once inside, they sat down on a couple of large rocks to catch their breath, for the second time that night.

"Can you please explain what's going on?" Paisley questioned again, with a slight edge to her voice. "Obviously, we've left, whoever those men were, behind us, and surely they're not going to try to follow us down *this* hideous path, in *this* terrible weather and rough terrain!"

"Listen!" He said, and sat up—alert and quiet.

She listened. "Listen to what? I hear drizzling rain and an occasional faraway clap of thunder...*so?*"

"So, that's right, except—I hear another sound!" he said defiantly, with great seriousness.

This puzzled her as she rubbed her sore ankle, which she'd twisted, "Okay, I'll bite. What is the sound that *you* hear?" She rolled her eyes and stretched out on the ground, not in the mood to play guessing games.

He was only slightly amused at her intonation and said, "It's a helicopter!"

"A helicopter?" She sat up again. "So, what? What's the big deal?"

"Because," he said, even more serious this time, as he looked directly at her, "I'm afraid that copter is looking for us!"

Her voice went up an octave, as she said, "What? Why? What makes you think *that?*"

"Let me put it this way," Boone began, "I'm afraid we—you—have something, which someone really wants, and is determined to do whatever it takes to get it."

Still flabbergasted and mouth gaping, Paisley said, "We? Me? What are you talking about? Why would you think that? It's ridiculous!" then she leaned back on her elbow, and winced due to a large scrape just below it, and waited for an answer.

"C'mon—get up—we need to move again!"

She begrudgingly stood up, brushed herself off, and they left the cave and continued forward, "I *still* don't know what you're talking about!" She was annoyed.

They trudged up a small slope for several minutes, as the

rain began in earnest, again. After they'd traveled silently for a bit, he stopped, turned and eyed her carefully, and said in a quiet, but serious voice, "Not as ridiculous as you might think, I have knowledge that some bad people are looking for something in this area, and I have reason to believe that we—or you—have some sort of information pertaining to it, that they want."

She scoffed, and said, "Right," drawing the word out slowly. "You have reason to believe? Believe what?"

"Shhhh...!" He suddenly raised his hand to quiet her. "Listen!"

She did. He shoved her under some large plants at the base of a nearby tree and dove in after her. She hit the ground hard and scraped her chin.

"Hey! Take it easy!" she lamented.

The noise came slowly closer, until it was no longer speculation, as to what made the noise. There, hovering above some nearby trees, was a copter, with its rotors beating loudly, stirring the branches on the surrounding trees and kicking up debris, as it flew low over the area, circling around and crisscrossing the terrain.

The copter utilized a searchlight, which traced a moving pattern over the trees and brush. It searched carefully, as it hung low over the area, like some huge prehistoric bird. Through the heavy brush covering them, Paisley stared skyward in disbelief, assessing the ramifications of this turn of events.

For the moment, they sat huddled at the foot of the tree and Boone grabbed dead leaves and fallen branches, pulling them up, around, and on top of them, to better conceal them from view, while the copter continued to move closer raking the area with its light.

Eyes wide, Paisley turned to look searchingly at Boone and whispered, "*What* is going on?"

CHAPTER 27

Boone couldn't hear her with the noise overhead, but read her lips, managing to utter a scoffing noise at her question, and said into her ear, "You tell *me*! Is there something you're keeping from me? What do they want with *you*? Please, be open with me," he said, "but—we can discuss this later, right now we're both in danger and need to stay out of sight!" The chopper eventually moved away, and as it searched further away, the noise faded and the night became quiet once more, except for the sound of the rain droplets, as dripped their way through the heavy foliage, where they took cover.

When Paisley's heart stopped pounding, she asked, "Why would they be targeting me?"

"Well, for starters, how about the burger place where Kamorov was murdered, where *you* are a well known *and* frequent visitor? You were there *and* found the body! And it was *your* Aunt's house, which someone ransacked. Also, we can't forget Ivan—someone murdered *him* and we discovered he's connected to the currently deceased Kamorov!"

"Yes, but..."

"And last, but not least," he continued, "let's not forget to mention, all these people are *Russian*—including your Aunt! Then, there's the fact that people were chasing *you* tonight! Are *they* Russian too? It *does* make one wonder?"

Surprised by his comments, she said, "Wow! I didn't see *this* coming...you've *obviously* given this lots of thought!" She felt attacked.

Instead of answering, his attention was elsewhere, as he peeked out from their hiding spot, to see where the chopper was, as the noise of the rotors could no longer be heard. Paisley felt as if time slowed, like a train coasting to an inevitable stop. They remained silent, in their hiding spot for a while longer—just to be safe.

"I think it's time to move on," Boone finally said, and stood up, helping Ingles to her feet. She groaned as she stood, because for the few minutes she'd been sitting, her body had stiffened and now Boone wanted her to get moving again!

"Why move? Why don't we stay here until the sun comes up? It would be easier to move in the morning because with daylight, we could figure out where we are, and how to get back to civilization."

"Here's why," he said, "because while they're trying to find us from the air, I'm pretty sure they've also sent a ground party to hunt us down, and they're probably already hot on our trail."

"You have this all figured out, don't you?" she said hotly, "Meanwhile we don't *actually* know what's happening—you're just guessing!"

Stumbling on a vine, she was about to take a dive, until Boone grabbed her arm, in time to arrest her fall. Stopping, with his hand still tightly gripping her arm, he spun her towards him and looked her in the eyes, his voice, as serious as, the look in his eyes, "I *know* we must figure this out, but in the meantime, it could mean the difference between life and death, if we don't take precautions."

She stared him down. "Are you saying that we could be...killed?"

With a graveness in his voice she hadn't heard before, he answered, "I'm saying, *just* that...these guys aren't fooling around, so I'd rather err on the side of caution."

"Okay, now I'm *really* scared!" she said.

"Sorry," he added, "but this *is* a serious situation, and they're not here to play hide-and-seek, so *please* listen to me, follow directions, and trust me."

Chastised, she meekly nodded her assent, and they continued to plunge through the undergrowth for the next half hour. Pausing at the base of a cluster of oak trees, he stood still and listened for a minute. Finally, the rain had turned to a light mist.

"But how do you *know* they're searching for *us*?" she said, as if the previous conversation hadn't ended thirty minutes ago. "I'm wet and cold."

"Trust me, I know. Hearing the helicopter's rotors, my instincts told me it was no coincidence that a copter just *happened* to be flying around in this area, in a dangerous storm, with searchlights, unless they were looking for someone! I think these characters are capable of anything, if they have *that* kind of air power at their command!"

Confused, she waited a beat and said, "But who are they, and *why* are they after us?"

"No more questions." Instead, he took her hand to help her over a particularly large fallen tree, as they navigated down the steep slope, around other fallen trees and large boulders, buried in the dense undergrowth, slippery from the wet algae on their surfaces. They half-slid, half-ran, down a declivity into an area populated with giant oaks, birch, tamarack, and jack pines, which pierced the thick undergrowth, and towered into the night.

Almost impenetrable vegetation slowed them considerably, blocking attempts to determine where they were headed. The sky wasn't visible through the canopy of leaves, which acted as a giant umbrella, protecting them from the mist and intermittent drizzle. Paisley felt fatigued, as they slogged along in silence, for what seemed like hours, until her injuries began to slow her down. She was thirsty and hungry despite the large meal they ate earlier that night, which seemed like a lifetime ago.

She slowed, stopped walking, and asked, "Are we there yet?" Seeing her fatigue, Boone found a sheltered area where they could rest again, then stopped, and she eased herself onto a large rock.

"I hope you fill me in, on the who-and-why part," Boone said, as he watched her take off her shoes one at a time to dump out a little muddy water. Surprisingly, there had been no complaints from her about her shoe plight. He didn't share her shoe predicament, because of his high top boots.

Folding her arms, she said, "So, we're back on that topic again. Why would I know?" Her frustration was now raising its ugly head, a result of exhaustion and discomfort from weather and injuries.

"Because somehow, as I said, this is tied to you...*and* me," he added quickly, "but mostly you, and I need to know why."

"I don't see how," she said, "what information would *I* possibly have? May I have a sip of water, please?" she asked, still using her manners, even under difficult circumstances.

Handing her the bottle of water from his backpack, she drank more than a sip, before she handed it back and wiped her mouth with her dirty sleeve. Boone took a couple of swings, before sitting down on an adjoining rock, put the water back in his backpack, then pulled out a couple of protein bars and handed one to her. He ate his slowly, while they sat in silence, each with their own thoughts.

When he finished, he took the time to put the empty wrappers back into his backpack, before saying, "Referring to our previous conversation, sorry if I was a little harsh, but I want you to think carefully, to see if there's something—anything—a phone number, a picture you've seen...fill in the blank. Perhaps you overheard a conversation, received an odd telephone call that you didn't think much about at the time?"

"Nothing, comes to mind." She wondered where the forest animals were—probably in a warm nest—she was jealous.

"Your Aunt and Uncle are Russian...could there be a connection there?"

She leaped off the tree stump, albeit painfully, and said, "Not at all! How *dare* you even suggest my Aunt is connected, *or* my Uncle!"

"Calm down, I'm only throwing ideas out," he regretted his remarks. He stood, donning his backpack, and helping her up, he said, "Sorry, I didn't mean to upset you. Friends?"

She didn't answer, although she felt he *did* say it with sincerity.

"We need to make tracks out of here, Ingles."

After they walked for a few minutes, she reluctantly said, "Okay, apology accepted. I'll search my memory for an answer," and she fell in lock step behind him, as he shoved his way through the soggy brush and small saplings, creating a path forward.

Paisley was hurting all over. She limped, and her head still ached from the car accident. Nonetheless, she soldiered ahead, not wanting him to think she was a wimp. Finally, she decided it was time to speak *her* mind, and broke the silence, "Now *I* have a few questions for *you.*"

"Oh?" He smiled, despite the fact they were beginning to climb uphill, and waited, curious about what she would ask.

"Well, for one thing, I don't feel you're actually, who you say you are." There--she said it! "My guess is somehow, you are with the CIA, FBI, or some other covert organization, and you were sent here under false pretenses, I might add, sent to be a part of our police department, to either spy on us, help us in some covert way, *or* as cover for something else. Why? I haven't the foggiest!"

Smiling again, although she couldn't see it, since she walked behind him, he responded, "Now, if you would only put that much thought into what *I* asked you, we'd be fine! Anyway, we need to move a little faster, to stay ahead of them, or we'll be in *real* trouble!"

Boone panted, as he grasped for clumps of well-rooted weeds and small branches to help boost himself up the ever-increasing steepness of the hillside. He had to admit that despite her injuries, she certainly kept up well. She's a smart one, he thought—not to be underestimated!

"I'm working on it," she said, noting that he didn't respond to *her* suppositions about *him*, but merely changed the subject. Nice dodge! So infuriating!

"If you need to rest again, we can do that. I think we've covered enough ground, over the last hour."

Boone stopped, as they had reached an overhang in the rocks, so he ducked through the weeds, which marginally covered the opening to check for critters, but found none. However, he *did* wonder how she'd feel about the spiders?

"All clear," he said and invited Ingles into the cave-like

recess, pushing a large rock her way and said, "Have a seat!" He watched, as she ducked in, and positioned herself on the rock, and if she *did* notice the spiders, she didn't react.

"Thinking about what you said earlier," she began, "if I recount the details of everything that happened, from the day I found the body, maybe there'll be a clue in my narrative?"

"I'll help you zero in on things," he said, removing his backpack, as he sat on the ground.

"Oh, really!"and was about to disagree, when a thunderous clap of thunder startled them both, then a nearby bolt of lightning lit up the sky and the rain began to pour, once more.

"Yes, here's what I think," she said, once they recovered from the storm's sudden interruption.

"Yes, what *do* you think?"

Taking out his bottle of water again, he took a swig and offered it to her. "Maybe you stumbled onto something they want, which is the reason they ransacked your Aunt's house, went to your office, and in desperation, tried to run you off the road. Maybe they even want to kill you, *because* of whatever it is that they think you know?"

"You're joking! What reason would they possibly have to go *that* far?"

"We don't know what they're capable of, and we can't leave it to chance!"

She took a moment to ruminate on his theory, "Okay, I was there when the body was found, but in your office, *we* investigated the victim, and *we* looked over the fingerprints, I accompanied *you* to the autopsy, *I* identified the tattoo, and *we* interviewed Ben, Zolotov and Yury. I was about to comb through Kamorov's subpoenaed computer, but *we* had another murdered Russian, to investigate!"

"Can't disagree with you on any of those statements," Boone replied.

"Maybe it's *you* they're after, just as much as *me!*" She was over it for the moment, as she stared out of the cave's opening, into the darkness of the rainy night. Despite herself, she enjoyed the earthy smell of the wet dirt.

"I'm getting colder," she said, "even though I'm wearing my raincoat...it's soaked!" And, her teeth began to chatter.

"Move over here with me, and we'll lean together for warmth and try to sleep for a half-hour, before heading out again."

She didn't argue, as she moved next him, asking, "What time is it?"

He looked at his watch for the first time, while he set an alarm. "It's almost 1:00 a.m., on Saturday."

"That's all? It seems like we've been walking for days, and it feels like it's turning colder!"

Paisley shyly rested her head on his shoulder, while he pulled a poncho from his backpack to pull over both of them, and looked down at her, amused as she was already out like a light He listened to her snore quietly. Smiling, he leaned his head on his backpack, then dozed off. A half-hour later, he roused Ingles and handed her a poncho from his backpack.

"Why didn't you hand these out earlier?"

"Because we were already wet, these are to keep us warm—if possible," and donning their ponchos, they crawled from their hiding place into the steady drizzle.

They hadn't traveled far when Paisley said, "Wait!" Suddenly she stopped walking and excitedly announced, "I know *why!*"

CHAPTER 28

Saturday, May 20, 2017
Cuyuna Iron Range

Boone stopped abruptly and spun to look at her, "What?"

"A flash drive! It *must* be the flash drive! I found a flash drive at Ben's Burgers by the door to the freezer, where the body was found!"

Looking at her with a blank expression, he said, "Okay, please explain! Tell me, while we keep moving."

As they continued trudging along, she briefed him on the flash drive and her attempt to discover its owner by opening it, only to discover it was secured by an advanced encryption algorithm.

"Finally, I was able to decipher the password about the time I was supposed to be meeting you for dinner, at Casa Café." She began relaying the technical details of how she did it, but Boone told her to wait until they were back at his place.

"Remember? I already mentioned technology was *not* my strength," he said.

"But listen to this! After I opened the drive, I saw ten files, nine in English, with the tenth one encrypted, which is why it presented a problem for me."

Boone said, "Bingo! I bet that's it! When we are back at my place, I have a friend who can decipher anything."

"Excuse, me? I managed to figure out the password all by myself—it was *chemodan*, in Russian. Then I looked up the translation, which means luggage or suitcase, and I thought it was weird, so it made me curious about the document in the file."

"And you never told all this to me?"

"Well, I didn't really have enough information! The documents in the file, would need decryption too, but—there *was* a JPEG included—a picture of a crude map and a couple of area names in English, which I recognized...like Brainerd and Cuyuna. Because I had to leave work to meet you, I didn't have enough time to work on it! I'm out of breathe," she said, "can we stop talking and slow down?"

"Dave Kaufman, can decipher it for us," Boone said.

Paisley responded sarcastically, "So...we need Dave? The decryption expert?"

Catching her condescending tone, he changed the subject and said, "Right now, let's figure out how to get out of this predicament."

Boone came to a halt and listened carefully. "Do you hear that?" He stood still, listening.

"Not again!" She listened, "...hear what? You're always hearing things! All I can hear is..." and she was interrupted.

"Shhhh...listen!"

Rolling her eyes, she stood very still, and thought, what now?

"In the distance," he whispered, "I hear the faint barking of dogs!"

"Your ears are better than mine, because I only heard the wind in the trees."

"Move it!" he said urgently.

"You got it!" and she obeyed, wondering what the hurry was, as they both picked up the pace. "Sounds like thunder again," she added.

"Uh-oh! We may be trapped!" As they struggled upward, he said, "The way the ground drops off, it looks like a canyon rim might be up ahead, and I don't know if it's a short drop, or not. If it drops off sharply, we'll be trapped, but with the dogs approaching from our rear, we have no other choice, but to move forward."

They continued to scurry towards the rim until they were almost to its crest, and as they neared the edge he realized the loud roar they began to hear, was *not* thunder, but the rotors of a black copter, rising over the rim of the cliff from the canyon below. Boone knew at that moment, it was game over, as the searchlight from the copter washed over them, bathing them in its brightness.

The dogs continued closing in, while the copter trained guns *and* the spot light on them, as they stood near the edge of the cliff, which fell off, to the lake below.

"Aha! One of the many mine pits for which the Cuyuna Range is famous," he uttered sardonically, as he squinted through the drizzle into the lake, which sparkled with the reflected light from the copter's spot light.

"What are you talking about?" She yelled, in fear and frustration.

"Just a little history lesson Ingles, while we're waiting for these thugs," he yelled back, over the noise of the rotors.

"I can't see—the light is too bright, and I can barely hear you..." she yelled!

"When mining operations ceased and the mines closed in the early 60s and 70s, they filled most of them with water, and many of the old mine pits were turned into recreational areas. Still, there are many further away from the beaten path, and harder to reach—apparently, *this* is one of them!" He was irked at this turn of events!

Boone raised his hands, so Paisley did likewise, "Now, don't say a word," he yelled, "let me do the talking, if they ask questions."

"Okay." She nodded her head still puzzled over why he would give a mine pit speech, when they were obviously in danger. "I'm scared, Boone," she yelled back.

Four men converged on them from the shadows of the dense forest below the ridge, to where Boone and Paisley stood. The men tried to gain control of the barking dogs, straining on their leashes. Without a word, two of the men approached and confiscated Boone's backpack, gun, and knife, then patted both down, for any other weapons they might be carrying. Paisley, characteristically rolled her eyes, when they patted *her* down, but she didn't dare say anything!

Finding nothing else, the men bound both of them with plastic ties, pulled hoods over their heads, and prodded them towards the helicopter, which had landed in a small clearing. Their captors unceremoniously shoved them inside the heli, and pushed them to the back, leaving them sprawled on the copter's floor. Neither one said a word, nor did the men.

The rotors turned and accelerated, until lift was attained, causing the copter to rise into the low-hanging storm clouds.

Over the noise of the rotors, Paisley whispered to Boone in the lowest, calmest tone she could muster, "Now what?"

Answering in hushed tones also, he said, "Patience...we'll get out of this."

Of *course*, he was right! She felt better—she would trust Boone. They flew the rest of the way in silence. When one of the men moved to the back to keep watch on them, Boone slowly inched over, so he could move his cuffed hands close enough to Paisley's side, to tap a Morse Code message saying, to the effect, "It'll be OK," and hoped it would comfort her, *if* she knew the code.

She carefully leaned towards him and gently bumped him with her sore shoulder, in response. The man who guarded them, was none the wiser. She tried her best to discern where they were going, but it was no use, as there were zero points of reference. Instead, she attempted to guess the time it took to arrive at their destination, by counting out the minutes.

She wondered if Boone was doing something similar. As far as she could tell, the copter had been flying about thirty or forty minutes, when she felt it descend. There was a slight bump, jostling them as it touched down, and a few minutes later the rotors slowed to a stop and silence prevailed. During the entire trip, the men in front had not uttered a word.

Her heart raced again, as she wondered what was in store for them. She didn't have to wait long. The door opened and several men pulled them from the helicopter, onto the ground. Paisley tried not to make a sound, even though it hurt her damaged shoulder when she landed. With their hoods still in place they were yanked to their feet. The men pushed and shoved them forward, until they were stopped.

The sound of a rusty metal door groaning on its hinges, assaulted their ears, as both of them were shoved through an opening, and with a grating sound, the door closed behind them. They stood on a wooden floor for a moment, until the men pushed them forward another fifteen feet and stopped them once more.

Still, no one said a word, so neither did Boone, or Paisley. They stood still listening to the footfalls of heavy boots shuffling around. Paisley felt she would go crazy, if someone didn't say *something*! Could Boone be just as maddened, by their silence? She doubted it.

Finally, after what seemed like an interminably long time the boots came closer, followed by, what sounded like a trap door on the floor being pulled open. It clattered back onto the wooden floor, then they were led down a long steep flight of squeaky wooden stairs, which deposited them onto a dirt floor.

The air became stale and dank, as they were propelled forward, suddenly stumbling, as they found themselves on a dirt path, angling downwards. Paisley surmised they'd walked almost ten minutes, until they were finally stopped. A rusty creak emanated from hinges on another unseen door, sounding like something from an episode of the old radio show, *Inner Sanctum*.

She involuntarily exhaled noisily, when they both received a push hard enough to send them sprawling onto a dirt floor. The men bound their feet with plastic ties, and at last, the men yanked the hoods from their heads. Their captors, still mute, left the room clanging the iron door shut and locking it.

Paisley and Boone didn't move, while their eyes gradually adjusted to seeing light—even though it was dim! They remained silent, listening to the sound of the plodding footsteps disappearing in the distance, leaving them alone in utter silence.

They both lay on the damp earth of the cell, in abject silence, until Boone tentatively said, "Ingles? You okay?"

She uttered a weak, "Yes, I think so. I've landed on my shoulder twice now, and I probably bruised my already injured knee. Are you okay?"

"Ya, I'm all right..."

"What a relief! Since we can *finally* talk! What the heck is going on?"

Boone answered in couched tones, "Well, the people that we attempted to elude, have captured us."

"Of *course*! But, *now* what do we do?"

"The first thing we do is find a way out."

"Why didn't *I* think of that?" she asked, sarcastically. "Obviously, I second the thought, but *how* do we escape? I sure hope you have a plan, Mr. MacGyver!"

Boone ignored her comments, although it inwardly amused him. "How tightly are your hands bound?"

"Forget it! I can't even move my hands...the bands are cutting into my wrists, they feel numb, and I'm *very* tired and cranky."

"I noticed," he said.

The only illumination in the room, came from a dirt-encrusted low watt light bulb encased in a wire cage on the other side of the small barred window, in the iron door. The caliginous beam of light only penetrated the area enough, for Boone to visually examine their surroundings. They'd been placed in a cave, approximately twelve feet long, by seven feet wide, with a dirt floor. The ceiling and walls were dirt also, and bolstered with rough wooden beams.

"I think we're in the Cuyuna Region, as witnessed by the large water-filled mine crater, where they captured us. Our situation *might* be hopeful after all!"

She desperately wanted to believe him. "Good news," she said, her tone sounding lackluster.

Boone considered this for a moment before informing her, "I believe we're in an old mine shaft." Then laying on his side, he rolled to a sitting position and scooted across the dirt floor, until his back rested against the far wall. By this time, she managed to sit up, with her back against the metal door, watching Boone and his movements with interest"

"Now, time for Plan B," he whispered and maneuvered onto his knees, then bent himself back, so his fingers could connect with his boots, which presented the soles. Slowly, with his fingers, he edged out a sharp piece of metal from a camouflaged area, in the side of his boot's thick rubber sole.

Once he grasped it in his fingers, he asked her to lay on her side, while he scooted towards her, until the metal piece in his fingers aligned with her bindings. He began to saw, freeing her wrists and ankles. It surprised her when this worked, and relieved to be free, she rubbed her sore wrists for a moment, then used the metal piece to free him.

They both sat for a moment rubbing their wrists and ankles, trying to get the circulation back in their feet, hands, and fingers. When the feeling in Boone's hands returned, he put the piece of metal back in the sole of his shoe. Paisley stared at him dumbfounded, then finally spoke.

"I must apologize for calling you MacGyver. How was I to know you really *were*? I'm *so* thankful to be free of those plastic cuffs! But how did you just 'happen' to have, a piece of metal hidden in your boots?"

Even though she whispered, he could still detect the ironic tone in her voice, so he responded, "Oh, it's one of the things you do when you're in my line of work. I try to be prepared for all circumstances...I used to be a Boy Scout, you know," he said dismissively.

His answer puzzled her, "What do you mean 'your kind of

work'. I thought we were *both* in the same business. I *knew* there must be something you weren't telling me! And in your *other* line of work," she said sardonically, "do you have more tricks up your sleeve to get us out of here?" His "I'm always prepared, I'm a Boy Scout," answer, had slightly annoyed her.

"You'll find out," he said slyly. "First, we need to hurry, before they come back again."

"What if they come back sooner?"

"I think that because it's the middle of the night, we probably have some time. I'm guessing they won't be back until morning, or maybe even later," he said, assuredly.

"I hope you're right! So, what's the plan? I'm mighty uncomfortable in this dungeon!"

"This old mine shaft was probably blocked at the far side over there, opposite the door, so that's where we'll start digging, to see if we can find an opening."

Boone took a piece of metal out of *each* boot heel this time, and handed one to Paisley. She watched, as he moved his hands meticulously over every inch of the far wall, until finally, his hand brushed over a small piece of wood jutting out from the dirt. It was slightly lower on the wall and barely noticeable.

He began using the metal piece to scrape dirt away from it, and uncovered more wood. She joined him, and they both scraped at the wall, as a semblance of an upright wooden piece, took shape. Boone exerted more effort, until he noted a cross piece emerging, closer to the ceiling. "Hey Ingles, maybe there's something here, come look!"

CHAPTER 29

She leaned over to his side of the wall and saw several old boards uncovered, juxtaposed to a small piece of wood, exposed at the top.

"What do you think it is?" she asked

"I'm hoping these are beams for an opening of some kind? I need your help. Can you use your hands to scoop dirt from under the area where I'm digging? It'll give me more room to work, as I dig further."

"Done," and invigorated by the prospect of escaping, she knelt and began pulling dirt away from his dig, while ignoring her sore shoulder, knee, and headache.

Soon, Boone uncovered a crude, rectangular-shaped wooden frame. Ingles stopped to look and joined him to work in the middle portion of the frame. They hoped to find an opening possibly blocked, when the mine was abandoned. With fingers crossed, they began frantically clearing dirt—it was worth a try.

Paisley dug, then dragged the dirt away alternately, while Boone concentrated on just the digging. Shortly, his metal piece struck something hard, and clearing the surrounding dirt, a broken piece of glass was revealed. It was a shard from what may have been, a window pane in a door with dirt backed up behind it.

He showed it to her and they both quietly gave each other a high five. There was no dilly-dallying now because there were no guarantees their captors wouldn't return sooner, rather than later. Boone feverishly continued digging, until he pried one of the boards loose, pulling it free.

He pulled a second board free, enlarging a deep niche in the dirt wall about a foot deep, where the surface of a large rock appeared. Boone focused on digging dirt from around the rock to determine its size. It was an unuually large rock, about two feet in diameter. Paisley glanced over, to see why Boone had stopped digging.

"My gosh! What a huge rock!" she whispered. "Why don't we push on it, and maybe we can move the dirt in front of it?"

"Great idea," he said, "worth a try, but I'm pretty sure it weighs a lot!"

"You must be used to slamming things open with your shoulders, or kicking down doors," she said with a slight smile, "but, since this hole is closer to the ground, why don't we both lay down on our backs, and push with our feet to see what happens?"

"Hmmm," he murmured, "I guess we could try?"

He pulled more dirt out from around the rock to expose more of its surface. A moment later, they both lay down on their backs, their legs in the opening, scooting as close as they could, then pushed with all their might. The rock began to budge slightly, and then it gave a little more. With the next hard push, they shoved it out and onto the other side of the dirt wall, thus creating an opening.

Boone stood up, examining their work, and called out excitedly, "Pais! I think if we clear more dirt from the hole, we can make the opening big enough to make our exit!"

She lay on the ground, exhausted from pushing and pondered the fact that he'd dropped the Ingles, and called her, Pais! Only Millie called her Pais. She decided not to draw attention to it.

"Oh! Please, *please* let it be true!" she said with fervor, as relief spread through her body.

Over the next twenty minutes, they labored diligently to enlarge the space, until it was large enough to accommodate Boone! He wriggled in and determined it was safe, then said, "C'mon Ingles, let me help you through." Covered with dirt, and with hands and fingers raw from their furious digging, they brushed themselves off, marveling because they were almost able to stand upright.

"I don't know where this will take us," he said, "but it's better than staying in that cell awaiting some unknown fate," and turning, he asked, "...you okay?"

"I am now!" she answered, enthusiastically, "What time is it?"

"They took my watch, so I have no idea. Who cares! Let's get going before they discover we're gone!"

Boone attempted to cover the opening by shoving as much of the dirt as possible, back in the area they had just crawled through, in hopes it would delay their captors for a bit when it was discovered they were gone. When he finished, he grabbed Ingles' hand, leading her through the tunnel as fast as he could.

"Look at this!" Boone said, "We're in luck...there's an old light in here, like the one on the other side of the cave's iron door —it must be connected to the same wiring!" Another dust-covered caged light dimly glowed in the distance, allowing them to view almost fifty feet into the tunnel.

"Lucky we have light, because total darkness, would *really* slow us down!" Paisley said.

Like a giant labyrinth, the tunnel snaked along, with some sections in total darkness where a ceiling bulb may have broken or burned out, slowing their progress as predicted. Shortly, the narrow tunnel opened up, giving them a chance to recover lost ground.

"I feel like we're going around in circles," Paisley said. "Will there *ever* be an exit?"

"No one builds a tunnel like this, without an exit," Boone answered.

"Makes sense...hope you're right! I feel like I'm breathing dead air..." and as she said this, a gust of warmer air hit them when they rounded the corner.

A few more turns, and a small opening appeared, which they squeezed through, finding themselves in a cavern almost fifteen feet high, at its apex, and at least forty feet across, to an exit tunnel. They halted, completely stunned! There were at least a dozen of the caged lights along the walls, although not all of them were working.

"Wow, this is amazing!" She said, dumbfounded by the cavern's expansiveness.

"True, but there's no time to look around, let's keep moving!"

Forging ahead into the cavern, they encountered shallow puddles, and they splashed along, until the puddles deepened and they found themselves sloshing, ankle-deep through a fetid, not to mention foul-smelling, pond!

Paisley held her nose and groaned, "Please, tell me this won't get any deeper—we've endured enough already," she groused, "and now *this*? This smell is *horrid*!"

As they reached the opposite side of the cavern, the pond tapered to shallow puddles, and they warily ducked into a narrow tunnel, which caused them to bend over, as they proceeded. They worried that the tunnel might lead to a dead end. Still, they moved ahead in total darkness on a path strewn with rocks of disparate sizes.

At best, travel was difficult until the tunnel narrowed again, and caused them to walk with their hands on both sides of the tunnel wall, and then all they could do was crawl. This was painful, so they paused to rest a moment.

Magically, Boone produced a wooden match. When it was struck, it illuminated the darkness for a moment and they could see another sharp turn looming ahead. He lit several more, as they maneuvered through several tricky twists and turns, until after the last turn, there was a faint pinpoint of light in the distance.

Paisley, quiet as they maneuvered their way forward, believed the pinpoint of light to be another tunnel light. "Finally," she said, "we have light again!"

"I think we're seeing an exit point!" he countered.

"What?" Thinking her eyes were deceiving her, she realized, as they moved closer, it was real! "I can't believe it—I see the proverbial, light at the end of the tunnel!" Paisley's breathing became ragged...loud enough for Boone to hear her.

He stepped back and helped her forward, whispering, "Hang in there—we're almost free," and with renewed motivation, he pushed through the bushes that blocked its opening. He helped her through. Following her out where they could stand up straight, they were able to take deep breaths, of the clean, crisp early morning air.

Paisley spoke first. "Where did the matches come from?"

He laughed, "That's your first concern? Remember—a magician *never* tells how he does his tricks!"

"I think you enjoy tormenting me," she said and smiled, "anyway, I'm so ecstatic to be free!"

"Who's been tormenting whom?" he said, throwing it back at her and smiling, "Now, let's not linger—we need to move!"

"Do we have to?" she whined, "I'm still winded!"

"Unfortunately, we do," he said, so they pushed on.

The sky was cloudy with a sliver of murky sun, just visible on the horizon. He guessed it was around 5:30 or 6:00 a.m., not the easiest time to disappear! Using the dawn light as a reference point, Boone calculated which direction to take. He decided to head northwest—or at least what he thought was northwest!

The two of them set off once more, floundering through the deep brush of the dry riverbed, where they now found themselves. It led through a ravine and away from the cave's opening. They clambered up the rocky sides of the ravine and into a dense wooded area. For the next several hours, they struggled through a heavily forested area, in a northwesterly direction.

"At least the dense canopy of giant firs and oak trees, is protecting us from the elements. If only they hadn't taken my watch," Boone lamented, "because it had a compass."

"It must be close to noon, by now," Paisley said, "because I'm starving—and thirsty!"

Hunger began to dictate the necessity of locating something to eat and drink for them both, and an hour or so later, they came upon a small stream, tumbling over rocks into a small clear pond. Boone knelt, cupping his hands to gather water, and hesitantly tasted it. Deciding it was okay, he began to drink thirstily. Paisley watched, then knelt and did the same. Having sated themselves with water, they sat by the riverbank, resting and deciding their next move. Silence reigned for several minutes.

Paisley glanced around and excused herself. "I'll be back in a minute," and she went into the tall brush under the trees, muttering something about nature calling.

Boone, exhausted, said nothing. Instead, he lay back in the tall grasses, with his arm over his eyes and dozed off, but was startled awake when Paisley came crashing through the bushes. There was something cradled in her coat, and he sat up, curious as to what she held.

"Look! I have lunch," she called out with excitement, and when she approached, she held up a hand full of berries.

"Great...we have lunch," he commented, without enthusiasm. He was fatigued.

Ignoring his comment, she lowered herself onto the ground, carefully dumping out the contents of her coat onto a nearby flat rock, saying, "Not just berries, but mushrooms, too! Granted, I'd *love* a Ben's Burger right now, but for the moment, this will have to do."

"Whoa!" he said, putting out his hand as if to indicate halt, "We better not eat the mushrooms—they might be poisonous!"

"Well, fortunately" she said smugly, "I *know* these are fine, because my Aunt took me out hunting for Morel mushrooms, which are indigenous to Minnesota, and they're *not* poisonous—they're delicious! I've identified these as Morel, so we're in luck," she said with a big smile.

"Well, you can be my taster, and if you're okay, *then* I'll eat them!"

Paisley rolled her eyes, as she divvied up the berries and mushrooms, and after their feast, pointed out, "See, we're both still alive."

Boone acknowledged her pioneering qualities, then

suggested they find a hiding place and wait until sunset, before continuing on their way. After agreeing it would be prudent to travel at dusk, she ran off into the brush to gather more berries and mushrooms for later. There was a substantial growth of thick grass and undergrowth, beneath a nearby giant fir, and they disappeared inside the bushy branches and settled in for a nap with Boone taking first watch.

By dusk, they were both awake, feeling rested and relieved that there had been no sign of their pursuers, so they finished off the rest of the berries and mushrooms. It was time to travel again. Although the rain had subsided earlier that morning, the storm clouds had gathered again, and a brisk wind had risen, causing them both to feel chilled, as evening approached.

They still had no idea where they were; however, they began walking again in hopes of getting to civilization. Having only traveled a short distance, Boone spied a small wooden structure barely visible through the dense undergrowth.

"C'mon Ingles, it's time for plan C!" Suddenly, something else caught Boone's attention, and he warned Paisley, "Shhhh...stop!"

Startled by Boone's abrupt warning, she sighed, "Not again! *Now* what?"

He responded, "There's a farmhouse over there on that hill... just beyond that wooden shack in the trees...stay here, inside the tree line," and he headed through the trees to investigate.

This suited her just fine...she sat down on the ground happy to have a chance to rest, yet wondering what he was doing. He returned in a bit, with a big smile and said, "Stand up please, I've gone shopping! I hope I picked the right sizes?"

CHAPTER 30

Boone tossed some clothing towards her. Surprised, she caught the bundle, then held up the pieces—jeans, socks, a sweatshirt, and a tee shirt. Boone began to change into his duds right there, but Paisley quickly retired to the tall grasses. When she emerged, he smiled and whistled softly, and she rolled her eyes.

"Now that's what *I'm* talkin' about! I like a girl who can rock a sweat shirt with a 'Farmer Smith.Com, For High Quality Hog Feed' logo, emblazoned on it!" She never heard him laugh so hard, and looked down at her sweatshirt and laughed, too.

"The pants are a little tight, and the sweatshirt is *much* baggier than I prefer," she commented, "but at least they smell clean, and they're dry! Where did you get them?"

His outfit consisted of a pair of well-worn blue denim bib overalls, a black and blue plaid flannel, long sleeve shirt and a gray flannel quilted jacket with a hood. His were ill-fitting too, so Paisley also had a good laugh!

"As I approached the farm house to check it out," he said,

"there were no lights and no cars to indicate anyone was home, so when I spotted laundry hanging on a clothes line out back, I crept up, and 'borrowed' our outfits."

She could tell he thought it was clever, and smiled, then said, "It feels great to have clean, dry clothes—even if they don't fit, but I want to return our fancy duds, when this is all over, or I'll feel guilty. Now, what do we do with our old clothes?"

"Hmm...Let's bring them along for the moment, until we find a place to stash them—we don't want to leave them behind in case our mystery captors are using dogs again!"

They each rolled their old clothes into a ball, and with the fashion show ended, Boone turned and led her up the next hill-side, which was flanked by birch and pine trees.The trees kept them well-hidden from the farmhouse, until Boone stopped suddenly, once more, and grabbed Paisley's arm to hold her back —she froze!

"Again?" she asked, in a whisper. Her heart pounding, she said, "I'm beginning to develop SFS—Sudden Fear Syndrome— from your frequent alarms!"

He chuckled. "Okay, but don't you hear it? It's the sound of cars on a road!"

"Yes! I just heard one pass by...should we worry?" Her heart sank.

"Not this time, we're home free—to a point, of course—it's the sound of civilization!"

He gave her a high five, and they ascended another embankment, pausing in a small cluster of trees to dust themselves off and assess their situation.

"What's our next move, now?" she asked.

"Straighten yourself a little," Boone said, "because I think we're going to that bar across the road, and we don't want to stand out anymore than we already do...see that sign—The Bridge Tavern? It looks like a place where we can go."

"What about our old clothes?"

"I know! You stay hidden here, and I'll go across to the bar with the clothes, and find their trash bin. I'll dispose of them there."

She was skeptical about this plan, but in just a few minutes, he was back by her side. Relieved by his return, she brushed herself off and tried to comb her hair with her fingers, then said, "Any dirt on my face?"

He stared at her in a way that made her feel self-conscious. Her cheeks felt warm, and she knew she was blushing—he could see it too, she realized.

Using his fist tucked into his sleeve, he brushed a little smudge off of her cheek and grinned, "You look perfect!" He rubbed his face hard with his sleeve, and asked for *her* approval, too.

Giving him a nod, she grinned, "You'll pass, but you *do* have a bit of a five o'clock shadow."

"Alright, I'll make it work...here we go!" Boone said, and led the way across the highway, into a small field next to a parking area, as music drifted across the breeze.

They stood for a moment on the edge of the parking lot, taking stock of the place, when Paisley broke the silence, "Do you *really* think we should go in?"

"I believe we'll take our chances. Yes, we'll go in and listen to the music. Although we can hear it out here, we'll be warmer in there. We must continue to stay undercover, because we have no idea if they're still searching for us."

Crosby, Minnesota The Bridge Tavern They headed across the parking lot towards a set of wooden steps, next to a wooden ramp, which led to a large, well-worn wooden deck, with a sliding glass door entrance. Boone and Paisley ascended the broad steps. The place had the flavor, of a western saloon, and ducking inside the dimly lit bar area, the strains of a country song came from a larger side room to the right.

A few colorful characters in their cowboy gear were seated on stools at a wooden bar, while others were seated in a few of the booths and scattered tables in the small area in front of the bar. Bikers, decked out in their leathers, were seated at one of the tables drinking beer, engrossed in lively conversations.

Boone gave a slight nod to those sitting at one of the tables. Entering, he said, under his breath, "Ingles, let's slip into the restrooms where we can wash up a little." She nodded, and they went their separate ways.

Inside the Girls Room, Paisley looked in the mirror and was shocked to see herself. What a mess, she thought! Washing her face and hands, she attempted a re-do of her hair. Glancing around the small space, she spotted a rubber band on the floor and used it to put her hair in a ponytail—so much for germs! She longed even more for hot shower, as she finished primping.

Reuniting with Boone, they headed towards the music emanating from inside the large room to the right of the bar area, then opened the glass door and entered. They found themselves in a large high-ceilinged room with tables in the back of the room, a wooden dance floor (replete with dancers), in the middle of the room, and a stage for the band at the front of the room.

Paisley was stunned, to see a country band in person. The music was catchy, and she thought she even recognized the song —well, maybe she didn't recognize it, but it *did* sound familiar! Boone slid in between a couple of dancers, pulling her onto the dance floor.

He began to do the two-step. She was totally taken off

guard. This would have worked out fine, except she didn't know *how* to dance. However, she caught on, with a little coaching, and soon they were two-stepping with the best of them—well almost! She loved it, as they circled the floor and danced by the stage, where she could look at the musicians and see them play their instruments for a moment, as they danced by them.

"This is the perfect vantage point to scope out the place," he whispered.

Next, they tried a polka, which didn't go very well, and then they danced a mediocre waltz. Finally, they left the dance floor for a table in the far corner and sat down. She was surprised he knew how to do these dances. Regardless of *her* lack of dance ability, she *loved* the music and the fact that the customers were having so much fun!

Happy to sit down and rest a moment, she said, "Next time, take it easy with my sore arm, and as much fun as that was, I'm beginning to feel faint from hunger *and* exhaustion— again. However, the music *is* great! I never listened to country in California, so who knew I'd like it so much? When our 'adventure' is over, I would *love* to come back to this place!"

Boone was surprised by her comments. He'd always liked country music, and he had to agree—it was an excellent band. But, he was also in need of sustenance, as they had little to eat since the escape—except for the wild berries and mushrooms. Boone rose and skirted the dance floor, returning with two large ice-filled glasses of water.

After they both took a couple of long chugs, he said, "I'm goin' back to see if I can rustle up some grub, little lady."

She laughed, "Who *are* you? I see you like to act—you're a chameleon—adaptable to any environment!" She watched the different musicians play several more songs while she waited.

When he returned, he said with a grin, "I convinced the

waitress that our car broke down, and when some guys stopped to help, they stole our wallets and phones, instead! She's gonna bring us some chow!" He chuckled.

With his explanation of how he managed to procure the food, her only comment was spoken with admiration, "Ohhh!... You're *good!*" And the next thing she knew, they were eating hamburgers and slurping wild rice soup—on the house—and when they finished their meal, she commented, "*That* food, was delicious. You know, it's hard to believe I'm actually having fun, even though we're being hunted by" our ex-captors!"

Boone smiled and sat back in his chair, "I agree, but since you brought up our predicament, we need to assess our situation. We have no idea how far behind us, our ex-captors are!"

"I'm hoping, by the time they discovered we escaped," Paisley said, "that they had trouble in the tunnels, with the twists and turns. I also hope they spent *lots* of time in the maze, trying to figure out where we exited"

"Yes, unless of course, they already *knew* the location of the exit, and started from there! However, we won't take any chances...we *must* assume those guys aren't far behind."

"Can't we hide out tonight and rest someplace dry," she pleaded, "it would be so nice, not to camp out again, or be on the run. I'm beginning to feel like a criminal on the lam!"

He laughed, "You've been watching too many whodunits," he said, matching her corny phrase. "The Bridge will give us cover for the time being...right now we're hiding in plain sight...until this place closes!"

They sat for a while in the darkened corner of the room, watching the various dancers. The waitress even brought them each a can of pop, and after a very long sip, Paisley felt like she'd died and gone to heaven! As night faded from dusk to complete darkness. Boone told her to stay put and left to investigate the

Bridge Tavern's surroundings. He slipped outside and walked the perimeter of the building, looking around the area, for a spot where they could take cover for the night, and get some much-needed rest.

Returning shortly to their table where Paisley patiently waited, he helped her to the dance floor again, for a slow two-step, to a Merle Haggard, country classic song. While they danced, he whispered his plan to her before the music ended, and without drawing attention to themselves, they casually danced towards the back door, making a furtive exit. Outside, it was cool, dark, and without a moon. Boone led the way around the back of the Bridge Tavern to the perfect hiding place. He'd found it on the westside of the building.

Boone trotted down a dirt ramp, which sloped to old basement doors at its base, and proceeded to pull the doors open, motioning Paisley to follow. They entered, and he closed the doors behind them. Boone reached in his pocket, producing a match book he'd picked up from the bar, then lit a match.

Paisley peered around the shadowy cellar and agreed it was a perfect hiding spot. Although, even with the light from the match, it was very dim inside, as their eyes adjusted. Old chairs lurked in the corners, next to tables stacked haphazardly against the back wall, casting shadows in the gloom, like discarded ghostly sentries. The large cellar ran under the dance floor and bar area, where faint strains of county music floated down from above, serenading Paisley, Boone, and the boxes full of storage items.

Boone moved one of the larger boxes in front of the door and piled more items against it. "Now we can sleep," he said, and rummaged around by the light of yet another match, finding old burlap bags, which he piled into makeshift mattresses.

"We can use these discarded tablecloths as blankets," Paisley said. The mustiness of the burlap wasn't pleasant, but Paisley didn't care...she just wanted to sleep.

They dozed off on the make-shift beds. However, Boone, a light sleeper, was awakened during the night by the sound of a helicopter. It was distant at first, but minutes later, it had moved closer. He glanced at Paisley...the noise didn't wake her. He sat still, until the noise of the helicopter faded, then breathed a sigh of relief, happy with his decision to stay off the roads for the night, and fell back into a restless sleep.

Boone woke early. Since Paisley still slept, he unblocked the cellar door and cautiously peeked outside, relieved to see it would still be a while before the sun rose. He closed the door, struck another match, then headed towards Paisley, gently shaking her. She opened one eye, but It took several minutes until she was fully awake and could stand.

Sunday, May 21, 2017 Groggy, as if she'd barely slept, it surprised her when she saw Boone up and ready to go. She stretched for a moment, then stood up and stretched again and began helping Boone replace things. He'd managed to find a candle, which made it easier to see. As soon as they finished, he slowly drew the door open a crack and glimpsed outside. It was still dark—a perfect time for their departure.

Dousing the candle, they slipped through the door, closed it and ascended the ramp. The two of them headed towards the back of the property, where Boone spotted a couple of old vehicles the night before when searching for a place to hide. It appeared to Boone that the old beaters, were used to haul supplies to The Bridge. Either one would be perfect to drive away from the area.

A seasoned nondescript old Ford truck seemed like his best bet, so he checked the wheel wells for keys, while Paisley stood watching. Her arms were folded, and she bounced up and down to warm herself in the chill of the early morning air. Boone quietly opened the rusty battered door. It made a terrible sound, which he ignored as he slid into the front seat. Checking on top of the visor for keys—he found nothing. He checked under the seat—nothing. Deciding to start the car the old-fashioned way, he pulled a couple of wires from the ignition, then struck them together until the engine sparked, chugged, and finally turned over.

Leaning over the seat, he shoved open the passenger door, "Hop in," he said with a smile, "time to get outta Dodge!"

She climbed inside, and they drove away. Boone drove the back roads while keeping an eye out for any car that might look suspicious. Thankfully, there was no daylight yet, to illuminate their hasty retreat. She sighed with relief and settled back on the ragged seat, as she breathed in the smell of car oil from the empty cans, carelessly tossed on the floor in back, by whomever owned the truck.

"Well, well," he searched the compartment between the seats, "look what *I* found in here!" He held up a battered cell phone and showed Ingles, that it still had a little battery life. "So —how about looking around to see if you can find a charger?"

CHAPTER 31

P aisley complied with Boone's request, and in a minute or two, came up with a charging cord, from under the oil cans on the floor, behind the front seat. "Bingo! I can't believe our good luck...uh-oh, scratch that idea...this truck is old and has no place to plug in a cell phone."

"Figures," he said. "I'll try a making a call anyway," and of course, he couldn't get a cell signal, so he turned it off.

Taking as many back roads as possible, he looked over and noticed Paisley had dozed off again, so he let her be. A road with a mile marker, indicated a town up ahead, and as it came into view, he picked up speed. He woke her to give her the news, and excited, she picked up the cell phone again and turned it on.

"Hey! I finally have a signal, it's weak, but it's there," she said excitedly, handing the phone to Boone. He called Dave Kaufman first but was annoyed when it went straight to voicemail. Uttering an expletive, he called Commander Walters, head of the task force.

"Wally! This is Boone!" he said, relieved, "Lucky I have your number memorized—I've lost my phone! Listen carefully, I'm with Detective Ingles, and we're both safe. We've had quite an adventure, but I'll fill you in later, as soon as I can figure out where we are. We'll be heading to Pinecrest, and I'll want to speak to Dave right away." Walters verified the arrival of the special forces, in Brainerd. They had assembled and already set up the Command Center, but Dave had gone to Boone's place.

Suddenly, the phone filled with static, and the Commander's response was unintelligible. As the signal grew weaker and the connection became spotty, Boone said, "Later—over and out!".

It was almost dawn, yet the early morning felt somber, with clouds from the previous storms, still stretching into the distance, like a giant puffy gray comforter. The small town was soon in sight, and Boone knew where he was. He diverted the truck onto a back road to Pinecrest, which zigzagged through the back streets, until they arrived at the back alley, which ran behind his cabin.

Brainerd Paisley, who had napped again, began to stir and lift her head to determine where they were, while he pulled the truck close to the back of the cabin and stopped. She began to exit the truck, but Boone stopped her saying, "Stay put while I run in, to apprise Kaufman, about our disappearance, and other important matters."

"Oh no! Not without *me!*" she said.

Hesitating a moment, he reconsidered, then motioned her to follow him, and they ran around to the front door and up the steps two at a time. Reaching the front door, he was about to knock, since he didn't have his keys, then noticed it stood slightly ajar. Puzzled, he put up his hand, indicating to Ingles, to stay still, then put his finger to his mouth, indicating silence.

He pushed on the door and opened it, as quietly as possible, while his heart pounded with anxiety, then he took two careful steps inside, Paisley at his elbow. Signaling her to stop again, he crouched and stealthily peeked around the corner of the wall, into the living area. What he saw made his blood run cold, and he involuntarily gasped.

She whispered, "What is it?"

"Don't come in—its Dave! He's dead...it's gruesome!" Anger rose inside of him. *Who did this?* He pounded his fist on the wall in frustration!

"I'm not afraid!" and she came around the corner and gasped, then clapped her hand over her mouth. All she could say was, "Boone, I'm *so sorry.*"

She remained by the door, wondering what he was going to do. Dave laid in a pool of blood, still exuding from his slashed throat, like slow-moving Ketchup. She put her hand on Boone's shoulder, as he squatted with one arm on his knee while the other hand closed Dave's eyelids over his unfocused eyes. Then he wiped his own brow. How could this have happened? He had no words.

Paisley *swore* she heard his voice crack as he asked her to dial 911. He just stared with shock and disbelief at his close friend, so brutally murdered, laying dead on his carpet. She could smell the coppery odor emanating from the pooled blood, while her heart went out to Boone, as he spent a few moments grieving.

Fading back into the hallway, she gained her composure, then stepped back in the room and picked up the phone on the desk, "Yes, 911? I'd like to report a murder."

Meanwhile, Boone mentally compartmentalized his emotions, which enabled him to spring into action. He looked around, viewing the room as a crime scene, as per the bureau's procedures. With a determined look on his face, and lips grimly pressed together, he went to his office and gathered his satellite phone, computer, guns, and ammo, from a hidden compartment in his small closet.

He put clothes, watch hats, and heavy jackets into a duffle bag, while Paisley hurriedly retrieved several of her belongings, left from her stay the other night. Handing her a duffle bag, she stuffed her things inside.They both headed outside with their gear, tossed it in the back seat of the truck, then Boone said, "Wait here, Ingles."

"Yes, sir!" She climbed into the truck and moments later, Boone slid onto the seat, taking extra precautions, by looking up and down the street, to see if they were being surveilled.

"Whoever went to the trouble of killing the people in our immediate circle, is *not* going to give up and go home—so, I'm taking some precautions!"

Feeling it was safe enough to leave, he sped down the alley, skidded around the corner and headed down a street, which would take them out of town, as fast as possible. They hadn't gone far, until just as Boone suspected, a black sedan with darkened windows, pulled out from a side street and followed at a safe distance. He expected this and quickly devised a plan. Ducking into a side street, he drove back to his cabin, where the police cars had just pulled in and parked in front of the cabin, knowing this would cause the mystery car to hang back.

He quickly circled around the back of his cabin, and coming around again, he pulled behind the unsuspecting sedan. They were close enough to the sedan, to enable Paisley, to get a license plate number. This spooked the sedan, and it tore off down the street and around the corner, with Boone on its tail, until Boone swerved into a side street, and headed in the opposite direction, and turned into a small commercial area. He parked behind a row of cars, at a local repair shop.

"Hey, Ingles, time to change vehicles," and after looking through the parked cars, he chose a van this time. It was an older model painted a sable color—like most vans—and he jimmied the door. Fortunately, he found the keys under the driver's seat this time, and after transferring their gear to the van, they waited for half an hour, until the sun attempted to rise.

Driving a block or two, he removed a new phone from his duffle bag and dialed the police station's dispatch operator. He read her the license plate information, along with the sedan's description. "Please pass on the information to one of the detectives," he said to the operator.

"Where to now, Mr. Boss Man?" Paisley quipped, although she wasn't sure he was ready for lighthearted humor. He managed a slight grin, but she apologized anyway, "Sometimes levity helps," she said

"No worries."

His attitude under these circumstances impressed her, and she began to feel guilty because after all, it was only because he tried to help *her*, that all this trouble transpired! Boone turned into a fast-food place and ordered a quick breakfast for both of them. There were dark glasses on the van's dash, which he donned, and as soon as the food was ready, he paid for it, and they left. The sky darkened, as more clouds moved in, which gave them more cover.

Pinecrest, Minnesota "We have another stop to make," he said. "...we're going to the police station."

"What for?" Her eyes widened with surprise, when he pulled up to the back entrance of the precinct.

"Go to your office and retrieve all copies of whatever you were able to decode, along with the flash drive and any other pertinent information. Also, please bring your computer—I hope it wasn't in your car?"

She thought about this for a moment and said, "Won't it be dangerous for me to go in there now? Aren't we likely to be detained by the officers working today? What if they already have the report of the murder, in *your* apartment?"

"Don't worry about that stuff, I'll make some calls on my SAT phone, while you're retrieving the materials. It'll be fine."

"Okay," she said stepping out of the car, "I guess you know what you're doing!"

Since Millie didn't usually come into work until nine or ten every morning she felt safe entering through the side door. Hurrying down the corridor, she accessed her office and rushed to the safe. She put all the contents, related to the case, in her beloved briefcase, along with her laptop.

After looking around, she added the necessary cords, paper, pens, and pencils, and shoved them into a portable file case. Once she had everything, she hurried into the hallway, closed the door, and looked up and down the corridor. Suddenly, she ran back to her office and grabbed a small printer. Luckily, there was no one coming, so she let herself out through the outside door, and piled with equipment, she struggled it into the waiting van, placing it all on the back seat.

"Whew! Okay," she said, "let's make our getaway!" Boone chuckled softly and said, "Clearly, you've been watching too many cop shows!"

CHAPTER 32

Staying off the main roads as much as possible, the two detectives headed east, through Pinecrest. The heavily clouded sky cast a gloomy pall over the landscape, as they passed through Brainerd, continuing east onto MN-18. It would be about twenty-five minutes before they reached the small town, of Garrison, nestled next to Lake Mille Lacs. Boone appeared to be deep in thought about some purposeful mission, so they drove in silence. A light rain began to fall with the promise of heavier rain, as the day progressed. Finally, they approached Garrison, slowing when they arrived.

Garrison, Minnesota "Hey Ingles, here we are, in Garrison! It's a small town, with a population of around two hundred people. It's only a half- hour or so from Brainerd, and located next to the second largest lake, in Minnesota, called Lake Mille Lacs. It's huge— almost like an ocean— you can't even see across the lake, to the other side! I read this in a brochure, when I was here a month ago."

She thought about this, "You sound like an expert...does Minnesota, really have ten thousand lakes?"

He laughed, "It does!" Then added, "There it is! The Lazy Loon Inn! Two weeks after I arrived in Pinecrest, I stayed here when I went fishing with a few of the guys from the precinct... kind of a get acquainted thing. There's a small cabin way back in the woods, with a perfect place to park the van. It's *very* secluded. The beer in their bar isn't bad either," he added, and turned to her and smiled.

Accepting his smile, she countered, "Sorry to inject some practicality into this situation, but how do you propose we pay for this?"

"I always have several backpacks with small canvas pouches packed with money, a fake ID, and anything else I might need to get out of town—fast. Naturally, I grabbed one of my backpacks, so we're all set."

"Aha! More of your covert cloak and dagger stuff." She laughed.

Grinning, he glanced at her, then put on a ball cap and the dark glasses—validating her cloak and dagger comment—and drove just far enough past the cabin rental office, so she wouldn't be seen from the office window.

"I'll be right back...stay in the van," and he hopped out and entered the office, returning several minutes later. "Well, 'Mrs. Davis', looks like we have the end cabin, way down by the woods—Cabin 17—hope that meets with your approval?"

She stammered and sputtered for a moment, "But...?"

"Take it easy...it's necessary for us to disappear, and that's our alias...we are officially married *and* undercover, this is what we cloak, and dagger people do," he said with a grin. "Now, we have a little time to figure all of this out."

"However, not to change the subject," she said, "if we're

going to be working with computers, I hope the internet works in this luxurious backwoods hideaway, in the boonies!"

"Yep! You can count on it. Lots of business people come up here to get away from it all, and they're still able to use the internet to stay in touch with the outside world."

He drove the van down the dirt road, past all the cabins, and turned left onto a smaller dirt road, leading to the last cabin-- Cabin 17. It sat deeper in the woods than the other cabins, and was the farthest away from The Lazy Loon Inn's office. They climbed out of the van and carried the gear inside, then Boone hid the van behind the cabin.

The cabin itself was typical of the area. Made of logs, it had a wooden door with a window on either side, giving it a cozy backwoods look. They entered, and it seemed chilly, since the heat hadn't been used for a while, so Boone turned up the thermostat and started a fire in the fireplace...not so much for the heat, but to take the dankness and chill out of the room.

Paisley glanced around the cabin with its spartan furnishings, before setting her bags next to one of the two, overstuffed chairs. They were predictably upholstered with fabric sporting different varieties of fish, on a forest-green background. The one-room cabin had twin beds in one corner, and a kitchenette in the other.

She turned on a floor lamp with a yellowed parchment shade, laced with thin strips of leather, which sat between the two arm chairs. A worn oval braided rug sprawled across the floor from the beds on one end of the cabin, to the hearth on the opposite side of the room. A pinewood coffee table was positioned close to the two chairs, while a door on the same wall as the beds, led to a small bathroom.

Boone carried the equipment inside and set it on a kitchen table of dark stained wood, which had been pushed against the kitchenette's bar. There were two straight back chairs meticulously scooted underneath. He draped his jacket over one of the chairs, noting the crowning glory of the room, was the swag light made of intertwined deer antlers hanging over the table. It served as the only other light in the room.

The knotty pine walls held two pictures...one was a framed print of a deer standing in a forest, and the other was a print of a wolf in snowy woods, peering through the firs, with glowing eyes. Paisley, not enamored of the artwork said, "That wolf picture is creepy," and she pointed it out to Boone, who was bringing in the rest of the gear.

He eyed it, agreed, and changed the subject, "While you unpack the equipment and set things up, I'll jog to the little market by the road, buy some groceries and make a call to my men. What supplies do we need?"

She could see the coffee maker on the counter, and checked the lower cupboards to make sure there were pots and pans available for use also, then said, "Coffee, for sure, and something for sandwiches, I guess?"

"Got it! Now, please lock and deadbolt the door, and don't open it for anyone except me."

"Of course," and she carefully locked and bolted the door, as instructed.

Entrenched in Cabin 17, Paisley set the computer on the nearby kitchen table along with the small printer, connecting them both to their adapters, and plugging the adapter cords into a nearby wall socket. Okay, Detective Boone, she thought to herself, I hope you're right about the internet?

The computer was turned on and booted—success! Next, she inserted a flash drive. The information contained, was displayed, so she printed it out to have it ready for Boone. With printouts stacked on the table, she searched for something to do while she waited.

She decided to investigate the upper cupboards in the kitchen, but unfortunately, just like the *Old Mother Hubbard* rhyme, the cupboards were bare! Still bored, she ambled over to the stuffed chair and eased into it, deciding it was a comfy place to wait for Boone's return.

On his way back from the store, Boone called Riley, who already knew who it was, and answered, "Boone, hey—you okay?"

"Yes, my wild ride to find Ingles took a radical turn, but both of us are fine now. However, before I go into that, I need to know everything you've discovered from the surveillance, because I think we've reached the critical point for this operation."

Riley briefed him, "We intercepted emails, which Misha translated for us, and the surveillance men discovered a camouflaged encampment in uncharted territory, in the Cuyuna wilderness, about two to three hours, out of town."

Boone reacted to this information, by saying, "Well, *that* checks a few boxes for me, right there!"

Riley continued, "The wire taps on Zolotov's house revealed he had men stationed in various houses, all over the Pinecrest/Brainerd area, and now, his men are amassing in preparation for a covert migration to their encampment."

"Fantastic!" Boone said, mulled this over for a moment, then asked, "And, do you have the coordinates of this encampment with information, as to their purpose?"

"All we know is there are vans packed with military-type equipment. The men are dressed in *Spetznez* KLMK (mountain pattern) uniforms, and there are several vehicles containing some sort of electrical, or perhaps scientific equipment. They've been moving a little at a time, so as not to draw attention to their activities. Some of this information has been gathered by our drones."

"I assume their equipment is going to the encampment?"

"Yes," Riley said, "and our spotters saw computer gear and food supplies in some of the trucks, *at* their encampment, but some of the other vans and trucks were covered—so who knows?"

"Great job!" Boone said, pleased that Riley's team had been so successful. "What about the actual computer intercepts? Do they reveal what they're up to?"

"Of the computer intercepts captured, several are highly encrypted, and we're working right now on the decryptions, so we can forward them to your computer. Included in the text of the intercepts, are some sort of coordinates, but we can't make out what they are, yet"

"Perfect! Keep probing and send me those intercepts over the secure link, as soon as you can. Detective Ingles is a Computer Forensics Specialist, and she's with me now, so we'll work on it too."

Riley said, "Will do, Boone."

"I'll be in touch as soon as we have something. Meanwhile, gather the men and equipment, and be ready to go, as soon as I give the word. Sorry I've been off the grid for a bit, but Detective Ingles and I have been through a dangerous ordeal. It's a long story for another time, but suffice it to say, we are still in danger and forced to keep a low profile, and I believe *this* group is responsible!"

"That reminds me," Riley interjected, "you might be interested in knowing the men spotted two large helicopters—without any markings—hidden in a makeshift hanger in the woods, at their camp."

"Hmmm...thanks Riley. I'll be in touch, as soon as I have more info." He discussed a few more business items to be taken care of, regarding notifying the precinct and Ingles' Aunt. Boone gave Riley their contact information and relayed the story they were to be told. "Thanks again, Riley. Over and out."

"Roger that," and Riley hung up. Boone put away his SAT phone and headed back to the cabin, while Paisley dozed in her chair. Awakened by a knock on the door, she rose instantly, her heart pounding.

Tiptoeing over to the door, she asked, "Who is it?" in her sternest voice.

"It's Boone!" When she opened the door, Boone was laughing and said, "From the tone of your voice, it's as if you expected to hear, 'I'm the big, bad wolf, and I'll huff and I'll puff and I'll blow your house down'..."

She felt silly for being scared—but relieved—and laughed as her fearfulness evaporated. Boone carried the grocery bags to the counter, set them down, and emptied them. As soon as she set the can of coffee on the counter, she snatched it up and opened it. The delicious aroma of the coffee grounds floated up, and she breathed deeply, enjoying scent.

Filling the coffee pot with water, she glanced over her shoulder, "What took you so long?"

Boone apologized, filling her in on the call to his men, and explained that they had been worried about him, because, "Except for a short phone call from my apartment, all they knew was, I'd dropped off the grid for longer than expected. I recounted what happened, as succinctly as possible, and told Riley to cover for us at the precinct, including contacting your Aunt to let her know it would be best if she stayed in the cities to be safe until things are wrapped up here."

"How did you get hold of her?"

"Easy! Her number was taken off the house phone when your Aunt left several messages for you." Paisley began to ask another question, but Boone interrupted her mid-sentence, adding, "Yes, Millie was also contacted and told to be careful."

"Just like that?"

"Yes," he said, "just like that!" He hesitated for a moment, then a serious look appeared on his face.

"What? Why are you looking at me like that—what's wrong?"

"I didn't want to tell you like this, but maybe it's best." The look of fear on her face concerned him, but he continued anyway, "Riley disclosed something to me about your Aunt. When he talked with her, she wanted you to know...your Uncle...he passed away."

Paisley stood, staring at him, but he wasn't sure if she heard him. He started to repeat it, but before he could repeat the words a second time, a pained look fell across her face, and tears began to slide down her cheeks. She stood perfectly still, not making a sound.

Boone wasn't sure what to do and stepped over to put his arms around her for comfort. It felt awkward because he wasn't sure his comfort was wanted, but he did it anyway...his heart went out to her as he felt her sadness. They stood like that for a minute or two, until she lifted her head off his chest and stepped back from him.

"I'm sorry," she sniffled, then wiped her tears with the palms of her hands and the sleeves of her shirt and said, "I'm okay now. I think we have work to do."

"You, sure?" he asked.

"I am. Whatever grieving there is, I can do it later. I know our job here is important."

Surprised by her answer *and* focus, he wondered under his breath, "Who *is* this person?"

The coffee was ready, and she poured two cups and set them on the breakfast bar. "How would you like yours?" she asked.

"Black."

"Same here," and she continued silently processing the devastating information, as she put the groceries away, then grabbed a plate from the cupboard, and arranged four dough-nuts on it.

"You *sure* you want to do this?" he asked.

"The doughnuts were a nice touch," was her answer, as she put the plate on the counter.

Boone, puzzled at the control she had over her emotions, picked out a jelly doughnut. Both sat on stools by the counter, quietly sipping their coffee and eating doughnuts, until she brushed her hands together dusting off the crumbs, and said determinedly, "Let's get started!"

CHAPTER 33

Boone removed Dave Kaufman's briefcase from the murder scene before Ingles called 911 for him. Its contents included a computer, hacking programs, and surveillance information, which had to be protected from falling into the wrong hands—even those of the police.

"Thank goodness the perp didn't take Dave's briefcase!" Boone said as he unpacked it and set the discs on the table along with other papers.

"Now, please bring me up to speed on everything you have concerning the flash drive and its cryptic message. My men are waiting to see what information it contains—I assure you—this mission is serious. I have two teams in place, and another team, who will work with me, and all are poised and ready to act as soon as we know exactly what we're confronting."

"Serious how?" she said. "You've divulged very little to me..." Her voice trailed off.

"First things, first, *you* tell *me* what *you* have, and I'll fill in the gaps," he said. "Now, what have you found on the flash drive...tell me everything."

She began, "The night I was late to Casa Café for our meeting, I decided to see what the flash drive contained, because I thought perhaps there would be a clue, as to its owner. Since it was password-protected, the thought crossed my mind that maybe it was linked to the murder." She was silent for a moment.

"So, you *did* open the drive!" He wanted to hurry her along with her story but sensed he needed to be patient.

"Well, I began to feel guilty, because after I found it, I didn't turn it over to the police." She looked at the coffee in her cup. "However, I'd already committed to discovering its owner, so I pressed on. Of course, hacking passwords don't easily stop me, because it's part of my job description, so I grabbed a password cracking disc and inserted it into my computer." She paused and sighed.

"And?" he urged her.

"Like I told you before, I discovered this was no ordinary password. I had to use my most sophisticated software, which uses complicated algorithms to do the job." She stood up and grabbed the coffee pot and asked Boone if he wanted more. He nodded, and she poured some for him, then topped off *her* cup. "I popped in the disc, let it run for a while, and finally it turned up a password."

Boone was getting impatient with this story because she'd already told her some of this. He grabbed another donut then said, "Yes, and the password was *chemodan*."

"This is the weird part," she raised her head and looked directly into his eyes and continued, "that's right—what I saw, was in a foreign alphabet—Cyrillic—and Russians use that alphabet!"

Boone wanted her to hurry past the part she'd already told him. "Yes, yes...you told me this, is that all?" he said. "I still wish you'd told me about this at dinner that evening!"

She looked sheepish, then replied, "Part of it was because I felt from the beginning that *you* were holding something back from *me*...maybe you weren't being forthcoming about who you were, or something—so I didn't feel it was the right time. I decided to work on it more before I came to you with any information. I only had the word *chemodan*, and I didn't want to look foolish."

"Even *that* information—little though it was—would have been important," Boone said.

"I'm so sorry," her eyes watered, and her lip quivered. "I know. I should have turned the drive over to the police, no matter what, regardless of whether it would hold a clue, or not."

She looked down at the computer and avoided looking him in the eyes. She felt uncomfortable, so she stood up and walked to the coffee pot for another refill. Seeing her distress at having divulged her unprofessional handling of the flash drive, he softened a little.

"Don't worry...it's fine because regardless, I know the flash drive will reveal the rest of the puzzle pieces."

He watched her return slowly to her chair, then added, "I'm sorry I wasn't more forthcoming about my identity and connection to this case, but with all we've gone through, I think it's time to bring you into the loop."

He waited for her reaction. This sudden change of direction surprised her.

"You mean I was right? You really *aren't* who you say you are!" She had an incredulous tone in her voice, as she realized her sixth sense was on target, adding, "So, probably Deedrick Boone isn't even your *real* name!"

For a moment, all sorts of betrayals scrolled through her head leaving her confused, angry, and somehow relieved. Surprised, Boone could see her facial expressions change, as thoughts flickered through her eyes. These thoughts were revealed, by a kaleidoscope of emotions, scrolling on her face, like an old-time silent movie!

"Let me explain."

"I'm all ears!" she said, struggling to get her emotions under control.

Giving her a kindly smile, Boone told her of his connection to Washington, D.C., the FBI, and CIA, and the reason he'd been sent to Pinecrest.

She was stupefied by the high-level list of acronyms and listened with rapt attention, for the next five minutes, as he admitted his affiliation with an FBI Counter-Terrorism Special Forces Unit, and his assignment to head up three tactical groups.

With this statement, her eyebrows rose in surprise, "This sounds incredulous...is this for *real*?" And realizing she was still standing, she sat down in her chair. She folded her hands in her lap as she listened to him, recount the facts about the contact's conversation, between Mr. Ohm, and an undercover FBI agent in the Minneapolis Bureau, four months ago.

"How did *that* happen?" She was dumbfounded.

"The FBI has a watch list, and undercover agents get tips all the time. A tip came in from a man of Russian descent who was here in the US on a student visa. He wanted to sell some crucial information on the black market. He described it as critical and wanted to sell to an entity, for as much money, as possible. "

"This is just like out of a *spy* movie!"

"I suppose it seems like that, but the information supposedly involved a weapon of mass destruction, which of course, might affect our national security, and possibly that of other countries. Information like this gets immediate attention from Washington, and *must* be taken seriously!"

"I'm sorry, but this doesn't seem real!"

Now, it was Boone's turn to stand up and refill his coffee cup. Taking a sip, he set it on the breakfast bar and began to pace, "I can understand how all this must sound, but it's true! I was selected to set up a meeting with him as soon as he contacted me."

"Oh, my gosh! That sounds dangerous."

"This is why I couldn't confide in you because the bureau was unable to discern his identity at the time, so I waited several months for him to make contact. The information our Minneapolis Bureau was able to glean, was credible enough by this time, for the Washington Bureau to take action, and I was sent straight to Pinecrest."

Ingles felt overwhelmed, "So, did you make contact?"

Boone continued, "I was told the information was linked to the Russian Mafia because there'd been a steady flow of Russians, over the last two years, to areas in Minnesota, and to Crow Wing County, specifically. With a hint of international terrorism, our government needed to move quickly, and this is why I'm here. And no, I never made contact."

"So, what *is* your real name?" she said, interrupting his story.

"Are you listening to what I'm explaining to you, or are you stuck on the name thing?" He could tell by her expression—it was the name-thing, and said, "As far as anyone here is concerned, Deedrick Boone is my real name. I have other aliases because of my job, and my real name is never used—it's for my safety—*and* the safety of others."

"Okay, okay," she said, "I'll admit, I'm disappointed with the answer, but for the time being, I'll let it go." She smiled and settled down again, as he clarified the importance of their findings.

He stopped pacing, putting his hands flat on the table, leaning over them, and told her, "I believe I was unable to meet with the informant, because..."

"Wait," she interrupted, as her eyes registered the answer, "...the informant was Gregore Kamorov, *wasn't* it?"

Boone nodded, "Yes, I believe Kamorov is—was—the informant. He called himself Mr. Ohm, and was murdered before I could ever talk, or meet with him."

"I *knew* it!" she said, triumphantly!

Boone took his hands off the table and sat on a stool by the counter, with his coffee. "Yes, it seems logical, but regardless, whatever is going on, it appears to be a *very* serious matter!"

"Oh, my gosh," she said, "it makes total sense."

"Furthermore," he continued, "if the information from this flash drive pans out, it will lend credence to my theory. Now, it seems obvious why the flash drive was an object of so much interest, that people were willing to kill for it...*and* it explains the attacks on *you*! Something is on the flash drive, which these people desperately want, so it's imperative for us to begin working right now to ascertain what kind of information it contains."

"Thanks for the clarification," Paisley said, amazed at these revelations.

"Well, let's get busy! It's up to us to save the world!" Boone quipped.

This caught her attention. "How can you sound, so cavalier? You just scared me to death with talk of an international plot, and now you're joking about it?" Her indignation was palpable.

Not really," he said. "We've got important work to do, and I was just trying to lighten things up a little."

Her only response was, "Dahhh!" Then she cracked a slight smile and said, "Okay, let's do it!"

With decryption software at her fingertips, Paisley sat down at the computer and slid a disc into the DVD drive, then began entering commands. Boone watched, as the computer displayed lines of gibberish on the screen, which made no sense to him. She continued to key in codes, and pull up various screens while letters, digits, and graphs, appeared and disappeared on the monitor.

Ten minutes later, working with the files as they scrolled down the screen, she set specific parameters, then sat back, "Now we wait for the software to do its work."

Boone picked up their coffee cups, went to the sink to dump out the dregs, then brewed a fresh pot of coffee. When it was ready, he poured them both another cup. Returning to the table, he set the cups down, far enough away from any possibility of being accidentally spilled on the computer, *or* the papers.

She grabbed her cup, took a sip and turning to Boone asked, "Do you have access to anyone, who speaks Russian?"

"I do," he said, rocking back on the two back legs of his chair.

"Good," she said, "because it will save a lot of time. Right now, what I've seen so far, looks like it's all in Russian, just like the password. We can send a copy to your interpreter for translation into English once we have the rest of the files from Kamorov's flash drive and computer decrypted and printed out."

"Sure, not a problem," he said.

"I'm presuming your translator is yet, another person, in your cadre of specialists, whom you have at your fingertips," she chided.

Bong, bong, bong! The clock on the fireplace mantel began to chime, and they both jumped. They were still on edge from their harrowing experiences of the past several days. The sudden unexpected chiming of the clock served to illustrate the point.

Relaxing again, Boone said quietly, "I speak fluent Russian, so *I* will be the one to translate it."

"*You?*" She turned and looked at him, mouth agape!

"Another piece of information I neglected to mention, I speak fluent Russian, German, Pashto and Arabic."

"*Wow*! I'm speechless!"

Boone looked at the clock then excused himself, "I have to make another call, Ingles," and he stepped outside to contact Riley on his SAT phone, while Paisley continued monitoring the computer.

"Riley, this is Boone again. Listen, we're almost finished with the decryption. I'll call the minute we know what we're dealing with, but in the meantime, it's a 'go' for our plan...set things in motion, *now!*"

Boone re-entered the bungalow with a cell phone.

"Where did that come from?"

"I have several special cell phones in different go-bags, in case the one I'm using has a 'mishap'. They're burner phones— just use and toss. If I can't toss it in time, and it's confiscated, the phones are coded, so if anyone tries to use them, all its information is automatically deleted—kind of like Mr. Phelps, from the old TV show, *Mission Impossible.*"

"What?" Ingles seemed confused.

"Should you choose to accept this mission...blah, blah, blah...then this message will self-destruct..." he said.

She just shook her head, "Oh. This covert world of yours, is new to me--but—I *do* find it exciting," she grinned, still having no idea what he was referring to?

While they waited for results, Paisley decided to avail

herself of the opportunity to find out whatever she could about the Russian Mafia in the Lakes Area. She logged onto Google with Boone's computer, typed in "Russians in the Brainerd Lakes," and perused the topics presented by the search engine.

There were a few Brainerd Lakes references, regarding hotels, and a Heartland Symphony Orchestra concert series—Russian Masters. Scrolling further, a Russian Vodka Mirror Sign for $35.00 could be found on Craig's List, etc. Before she tried a different search topic, something caught her eye, and there it was! It Immediately grabbed her attention The title read, "When the Cold War Paid a Visit to Brainerd, Minnesota", by a local reporter, dated Jan., 2012.

CHAPTER 34

Paisley eagerly read several reports, including some congressional records, which suggested the KGB hid weapon cashes, near Brainerd, Minnesota, and in other locations in the US, during the Cold War. It was even mentioned, that the Soviets had given these caches in Brainerd, the code names of 'Aquarium I' and 'Aquarium II'!

Regardless of the tone of the articles, it spurred Paisley to perform more specific searches. As the first article printed, she handed it to Boone to peruse. At the same time, she entered several more searches, which unearthed other articles, more specific in nature, and substantially more sobering in their content. These were also printed and tossed over to Boone.

"What the heck!" There was surprise in his voice, "If this is what I think it is, then we're *definitely* going down the right road!" After giving a low whistle, he said, "This positively merits, calling out the 'big boys'!"

"I'm finding more articles, Paisley said, "I'll print them out, and we can read them later, but for the moment, suffice it to say, I can give you the abridged version. Here goes. It seems *some* Russians may have discovered the probable location of one of these caches, which *might* contain a suitcase bomb, or other ordinates, with which to make some sort of weapon, of mass destruction...aka, a WMD!"

"It's certainly all coming together!" Boone said.

Pausing a moment to look at him, she continued, "And, *I* think these Russians are coming down the home stretch—to retrieve it!"

"Interesting...I totally agree."

"Well," she continued anyway, despite his seemingly lackluster answer, "I guess you *and* me, and your platoons, or whatever, must beat them to the punch! Sounds like the making of some superhero movie, right?"

"I think..." Boone started to say, but was interrupted.

"So, it's Boone—the Camouflage Man—and his band of sidekicks, who save the world from the evil Russians, from the Soviet Union! Or, is it just called Russia now? I forget," she laughed.

Looking at her with a smirk on his face, he said, "Are you through, miss 'how-can-you-joke' about this?"

"Oops! I'm sorry? I'm...just over-tired and overwhelmed by this thought, and when I can't deal with reality, I guess I fall back on humor, too—wrong time?" she asked, with a sheepish look on her face, "Too soon?"

He gave her another kindly smile. "I understand. I'm used to being in dire situations and forget this must be a lot for a detective, new to the PPD, to comprehend. However, I thought of another possibility."

"Like what?" She stood up and picked another donut, out of the box, since the ones Boone had put on the plate were gone.

"Based on the shady character of Mr. Zolotov and his group, this may not be for national reasons. I think they're planning to put it on the black market, for some staggering price, to sell to other, not-so-integrity-oriented nations *or* terrorist groups!"

"I never considered that, but you're probably right!"

"Because," he continued, "if a lawless terrorist group were to obtain this weapon, it would be the worst-case scenario. These bad actors would pay gobs of money to get their hands on a suitcase bomb—or *even* its fissile nuclear material!"

Paisley had taken umbrage with Boone's condescending statement, "…a lot for a new detective in the PPD, to comprehend…!" But before she could speak, the computer hummed to a stop…the decryption complete.

The silence felt ominous, and both were somber for an exiguous moment, until Paisley resumed downloading information about suitcase bombs from various websites. Boone sat passively reading the printouts handed to him. After several minutes, the decrypted information appeared on the monitor, in the form of discernible word-groupings.

The document was in *Russian*! Boone became agitated and scooted his chair closer to the computer, "Ingles, I need these documents printed!"

Putting more paper in the printer tray, Boone watched, as it began clicking, whirring, and making assorted other noises, while he eagerly waited. When the first page came up on the monitor, he reached for a spiral notebook and waited—watching the computer screen, as the pages printed. He was eager to begin translating the decrypted message.

When the printer stopped, and the printed pages sat in the tray, Paisley leaned back in her chair and stretched her arms in the air, realizing how tense her back muscles were from her concentrated efforts over the keyboard.

While Boone began typing on his computer, as fast as he could to translate the pages, he uttered strange sounds and expletives, as he worked, while also jotting notes in his spiral notebook. Paisley was rife with curiosity but didn't want to distract him in any way. He completed his translations, and sat in stunned silence for a moment, before asking her to move closer, so he could show her what the pages revealed

To her horror, as he read aloud, all their fears were realized, because the papers confirmed their worst nightmare. The object sought by the Russians, was indeed, a suitcase bomb, better known in Zolotov's, communications from his Russian boss, as the *chemodan*, or in English, the suitcase!

Boone's grasp of the Russian language astonished Paisley, and realizing he had these amazing skills, along with his newly divulged job description, she suddenly felt very small and inadequate.

"Okay," she said, for lack of anything else to say, and turned her attention to the computer screen. Both fell silent. Time had dragged for Boone, but *now*, having the information they sought, there was so much at stake! Now, time was of the essence!

"It's clear, according to these older articles from my research," Paisley said, "that the suitcase bomb the Russians are looking for, was one of many ordinates buried in different locations around the world, at least according to some government Intel!"

She grabbed another article and read bits and pieces to Boone, and both understood the ramifications of this information. Her gaze was fixed on Boone. "I guess it's time to act to prevent the worst-case scenario from happening," she said. "Do you have a plan D, since we've already used A, B, and C?"

Boone looked at her with such grim determination that she

paled for a moment, never having seen a look like this on his face, and she was filled with fear—he wasn't amused anymore!

"What are we going to do?" she asked, "I hope your plan will save Brainerd—and possibly the world?" He laughed out loud this time when he saw the serious look on *her* face. His laugh made her smile, too. She couldn't believe she said that—again! However, this was no time to be joking, but then again, she *wasn't* kidding!

Boone's face became serious again, and he said, "I need to contact my men...there's no time to explain everything right now, so please trust me and do what I say—no questions asked— I'll explain everything to you, as needed, and the rest later, because this *is* the time for action...deal?"

She hesitated for a moment and looked deeply into his eyes, replying with great seriousness, "Deal! Just tell me what to do."

"Come on then, let's pack up this equipment, and please make a couple of printouts of the translated info. While you do that, I have calls to make!"

He started out the door but quickly turned around to tell her he sent a special email address to her. She was to email a copy of the translated info to that address, then erase the message. He turned again and ran out the door to the van to grab his SAT phone.

"Riley?"

"Here, boss."

"Give me whatever you have, I'm finished here, and packing up now," he said, tossing a satchel into the back of the van.

"First," Riley said, "I want you to know, we've done a prelim investigation of Dave Kaufman's murder, in your apartment."

"And?" Boone grimaced at the mention of Dave's name, as it brought back the bloody mess he'd confronted, the night before.

"I think we've found the perp's car, and needless to say it

was stolen and wiped clean—of course! We're testing other samples taken from the car, but chances are, they belong to its owner, not the perp."

"Figures!" Boone muttered.

"Based on a description given to us by a man who'd been walking his dog around the time of the murder," Riley added, "the suspect had been hanging around a park close to the spot where the car was stolen. When the perp walked by the witness with the dog, the witness heard the man talking on his cell, apparently arguing with someone, in what the witness thought, was some sort of foreign language. He believed it sounded like Russian, but couldn't be sure."

"Was the guy close enough to get a description?"

"Yes, he gave a pretty good description, because he thought it was weird the way the man was behaving. The witness circled the park twice with his dog, It was the second pass where he heard the perp on his cell, and said the man was very focused on the phone call."

"Okay, maybe a lucky break, I hope!"

"We brought the witness in and showed him our version of mug shots, Russian style—that is, only the perps found to be in the US, from Russia—and Bingo! Our perp is a two-bit crook, probably on the payroll of the Russians. We're still researching his background, to find out more. We've got a couple of men trying to locate him now, but no luck yet. The Russian group here in Minnesota is a tricky and deadly bunch connected to the Russian Mafia, willing to kill whoever gets in their way."

"Okay, good job Riley. I want to get this low-life, at any cost," and he ordered Riley to have the men and trucks ready to roll, explaining the coordinates of the actual site are in an email, just now, being sent over the Agency's network. "Also, tell Sanchez to print out multiple copies for the men on the task force."

"Roger, that!" Riley acknowledged.

"Make sure everyone has their protective and tactical gear with them, according to whichever part of the operation, they've been assigned. And please bring a set for me—in fact bring another couple of sets in the smallest size. I'm bringing Detective Ingles, with me to protect her from any attacks by these animals. It's a *long* story for later!"

Riley answered, "Roger that, and I think the email just arrived, so I'll start immediately."

"Oh, and when you have a chance," Boone said, "log onto the secure site to acquire the tactical maps relayed to us, from our spy planes on duty, with their satellite equipment. Thanks to them, we have the exact location of the Russian's bivouac, and it will be our first strike point!"

"We'll be ready, Boone," Riley responded. "Now, what about the rest of the team?"

Boone said, "The rest of the team will focus on retrieval. If we can take out most of their forces with the first team, we'll have no interference in *our* extraction. I listed all the equipment to be flown to the retrieval location, including the nuclear physicists, whom I've arranged to have on call, along with the equipment they'll need."

"You got it, Boss, it'll be handled, stat."

Boone walked back towards the cabin and paused in his conversation. As he approached the cabin's door, it flew open, and Ingles came barreling out with equipment to put in the van. Brushing by him, she set the computers and printer by the truck, and hustled back for the last few backpacks.

Boone turned his back to her as he finished the conversation with Riley. "I'll be on my way shortly. I'll call you back, so we can discuss the rest our plan, and we'll go from there. It's imperative that we beat them to the punch! We can't afford to fail, because from what you told me, they could already be on their way, so we *must* arrive first—before it becomes a *real* situation!"

"Roger that!" And Riley broke their connection.

CHAPTER 35

Cuyuna Iron Range

"Off we go!" Boone said. "Now, I'll call Riley to verify plans for this operation while we drive."

Boone took out the SAT phone and called headquarters. His Task Force Leader, picked up, and Boone said, "Riley, what's new?"

Riley closed the door to the communications room for privacy and quiet, then said, "That was fast! Look, at this point, I think our best plan now that we know what's really at stake is to consider who we're up against. It's a bunch of Russians! We figured out what they're bringing to the table, and on this basis, we've determined what *we* need to bring, to that *same* table."

"Perfect!" Boone said, "So, hit me with everything you've uncovered about their assets. Who are they, and how do they operate?"

As Paisley listened intently to Boone's conversation, she could hear a tone in his voice, which revealed the confidence he had in Riley's abilities. She leaned her head back on the seat, exhausted from the morning's stressful work, and continued to listen, while Boone apprised Riley of the information just obtained from the decrypted documents.

Boone asked, "Are we still tailing Russians? If so, what did you find out?"

"The rest of the men, connected to this Zolotov character, are definitely Russians. There seems to be a whole boatload of them living here in Crow Wing County. Zolotov contacted them by phone and fortunately, Mishka was here to translate for us. We ascertained from the conversations, that whatever Zolotov had planned was critical, and he ordered the group to amass today somewhere, in the Cuyuna Range."

"Do you have the specific location?"

"We're still working on it. We planted bugs in Zolotov's home, to tap into their communications, and managed to attach a GPS device to Zolotov's car, but of course, one of the new guys in town picked him up in a black van with no visible license plate. It appeared to be a tactical vehicle!"

"These guys are cagey! Do you think they know w're surveilling them?"

"I don't think so," Riley answered, "but can't be sure...we have a man tailing them now. The Russians have been driving off-road through deserted areas, for several hours. We should know their final location soon."

"Perfect! Let me know their *exact* location, as soon as possible. We have pinpointed the area with our satellites, and now, we need to zoom in to the *exact* spot."

"Also, according to our man, Jim," Riley continued, "another group of tactical vehicles, are being followed. They left hours before the second group, and stopped in an area close to a cluster of old historical mine sites. They're setting up a camp near a large, ramshackle storage barn. Looks like they're waiting for the others to arrive. The conversations we intercepted, which Mishka translated, indicated there may be upwards of twenty, or thirty men expected at the camp, soon!"

"What the heck?" Boone exclaimed. "Are they sending a platoon? I didn't anticipate those numbers! It's like they're coming out of the woodwork—it's a Russian infestation! I knew this wouldn't be a cake-walk, but *this* is ridiculous! Well, in a way, I guess I'm not surprised, because what they're planning, *is* BIG!"

"And yes, Boone, there *is* a tracking device on one of the vehicles in that group, too." Riley added, "According to the reconnaissance by our head man, Dino, with Mishka translating, this is *not* a KGB-type military group, but more akin to a bunch of Russian Mafia mercenaries, assembled into a guerrilla group, and like rebels, they're ready to fight with whatever they can get their hands on, which is plenty!"

Even with the noise of the van's engine, the speed with which Boone drove caused the van to jounce along, adding to the din. Nonetheless, Paisley was still able to hear some of what Riley said. She felt like she was eavesdropping on something top secret! She was beginning to feel drowsy.

Riley said, "The men did a great job gathering Intel, which indicated these thugs don't have the newer weaponry, but instead, are using weapons such as the good old Makarov PNs, which holds 8+1, 9 x 18 mm rounds. They're older, but probably work better for *this* particular band of Russians!"

"Figures," Boone said, "because since the 80s, those weapons are easy to acquire anywhere in the US, and they wouldn't even need to smuggle them into our country!"

Opening her eyes for a moment, Paisley glanced out the window, then panicked, "Look out!" she yelled, as they careened around a twist in the road, narrowly missing a tree positioned too close to the road. Boone took the warning in stride, avoided the tree and looked at her, puzzled by her concern. She settled herself down again, after her scare.

Riley continued, "We also think the men have AK-47 C's—aka, Kalashnikovs, but from a distance, it was hard to tell. My men said it looked like the shortened version, which would be easier to carry because it uses shorter rifle rounds, (760 x 39)."

"Good to know, Riley!"

"Through our extensive research, we know these men are extremely tough criminals and will attack like a typical guerrilla force. We've seen and dealt with these types before!"

"I hear you on *that* one," Boone said. "Yes, they're low-tech, and use the finger-point-and-fire technique, instead of gun sights!" He chuckled.

"Well, that may be, but these men look extremely ferocious, and Mishka thinks some of them are from the Special Forces Unit, *Spetsnaz*! However, you'll be pleased to know, the radar imagery of the area where the first group traveled, enabling us to locate their exact bivouac, which matches the info from our drones. Several armored personnel carriers were spotted, which are also easy enough to acquire, in the US."

Boone ruminated on this for a moment, as he raced down the road, and furrowing his brow, he commented, "This is disturbing."

"And, I hate to tell you, Boss," Riley added as a sidebar, " but get this—we think they *also* have a couple of RPG's!" Riley put Boone on hold for a moment.

Paisley couldn't believe what she heard and whispered, "How did they manage *that*?"

"Easy," Boone said, in a serious tone, "the stuff is smuggled from South Africa to South America, and from there, up to Mexico, then across the Mexican border into the US. All they have to do then is pick up a transport vehicle and head for Minnesota, with their cargo."

At this information, she managed a weak whistle, "They certainly *do* mean business!"

Riley came back on line and proceeded, "Sorry for the interruption, but to continue, I want you to know, according to our assessment of the situation, as of this moment and in our best judgement, that we have the advantage in this operation."

"I would *hope* so, " Boone responded.

"The men, whom you've chosen are highly trained in the use of the latest technology. There are twenty-five men here at the moment, skilled in all the areas needed, so how would you like to proceed?"

Frowning for a moment, as the van continued to lurch along the road, throwing out dust clouds, he answered, "Here's what I think we should do. We'll divide the men into two teams, Alpha and Delta." Boone, knowing they had all the coordinates, continued, "Alpha will go directly to the location of the suitcase bomb, where all the equipment necessary to retrieve it will be located."

"Copy that," Riley said, "and I have the list of the equipment and vehicles already delivered to the area, where you'll be encamped, including everything needed for the actual extraction. We've been busy bees! I'll go over all of it with you when you arrive at base camp."

"Roger that." Boone said, and they disconnected. Once the conversation was over, Paisley couldn't help herself from asking, "Who *is* this Riley, guy?"

"Riley? Matt Riley, is first in command of my task force, and compiled the maps and information needed for our tactical operation. You and I furnished the last bit of data needed to make this operation a 'go'!"

She calmly said, "Roger that," knowingly using Boone's

lingo, and smiled to herself, then settled into the car seat to get more comfortable before asking, "What's your connection to Riley? Anything other than you work together? It seems like you're more than just teammates."

"Astute of you to notice, because Matt Riley and I go *way* back. We attended the same academy in Maryland, where we forged our friendship. Military school, with all its demands and expectations, can make or break you, and neither one of us, were the type to be broken. Therefore, we became very competitive, both of us graduating with honors. We were sent on a tour of duty in Iraq, and later to Afghanistan, but always in the same area. Although we served in different units, we *did* see each other frequently."

"Go on," she said, "surely, that can't be all?"

She was being jostled around on her seat, as the dirt roads became rougher. On occasion, she put her hands on the dashboard to counterbalance herself around turns. Having Boone talk gave her something else to concentrate on, making his crazy driving easier to handle. She encouraged him to continue.

"Okay, I suppose it won't hurt. Riley was a sharpshooter, and I served in a special unit, which handled security, and I became an embedded spy in the Iraqi citizenry, tasked with infiltrating groups associated with Isis and the Taliban, to gain sensitive information, on their leaders. I was also sent to some locations, to assassinate identified leaders. We both excelled in our ability to speak the languages."

Ingles, surprised by this revelation said, "*Wow*. Maybe I shouldn't have asked?"

"If it bothers you, I won't say anymore."

"No, it's okay...please...go ahead...I want to hear the rest."

"Well, I'll be brief. When the war was finally over, Riley and I returned to the US, and were individually recruited for a

Special Forces Unit with the CIA, which took us to Afghanistan, where we served in the same small elite group."

"But you're not in a unit now, yet I get the impression that you have contracted men you knew to help on this operation. Is this true?"

"Well, yes, it's true, but I haven't told you the rest."

"Okay...I'm still listening..."

"Riley married when he returned from Iraq, but with his kind of work, the marriage was short-lived, and his wife divorced him. He then went to Quantico for two years, and became a member of the FBI for a while, before contracting out."

She sighed heavily in frustration and said, "Aren't you going to tell me the rest about you? Did you marry?" She was annoyed that he was making her drag it out of him. Boone was quiet, concentrating on his driving. One side glance told her he was weighing his decision as to whether he should divulge more information.

"I'm sorry," she said quickly, "you don't need to answer. I didn't mean to pry."

He began speaking again, "I married five years after joining Special Forces, but like Riley, after three years, my marriage ended in divorce. Marriage is a casualty of this profession, due to the dangers and months spent in faraway places, where communication is difficult—if not impossible! It takes its toll and accounts for the above-average divorce rate for men in this line occupation. There are a few who manage to make it work, but they're few and far between."

Paisley wondered if he told her everything, but decided not to push any further since the information satisfied her for the time being. She was quiet and content...back to enduring the difficult ride. As she gazed out the window, trees, brush, and tangled undergrowth flew by scratching the sides of the van, its windows, and roof, as they bounced along.

"Hopefully, we'll be there soon," she said.

Exhaustion from the intense events of the morning, and fear of what was next, nagged at her after listening to the conversations between Boone and Riley. Boone was as intent as ever, pushing the van through the difficult terrain towards their destination, at breakneck speed.

Yanked from her thoughts when the van careened to the left, she could tell they were on another dirt road, barely driveable, and covered with saplings and vegetation. After a few jarring minutes, they emerged into a clearing occupied by a large encampment.

Three or four large tents were set up in the clearing, along with an extremely large tent, and finally, a group of smaller tents to accommodate each of the men. Tactical vehicles and trucks of various sizes appropriated for the mission were parked at the perimeter of the clearing, along with giant tractors and other machinery.

"Are we at the site of the suitcase bomb?" Paisley asked, apprehensively.

CHAPTER 36

Cuyuna Range, Base Camp
"No, we're far enough away for safety," Boone assured her and smiled, stretching his arms to the sky as he tried to unwind from the arduous drive.

"The entrance to its actual location is about a half mile or more away. I requested our command center to be set up here, where we'd be more camouflaged by the densely wooded area." He added calmly, "I'd like you to sit here for a little bit while I check in with my men."

He spoke with such kindness as she gazed into his eyes. Who *is* this man? There are so many facets to his personality, she thought. Leaning back against her seat, with one foot still dangling out the door, she watched him stride towards the tents, where men were milling around. Mulling over all the things Boone needed to plan for this mission, she chastised herself for asking so many personal questions, as they drove to this camp when he needed to focus on more critical things.

The camp perimeter was shaded by sentry-like jack pines,

aged oak trees, which towered into the cloud-filled sky, and birches, with their dappled bark. Paisley wasn't very knowledgeable when it came to plants and trees, even though they seemed to be waving their branches at her. She enjoyed taking in the beauty of the area, with the tents set up, as if it were some innocuous family camping trip. The large transport trucks and armored vehicles stationed at the clearing's perimeter belied the innocence of the campsite, and brought the reality of the mission into focus. It seemed a bit surreal.

"Have the communications team give you all the latest info on the status, of the Russians," Boone ordered, "...and now, what's our final plan?"

Riley referred to his notepad. "Here goes! We have a tracker on Zolotov's vehicle, so the minute it leaves Brainerd and heads to *his* compound, Delta One, led by Carson, will follow it out of town and capture it as soon as it's in an unpopulated area. The team will have Zolotov in captivity, thus cutting off the head of the snake. Mishka will translate for Carson, if necessary "

Boone, Riley, and a team of men filed into the main tent and sat at one of the tables. Riley continued, "Delta Two, led by Perez, will infiltrate the area around the Russian encampment and ready themselves for a firefight, then Delta Three, led by Chaser, will rush the compound and attack. Also, Vasily will go along to translate."

"Will the transport heli be on hand in a secure location? It has to be ready to pick up our men, their prisoners, and casualties, from the aftermath of the attack," Boone added.

"Yes," Riley said, "and then it will be the Russians' guerrilla-like, blunt-force old-school warfare tactics against our new technologies and strategies—*and* I predict we'll win!"

"Now that's a plan! Copy that!" Boone said menacingly, and they all agreed.

Shortly after leaving the main tent, Boone looked back at the van, caught Paisley's eye, and beckoned her to join him. She hopped out of the van and hustled over to stand next to him, while he introduced her to the small group he'd just addressed. The men stared at her with curiosity. He introduced Tom Mitchell to her as he was to see that she was outfitted with the clothing she would need for the rest of the day, and the next. Boone also requested Mitchell to give her appropriate weapons.

Boone turned to her, "Follow Mitchell. He'll take you to your designated tent, where you can change clothes...try and nap if you can...we have big things to accomplish, soon enough," he grinned and walked away towards a larger tent, leaving her standing with Mitchell.

Mitchell appeared to be in his middle to late forties, of medium height, but stocky, with a military haircut and prematurely graying sides. He had a tanned weather-beaten face, out of which, gray eyes gazed and seemed to inspect her. His pleasant smile caused his eyes to squint, and he said, "They call me Mitch around here. C'mon little lady, let's get you settled," and he ambled towards a small oak patterned camouflage tent, while she trailed behind him.

"Yes, sir," she said quietly under her breath and attempted *not* to take umbrage at the 'little lady' comment as she followed Mitch to her tent.

With the flap thrown back, she entered and looked around, then noticed a table stacked with clothes, and a cot with a pillow and sleeping bag. "Well, this looks cozy," she said.

Mitch chuckled at her comment and added, "Nothin' but the finest!"

"So, what now?"

Mitch strolled to the table stacked with folded clothes and handed Paisley one of the stacks, consisting of camouflage pants, a shirt, socks, boots, and a warm puffy jacket for the chillier nighttime weather.

"Put these on for the time being. The second stack contains extreme protective wear, which you'll need for tomorrow."

"Thanks," she said, and Mitch left her tent. She changed into her new clothes, then relaxed onto the cot, even managing to nap.

It was early evening, and she was awake and ready, when Boone finally came to her tent. "Time to eat," he said, and led her to the mess tent, where all the men gathered for a dinner of MREs.

Boone explained, "MRE is the military acronym, for Meal, Ready-to-Eat."

"Hmmm...." She replied, "...interesting!"

When the meal was over, they all congregated in the largest tent with the rest of the men, as Boone elucidated the plan, which he and Riley devised earlier that day. She took a seat in the back.

Boone reviewed the three parts of the plan, "Delta Team One—ambush their leader, Delta Team Two—guard the compound perimeter, and Delta Team Three—attack the compound. Alpha Team One, we'll stand down until I can confirm the capture of the Russian leader, Zolotov, at which time I will notify *and* give Riley the go-ahead to attack the Russian camp. We plan to surprise, disarm and capture or kill them—*if* necessary. Our Alpha team must *not* be prevented from retrieving the suitcase bomb."

With murmured approval and the nodding heads, Boone continued. "I'm heading Alpha Team. Our mission is to retrieve the deadly package from the bomb site, and fly it out by helicopter, to a top-secret location."

He has charisma and command over the men, Paisley

thought, as she listened to him speak. Sitting towards the back of the assemblage, she was sobered by his speech. His normally placid face seemed to transform into a more angular, tight-lipped visage. His voice exhibited a lower, gruffer tone matching the intensity in his eyes, and the gravity of his message.

She could hardly believe this was the same man, with whom she had investigated a murder in a fast-food restaurant a mere week ago! She was riveted to every word he spoke. His leadership abilities made him seem taller than his six feet, and more muscular in the short-sleeved navy blue T-shirt, and khaki-tan cargo pants. With his sidearm in the holster attached to his belt, it *did* make him look sort of like a super hero!

It seems like ages have passed since Boone and I teamed up. Who knew the investigation would escalate and morph into this dangerous course of events. It's as if I'm in an action-adventure movie she thought. I'm sitting here in a camp, dressed in camouflage gear with a group of men divided into covert teams—it's ludicrous! There hasn't been time yet, for me to process the week's capture and escape from the men who tried to kill us—it all seems like a bad dream! Her attention drifted back to Boone, who was still discussing the plans.

"Mitch will stay here at camp in the communications tent. He'll be in contact with me and Delta Team to relay any updates, or changes. The following men will ride up to the site in the morning, which we'll call ground zero," and he called their names.

"Alpha Team Three oversees the transportation of equipment to the location, and will set up the tactical equipment at the retrieval site, tomorrow."

The men murmured among themselves again, then Commander Walters stood up, consulted his notes, and addressed the group, "The men on Alpha Team One, who will be entering the old mine pit with Boone, once it's penetrated, are: Smith, Porter, Max, Torres, Sonny, Rod, Manny, and our nuclear physicists. They are Dr. Akio Moto and Dr. Bruno Steinhoff, and their two assistants, Dr. Kent Rollins and Dr. Sanjay Kapoor."

An enthusiastic round of applause ensued. Boone held up his hands, signifying quiet, and asked if there were any questions. There were none. He pointed out the information packets on the table at the back of the tent, and the group craned their necks to look at the large table, laden with stacks of folders.

"Each man must take one, because they contain a detailed copy of the plan, along with maps and a list of gear to pack." The men began to stand when Boone again put up his hands for quiet, and the men settled back into their seats. "Before we adjourn, our physicists have equipment to pass out to those, who'll be working with the heavy equipment needed to penetrate the cave for tunnel excavation, including those who will approach the suitcase bomb."

While the men assigned to bomb retrieval assistance conferred with the physicists, the rest were encouraged to retrieve their folders, grab some coffee and relax for a moment. Boone ambled over to the table containing the coffee urn, poured a cup for himself, then sipping his coffee, observed the men kibitzing, as the physicists in the back of the tent, assembled the equipment to pass out to the designated men.

CHAPTER 37

The physicists Boone chose were the best in the country. Dr. Akio Moto was lead nuclear physicist in the National Nuclear Security Administration (NNSA), sub-department: The Office of Defense Nuclear Nonproliferation (DNN). He attended the University of Michigan in Ann Arbor, graduating *magna cum laude* with a PhD in physics, and receiving a doctorate in Nuclear Engineering.

Presently, his work concerned detecting and securing nuclear material, which may, or may not, be connected to proliferation of WMDs. He also managed terrorism incidents on a worldwide basis, which required securing dangerous nuclear material, thus making him the perfect fit for Boone's team.

Dr. Moto's assistant, Dr. Bruno Steinhoff, was born and raised in Bonn, Germany, and aspired to be a physicist. He moved to the US, received his PhD in Nuclear Engineering, and a doctorate in Nuclear Medicine, at Stanford University, in California. Dr. Steinhoff also worked at the DNN. He dealt with the study of how the body reacts to radiation, along with methods used to properly handle and dispose of radioactive material, until he was assigned, along with Dr. Moto, to Boone's team.

"Good evening," Dr. Moto said, as he introduced himself and Dr. Steinhoff to the group, "follow me," and he led several of the groups to the back of the tent where he passed out a piece of equipment to each man, called a dosimeter. He explained, "It's a device to be worn on the belt to measure radiation exposure."

"These devices," Dr. Steinhoff told the group, "are called thermo-luminescent dosimeters (TLDs) and are made of translucent polyurethane. They're used to record the accumulated exposure to radiation, in millirems (mRs). The TLDs are rectangular objects approximately the size of a small deck of cards, and thus won't impede your movements while you work."

Dr. Moto continued with more information. "When the mission is complete, you'll turn in the TLDs to an onsite lab back at base camp, equipped to read the accumulated exposure levels. At the site where you'll be working, it's possible that gamma rays, or other forms of radiation 'could' be present, with gamma rays being the most dangerous kind associated with nuclear material."

Dr. Steinhoff also passed out self-indicating pocket dosimeters (SIPDs), which were in the shape of a shortened writing pen to be carried in the pocket. "This dosimeter," Dr. Steinhoff said, "will provide each man with an immediate reading of the exposure level, due to possible gamma rays."

The men listened intently, while each Doctor took turns instructing the men on the use of dosimeters. They were given information on other dangers they might encounter during this mission. In conclusion, Dr. Steinhoff produced one last piece of equipment, called a Radiac.

He explained that the Radiac was a handheld about the size of half a medium shoe box, with a grip on top to be used in a sweep-as-you-go manner, for monitoring the entrance into the unknown area to check for alpha rays, beta rays, and gamma radiation. Both physicists declared the goal of the mission was to get in and out as quickly as possible with the least amount of exposure to radiation.

When Drs. Moto and Steinhoff finished briefing the team, Boone clapped his hands together and called the men to rejoin the rest, then said, "I don't want to adjourn before I introduce a new face to the group."

The men sauntered back to their chairs. Boone began, "Mitch has met her already, and I'm sure you've all wondered who she is and why she's here. Ms. Ingles? Will you please stand for a moment? This is Ms. Paisley Ingles," he said, and motioned her to stand, which she did...hesitantly.

Her cheeks were flushed, as Boone continued, "She's a detective, *and* a Forensic Computer Specialist. We worked together on a recent murder investigation. Her discoveries resulted in endangering her life, and subsequently mine, then led both of us down a path to the discovery of the Russian Mafia plot to retrieve the suitcase bomb, which had been buried over forty years ago."

Standing, with all eyes on her, she was uncomfortable and felt very small. But Boone didn't stop, "Without her help and ability to decrypt the Russian messages, we would not be running this operation right now!" The men stood and gave her a polite round of applause. "She's also going to accompany us tomorrow!" he added. "Okay, the meeting's over. Take your folders, prep for tomorrow, and plan on rising early."

The men all drifted off to their assigned tents for the evening, to a background of excited chatter, allowing Boone to approach Ingles, and present her with a folder, as well. She was still standing, with a stunned look on her face.

"Is everything okay?"

"I'm still in a state of disbelief at the accolades you bestowed on me," she said.

Amused by her reaction, he patted her on the shoulder adding, "I meant what I said."

That broke the spell and she began to say something, but he put a finger on her lips and said, "We rise early tomorrow... let me walk you to your tent. You can read over the information in your folder, so you'll know what *your* part is for tomorrow. I'll make sure you're up in the morning, in the meantime, please get some much-needed sleep."

She looked at him gratefully and did exactly as he said. Bone tired, after reading through her folder, she crawled into the camo sleeping bag, arranged her head on the pillow provided, and far from being revved up from coffee and the meeting, she was asleep before she could conjure any more thoughts.

Instead of retiring immediately, Boone held another short meeting with Drs. Moto and Steinhoff, and their assistants. They conferred for the last time, concerning the methods of extraction to be used to ensure the safety of everyone, during the delicate extraction operation. When the meeting ended, Boone rose wearily and shook their hands, declaring it time to retire.

The men hustled through the silent camp to their own accommodations. Boone sat for another hour, pouring over papers, maps, and stats. Later, flashlight in hand, he headed for his tent. The silence in the camp was palpable, and he gazed up-

-noting the crescent moon, as it slid up and over the sentry-like trees, then passed through some dark wispy clouds creating an etherial tableau.

Boone arrived at his tent, then he stopped and gave the moon one more glance, before stealthily entering, and crawling into his sleeping bag. He doused his flashlight. Exhausted, he drifted off to sleep to the sound of owls, hooting in the silence of the night, with no one else—as far as he knew—awake to hear their incessant questions.

Monday, May 22, 2017 Before the sun made its appearance, Boone and his men were up, and prepared for the move to the target location. Paisley dressed and was ready to go when Boone pulled back her tent flap and beckoned her to follow him as he headed towards the mess tent.

"Ms. Ingles, I need to talk to you about today, but first, we'll have breakfast."

"More MREs?"

He turned to her and replied "No, real food. Instant oatmeal, toast, juice, and coffee."

She laughed. "Works for me!" Breakfast didn't last long, because there were many things to do before leaving. Boone spoke to a few of the men, then approached her when she finished her meal and invited her to follow him to a corner of the tent, where they could speak privately.

Boone didn't beat around the bush, he stated, "Mitch and Sparky, will stay here at camp in the communications tent, and monitor everything between Alpha and Delta teams, but you have two choices."

"Which are...?"

"You can accompany me, as my onsite Communications Coordinator, which consists of documenting the extraction, *or* you can stay here with Mitch and Sparky in the COM tent?"

With a huge smile, she said, "I'll go with *you*, of course!"

With a serious look on his face, he continued, "Before you answer so fast, I must tell you, this is a very dangerous mission. We'll possibly be dealing with radiation, and injuries may occur if things don't go well, so I want you to consider the risk before you answer."

Without hesitation, she replied, "The answer is still the same," and with a broad smile, she added, "I didn't think you'd ask me...and after all I've been through, I *sure* don't want to miss the grand finale!"

"I had a feeling you might feel this way." His broad smile told her he was happy to have her on board, and to her, it was a huge acknowledgment. "C'mon then, grab your gear, and we'll put it in our van...got your weapons?"

"Yep," she said, as her hand touched the KA-BAR knife nestled in its sheath on her left leg, and felt her waist with the inside of her right wrist, where the Glock 26 Gen 4 (9x19 mm), she'd been issued was holstered.

"Okay," he said, "let's get the equipment you'll be using for this mission. We'll take the other computer from the communication tent, the digital cameras, and the SAT phone, and you'll be all set, as my official Communications Assistant and Documenter. Here's your TLD and SPID dosimeters, one for your belt and the other for your pocket." He proceeded to explain their use since she hadn't been instructed the night before.

As soon as she caught up to him, she commented, "By the way, there was something I wanted to ask you last night."

"Shoot," he said, staring at her with those penetrating blue eyes.

"Well," she hesitated, now his blue eyes were making her feel flustered again, but she found her voice and continued, "You introduced me to Mitch and mentioned his assistant, Sparky, and I was curious...is Sparky the man's real name, or is it just a coincidence?" Suddenly, she felt silly for asking and blushed under his stare.

"Nope, not his real name."

"Then why do they call him Sparky?" She cringed as she said it.

Boone let out a huge laugh, taking her by surprise, then replied, "Trust me, you don't want to know!" and he continued to chuckle.

"Hmmm," She replied. Now she *had* to know and vowed to herself that she would bring it up again sometime. It piqued her curiosity, especially since her question made him laugh so hard! She was sure it must be a story worth hearing and fell in behind him as he turned and headed inside the COM tent, and immediately began chastising herself for bothering him with such a stupid question.

After a few minutes, they exited the tent, and Boone rounded up Alpha Team to announce the good news he'd just received from Riley, concerning Delta Team.

When everyone gathered around, Boone spoke, "Overnight, Delta Team successfully captured Zolotov and his entourage, and the rest of Delta Team was given the go-ahead, to deal with the Russians' camp."

The men cheered excitedly, and one of the men yelled, "What about their camp?"

Boone held up his hand for silence, and the men quieted down, "The Russians did *not* voluntarily surrender, but instead, met our men with serious resistance. Suffice it to say, our attack worked as planned, and we prevailed. Several of our men were injured, but not critically." Applause broke out. "However," he continued, "I can't say the same for the Russians! As it stands, we don't have to worry about their interference with our extraction process, anymore!"

With this information, a great cheer went up, and there was high five-ing all around. The tone became serious again, as Boone announced it was time to leave. The men dispersed to their assigned vehicles. The equipment relocation team grabbed their back packs and weapons, then climbed into the armored vehicles.

A two-trailer semi, loaded with digging and excavation equipment, lumbered onto the dirt path behind the armored vehicles, followed by an oversized trailer carrying scientific monitoring equipment, clothing, and radiation shielding.

The radiation containment units followed, along with the physicists, their assistants, and guards. Boone gave the signal, the engines roared, and the caravan was on its way to the designated site. The van with Boone and Ingles was last to leave.

The caravan headed onto the trail, which had been cleared for passage over the last several days, by the task force engineers. This made it possible to use a more direct route to the site, without drawing attention, by traveling on conventional roads.

The caravan lumbered along for almost an hour, before making its way through a dense copse of trees and tall ground foliage, until the trail finally emptied the convoy into a large area cleared of small trees and brush. This is where tents would be set up and vehicles parked to unload the equipment.

A second team, which arrived earlier had located the entrance to the hidden mine shaft, where the suitcase bomb was concealed. They used the GPS coordinates from the decrypted information, supplied by Ingles and Boone, and verified by Riley's surveillance teams. Back hoes and bull dozers cleared the large boulders and dense foliage, from the old mine shaft's entrance, revealing the long-concealed mine opening.

The opening had been camouflaged by an overgrowth of brush, rocks, fallen trees, and whatever else nature had wrought over the years, to render it invisible. Without the coordinates, it would have been impossible to locate. When the entrance was cleared, the foreman contacted Boone, who hopped out of his van, ready to give the order to penetrate the opening, and prepare it for exploration.

Paisley stepped out of the van, and shaded her eyes from the refulgent sun, which had just breached the horizon. She viewed the panorama before her. Overwhelmed, she took in the scene, with all the men and heavy equipment in the small clearing. Furrowing her brow, she brushed a few stray tendrils of hair back under the camo cap she was given, and for a moment was filled with trepidation, wondering if volunteering for this endeavor, *had* been the right choice?

The heavy equipment was silent, and the men also grew silent. The area was now staged, and at this moment of stasis, it was as if all the characters were in place waiting for the opening curtain, so the play could begin.

CHAPTER 38

As suddenly as the activity had ceased, it began again. Small cub tractors resumed digging, as back hoes lowered their shovels and scooped dirt, to carry it away from the expanding cavity, in the entrance of the mine's tunnel. It took all morning for the dirt and debris to be removed.

Drs. Moto and Steinhoff gave their assistants a couple of Radiacs to sweep the tunnel, prior to the excavators progressing further inside. When declared safe, the engineers began the process of bringing in wooden beams, to shore up the tunnel walls.

In the meantime, Mitch and Sparky had moved to the site also, and ushered Ingles into the small COM tent, which had been set up, about the length of a football field from the hub of activity, at the tunnel entrance. The COM tent was smaller, but when the tent flap was pulled back, and Paisley glanced at its contents, surprised to see, as much state-of-the art equipment, as the larger COM tent at base camp.

When she entered the tent, Mitch welcomed her with a

high five, showed her where to set her equipment, then formally introduced her to Sparky. True to his name, Sparky, appeared thin and wiry, with *extremely* curly red hair standing up, in all directions, looking as if he just stuck his finger in a light socket. At this moment, she *knew* why he'd been called Sparky! She smiled, as he pumped her hand instead of just shaking it. His exuberance was catching—she liked him!

Mitch escorted her to an aluminum table where there was a gunmetal gray foldout chair with a padded seat. Sparky left for parts unknown—presumably to run a myriad of cables needed for communication, into the tunnel.

"Here ya go, little lady," Mitch said cheerily. "Let me know if you need anything. Coffee, maybe?"

There he goes with the "little lady" bit again, and once more she smiled to herself, but took no offense. "Thanks, Mitch, yes, no cream or sugar, though—I take it black."

He brought her a cup of what he called the "good stuff ", saying, "There ya go!" He set the cup on her table, sans the "little lady" comment this time. Maybe this was progress, she thought?

She put her backpack on the table, opened it, and plugged in the equipment supplied to her, to make sure everything was charged and ready to go. She asked Mitch a question, but he didn't hear her over the noise of the tractors, backhoes, and the roar of truck motors outside the tent.

It was all *she* could do to ignore the noise, as she sipped her coffee. She'd have to acknowledged Mitch—his coffee really *was* the good stuff—she'd tell him later! After her equipment charged, she organized everything needed on the tables until time to use it.

Paisley stepped outside for a moment to stretch and release a little tension. However, the heavy equipment kicked billowing brown clouds of dirt into the air, to be inhaled by everyone in the vicinity, except the men closest to the source, who wore protective masks. After a couple of little coughs, she retreated into the COM tent. Shortly after re-entering the tent, the noise diminished until there was silence. The cessation of noise was deafening.

She packed her equipment and glanced over at Mitch, and quipped, "Hey, now we can think again!"

Mitch stood, came around the equipment table, and responded, "Now it's *too* quiet to think," and gave her a hearty laugh and a wink.

Several moments later, they both turned, as the tent flap was thrown back. Boone burst in, "Good news!" he said, "The excavation equipment was no more than a hundred and fifteen feet into the opening when the shaft widened and opened into a large cavern!" He gestured with his hands, "And, the foreman judged it to be, approximately ninety feet wide, and easily one hundred and fifty feet deep, with craggy rock walls and jagged outcroppings. It reached upwards of thirty feet to the ceiling, at the chamber's highest mid-point!"

He was excited! As Boone stood there in expectation, it was obvious Mitch wasn't going to say anything. Boone waited for the right questions to be asked. So, Paisley, resignedly elected herself to ask the obvious questions, breaking the silence by saying, "Is that good? What happens now?"

Boone came to life again, "Well, the wooden beams have been placed to shore up the tunnel for safety, and Halogen lights are in place along the tunnel walls, from the entrance all the way to the cavern's opening, and so far, no radioactivity has been detected—a *very* good sign!"

Boone stood there looking at them, hands in his pockets and

a big smile on his face, which she noticed, *always* made his eyes sparkle.

"Then it's time to enter?" she asked tentatively.

"Yep!" he said, and Mitch, who had turned on his SAT phone while they talked, patched a call through to headquarters, then handed the phone to Boone so that he could give Riley the good news!

After his call, Boone noticed a look of concern on Ingles face, "C'mon...walk with me to the opening, so you'll have an idea of what to expect," he said. The tunnel wasn't far, and as they approached, Paisley didn't see anyone until they'd entered the tunnel's opening, where some of the men had already gathered. As the group ventured further inside, more men assembled at the cavern's opening, gazing around in amazement at the enormity of the chamber.

Ingles said reverently, "Amazing!" while squinting into the dim interior of the cavern, with its cathedral-like ambiance, then asked hesitantly, "Where's the suitcase bomb?"

"It's in the very back of the cavern. You can't see it from here," Boone whispered and called out to get everyone's attention, "It's time to head back and get the show on the road," and he led the group back to the tunnel entrance. Calling the rest of the crew from the clearing, Boone announced, "It's time for a dosimeter check," and directed those with dosimeters, to line up at the lab trailer. They checked the men for radiation, and everyone checked out fine—exactly what the physicists hoped—then the men dispersed.

With the four physicists assembled, Boone said, "The tunnel is cleared. Now it's time, Dr. Steinhoff and Dr. Moto, to use your robot to investigate the cavern and verify whether or not there *is* a suitcase bomb. And if it *is* there, the area around it can be tested for radiation levels."

They shook hands with Boone and retrieved the robot, from the lab trailer. Drs. Moto and Steinhoff, assisted by Drs. Rollins and Kapoor, climbed into a waiting golf cart, which pulled a small open trailer carrying the robot.

The remote controlled robot, like those used by bomb squads, had been outfitted with a video recorder, munitions detectors, and radiation detection equipment. It would be able to check more closely, for possible booby traps, or other dangerous explosives, which might be buried in the immediate area and could create an explosion, or cause a delay in the retrieval of the suitcase.

Everyone waited nervously at the tunnel entrance, as Dr. Moto said, "Please, Dr. Steinhoff, will you help me get this robot ready to go?"

When the robot was removed from the cart, put on the ground and turned on, the controls were given to Dr. Kapoor, who was in charge of the robot's movements. Dr. Kapoor guided it remotely down the tunnel and introduced it into the cavern. It took twenty minutes to reach the back of the cavern, where the robot gave them their first view of the bomb. The robot thoroughly checked for radiation emissions, gleaning other information, along with photos and video, then transmitted the findings to the physicists, at the cavern's entrance.

After twenty minutes, Dr. Steinhoff addressed Boone. "The robot has transmitted the information and now we must analyze the photos, video, and radiation information before we call the robot back."

"That's fine," Boone said, and put a hand on his shoulder. "We'll await your findings before we make any decisions."

The three physicists walked to the nearby lab trailer and disappeared inside, while Dr. Kapoor waited at the controls, and the robot waited in the cavern. Thirty-five minutes later, the physicists emerged from the lab and approached Boone. He paced back and forth, but halted when he saw the Doctors head his way.

With expressionless faces, the physicists stopped in front of him, and he held his breath, wondering if the project could go forward. "Well," Boone said, expectantly.

Dr. Moto spoke first, while he looked up at Boone, who was quite a bit taller, "It is good news, Mr. Boone," he said, then looked around at the group that had formed. "Because according to the Radiac information, and corroborated by the robot, no real measurable alpha or beta rays were detected, just a small amount of harmless radiation was found, but will not prevent retrieval. Good news!" Dr. Moto, said again.

"Yes, this *is* good news!" Boone reiterated the phrase with a sigh of relief and nodded his head in agreement.

"When fissionable material begins to degrade," Dr. Moto continued, "it emits alpha and beta rays, which in turn causes more degradation, which in turn allows 'some' of the dangerous radiation to be emitted. But, my robot's findings confirm only a small amount of relatively harmless, low-level radiation is present."

"What a relief!" Boone said.

"Yes, we are in agreement now, and we can continue our plan to approach. From the robot's photos and video, we confirm it to be an old Russian suitcase bomb!" He gave a slight smile, and though his expression remained unreadable, he gave a subtle bow.

Elated, Boone requested Dr. Kapoor to retrieve the robot, take it to the lab trailer to be decontaminated, and probed for other information it may have gathered. When the robot made its way back from the cavern, the physicists headed to the lab.

Boone's eyebrows raised, as he uttered under his breath,

"Well, I'll be darned!" He removed his cap, ran his fingers through his hair, then settled the cap back on his head, and mumbled again, "I'll be darned!"

It was time for Boone to join the rest of the crew. Dr. Steinhoff trailed after Boone, chattering away, as Boone headed towards his group of men lounging in the shade of a huge fir tree. They were attempting to escape the sun's rays as it had reached its zenith.

Steinhoff continued to talk, as they walked along, "...And, this means these findings are a good indication that there is very little deterioration of the fissile material, contained in the bomb! Although, we don't *really* know how much there'll be until it's deactivated."

Boone, only half-listening to him, said, "Yes, uh-huh..."

Steinhoff added, in a somewhat hurried mumble, "...And, we didn't detect alpha or beta radiation levels in this scenario, perhaps due to the fact that the temperature held at a constant all these years such that..." and his voice trailed off, when they arrived at the tree, where the group waited.

Steinhoff stopped walking and his eyes drifted around the group, now standing in front of him and listening. He stopped talking, mid-sentence, when the blank looks on the faces staring at him, told him they probably weren't interested in hearing the scientific theories, upon which he was about to expound.

Boone shuffled from one foot to another impatiently, and given an opening to speak, saved the situation by saying, "Yes, well this is very good, thank you, Dr. Steinhoff. Now, let's take a short break for lunch, then we can carry on with the retrieval."

As the men headed away conversing quietly with each other, Boone turned to Dr. Steinhoff and said, "Please let the other doctors know that we're going to eat first, and then the retrieval team can suit up, and we'll head to the mine shaft." The Dr. nodded and hurried off to the lab trailer.

It had turned warmer, as the sun migrated over the tree tops, accessing a commanding view of the workers below, and its intense heat, beating down on the camp, caused some of the men to sweat profusely. They had gathered by a metal tub of ice, which contained water bottles. Other members of the crew strolled over also, to procure water, and find a little shade under nearby trees, where Boone was about to address the team, concerning the next phase of the process.

With everyone accounted for, Boone began to speak, recounting all that had transpired since the physicists' analyzed the robot's findings. The men listened intently while he announced procedures for the next phase. He ended by saying, "It's time for a lunch break. The food is arranged on the tables back by the trees, near the other bottled water tub. Be ready to go at thirteen hundred hours." The group scattered for the tables.

Cuyuna Range, The Cavern At thirteen hundred hours, those involved with the actual retrieval of the suitcase bomb, were assembled, wearing their protective gear and ready to go. Everyone who was to enter the mine shaft assembled at its entrance, including Paisley. Although assurances were given, about the relative safety of the mission, according to the information revealed by the robot, there was still the possibility of unknowns. Thus it remained an extremely dangerous operation.

Boone stepped towards the physicists and said in a somber tone, "I'll have my men follow you gentlemen, into the cavern, a short distance behind you, with Halogen lights. Once you get further in, they'll set them up to provide better illumination of the interior, closest to the bomb."

"That will be fine," said Dr. Moto, "we will still be taking readings with the Radiacs as we go, and will relay any pertinent information to you." Dr. Steinhoff stood, nodding.

"Great!" Boone looked around at each person standing with him. He paused a moment, then with conviction said, "Let's do this!"

All who were selected to enter the cavern, including Paisley and Boone, were dressed in protective gear, specifically made to block radiation. A tense feeling pervaded the retrieval contingent, as it became very real for each person, now that the moment had arrived. Entering the cavern was a step into the unknown, and whatever information the physicists gleaned, could affect the suitcase extraction, and possibly expose them to unknown dangers.

Nevertheless, they hoisted their equipment and began traveling down the mineshaft's tunnel. The physicists were in the lead, keeping an eye on their Radiacs, as they cautiously moved forward. Each participant wore high-powered LED lights on their protective hoods. The mood was somber.

CHAPTER 39

The group grew silent, moving cautiously forward until halting at the cavern entrance. Poised at the opening, Paisley felt the dank air accompanied by a musty smell, that bothered her. She involuntarily shivered, as she kept pace with the retrieval coterie, while they continued into the cavern. Their footfalls on the gravely cavern floor echoed throughout the subterranean area as they progressed.

The physicists walked ahead of the rest until they were approximately fifty feet into the cavern's interior. Dr. Moto stopped and signaled that he'd spotted the suitcase bomb, barely visible, next to a stony protuberance at the farthest end of the chamber. An adjacent rocky ledge jutted out from the cavern's back wall, acting as a partial shelter for the suitcase bomb. The physicists, having come to an abrupt halt, conferred for a moment or two and concurred there was still no measurable radioactivity detected.

Boone, standing partway into the chamber, radioed Mitch to have the light crew move the portable Halogen light-bar stands through the tunnel and set them up near the center of the cavern. After they placed the light-bars, the small group proceeded further into the interior area. As Paisley traveled through the cavern, she gazed around the space, awed by the cathedral-like ceiling, which accorded a tomblike feeling, as if primitive spirits had been protecting others buried here, in past ages.

The LED lights caused a dark, eerie moving mural, to be displayed on the cavern walls, and large grotesque, animated shadows moved forward in sync with their group. The air omitted other ancient odors, which spoke of dark secrets hidden over many decades, if not centuries. Paisley pondered this realizing, as she moved forward with the others, that her thoughts spooked her. Instead, she attempted to focus on the task at hand, until they came to a stop, halfway into the cavern.

Boone called Mitch on his SAT phone, "Give my orders to the men outside the tunnel, to send in the bomb retrieval equipment for the physicists, then check on the CH-53 transport heli and its two companion choppers, to make sure they'll be arriving soon."

"Copy that," Mitch said, "and what about the campsite?"

Boone paced back and forth and said, "Tell the men, I said it's time to strike camp!"

"Roger that!" Mitch said. Boone continued to pace, as Paisley watched him shift from foot to foot, looking as anxious, as he was, impatient.

Several minutes later they both spied what looked like the golf cart, which had made its way into the cavern, stopping where they both stood.

"Hop on," he said to her "here's your equipment...we'll ride forward to where you'll be stationed. All aboard!"

She wasn't amused by his comment, but he didn't seem to

notice her reaction...she hopped into the cart, and they slowly drove further into the chamber, before stopping to disembark. The camera equipment was unloaded onto a small collapsible table, set up to provide a work surface for Paisley's equipment.

All she could think about, was how incongruous the golf cart's presence seemed inside a cavern, under the present circumstances. The physicists stood near her table, patiently waiting for their equipment, while she set up her video camera and tripod, adjusting its legs to level it on the uneven cavern floor. She opened the computer, powered it on, then typed information into it, concerning the actions taking place, since as of now, the operation was underway.

Awed by the enormity of what was happening, Paisley suddenly felt overly warm and began to sweat in the jumpsuit she wore for radiation protection. Watching the events taking place around her, caused her anxiety level to rise, as she realized the possibility of catastrophic repercussions.

Her legs began to shake and feel wobbly, so she put a hand on the table to steady herself. Everything began to spin, and it was as if a black curtain began to engulf her, turning everything dark. She began to crumple.

Boone glanced over, noticing her blank stare and ashen face, through her face plate. He immediately grabbed her around the waist, without drawing attention from the others and said quietly, "Are you okay?" She rallied, and nodded. "You don't have to do this if you don't want to," he added, "I just thought..."

"No! I'm fine!" she whispered obstinately, "I just felt over heated, for a moment." She furtively glanced at the others to see if she said this a bit too loud, but no one seemed to notice, over the noise of the golf cart, returning to the entrance of the tunnel. Gaining her composure, she shoved down her fear and strength-ened her resolve, "I'm not giving up now, Boone," she said softly, in a kinder voice.

So, once again she persevered, as always, by rising to the challenge. Whenever her parents or teachers told her, "You can't do that," she doubled down with even greater determination. It was a trait her parents had difficulty dealing with at times. With a silent whisper of, "I'll show *you*," she readied her cameras and computer then made sure she had radio contact with Mitch. She looked Boone in the eyes, and said with a smile, "I'm ready!"

Boone watched, as she began capturing the physicists with the video camera, while they began their approach to the bomb. She's a feisty woman, he thought.

She took many digital pictures of the physicists, knowing it would soon be time to move forward to capture pictures of the bomb. Her camera quietly clicked away, as if she were on just another ordinary photo shoot. Boone surmised there would be thousands of photos to examine when *this* was finished.

For the team closest to the suitcase bomb, which included Paisley, the physicists, and their assistants, state-of-the-art protective suits were worn. The suits were made of a special fabric infused with lead threads, designed to protect them from dangerous radiation, which 'might' be present, as they approached the bomb. Special goggles and breathing apparatuses were worn by all four of the physicists, who would secure the bomb—it was necessary to take every precaution!

The physicists ceased moving forward, a mere fifteen feet from the bomb and conferred. Meanwhile, moving through the cavern's entrance was another piece of equipment, making its way into the chamber, on a motorized cart, moving forward on caterpillar tracks. It was a large lead sheet, approximately three feet by five feet.

"What's this coming our way?" Paisley asked, as her camera captured the cart and its contents.

Turning his head to see what she was looking at, Boone answered, "It's a lead sheet to be inserted between the physicists and the bomb...it'll block radiation, yet still allow the physicists to reach around it when they open the suitcase for examination."

The cart stopped near the bomb, and Boone, from his vantage point, proceeded to wave another smaller heavy-duty tractor, with huge mechanical arms, into the chamber, slowly pulling a large trailer behind it. The cart held a box, approximately five feet long, five feet high and four feet wide, that looked much like an oddly shaped metal coffin.

"What's *that?*" she asked incredulously, as it lumbered into the cavern. "It must weigh a ton! This is the weirdest parade *I've* ever seen!"

Her digital camera clicked away, then she changed to video. Clearly, the physicists waited for whatever-it-was, which was headed their way. She turned back to her view of the bomb, with her camera lens set for close-ups, to take as many pictures of the suitcase bomb as she could, but the physicists were blocking her view. She was curious to see what it looked like.

"I have no idea what it weighs," Boone finally answered, as he walked up behind her. Leaning slightly towards her, he quietly added, "However, I do know it's made of thick lead, which is why tank treads are needed. They're aggressive enough to provide extra traction when transporting extra heavy equipment over all sorts of terrain. The three suited men walking beside it will help guide it, as close to the bomb, as possible."

The tractor and its container rumbled lethargically past Paisley and Boone, while she documented it with pictures and video. It ambled noisily towards the physicists, with Boone in its wake to help with its final positioning. She took the opportunity to move forward to take as many pictures as she could, using the high-powered close-up lens. Still no photos of the bomb yet— the physicists and equipment were always in the way.

She returned to the table where the computer waited and quickly typed in the time and actions taking place, along with other relevant information, before returning to her position, which was within twenty feet of the action. Boone and the physicists conferred for a few minutes and then walked back to where Paisley stood.

After calling Mitch on his SAT phone to tell him they would begin in approximately ten minutes beginning, Boone looked at Paisley and asked, "Are you ready? We have a few more minutes before they begin."

"Yes, I'm fine now, it's still scary, but I *am* doing this!" She was quiet for a moment, just watching the odd tableau in front of her, then looking at Boone she asked, "What's *that* thing's purpose?"

"That," he responded, as he stood next to her with folded arms, "is intended to be the final resting place for the bomb. Its sides are of a special lead, antimony and steel alloy, which prevents radiation—especially deadly gamma rays—from passing through its walls, due to its density. I believe small lead containers used to carry radioactive material, are called lead pigs, so I guess this is the largest lead pig we'll ever see!" Boone said with a grin, shifting his weight to his other foot and giving her a sideways glance.

She lowered her camera and smiled then began taking more pictures, with the video camera perched on the tripod.

"You're telling me that all they have to do—stick the bomb in there, and *voila*? Or, maybe an abracadabra and the bomb is gone?"

"Yep!" Boone stared at the scene in front of him. He also was mesmerized by the sight, "Will you look at that!"

At that moment, Drs. Rollins and Kapoor, and the two assistants, redirected the bright Halogen lights towards a brown leather object. The suitcase bomb was bathed in the brilliant light, and as she shot the video, she was shocked to finally *see* the bomb. It looked nothing like what she'd imagined. She expected to see an actual *suitcase*—like you'd use to travel! But instead, what she was looking at took her by surprise!

The suitcase bomb looked like an over-sized worn leather back pack/duffel bag, with a flap covering the top and fastened by two straps on the front, with buckles! Two thicker straps on the back, would enable it to be worn, like a backpack. Its height was probably a little over three and a half feet, the width about two feet wide, and maybe a foot and a half deep. It did *not* look at *all*, like a suitcase! It was more like a large duffel bag!

"Shocking!" Paisley whispered to Boone, almost in a reverent tone, "Just think—I'm standing here taking pictures of a nuclear device, that for all I know, *might* explode—it's hard to wrap my mind around *this*! And, I was waiting to see an actual suitcase! I don't understand? Oddly enough, I'm kind of disappointed—I expected something more exciting."

Boone replied in a similar tone, adding, "They call it a suitcase bomb because it can be carried in the same fashion as a backpack...although it probably weighs quite a bit more! Look— I think the show is about to start."

She turned back to the action, "What are they going to do?"

"The plan is to carefully open the bag carefully, then check the electronics and, if possible, disconnect any power source that may still be working, so there *won't* be an explosion. Our lives are in their hands!"

"And then what," she said again and readied her camera to take pictures of this next step.

"The tractor will disconnect from the wagon," Boone replied, "and the two mechanical arms, will carefully lift the backpack and deposit it into the lead box, which they're moving closer to the bomb, right *now*!"

Her cameras captured everything. "What's the purpose of the lead box, if the bomb is already disarmed? Why don't they just let the tractor roll it out?"

"Because it doubles the protection when its inside the lead box. Just because it's disarmed, doesn't mean the radioactive material inside is safe! So, to assure the fissile material can't cause harm, the bomb will be immersed in the lead box, which contains Grade 1 water, which will diffuse any other electronics, while also blocking radiation."

"Grade 1?" she queried?

"Yes, also called UPW, which stands for Ultra-Purified Water."

"Oh, my *gosh*!" she whispered inaudibly. She contemplated this new information, and once again, became aware of the immense danger of the operation, which she was busy documenting on film *and* video.

CHAPTER 40

For a moment, she gazed around at the other men who concentrated on their tasks, took a deep breath and refocused. Her video camera remained perched atop the tripod, at a perfect angle, and captured everything taking place.

She turned to the computer, entered more information, and communicated several times with Mitch, back at the COM tent, letting him know preparations were in place, to evacuate the bomb, and things were running smoothly...it was time for the final phase of the retrieval.

The physicists and assistants, with their protective gloves, reached around the lead shield, and carefully removed the debris from the top of the leather bag, containing the bomb. It took a moment to accomplish, and then the bag sat in a circle of light where Drs. Moto and Steinhoff could examine it closely.

Those present fell silent as they uncovered the bomb. The tension in the cave was palpable. Paisley stepped into the golf cart, which drove her closer to the physicists, to get a better view of the procedure with the camera.

There was a moment of stasis in the cavern, and everyone, including Boone and Paisley, held their breath. There was dead silence, except for the sound of the camera's shutter, as it took a series of pictures, before the cart turned and re-deposited her by her work table.

Safely back, she noticed a tangible reverence in the air, as everyone realized the danger this comparatively small object might be capable of unleashing. According to the newspapers and other information she Googled two days ago, hypothetically, the bomb *could* have up to a ten-megaton capability, should it ever be detonated!

The bomb itself, was judged to weigh, in the vicinity of fifty to sixty pounds, would be awkward to carry—but not impossible! It was portable, like a heavy suitcase, hence its name. However, it *was* possible the fissile material contained within, had degraded, but could still cause huge problems with the extraction. The latter scenario didn't seem to be the case—so far —as no leakage was detected.

With the lead sheet in place, the physicists worked as quickly as possible. First, the leather fasteners were cut off the flap and away from the bag's sides, with a small knife-like tool. Under the flap, there was a lid, which covered a larger rectangular shaped container. Once the leather flap was pulled back and out of the way, the container's lid was carefully unscrewed and lifted so the wiring could be observed.

All four physicists examined the wiring configuration, then stepped back behind the shield, where they conferred for several tense minutes, deciding which wires to cut. With the decision made, Dr. Moto wasted no time in severing a red wire on the left side, while Dr. Steinhoff, severed its mate on the right. The electrical circuit, which had been in hibernation all these years, was broken!

Those in the cave, stood in silence during this time, praying each in their own way, that the physicists, all tops in their fields, would be successful. As soon the last wire was cut, Dr. Moto rolled his hand in the air to motion the small tractor, to move in closer. Straps were attached to the bomb and then to the tractor's two arms, which gently hoisted the bomb aloft and lowered it into the Ultra-Purified Water in the lead container.

The assistants replaced the lead container's lid and locked it into place. An audible sigh of relief, and a smattering of applause broke out, as the cart with its lead container moved deliberately towards the cavern's entrance to. The cart sluggishly made its way through the tunnel, exiting into the clearing, to a partly cloudy afternoon.

A cheer went up from those outside, who had patiently waited for the ordeal to end safely. Within a few minutes, the box was hoisted into a waiting helicopter, while the physicists headed to the decontamination trailer. Inside the trailer, the physicists were individually 'frisked-out', which entailed having their clothing 'frisked', by using a Radiac to scan their suits at the rate of about two inches per second.

Following this, regardless of whether or not any radiation was found, the clothing was put in yellow poly bags, and jay-sealed (ends twisted and taped, then folded over on themselves and taped again). The tools would be either decontaminated or disposed of, by two men from the NRC (Nuclear Regulatory Commission), who oversee explosive ordnance disposals.

Once the Doctors went through their frisking process they exited the lab and boarded the CH-53E heli with the deactivated bomb, and left immediately, heading to a secret location.

Boone, Paisley and the rest of the men in who had been in the cavern, were the next to undergo the frisking procedure.

When Boone and Paisley finished the decontamination process and left the trailer, another Sikorsky CH-53E, Super Stallion helicopter (for carrying *lots* of heavy equipment), was warming up in the field. This was the biggest helicopter she had *ever* seen, and as she glanced around at the used-to-be camp, it shocked her to see the all the tents were gone. The last of the heavy equipment, was being driven up the ramp, and into the gaping cargo bay,

She was awed by the size of the enormous helicopter, "It looks like a giant grasshopper sitting on the ground, ready to flit off at the slightest movement," she said to Boone, as she watched the men boarding along with more equipment and gear. The only thing left, were two transport vans.

"What about us?" she asked. She was drowned out by the roar of the helicopter's engine, as the enormous flying beast stirred up dust and debris with its whirring rotors, in preparation for lift off! Boone didn't answer right away but instead, walked over to gather his gear, before heading towards one of the transport vans. He turned his head to look back at her and motioned her with his free hand, to do the same.

Tired to the bone from the stress of the day, she picked up her gear, which somehow was magically packed, and shuffled after Boone, hanging onto her backpack's straps with one hand, and her cap with the other, as the rotor wash attempted to relieve her, of both. The dust and debris made her cover her eyes, and when it subsided, she was left standing there, with a whole new hairdo! She caught up to Boone, brushed herself off, dumped her gear on the ground next to his, then leaned against the van.

Boone grabbed her gear and tossed it in the back of the van

with his, "C'mon! Jump in!" He stood aside, helped her into the van's second seat, then climbed in next to her. Shorty, their driver, started the engine, they buckled their seatbelts, and both transports pulled away, leaving the site, as pristine as it had been before the arrival of Alpha Team.

"It seems like we've been living some sort of unbelievable dream!" she mused aloud, while gazing out the window, as trees and brush passed by. She felt the familiar lurch of the van once more.

Boone heard her say something, but had just called Riley, "We're on our way back to base camp," he said, and she faintly heard Riley say, "Roger that, Boss."

"What happens now?" she said wearily, leaning her head back on the seat.

"Well," Boone paused for a moment, "mission accomplished! We go home." He grinned, then fell silent, staring out the window the rest of the way to base camp.

Paisley, dozed off in the van, which wasn't easy to do, because of the bumping around on the rutted road. Nevertheless, she felt mildly refreshed from her catnap anyway, when she stepped out of the van, upon arrival at base camp. She stretched her arms and legs before grabbing her duffle bag.

Next, she surveyed the area and noticed Alpha Team's gear organized and placed in several piles at the edge of the clearing. When she glanced back at the van, Boone disembarked, and a feeling of elation came over her as she remembered the mission was over! Boone caught her eye, grabbed his duffle, and strode towards her. He gave her a smile, but his face betrayed the strain he'd been under for the last few days.

He said, "Well, we made it!"

She wanted to run up to him and convey her excitement at

finally having the mission complete but restrained herself and just smiled pleasantly, replying, "Yep!"

The rest of the base camp team busied themselves, by loading their gear into their respective vans.

Boone grabbed his duffle and back pack, saying, "C'mon, grab your bag and come with me."

She did what he asked, and they began to walk in the direction of another van, but he put his arm around her shoulder and pulled her with him, veering away from the UH-1N Huey, which was warming up. It was a twin-engine, medium-sized military helicopter, and would transport some of the men who weren't taking the transport van.

"We're getting on the other copter at the far end of the clearing, it's a Sikorsky MH-60G PAVE. It will fly us back to Pinecrest," he informed her.

"Well, I guess it's nice to know people in high places," she said with surprise, "because I've *never* been on a helicopter without being tied up and a bag over my head!" She smiled

He laughed out loud, "Trust me—you'll love it!"

"What about the rest of the men?"

"They'll be taking the transports back. They're going to a different location."

He helped her into the copter, tossed in their gear, then walked back to the men waiting to board their transports. He gesticulated with his arms as he spoke to them, congratulating them for the final time. They shook hands all around and patted backs, then he waved as he headed back to the copter.

"What was that all about?" She yelled, as he climbed in and seated himself next to her. The rotors were turning and the noise became loud enough, that it was time for headphones. He handed her a set, and she put them on.

"Now, what did you say?" he asked?

"I was asking, what was going on out there?"

She adjusted her headphones. They seemed oversized to her, but what did she know—better than a bag over her head, for sure!

"I thanked my men for a job well done, and once they arrive at their destination, I gave them a few directions"

"Then I'm guessing that you're very pleased with the operation," she said into the microphone connected to her head set.

He nodded. Boone leaned forward to talk to the pilot for a minute, and then the helicopter slowly lifted off the ground and began rising into what had become a cloudless late afternoon sky. Before veering into a long turn to the left, the copter tilted towards the side where Paisley sat, which gave her a panoramic view of the area where they'd just been. It was thrilling!

She was mesmerized by the view...she could see for miles, over the verdant wilderness beneath her, with the lakes shimmering like diamonds, in the late afternoon sun. The helicopter straightened out, and she turned towards Boone, noticing his brow no longer furrowed, his jaw unclenched— but he still hadn't shaved—there was *much* more than a five o'clock shadow!

Boone sat in his seat looking relaxed, so she ventured again, "How do you think things went today?"

"In my estimation, it went *very* well," he said turning his head towards her. "The suitcase bomb was indeed there, and Drs. Moto and Steinhoff, with their impressive expertise, opened and expeditously disarmed it, preventing little—if any— radiation from escaping. Even so, the fact that the bomb was basically still intact after all these years was shocking to everyone."

With her elbow on the armrest of the seat and her chin in her hand, she listened intently to his summation, then joked, "So you *did* save the world after all!"

They both laughed. "But what exactly happened to Delta Team?" She wasn't sure if she was treading on thin ice by being so inquisitive.

"Here's what I'm permitted to say," he began, using air quotes on the word permitted.

"Air quotes? Seriously?" She chuckled.

He ignored her comment and continued thoughtfully, "Mitch relayed the info he received from Riley, concerning the ambush of Zolotov, and the subsequent defeat of the Russian contingent. As it turns out, they didn't give up easily...there was a tremendous firefight, but Delta, comprised of my finest recruits, forced some of them out of their buildings, with a barrage of flash bangs, grenades, and guns...now they're prisoners!"

"What about the RPGs?"

"Because it was a surprise attack, we destroyed the RPGs, before they could be used. Unfortunately, when that happened, it sparked a conflagration when it set fire to the munitions stored in their outbuilding. The men inside never had a chance, and everything was destroyed. Only fourteen were captured— wounded, but alive. Three of our men were wounded, one seriously, but it looks like he'll recover. So, overall, it was a *massive* success!"

"Where are the men from Delta Team now?"

"They've already been picked up, along with their prisoners, and their equipment, by the another CH-53E heli. The Delta Team causalities, are being taken to a hospital, and the rest have boarded separate helicopters bound for parts unknown, aka, the enforcement facilities of the FBI's special forces, where they'll be debriefed."

"And the prisoners?"

"They're off to an undisclosed location for interrogation,

along with their weaponry, vehicles, and communication mate-rials, and anything saved from the fire that destroyed their head-quarters. This all took place at night, so our helicopters could travel back and forth covertly, because, as you can imagine, they would draw a lot of unwanted attention!"

"Well, *that's* certainly an understatement!" she said as she gazed out the window and listened.

Boone changed the subject. "How are *you* doing, Ms. Ingles?"

She smiled slightly at his use of Ms., and twisted her hands in her lap, thought a minute then said, "I'm relieved and worried, at the same time."

Surprised by her answer, he looked at her with concern asking, "Why is that?"

"Because I don't know what happens next, my life is topsy-turvy, and my direction is gone! I have no idea how my Aunt *really* is, I haven't had a chance to grieve over my uncle's death, or Aunt Olga's dog, or even your friend Dave, who was murdered! I have no idea what will happen with my job and..."

"Stop!" he said and put a hand on hers to prevent her from continuing. Startled, she turned and looked at him.

"I know it won't be easy, but I've seen what a strong person you are, and I know you'll be okay." He saw a tear roll down her cheek and brushed it away with his finger.

"Sadly, I don't feel like I'm that person you're talking about right now." She looked down at her hands.

"Look at me...what would you say if I told you I'd like to treat us both to a delicious steak dinner when we get to Wash-ington, D.C.?"

"What?" She sat up straight, in her seat,"What do you mean, in Washington?"

"Oh, didn't I mention it? We're going to Bureau Headquarters, in Washington, D.C., for debriefing concerning our recent adventures."

She brightened! "No! I think you must have forgotten to tell me that part!" However, she deflated again after remembering her responsibilities. "Sorry, but I can't. I have to go back to work and get everything straightened out there."

Boone put his head back on the seat, "Nope! The arrangements are already made. Captain Bower, at the precinct, knows and sends his regards, and your Aunt was also contacted. All is well, and all are excited for you. Besides, how does a nice big, juicy steak dinner sound? I thought we could go out and grab one at some fancy restaurant, after all, I think *we* deserve it!"

Although there was still a frozen look of surprise on her face, she answered, hesitantly, "Okay," then added jokingly, "although— the MREs weren't really *that* bad..."

"Great!" he said, while giving her an amused look, and continued, "By the way, you said you've never been on a helicopter before we were captured?"

"Not ever! This whole week or so has been full of not-evers." She also copied Boone, by using air quotes, for not-evers.

He laughed, "Okay, okay—I get it, no more air quotes! However, now it's time for us to put our heads back on the seat and at least get a cat nap before getting back to civilization, such as it is."

She wanted to ask more questions, but fatigue was taking its toll, and with no words left to say, she laid her head back and listened to the rhythmic whomp-whomp of the copter's blades, as they lulled her into a much needed, restful sleep.

CHAPTER 41

Thursday, May 25, 2017
Brainerd, Minnesota

Three days after their return to Brainerd, Ingles barely had time to visit with Aunt Olga, or go to dinner with her two best friends, Millie and Sue, before she had to pack and be ready to say goodbye, once again, to travel to DC. It was different to see Boone again when she met him at the airport, after everything they'd been through .

"Hey Ingles! How are you doing?" This was the first thing he said to her.

"I'm doing great," she said self-consciously.

"If it's all right, may I call you Paisley? I'll use Ingles when we're at headquarters, but since we've been through so much together, I feel it would be nice to be a little more personal," he grinned.

She was shocked, and mumbled, "Sure, why not?" Then laughed and replied, "But, I still want to call you Boone, if that's okay with you—I like that name, and it feels personal to me!"

"I'm fine with that, too," then he gave her a friendly hug, and said, "Let's go!"

They boarded their plane at the Minneapolis/St. Paul Airport—their destination—Washington, D.C., where they had an appointment with the FBI, at the J. Edgar Hoover Building, and she could hardly believe it.

Washington, D.C. The plane departed shortly after noon, and descended two hours, and twenty minutes later, into the partially cloudy afternoon, at Dulles Airport. Not even cloudy weather could dampen the enthusiasm Paisley felt, as she recognized the historic buildings, while speeding through the crowded DC streets, in a wild Taxi ride for twenty minutes or so, to their hotel, The Four Seasons!

The Four Seasons, was a beautiful red brick building, with a brick tower, displaying a large clock, standing like a sentry to guard the hotel and its grounds. This chose this particular hotel for its proximity to FBI Headquarters. Once inside the hotel, Boone motioned Paisley towards a tufted loveseat where she could sit, while he checked them in, at the desk. She was happy to have a chance to rest a moment and glance around the lobby as she waited.

A tall, leafy-green plant sat on a low table next to her, and she noticed several other chair and couch groupings nearby, with palms placed strategically around the room, their large fronds fanning out into the lobby. For Paisley, with her active imagination, these palms conjured up pictures of sinister-looking men—probably spies—carefully parting the fronds, to keep from attracting attention, as they eyeballed the passersby. Several men sat on a loveseat across the lobby, looking suspicious, as they peered surreptitiously over their newspapers, looking for—she was *sure*—their contact!

She was jolted out of her spy fantasy by Boone, who said,

"Hey! Paisley! I was trying to get your attention...didn't you see me? We're checked in, so we can go to our rooms now." He looked at her quizzically.

She turned to look at him, "I'm so sorry, I was distracted by the people in this busy lobby," she lied. "It's *so* elegant!" She wasn't about to tell him of her spy scenario!

"Yes, apparently, the Bureau spared no expense for us...either that, or they're going to charge it to my card later," he grinned, "and if that's the case, I'll just put it on my expense account," he said, laughing.

There's that wonderful laugh of his, again! His laugh sounded so genuine she wanted to join in—she hadn't known a man who laughed quite like that—he *does* intrigue me, she thought!

They headed for the elevator, which took them to the fifth floor, while the bellman carried their suitcases. Paisley wanted to handle her own small suitcase, but, the bellman insisted on taking it and led them to Room 517, opened the door, then handed her the key card. Boone tipped him, and the bellman left. She wheeled her suitcase inside.

"Well," Boone said, "just so you know, my room is right down the hall, Room 521, and since we have to leave early tomorrow for the FBI, I thought we'd order-in for tonight, and call it a day."

"Sounds perfect," she said.

"Get yourself settled, and we'll meet in my room...say, in an hour?" He smiled and turned for the door, then turned back and said, "See you in a bit, Paisley."

She nodded and grinned, grateful for a little alone time to relax. An hour later, she joined him in his room, and they called room service, ordering hamburgers and fries. The hamburgers were a fantastic gourmet delight—they were so big, she could hardly open her mouth wide enough to take a bite! "Thank goodness for the extra napkins," she said. The fries were sprinkled with some sort of secret seasoning of the chef's, and were the best she'd ever had! Or, maybe she was just super hungry, she thought!

Following their delicious repast, Paisley commented, "I think this hotel has a place where we can order an old-fashioned milkshake, so why don't we go down to the little outdoor terrace cafe, and talk about the plans for tomorrow—the brochure indicates, it has a great view!"

"Sure! Why don't you grab a jacket, just in case, and we'll meet at the elevator?"

"I want you to know, I have an ulterior motive." She paused, then continued, "There are still loose ends for me, about this whole operation—I'd like to tie them up."

Boone nodded his head, "Sure... good idea!"

The little cafe on the terrace, was all that the brochure made it out to be, situated on a second-floor balcony, with a breathtaking view of the city lights. When the server arrived, they both ordered milkshakes. Boone chose a White Cow, and Paisley ordered a Mocha Java.

As soon as the server left, she began with her questions, and looking Boone directly in his eyes, she opened with, "I'm curious about exactly why you came to Pinecrest. You told me a little bit, but not everything, so—*now*, I'm all ears!"

CHAPTER 42

P aisley jumped, when her phone began to vibrate, and held up a finger in front of her, to signify wait a moment, then reached in her pocket and answered, "Hello?"

"Paisley, it's Aunt Olga, just want to know...you arrive? You okay?"

Paisley turned down the volume on her phone because Aunt Olga always talked on it with a loud voice as if it were the only way she could be heard.

"Oh, yes—I did. I'm sorry I didn't call you sooner, but the time difference and all...yes, everything is fine...are you okay?"

"I'm good, love you...Bye-bye..."

"Is everything okay?" Boone asked, when she abruptly ended the conversation,

"Yes," she grinned, "I'm sorry, Aunt Olga called, because I forgot to tell her I arrived," she smiled and put her phone away, "now, you were saying?"

"Well," Boone began, "to make a long story short, in 1990,

333

the FBI, did come to Brainerd to investigate the rumor of a suitcase bomb hidden somewhere in the Brainerd Lakes area, by the
KGB, during the Cold War. The agents searched around for a
few weeks, but nothing ever came of it, so they left. Still, a few
stories were printed in the local newspaper about it—some of
the same stories you found. There were also hearings in
Congress about the situation, and needless to say, we had *our*
files on the investigation, in our Counter- Terrorism Office, here
at the FBI."

"Yes, that was strange when I searched for articles, I thought
it was preposterous, at the time!"

Boone continued, "However, because we were contacted by
this unknown informant, Mr. Ohm, he *did* need to be taken seriously, given the accusations made, back in the 90s, in case
somehow they were connected."

Her eyes grew big, "Oh, my gosh! How strange that Gregore
Kamorov turned out to be your informant, Mr. Ohm!"

Ignoring her, he continued, "Because I spoke Russian, it was
the determining factor in choosing *me*, to come to Pinecrest. As
I said before, I thought he didn't contact me because he was
spooked, but of course, now we know it was because he'd been
murdered—so no wonder!"

She listened with rapt attention, to everything Boone said,
and asked, "But who *did* murder him?" She thought a moment,
then added, "Wait—let me guess! You figured somehow, that
someone found out Kamorov wanted to spill the beans, and *they*
killed him! Am I right?"

Without giving an answer, Boone called the waitress over
and ordered another milkshake. "Would you like another one,
Paisley?"

"No, I'm good." She still wasn't used to hearing him call her
Paisley.

He continued answering questions, "It wasn't exactly like you're saying. Kamorov's murder seemed just a coincidence at first—except for the fact that he was Russian. "

"But *after* the murder, you *knew* Kamorov was the one you were looking for, didn't you?" she reiterated, and sat back in her chair, "but, *you* couldn't tell *me* that at the time."

Chuckling, he said, "No, it still wasn't that evident. At first, I believed the murder to be random, but it was something to keep me busy, while I searched for the informant. Once I found out Kamorov moved here from Russia, then it looked more suspicious, but there was still no proof."

"Whoa, that must have been a surprise! So, case closed!" She sipped some more of her milk shake and looked out pensively at the city, as the waitress brought Boone's second shake.

"Not really," he continued, "because, since I had no proof, I was still just guessing. Perhaps, it *was* just a normal homicide? But, then we interviewed Pyotr Zolotov—another Russian! A coincidence? Maybe, but still, during our investigation, nothing came up right away, remember? And the next thing I knew, you were obviously under assault from someone, but I couldn't figure out who or why?"

"I couldn't figure that out either," she agreed.

It was getting chilly, so she stood to put on her jacket, and Boone rose to give her a hand.

"But, of course, *now* I understand how the 'thumb drive' turned out to be the connection," he said, "they all called it a thumb drive, instead of a flash drive." He looked at his new watch. "Perhaps we should make a night of it," he suggested, "since we have a big day ahead of us tomorrow."

"Okay, that sounds good to me, but what about Ivan's murder?"

They started walking towards the hotel's terrace door, "Yes, that raised even more suspicions. Thankfully, you were smart enough to notice the tattoo on Gregore's arm, and it turned out there *was* an identical one on Ivan—the tattoo connection was *impressive*. This is when I was sure, that the informant had been Kamorov. They were all in the same Mafia organization— and it required each member to have the green coiled snake tattoo."

"Well, thank you." She accepted the compliment with a smile.

"On what little information I had from the beginning, I called the Bureau and started the ball rolling, to plan for every possible scenario, and that's when Riley flew out here to stage everything. He put in wiretaps, and had the Russians tailed, to see what they were doing. It became obvious it was something critical, but we still didn't have a clue so we planned for the worst case scenario—that the hidden suitcase bomb had been found."

"Hmmm...that's amazing! I had no idea all that some of that went on behind the scenes. Why didn't you confide in me?"

He laughed out loud, as they left the terrace, entered the hotel, and headed for the elevator, "Because it was on a need to know basis, and at that point, there wasn't a need for you to know!"

Turning to stare at him, she said, hands on her hips, with faux indignation, "*Really!*" Then they both laughed.

By this time, they were inside, and had reached the elevators, "I'm sorry," he said with a sheepish grin, amused by her reaction, but the night they followed you, I feared something was *very* wrong. Then, of course, they hunted both of us down, we were captured, and landed in the enemy's lair. From that point on, I knew our lives were in grave danger, and there was no time to chat about my back story—we *had* to escape!

"I understand now...I was sort of a brat, about it all...sorry!"

"True," he grinned, "however, when we made it to my place and found Kaufman murdered, I had to get in touch with Riley. The team had already set up the ground work, the surveillance, and wiretaps, and so, it was time to rock and roll."

"I thought we were the ones that produced the critical information when we decrypted the flash drive?" Paisley was puzzled.

The elevator door opened, they stepped in and Boone pushed the button for the fifth floor. The doors slid shut, and they were alone in the elevator, he ignored her question.

"My team was prepared from the beginning, because the agent from Minneapolis, got the tip from the informant, stating the item which was being negotiated by the Russian Mafia, concerned weapons of mass destruction!"

"Oh, yes—the original FBI guy..."

Boone continued, "When Riley and the men arrived, they amassed covertly, in a strategic location outside Brainerd. This transpired at night, so as not to draw any attention."

"So, I guess I wasn't much help in all this?" Paisley said, with disappointment.

"To the contrary, Ms. Ingles! *You* were the one with the most important clue of all—your decryption of the final piece of the puzzle. The flash drive information verified it was a suitcase bomb, and most importantly, it gave us the exact coordinates to its location!"

The doors opened on the fifth floor, and she stepped out followed by Boone, then stopped and turned to look at him, "But I still don't see how all this connects to the Gregore Kamorov murder? Why kill him?"

"Okay," Boone said, crossing his arms, "Kamorov, a computer geek, lived in Zolotov's house and was helping with technical things needed by Zolotov, for computer communications with the Russian Mafia leader. However, Kamorov somehow gained possession of Zolotov's flash drive, hacked into it, discovered the plot, and decided to sell it to the US government, for a hefty price."

'Aha! Kamorov tried to extort the US, and we still don't extorted by , and we still have no idea, who killed him?" she asked. They were standing in front of the elevator by themselves, still discussing things, when a couple walked up to the elevator and pushed the lobby button. Boone led Paisley down the hallway towards her room, before answering.

"Yes, actually we *do* know who the killer is/was. While we were being chased around the countryside, the police discovered a body floating in one of the old mine pits, filled with water to create a lake. It was the body of a man named Lenny Starko— also of Russian descent—*and*, with the same tattoo as the others!"

She said, "The tattoos really helped to link these guys to one another, for sure!"

"True! He'd been shot in the head, with a gun belonging to Zolotov. There are other facts that point to Starko, as the killer of my friend, Dave. It was done with the same knife, used to kill Ivan."

"So, it seems like this Lenny character, had become a liability to Zolotov, because why else would he kill him? Right?"

Boone added, "Yes. When Lenny searched Ben's Burgers and couldn't find the flash drive, he went to your Aunt's farmhouse and searched, still coming up empty handed. Then he figured Ivan had it, and killed him to get it. This was drawing too much attention to Zolotov because sooner or later, Lenny would have been linked to Zolotov's group. Starko was a cold-blooded psychopathic killer."

She was shocked, "What a mess! So, Lenny killed Ivan, too? And what about Yury Panuken?" They were walking slowly now, so she could finish her questioning.

"Yury was totally innocent, without any knowledge of what was going on, he was focused on his education. He has since relocated to another college near the cities, to continue his studies, and hopes to graduate and become not only a doctor but a US citizen!"

They had reached her door, "Good for Yury! You've sure been busy piecing this together," she said, as she stood by her door.

"There are others taken into custody, as well."

"Good! I'm relieved they're all gone!" She slid her key card into the door to unlock it, then turned, to say good night.

Boone said, "Wait, hold on a minute, not so fast, there's more." Boone put his arm out to hold the door open, "Unfortunately, Zolotov's top man, managed to escape when they raided Zolotov's house, and he's still being hunted. Chances are, he's headed for Canada with false passports, and will make it back to Russia, through some circuitous route."

"Isn't there a way to find him?"

"The police took every shred of evidence, from Zolotov's house, and other places occupied by the Russians, and turned it over to the CIA. Hopefully, the information will lead to the head of the Mafia organization in Russia, who set this project in motion. The Mafia leader, whose name is Tazvoshenko, may have *also* killed the man originally responsible for discovering where the suitcase bombs were hidden years ago, in all the different locations around the world. So, as you see, there's still a lot more to investigate."

"Hmmm...that's disturbing," and she frowned at this disquieting news.

"By the way," he continued, "we'll meet tomorrow morning in the lobby, at 8:00 a.m. Will that work for you?"

"Yes, of course, and thanks for the milkshake, *and* for filling in the blanks. What an adventure this has been—it wasn't the simple murder that I thought we would solve!" She grinned and said good night.

"Good night, Paisley...just so you know, I couldn't have had a better partner, and I feel this isn't the last time we'll have the opportunity, to work together..."

"If you say so, '*Deedrick*'," she countered, and they both laughed, at her use of *his* first name.

EPILOGUE

Monday, June 12, 2017
Pinecrest, Minnesota

Two weeks and four days (to be exact), after Paisley's amazing trip to DC, she went back to work, surprised to see how many of her fellow officers knew of her exploits—news traveled fast! Of course, everyone had seen the articles in the Pinecrest and Brainerd newspapers, *and on* TV. However, what people *didn't* know, was the FBI dictated what they wanted to have reported, which differed significantly from the *true* story, which was classified, by the FBI.

Only Paisley, Boone, and the FBI, knew the real truth, and Paisley and Boone were sworn to secrecy because of it being a national security matter. As far as the public knew, Paisley and Boone had identified the killer of Gregore Kamorov, and several others, as Lenny Starko. The articles described in detail, their great detective work in discovering the killer's true identity—he was a Russian terrorist!

The news media quoted them: "We chased the subject

through rough terrain for several days, until we discovered his body, floating in an old water-filled mine pit, in the Cuyuna Range, with a self-inflicted gunshot wound. His prints were matched to those found, at the murder scene of Gregore Kamorov and Ivan Belenski." The media described the two Detectives, as heroes.

A picture of Boone and Paisley accompanied the newspaper stories *and* the TV news reports, along with a description of their trip to FBI headquarters, where they received special recognition and certificates for their great work in ridding the country of a terrorist. The only people to know about the suitcase bomb, were the FBI's Special Unit, Boone, and Paisley. The case was now officially closed.

Stepping into her office on Monday morning, for the first time, since returning from DC, it comforted her to have several computers waiting to be worked on—not to mention—Millie to greet her!

"Hey Pais, how's it going!" They hugged.

"Well, after a month now, I think I've finally caught up on my sleep, and I'm back to my normal life." She put her purse on the floor and reached for the computers on the shelf.

"Oh no—you're a celebrity now! You don't *get* to have a normal life!" she laughed.

"Really? Please, Millie, I'm trying to move past all that..."

"Then how about going out for a bite to eat, with me and Sue tonight? It's been a while..."

Paisley looked at Millie, and said, "I'm *totally* up for doing that, although I *do* hate leaving Aunt Olga alone. I've stayed home with her in the evenings since her husband's death for month now, and I don't think she'll mind if I'm not there for *one* evening."

Brainerd Millie chose Applebee's. When Paisley arrived,

Millie and Sue were already there. They laughed and talked and had a great meal, then ordered coffee and began to chat.

Millie said, "Well, you see...I had a small part in your case too, because *I* identified the snake tattoo!"

"True," Paisley said, "and it turned out to be a *very* valuable clue!"

Sue, not to be outdone, said, "Well, I *also* had something to add to the case!" She smiled.

Paisley and Millie looked at her with surprise, and Paisley said, "What was that?"

"Well, after the murder of Ivan Belenski, I saw his picture in the paper, and recognized him from the library...he came in the day after Kamorov was murdered and used a computer. I contacted the police—in case it might be important—and they discovered somehow, I don't know how—his connection to Zolotov!"

"No way!" Paisley said, "No one told *me* about this, but of course, I haven't been out with you guys for the last month."

"Oh, yes!" Sue continued,"They got something off of the computer he'd used. They disconnected it and took it for evidence! You were gone by that time or you probably would have been the one to work on it, Paisley!"

"Well, what do you know, my two friends are amateur detectives, too!"

They all had a laugh over this and were congratulating each other, but Sue's laugh was *so* infectious, that they were almost unable to stop—tears rolled down their cheeks before they could get their laughter under control!

Paisley said, "It feels so good to laugh that hard, again."

At the close of their evening, they ordered more coffee and Sue asked Paisley a provocative question, "What are your plans? Will you stay at the police department?"

"I have a question, too," Millie said coyly, "...so what's going on with you and Detective Boone? I hear he's still in town!"

"Here's the answer to both—I don't know!" Paisley blushed in spite of herself.

"Way to avoid the question," Millie said.

They all grinned and Paisley added, "Well, you never, never, know!"

June 15, 2017 Somewhere in Russia

In his *dacha*, hidden in a remote area of Russia, Tazvoshenko and several of his loyal followers were hiding to keep the disappointed (to say the least), evil characters from finding them to deliver retribution, after Tazvoshenko's failed attempt to acquire the suitcase bomb, as promised. The disgruntled despots, who bought into the project, never recovered their investments. Now, there was a huge price on Tazvoshenko's head—their goal was to annihilate him *and* the few men still with his decimated Mafia organization.

Tazvoshenko eagerly awaited the return of Lev, whom he'd sent to the US to locate the two Detectives, Paisley Ingles and Deedrick Boone. These two had disrupted and destroyed his men, his project, and his Mafia organization, leaving nothing for him, except a desire for revenge, at all costs.

Weeks later, when Lev finally returned from the US, he gave Tazvoshenko the information, for which he'd eagerly awaited. They sat down over cups of Espresso. Lev began, "The female has been living with the Shenkovskys, in Brainerd, Minnesota!"

Shocked by this, Tazvoshenko said, "Are you sure?" Lev nodded and Tazvoshenko smiled a slow, evil smile, which turned to rage. "Perfect!" He pounded the table with his massive fist, almost overturning their espressos. "I will get revenge for newest betrayal *and* destruction of my Mafia business! Also revenge for an old betrayal—by the Shenkovskys! How do you know it's Shenkovskys? I search for them many years. They stole from me. I *knew* I'd find them someday!"

"I *thought* you would be surprised," Lev said. "Lenny Starko, ransacked their house to find jump drive that Detective Ingles had, and guess what he found instead? A picture of them —the Shenkovskys! The two of them are in old photo," and he handed the old black and white photo to his boss. "Starko gives it to me. He is dead now. Bah!"

"Yes, good! He was part of problem, too! Eventually, they will *all* be killed for what they did, now *and* in past! I *will* never give up—I *must* have my revenge! No matter how long it takes!" He stood with a rage so terrible, let out the most thunderous roar, and shook his fists in the air, frightening Lev and causing him to recoil!

THE END

AUTHOR'S NOTE

THE SUITCASE, is only a story, which I concocted, *but* there are several **FACTS**, in my fictional story. I was inspired to create a "what if" scenario, based on information I came across, while doing research. My research turned up information on a high-ranking Russian defector, who testified in government sub-committees, concerning sites containing caches, stocked with Russian military equipment, which were situated in locations, in Europe, *and* the United States, during the **Cold War**.

Many sites were located in places like Switzerland, and Belgium. The Russian defector indicated caches were also located in the US, and named Montana, New York, possibly Texas and California, but specifically, the Brainerd, Minnesota area.

Congressional committees looked at this information, and taking it seriously, discussed sending FBI agents to Brainerd, to look around. The FBI visited Brainerd and looked around, but had no specific locations, as to where the caches might be found. The caches in the US, were said to possibly contain munitions, equipment, and/or material involving a weapon of mass destruction. It was felt the caches were so old, that anything contained would no longer be dangerous. Bills were presented in Congress, but nothing came of it.

Anyone interested in reading more about the topic, may Google, these sites:

RUSSIAN THREAT PERCEPTIONS AND PLANS FOR SABOTAGE AGAINST THE UNITED STATES

https://fas.org/irp/congress/2000_hr/hr_012400.htm

Test-H.RES.380-106th Congress (1999-2000): Expressing the...

and:

www.congress.gov/bill/106th-congress/house-resolution380

ABOUT THE AUTHOR

Long Minnesota winters, spurred a new author to write her first book. Mystery is her genre, and her first book is a mystery/thriller: **THE SUITCASE.**

TV Scribner, currently lives in Brainerd, Minnesota. With a Computer Engineering degree, she worked as a technician, *and* a reference librarian. When she's not at her computer sleuthing, plotting and solving mysteries, she takes ballet, plays guitar, sews and stays in communication with her eleven adult children and thirty-five grandchildren, all of whom live in different states. Currently, she's working on the next book in her **Paisley and Boone Series**, titled **THE DRAGONFLY NECKLACE**.

FIND OUT MORE ABOUT UPCOMING BOOKS
Sign up for the NEWSLETTER at this website:
www.tvscribner.com
Email: tvscribner@yahoo.com

facebook.com/tvscribner
twitter.com/tvscribner
instagram.com/tvscrib